Tabl

MW01223608

Foreword

A simple look into Jesus' life shows that he represents a God that is there amidst the chaos of life. Yet many people who claim to know God have no idea how to communicate that truth in the context of our world and the vast issues that plague it.

As a youth worker, I have heard many stories of hurt and pain where God seemed absent. Many times I struggle to find hope in these situations and feel inadequate to represent God's heart.

In reading this book, I felt a sense of how God can and does work. His message can and does give hope to those facing destitute situations. This book serves as a reminder to not try to bring order into people's lives through a moral code or ethical guidelines—but to introduce them to my friend Jesus.

I plan on making this story a regular tool of mine in working with youth. At times, when stories mean more than logical advice, Twyla's book is a modern-day parable that fits much better than many of my theological formulas ever could.

I hope that your are as challenged and motivated by this book as I was. When you are done, pass it on to a young person in your life.

—DANNY FERGUSON, youth pastor

The Road

"For wide is the gate and broad is the road that leads to destruction and many enter through it but small is the gate and narrow is the road that leads to life and only a few find it."

Matthew 7:13–14

Amber White laid her head down. She was supposed to be standing, but she couldn't. Her legs were weak and shaky, her stomach nauseous. She knew if she tried to stand, she would vomit—not the wisest move in front of the judge who would be deciding her future. How had things gotten so out of control? A shiver ran through her body, her stomach lurched, and her head spun as she contemplated the ominous idea of having to spend numerous nights at Klahanee, the women's prison where she had resided for the past three weeks.

The noises she'd heard just last night put a new fear into her. She asked her cellmate, Lauryn, about them, and she calmly replied, "Pen abortion, sweetie." Amber didn't know if she was trying to freak her out or if it were true. Either way, she wanted out.

The judge's pounding gavel brought Amber back to her present surroundings. "Amber White. Is that your name?" The judge's voice held no tolerance.

"Yes, ma'am, I mean, Miss, er, Your Honor." The words could barely be forced out of her mouth. She wanted to hurl. The judge lifted a condescending brow and looked disdainfully at Amber; she felt the displeasure she emulated. The judge perused Amber with cold eyes, her face set hard.

"When my bailiff says 'all rise,' you, Miss White, are not above the law, as I am sure you must be aware of by now."

"I ... I, Your Honor, I can't stand. I don't feel well ... " She didn't dare finish her explanation; it only seemed to anger the judge more.

"Young lady, rise." Her voice was powerful. Amber stood, wondering if anyone ever disobeyed that tone.

Delores Grace was the honourable judge. Amber wasn't sure which name was her first and which was her last. She figured her to be about fifty years old. She saw no wedding ring. It wasn't surprising that she wasn't married. She probably didn't have children either, which explained her lack of tolerance. Delores Grace wore her hair pulled back tightly into a bun. It was chestnut brown with two gray wisps that loosely framed her face, hanging to her jaw line, defining the prominent bone structure. Her large, round eyes added a touch of softness to stern features. She must have been striking in her youth. Her eyes were steel gray, and Amber was positive they could see clear into her soul and would show no mercy.

Amber stood then dared to let go of the table in order to stand respectfully before the judge. Everything darkened. Voices webbed together, becoming incoherent mumbling. She was falling slowly, as in a dream, helpless to do anything about it. Salvaging dignity was hopeless as blackness ensued.

"Amber, oh, you had us so worried."

Amber focussed on her mother's expression; it seemed permanent. She smiled to herself, remembering her first night at the jail. Lauryn had commented, "Does your mom always look so constipated?" That described "the look" perfectly. Eyebrows furrowed; eyes half shut from straining; lips pressed flat into a thin, straight line. Yep, that described it.

"Amber, it's me."

"Yes, Mother. I know. I fainted. I didn't go blind or stupid." She used "the tone." It was the way she addressed anyone who got in her face—especially Dr. Gordon Forbes, because she was none of his business, and she truly despised him. She used it with her parents because they would never understand.

At Amber's first meeting with Dr. Forbes, she was repulsed. His jet-black hair was slicked straight back with half a tub of gel, or was it a month of built-up grease? His pimp-style moustache added to her appal. He thought he was so hip.

He was charming, too, as he slid his chair around the desk, leaning close enough for Amber to smell how many days since he'd last brushed his teeth. He placed his hands on her legs as he spoke. Sure, that was innocent enough; then he rotated his hands, turning his fingers toward her inner thigh, crooning, "You know, Amber, I can only help you if you let me."

She braved telling her parents. They chose not to believe her, their own daughter, over an obvious slimeball pervert. Her problems had only been mediocre then. They were unfathomable now, swallowing her whole, and she contemplated giving up completely.

Her mother's voice cut into her despair with its usual naivety. "Amber, you know we just have to have faith. I'm sure God will deliver you from this if you just let him. Surely when your true character is revealed this will all go away, and we can put this horrible nightmare behind us. Anyone can look at you and see you aren't capable of the charges against you."

Catherine must have deliberately chosen to be naive, that was the only explanation. She lived in a bubble. Anything she didn't want to deal with remained outside the bubble, which included Amber's charges. It made her want to scream, "Murder! Mother, I am charged with second-degree murder. Say it!"

When Amber was arrested, her parents hadn't even known

where she was living. She hadn't seen them in at least three months. She was admitted to Klahanee with an excessive narc habit, her drug of choice, crack. It was cheap and easy. Catherine and Michael must have worked hard trying to convince themselves there was good left in her. They needed to believe her problems were someone else's fault. She knew better; she had made the choices.

"Mother, you just don't get it, do you? I might not come home. The judge isn't exactly eager to see me go home. And you can pray all you want, but my future lies in the hands of that steely-eyed judge, not God's. I'd be willing to bet that judge hasn't given out a break in … well, ever! Be realistic!"

Catherine looked at the ground. Amber knew her parents couldn't accept that she no longer shared their faith. What did they expect? God had abandoned her. She was too destitute to chase fairy tales. She needed something tangible.

"When did you stop having faith? What made you decide to recant your beliefs? Was it when Adam—"

"Stop. Don't." At the mention of his name, the particular moment came uninvited. She closed her eyes, shutting them tightly, willing the image to go away. She had enough on her plate; she didn't need past demons coming to haunt her as well. The memory taunted her, plucking her raw emotions. Had that one event rolled into her present afflictions like a tumbleweed?

Catherine and Michael stayed a little while longer in the first-aid room, straining to make small talk with their only daughter. Before leaving they explained that the judge had postponed the trial until the next morning when, hopefully, "Miss White will have herself and her body under control."

Her parents each bent over to place a kiss on Amber's forehead. Catherine barely held back a sob as her daughter turned her face from her. She just wanted to make it better; her daughter only perceived that as stupidity. In her wisdom she called it sanity.

She looked intently at Amber, allowing herself to drink in her daughter's gentle features. Her sunny gold hair tumbled in layers halfway down her back. She remembered, as a young first-time mom, taking so much pride in her daughter's hair. She had secretly prayed that God wouldn't hold her vanity for her daughter's hair against her. How gracious he had been. She still had a head full of that beautiful hair—the same color as those adorable babies you see in commercials.

Amber was also blessed with enormous almond-shaped eyes that were a shade of emerald green so deep the oceans would be envious. A perfectly round teacup face and a sharp, petite nose. At the tender age of nineteen Amber could pass for fifteen or twenty-five when all done up. Catherine haplessly wondered when she would next see her daughter without prison bars or Plexiglas between them. With that thought, she made a quick decision. For the first time in way too long, she embraced her.

She didn't care that the body she held went rigid at her touch. She didn't care that it may have made her daughter angrier. She didn't seem to say or do anything right where she was concerned anyway. So, she held her. Her little girl. This was her moment, and she would hold on to it.

Releasing Amber from her forced embrace, Catherine made her way to the door. There she hesitated, and as she did, she was certain of what she heard. It was faint and unmitigated, but to Catherine White the small held-back sob that escaped her daughter's hardened exterior was a triumph. She closed the door just in time to conceal the sniffle that would shortly turn into weeping.

Michael wrapped his arms around his distraught wife. How much longer would they have to suffer? What lengths of suffering did their daughter still face? Initially, he and Catherine had believed Amber's problems to be manifestations of depression from the accident with Adam. She had never stopped feeling guilty; he knew that. He knew she had tried drugs to dull the pain. All they could do was pray for their lost child. Pray without ceasing. Pray God would send his angels to protect her, to keep her safe. He and his wife had spent every night for the last three years kneeling at their bedside hoping, believing. It was Jim Farrell that approached them one evening, noticing the dark circles under their eyes, the permanent crease in Catherine's brow, and the new patches of gray in Michael's thick, dark hair. He spoke with love and honesty, as a friend who had truly grieved with them. His son had died tragically. Their daughter had witnessed it and was lost in the emotional aftermath. Jim opened his Bible to Proverbs; no man imparted more wisdom than Solomon, and so he shared, "Trust in the Lord with all your heart, and lean not on your own understanding. In all your ways acknowledge him and he will make your path straight." God created the picture, and each day he added a new piece to the puzzle; God was working, that had to be enough. "In all things God works for the good of those who love him, who have been called according to his purpose." It is not God's will that any should perish. God could use the outcome of any situation for good; they only had to be willing.

Michael claimed to trust God, but only one outcome was acceptable. Michael and Catherine began to pray with renewed hope. God had not forgotten them. They clung to their faith with eagles' talons. Nothing could separate them from the love of Christ.

Two short days later their prayers would change again. They got the news. Their daughter was being charged with murder. They did not ask, "Why us?" The Lord was tearing down in order to start new. "Blessed is the man who God corrects so do not despise the discipline of the Almighty. For He wounds but He binds up. He injures but His hands also heal" (Job 5:17–18). In the initial days that followed, they relied on those verses.

Now, with the Lord's strength, they had made it to the trial. If they had hoped for any leniency, it was becoming apparent there wouldn't be any. Michael found himself wondering what it would take to restore their daughter. Catherine spoke, cutting into his thoughts.

"I think I heard Amber stifle a sob as we walked out." It wasn't at all unusual that they had both been thinking about Amber in silence. Michael mused out loud, "I know. I thought I heard it too. I thought it might have been impatience." He looked over at his wife and managed to give her a weak smile.

It was amazing how much they looked alike, Catherine and Amber. He recalled them entering one of those mother/daughter contests back when Amber was fourteen. They were runners-up. A Korean family had won, he remembered wistfully. As he looked at his wife now, he couldn't possibly imagine loving her more. He remembered how radiant she had looked then, so fresh. No question, she was beautiful. Catherine smiled back at her charming husband.

"I'm seeing a change in her, Michael." The gradual decline of Amber's conscience had been difficult. No remorse, no guilt, only justification. "It was self-defense," they had heard her repeat.

They refused to discuss the option that Amber might be found guilty, despite her claim of self-defense. A jury could still find her guilty, especially if she showed no remorse. That sentence would carry a life term.

Michael hugged his wife a little closer and whispered, "I hope you're right." Amber and her father were so much more alike that way. They thought of the negative first. Catherine preferred to think as taught in Philippians 4:8–9: "Whatever is true, whatever is noble, whatever is right, whatever is pure, whatever is lovely, whatever is admirable. If anything is excellent or praiseworthy, think about such things."

Michael and Amber thought realistically and suggested

often that Catherine should do the same. She would retort, "I have faith."

"And where has that faith gotten you?"

She closed her eyes tightly, holding back the tears. "Oh, God, everywhere, through every night, through every day, through each phone call, through each day of this trial. You will get me through whatever else is to come. Thank you, God."

"'Those who hope in the Lord will renew their strength. They will mount up with wings like eagles. They will run and not be weary. They will walk and not faint.' Isaiah 30:41."

Wearily, the couple walked to the car, fervently praying for strength to cope, hope to prevail, and for the faith to trust God with whatever the outcome of their daughter's future.

The drive to Nan's to pick up Lincoln was silent. It was getting harder to deal with his questions. Amber insisted that Linc never know the truth. *"Promise not to tell him anything," she insisted. "Even if I have to go to jail for life. Promise you won't tell him the truth about me. Ever."*

Catherine waited in the car while Michael went inside and got Lincoln. She smiled to herself; both her boys appeared exhausted. They had only been driving a few minutes when she looked in the backseat at her sleeping son. He was seven years old now. She wistfully remembered Amber being that young, that angelic. They never could have foreseen the tragedy that would unfold and become their lives.

Michael believed it wasn't just the accident that had contributed to their daughter's destruction, but a tapestry of events that had not been dealt with. She got worse after seeing the psychiatrist, harder. They had expected different results. They believed the doctor's explanation though.

"It was painful for her," he explained, "to relive the experience, but it was necessary in order to get to the healing." They accepted his answer. After all, what did Michael or Catherine know about psychiatry?

The doctor further explained, "The reason she may appear distant and hostile is, since the accident, she has started experimenting with drugs"—something they were suspicious of but not certain. The doctor explained, "Drug use adds to her destructive behavior, producing further guilt." His final words, "Be glad she isn't suicidal." So they were.

The doctor successfully dissuaded them from their concerns. It wouldn't be until this last predicament that they would reevaluate the psychiatrist's answers. Perhaps their daughter was right when she had insolently proclaimed that he was the sick one.

Catherine contemplated the accusations one more time. In her mind she needed reassurance that they had done the right thing. The psychiatrist came highly recommended through the school. Had other children experienced what their daughter claimed? Had other parents disregarded accusations from their troubled offspring, already overwhelmed by the circumstances that led to a family needing a shrink? As the parent of a troubled youth, Catherine felt at times like she was the one under the microscope. What mistakes does one have to make as a parent to raise a child like Amber? It was all so condescending. She felt the questions, even if they weren't asked. She didn't want to be the one to rock the boat by confronting a court-appointed psychiatrist about indecent behavior. Maybe other parents had faced the same dilemma. It was her optimism that always gave people the benefit of the doubt. Her stomach shrunk and ached as she thought, *Everyone except my own flesh.*

Amber heard the door close. She finally turned back over to lie on her back.

Why? she thought. *Why did Mom do that? Stop thinking about it,* she told herself. It was too late. Bitterness burned, purifying the self-pity that began much too long ago. How had things gone so bad? Never mind the many people she had hurt along the way or the silent torment of her parents, who had to suffer along with her. This wasn't their fault. They really didn't get it. Worse still, they believed there was still good in her. They didn't know all of the wicked things she had done. But she knew. She remembered every detail. There was so much. What would they think of her if they knew the truth about their little girl?

Then there was Lincoln. Oh, how her heart ached when she thought about Lincoln, her darling little brother. Those adorable round cheeks. His huge grin with thick, squishy lips and the way he lisped when he spoke. His tousled blond locks and huge blue eyes, round as saucers. He was adorable. He equally adored her. She could probably confide every sin to him. She closed her eyes and heard his voice, "It's okay, Amer. I did bad things too," he would say. What must be going on in his little mind? He was seven years old now, and she had felt more like his mother sometimes than his sister. She pulled the thin blanket up to her face. She tried to force herself to think about something else.

She was restless. Dark thoughts came as though sensing an opening. They came uninvited. They came with purpose, to destroy her.

How am I going to survive this? What am I going to do? How did I do something so horrible? What made me do it?
Then the rationale.

I had to. I had no choice. It was him or me. The more thoughts that raced in her head, the more she became filled with despair. Images tumbled in her mind like whitecaps on the ocean, pulling more thoughts and memories from the recesses of her soul. Thoughts turned and rolled and pulled her under. She deserved to be where she was. She was terrified.

Think positive thoughts, she told herself. She tried to think about something else. Maybe she could conjure up a long-forgotten Bible verse. The lone verse that stuck out in her memory wasn't helpful: "All sins are punishable by death." She couldn't remember it ... *"For the wages of sin is death but ..."* something, something. Oh, why couldn't she remember the rest? Resigning to self-destruction, she decided it didn't matter what the rest of the verse was. The part she remembered summed it all up for her. She half smiled to herself as she thought, *Now if I had remembered that verse before committing my sins ...* Again, the thoughts came. They came to haunt her, and the smile, though it had been a cynical one, quickly faded. She decided to take a stroll in her mind to absorb the reality of what had led her to this doleful place.

Amber vividly remembered the night.

The stars in the sky are brilliant. There must be a million of them.

Amber sucked in a deep breath of air. The night air was intoxicating, not cold like it usually was in mid-October. She stood on the balcony of their family home. It was a decent home, nothing like the homes on the South Hills, but wonderful for their family. Lincoln was three years old. He walked out on the deck to his big sister. With a goofy grin, he exclaimed, "No smoochin' boyz, Amer." She looked back inside to see her dad grinning. He had obviously put him up to it.

"We are friends, Dad, that's it," she said, facing the open French door. Michael shrugged as if to say he had nothing to do with it. She quickly returned her attention to Linc.

"Okay, little man, but I'm sure gonna smooch you all over!" She chased him around the deck, catching him and tickling him. He squealed with delight. They were still like that, laughing and tickling on the porch, when Adam pulled in. Amber wasn't really allowed to date yet, but Adam was different. They had grown up together. They always laughed at how they had known each other since they were in diapers. Adam was a

March birthday, and Amber was born in October. Adam was the youngest of two sons born to Tina and Adam Farrell.

Jim Farrell, a construction engineer, ran his own business as well as doing extra "fix-it" jobs for the church. He was teaching the boys the trade. Adam had different goals and aspirations. He was an A student, and he hoped to become a pastor.

Adam always did the right thing, and he managed to have fun doing it. He talked Amber into all kinds of adventures: cave exploring, rollerblading, repelling, or hiking up a trail and enjoying a spectacular view. He was sensitive too, an attribute Amber had only just begun to appreciate since they had become sophomores. That's when she found out how disgusting boys really were when they "thought" they were men.

Adam had called and asked her dad if he could take her to the movies for her birthday. He realized he was two weeks early, but he had just gotten his first pay check from his new job and wanted to take Amber out.

Adam was so nervous for some reason. It was just Amber. What was the big deal? They were best friends. He and Amber often made fun of their parents, who secretly hoped they would marry one day. He had "almost" hoped Mr. White would say no when he asked. The thought that he might say yes made Adam's stomach flip-flop. He kept telling himself, It's just Amber. Relax or she's going to laugh at you. She didn't laugh though; she squealed with delight like a child over candy.

As he drove up into the driveway in his father's F-250 pickup, he spotted Amber up on the balcony, laughing gaily with Lincoln. Adam all too quickly became aware of why he had been nervous. Amber was beautiful—not just pretty, but radiant. She exuded light.

He was fumbling and feeling goofy already, and he wasn't even out of the truck. As he walked up to the house, he breathed a quick prayer. "Lord, help me be a gentleman and entertain pure thoughts. Please give me back some control over my legs." His lovely date greeted him with an exuberant embrace.

"Adam! Thank you so much for inviting me out. I can't believe you actually got my dad to agree to this."

"He was totally cool about it." Adam tried to sound nonchalant. "You look—wow." He strained for calm in his voice, then, with an exaggerated, deep breath, he continued. "You should tell your parents we're ready to go."

Amber walked into the house and heard Lincoln and Adam goofing around behind her. She looked over her shoulder at Adam and saw the huge grin on his face. His eyes sparkled. She had never noticed before how serene blue his eyes were. She surprised herself at how much she suddenly realized about Adam. Like how his young, developing body was sporting a lot more muscle. She realized she adored the messy way he wore his hair, the earthy way he smelled. Wow! Amber was jolted by the reality of her thoughts. This was her best friend. What was she thinking? She really shouldn't let her mind wander.

As she entered the kitchen, Michael looked adoringly at his daughter. He took a deep breath, preparing to say something. Before he could speak, Amber started rambling and gushing. She was a geyser of excitement, diffusing any negative remarks he may have been prepared to make.

"Oh, Daddy! Thank you so much. What a fabulous birthday surprise. I know you know you don't have to worry, but I want to reassure you. I intend to be fully responsible with this privilege. The movie starts at 8:05, but it's three hours, so it won't be over until eleven. I'll take the cell phone so I can call you if anything should happen. Okay? I love you, Daddy." As suddenly as she had breezed in, she, like the wind, whirled out.

Michael barely got out, "I love you too, sweetie," and was not sure if she heard because she was already out the door, arm in arm with the young man he was trusting his little girl with. He folded his arms across his chest and leaned against the counter he had been wiping down before Amber had burst in with all her joy, making counter-wiping seem quite dull.

Amber didn't slow her footsteps as she hurried out to Adam.

"Let's go." Her enthusiasm and excitement were contagious. Without giving it a second thought, she looped her arm through Adam's and, in the same motion, bent to kiss her brother good-bye. She did not even dare to look behind her, afraid her father might add some stipulation or notice that she had said the movie was over at eleven and change his mind.

Once outside, Amber's attention quickly returned to Adam. It warmed her heart to watch him talk and play with her little brother. Lincoln was her good guy/bad guy test. If a guy was interested in her, he better be interested in her brother. Nothing proved a young man's character more than pretending to lose a fight to a three-year-old or thinking to bring him a sucker.

That wasn't a test for Adam. It was just who he was. She looked up at him then. Wouldn't it be funny if their parents had guessed right all along and she and Adam ended up together? She had to stop thinking like that. Adam would think she was such a freak. He would never think about her that way. Well, maybe after tonight he would. She started thinking of ways to catch his attention, not knowing she already had it … all of it.

Adam gallantly got the door for Amber.

"When did you become a gentleman, Adam Farrell?" she asked flirtatiously. Red immediately seeped into his cheeks. He bowed his head, hoping Amber hadn't noticed how easily he had blushed. He continued helping her into the Ford. The long-time friends reminisced about other outings, like the time Amber got her long hair stuck in the escalator. Adam had to hit the red STOP button and save her. Repelling with the youth group, Amber got her hair stuck in her rope. Adam used his Swiss Army knife to cut out a small chunk.

"How will I lose some hair tonight?" she teased.

"Car door?" he quipped.

They laughed.

The movie was out right at eleven, just like she had told her dad it would be. This time, as Adam helped her into the truck, she just came right out and asked, "Adam, do you ever wonder if maybe our parents are right and that you and I will end up married?" Adam was stunned into silence. He couldn't believe she had just blurted it out. He had hoped all night he would get a chance to talk to her about how he felt. Having no idea what to say, he said nothing. Here she was, out of the blue, asking him. He wasn't sure why she was asking, so he wasn't sure how to answer.

"I hadn't. Not until tonight. I think I have always taken for granted how amazing you are. I don't want to do that anymore. Thank you so much for this night." She held her breath for only a moment, then she bent over and ever-so-gently placed a kiss right atop Adam's totally shocked, half-opened mouth. He recovered quickly and slid his hand up to Amber's face and took full control of the kiss. Then, utterly shocked at what had just happened, he exhaled heavily, exclaiming, "I was planning to do that eventually." They both burst out laughing nervously, neither looking at the other for a moment.

Amber wanted to savor every moment of the night. "Let's go up Southside Hills. The view is amazing from up there."

"Amber, I promised your dad I would bring you straight back. Detouring wouldn't be wise if we want to be able to go out again. Your dad said you're not even allowed to date yet—"

"We don't have to say anything yet, Adam. Please. I don't know what my parents would say."

"Amber, if you're not going to tell them, then we will just have to wait," he answered seriously. Amber was immediately irritated.

"Mr. Goody-Two-Shoes, Adam!" she started, with irritation in her voice. Then she changed her mind and her tone. She would try killing him with kindness. "Adam, please, just give me some time to tell them. All right? Please. I just want some time with this. Don't you? What if things don't work out? Our parents will be so disappointed. We can talk about it at the top of the hill," she suggested coyly. Adam did not reply, but when she looked through the windshield and read the street signs, they were indeed heading up Southside. She couldn't hold in her excitement as she squealed. She undid her seatbelt, scooted over a seat, and encircled Adam's arm with both of hers. Her joy was infectious.

Adam wisely wondered, "What am I getting myself into?" But for this one moment he wouldn't care. With this beautiful girl snuggled up to him, holding on to him with such anticipation and delight, he would break the rules, just this once.

Amber had been up here once before, a long time ago, with the youth group. It was awesome. They didn't come up to this lookout anymore though; now it was overrun with people making out in their cars and others selling drugs.

As they wound around the last bend and entered the huge lot, not a single vehicle was in view. Adam drove the pickup to the edge of the hill where the view was the best. It really was amazing. High mountains encircled green countryside. The houselights were few, randomly dancing along the hillside. The night sky held a million stars. And the full moon was a huge orb floating on a sea of black glass. They had been taught that each star told a story; God knew each one by name. She was in awe.

"Adam, please stop just one minute. Let's get out. We only have to take one breath of fresh air, then we can get back in the truck and go home and not another word from me. Promise."

Adam mused to himself, "This girl must have had some idea of my feelings for her because she already has a knack for manipulating me." Regardless, he pulled over. How could he not? They got out of the truck and awkwardly held hands as they walked around to the front to take in the view. The air felt so clean. They simultaneously took in a deep breath, and then Adam took her hand and led her back to her side of the truck.

Amber just couldn't resist. "Don't you want to kiss me?"

After a moment of considerable thought, Adam finally answered, "I think we should just take things slowly."

Amber was immediately irritated. "Adam, we have been friends since we were in diapers. We know everything about each other. How slowly do you want to take things?"

Adam kindly but firmly replied, "You promised not to say another word, Amber. Let's go." He started walking to the door. He was relieved when he heard her footsteps right behind him. They climbed in the truck, and Adam started it up. Before putting it into drive, he leaned over, shocking Amber as he sweetly and nervously touched her mouth with his. He stopped for a moment to gaze into her eyes. Then he reached up and gave one of her curls a little tug. They drove off in sweet silence.

The corners up to Southside were steep and winding, and a vehicle easily picked up speed while going down. The rich and spoiled, with their souped-up cars, picked up speed on the way up as well. It was a vehicle such as this that came around the corner, trying to reach top speed. Only, it was on their side of the road. The car began to skid out of control. Tires screeched. The smell of burning rubber filled the truck. The oncoming car was doing a one-eighty, sailing right into their path.

Adam swerved to miss the oncoming car. It seemed to be on a guided missile course. Amber grabbed the dashboard and dug in her nails. She stole a moment to look at Adam, and then she felt the impact. The shrill scraping of metal on metal. Crushing. She sucked in her breath. She felt her face smash into something hard. The truck rolled end over end. She heard screaming. Was it her? Blackness surrounded her.

Amber opened her eyes. She looked around as best she could. Her face felt tight and swollen. Her neck was immobile. Her chest heaved in a ragged breath, seeking much-needed oxygen. She couldn't move. Every part of her body ached. She looked out the window and realized they had rolled at least fifty feet down a steep embankment. Amber forced her neck to turn, enabling her to get a better look out the window. She could not see the speedy yellow car that had run them off the road. She slowly worked the muscles in her neck to turn her head the other way. She reached over, feeling with her hand at the same time, opening her mouth to speak. She needed to ask Adam how he was. Even her jaw didn't want to cooperate. She continued to turn her head slowly until she could see Adam.

She was immediately gripped with dread. She felt pain in her soul. She no longer felt her own anguish. Amber fumbled to undo her seatbelt and reached over to him. "Adam. Oh, Adam. Not you! Not now!" She gently touched his face then closed her eyes. Disbelief crept in. She refused the tears that wanted to fall. Somehow crying would mean this was all real. She refused to believe. One moment, that's all it had taken.

Amber felt around for her purse, then the cell phone that was inside it. She dialled 911. The lump in her throat was hard and tight. It ached, needing to be released. The dispatcher was talking. She was getting frustrated. Her breath came in short, quick gasps.

She held her breath long enough to hear the lady on the receiver, "We have a unit on the way." Amber forced herself to look at her beloved friend, not noticing the continuous trickle of blood coming from a large gash in her own forehead. She felt nauseated. Was there any hope? She looked away and closed her eyes, pressing them tightly. She refused to look. If she didn't see it, it wasn't real. The stench of blood filled the cab. Without warning, she vomited.

The moon was all that shed light on the surrounding blackness. The pale light added shadows of evidence. The crushing blow was from a huge boulder. Adam's skull, on the left side, was caved in. It looked hollow, like the soft spot on a baby's head, only bigger, farther to the back, and lower on the side. He must have been looking far right, at Amber, for the rock to do such specific damage. His body slouched in the seat. The roof on his side was caved in. She reached out a shaky hand to touch, but she quickly lowered it. Realization set in, and she screamed.

"God, God." She began to sob uncontrollably. More words came, but they were barely understandable. "Don't take him. He's the wrong one. Take me. Take me, God. Do you hear me? It's not too late. He's the obedient one. I made him take me up here. It's not his fault. You're punishing the wrong person." She raised her head and hands. With fingers pressed firmly together, she begged God again. Streams of tears fell from her eyes. "God, give him back. I beg you. You're supposed to be merciful, loving. The dead can't do anything for you. He served you. He was going to be mine. He was going to be mine." She repeated her outcry, groaning with soulful pain that only the Spirit of God could discern. Her heart was sick, her soul vanquished.

Defeated, she laid her head back. Her brain was a minefield of thoughts: guilt, anger, and despair. She would not settle for this. It was wrong.

She could hear the ambulance. Soon the attendants made their way down the steep bank to where the truck rested.

"Lay down, miss," a man said to her kindly. "We're going to get you out of here. You'll be fine." Exhaustion and relief took over. She reached her hand up to her face and discovered the hardened blood. Running her fingers along her forehead, she felt the four-inch gash. She felt her eyelids shut. What a coward she was. She didn't even ask about Adam. She didn't want to know. She would keep believing the doctors would fix him. She kept telling herself that once they got to the hospital, he would be okay. Surely God wouldn't take one so young and devout. He was certainly a better Christian than she was. If anyone deserved death, it was her, not him, and surely a just God...

When Amber regained consciousness, she was in an enormous white room filled with bright lights. Her first thought was God had seen it fit to answer her heart-wrenching plea. She looked around, stiff and sore, and then closed her eyes again. She quickly opened them as the trauma played out behind her eyelids, frame by frame, second by second. Then the horrifying vision of Adam; it wouldn't go away whether her eyes were open or closed.

"Mom! Mom!" The attempt to get the words out took her breath and sapped her meager energy. No one answered. Panic gripped her chest. Her stomach twisted. Her heart pounded. She could hear the frantic rhythm in her ears. Her fists clenched the sheets that ensconced her body. This time the sound that escaped was a scream. "Mom!"

To Amber's relief, the double doors came flying open, and in ran her mother, her father, a doctor, and two nurses. The nurses tried gently, yet forcibly, to grab Amber's arms and take her vitals. A doctor shone a light in her eyes; someone else had a stethoscope placed on her chest. Her mother looked agonized as she gripped her father's arm.

Michael White stared at his daughter, knowing her condition was the least of his worries. He was more troubled about how they were going to tell her, her lifelong friend was no longer with them. Sure he could tell her he was with Jesus now. That hardly gave a fifteen-year-old comfort. It offered no solace in the wake of what she was facing. How were they going to deal with this? How would she deal with it?

Catherine was relieved their daughter was in stable condition. That relief was minimal knowing the heavy hearts Tina and Jim must have. They had been friends for a long time. Crossing paths in the hospital hallway, Catherine had immediately hugged Tina and sobbed with her. The two men had barely made eye contact, uncertain of what to say. They would see this family every Sunday.

Michael found himself feeling guilty. While his daughter may have some obstacles and issues to overcome, she was alive. The Farrells were being escorted to the hospital morgue. They would have to identify the body. They had no hope. Adam was pronounced dead at the scene. Their son was gone. He would never come home.

Amber willed herself back to the present. Looking around her dingy eight-foot cell, she sucked in a deep breath. The stench was reality; it stung her nostrils, and her stomach tightened. She was all alone in this. She thought about Adam often, but that first year she remembered him daily. God had made such a mistake. He saved the wrong person. She was sitting right next to Adam. Had the truck rolled a foot to the left, they would have missed the boulder completely. Two more feet to the right, she would be the one in a pine box. She would bet her miserable life Adam wouldn't be on trial for murder.

No more of that, she tried to convince herself. She should never have allowed her mind to wander back to that day. It always made her feel depressed and guilty. There was no fix in a courthouse that would enable her to forget everything that needed to be forgotten … nothing to dull the pain. The hours dragged on. More dark thoughts attacked Amber's mind. The memories wouldn't leave her head. Solace was intangible. How long did she have? How long till she would know her fate? How much longer did she have to hope? Hope for what? A miracle perhaps?

Fork In the Road

"Who leave the straight paths to walk in dark ways."

Proverbs 2:13

mber lay awake in her cell. It was three a.m. She found herself awake in the middle of the night on numerous occasions. Sleep never came easily, and always for the same reason:
memories tugged, begging to be replayed, leaving in their wake
streams of events that decayed all she was and ever hoped to be.

Amber hadn't slept through the night since the accident three
months ago. From where she lay she could see the barren trees,
their long, spindly branches looking as cold as the air felt. The
dull howl of the January wind was barely audible through the
thick window, adorned by an old-fashioned wood pane. She
wrapped her arms around her thin body and tried to shut out
the cold. Getting out of her warm bed, she felt the freezing
floor beneath her feet. The thick flannel nightgown she wore
clung to her body and did nothing to stop the cold from clawing
at her bare skin, allowing the cold to seep into her soul. She ran
her fingers along the pane and felt for a draft; there was none.
She walked over to her vanity, grabbed the stool, and placed
it in her closet. She climbed on top of it and then quietly and

carefully pushed on the ceiling. The corkboard gave way to the pressure, and she reached for her treasure.

It was an old wooden cradle made for her by her grandfather. In it she kept her favorite pieces of memorabilia: pictures of her brother, family, and friends. There were letters from friends she had made at camp; some were funny, some were sad. Sometimes when she had trouble sleeping, she would sit and look through her special box. She had started it a long time ago, but it was only lately that it had become so significant. How long would this pain go on? She wondered if a person ever actually got over a tragedy the magnitude of which she was suffering. Amber knew her parents expected her to handle the situation better than she was, but they just didn't understand. She had seen it all. She had seen his face. She had smelled the blood. She had to live with the sounds of crushing metal as the truck rolled down the mountainside. She couldn't just forget.

Amber picked up a picture of her mother and father. They looked so young. She was in the picture. She couldn't have been more than two years old. Her parents looked like hippies leaning up against their Volkswagen van. She looked like a flower-child with a daisy wreath placed atop her curly golden locks. She adored the picture. It seemed to capture the innocence that one could easily believe, if they chose, would always exist.

She had hoped to be a nurse. She was smart enough, but her grades had plummeted over the last few months, and she wasn't sure if she was going to be able to recover them before the end of the term. Truthfully, she wasn't sure she wanted to. It was too hard. Amber closed her eyes. She tried praying, but she didn't know what to pray for.

"God," she began, "God, please get me through this." She opened her eyes and shook her head. She raised her face toward heaven and waited. Nothing. Just what she had expected. It had been like this for a while. She had already apologized to God for accusing Him of taking her friend. He hadn't forgiven her. How long was she supposed to hang on alone? She let out a deep sigh, feeling once again as though God had left her out of His plan and was still angry with her for words uttered in despair. She carefully put her cradle back and replaced the corkboard.

As she headed back to bed, she heard a tick against her window. She froze and then quickly turned off the light. Amber's overactive imagination was playing tricks on her again, she supposed. She crawled on her hands and knees over to the window. Barely lifting her face, eyes wide, she peered through the glass. A short scream escaped. She threw her hand up to her mouth to muffle the noise she hadn't been able to control. Only the windowpane separated them. It was Dave.

"You scared me half to death," she accused through the thick glass. Dave had climbed the trellis outside her bedroom window. He had a huge grin on his face. He motioned for her to open the window. The strong stench of alcohol filled her lungs, not the fresh air she had expected.

"Are you crazy? What are you doing?"

"Let me in," he insisted without answering her question.

"If you're caught in here, you and I are both as good as dead. Why are you here?"

"I was just walking home. I noticed your light on, so I thought I'd see what you were doing."

"I am doing nothin'. It's three a.m. I was going back to bed," she retorted impatiently.

"You want to come out?" he asked casually, but it annoyed her that he blatantly ignored what she had just said. Furthermore, she didn't know Dave that well, and she could tell he had been drinking.

"No thanks." Her voice sounded a lot more sure then she felt. She was grateful.

"Aw, come on. We'll go for a walk. You're having trouble sleeping obviously."

She began to think. He was right about that, and the way he slurred his words did sound kind of funny. Noticing her hesitation, he begged, "Please, please, please." She was beginning to feel flattered by his enthusiasm. *What harm could it do?* she thought. Hopefully the fresh air would help her accomplish sleep.

"I need to change first."

He smiled and said, "I'll wait right here."

"No, you won't."

"You want me to turn around?"

"No." She was emphatic. He looked at her, his brows furrowed in question. "Wait downstairs." Her high-pitched tone was a sign that she was getting annoyed. He didn't seem to notice and asked another foolish question. "What if you leave me alone down there and don't come for me?"

"You'll just have to trust me then, won't you? You know, if you can't trust me, it's a sure sign that I should not trust you." He was through the windowsill in a flash and said, "I will be waiting."

Amber pulled on her jeans quickly, knowing it would take nothing for her to lose her nerve. What idiotic thing had she just agreed to do? She threw on a sweatshirt and walked over to her window, convincing herself that agreeing with him was probably the quickest way to get rid of him. She looked out the window as she prepared to make her descent, and, to her dismay, Dave lay sprawled on his back, passed out on her lawn. She had to help him now. At the very least she would have to get him off her property. She quietly and quickly made her way down the trellis, jumping the last three steps.

"Dave." She shook his shoulder. "You can't sleep here. Dave, you have to get up. Come on. I'll walk you home." He stirred, gazed at her, then smiled and promptly closed his eyes again. "No, no, come on." Amber, determined to get Dave off the property, pulled his arm over her shoulder and started dragging him. He began to rouse and fumbled with his footing. She pulled on him and helped him along. At least he was off her parents' lawn now.

Grateful for the assistance he was receiving, Dave slurred a gratuitous, "Thanks, Amber." He leaned over to try and kiss her. She was appalled. She scrunched up her face and, remaining polite, insisted, "It's no problem. You live close. Besides, what was I supposed to do? Leave you passed out on my front lawn?"

Dismal thoughts caused Amber to shiver. Dave noticed immediately.

"Something wrong?" Was he testing her? Or was he waiting for her to admit it?

"It's cold, that's all," she lied.

"Well, I really do appreciate you helping me out like this."

"So are we even?" she blurted out.

"For what? Oh, for me taking the rap for you getting caught with a doobie?"

Amber looked around to see if anyone could hear their conversation. Obviously no one could, but the sound of those words coming out of Dave's mouth were so convicting. Was it really her he was talking about? The incident he was referring to had taken place last Friday. Amber had tried smoking pot once before, that one time with Stan. She slept really well after that, which is how she convinced herself to do it a second time. Since the accident her sleep had been constantly tormented by nightmares, but not that night. It was easy after that to convince herself that if she only used it to help her sleep, she wasn't really doing anything wrong. She had a handful of new friends who readily echoed her whimsical theory.

After school on Monday, at her locker, a buddy handed Amber the joint she had requested and paid for. She was ready to put it in her bag for later. Dave had noticed the teacher rounding the corner; he was more accustomed to hiding things. Dave grabbed the joint from her and ran down the hallway to the bathroom, where he flushed it down the toilet. Though the teacher hadn't actually seen anything, he got detention for the rest of the week, based primarily on previous run-ins with the same teacher. Dave hadn't bothered showing up at school at all.

Amber wondered if this would count as payback. By the

tone of his voice, she understood that he wasn't going to let her off that easily.

"Go with me to Amy's party tomorrow and we're even."

"You can ask, but I will never be allowed to go."

"It seems to me, Amber, that you are becoming more clever all the time. Find a way. Come on. It will be fun."

"I don't know, Dave."

He leaned on her, using his body weight to push her gently, playfully. "You know what I'm going to have to do, don't you, Amber? I'm gonna have to tell your mommy and daddy the naughty things you've been up to."

Amber saw no humor in his statement. Despite Dave's chuckle, she felt threatened. She thought about his question for a moment. She was still contemplating how she was going to get out of this mess when Dave interrupted her thoughts. "Listen, you come with me, and we're even, I swear. Come on." Dave looked at her and smiled reassuringly before he continued. "Amber, I was just teasing. I wouldn't tell anyone. I just really want you to come."

It might be easier to go just to appease him. Put an end to this, or who knows what he might think of threatening her with the next time he had too much to drink. Besides, she convinced herself, she could always change her mind.

"Okay, fine. I'll go, but I am going to be home by midnight, you got it?"

"I think I got you," he answered boyishly. She narrowed her eyes and hardened her stare. Dave smiled at her, undaunted by her expression. "Okay, okay. You win. Home by midnight." He played along. Amber ducked out from under his arm. Away from his foul breath, she watched as Dave fell to the grass. At least it was his grass this time and not hers. He just lay there on his back.

"Sorry," she said with a chuckle. She hadn't realized how heavy he was and how much of his weight she was shouldering until he fell. "Goodnight!" she called as she headed for home at a sprint. "Are you just going to leave me out here?" he called after her. "Help! Help!"

Amber was halfway down the block, but she still heard the commotion.

"Shut up, you idiot! Get in here. You tryin' to wake the neighbors? Look at you. What a loser. Drunk again. Pathetic, just like your father."

Amber stopped, shocked. The tirade continued, laced with expletives Amber had never heard before. Then the door slammed.

Amber slowed to a walk. She couldn't believe what she had just heard. Walking home slowly, she contemplated. She had never heard a parent speak to a child like that. Amber quietly climbed back in her window. The house was still and silent. She lay back down in her bed; the relief of sleep she had hoped for would not come. She kept thinking, *Am I really going to go with Dave to the party tomorrow? Can I deceive my parents and sneak out of the house? What if I get caught?* Woven into these thoughts were all the horrible things she had heard from Dave's mother. Her degrading words reverberated in Amber's ears. She started rationalizing. Guilt and sympathy propelled her decision. She didn't want to disappoint him. He seemed to suffer enough disappointment. Further, she really did owe him, big time. What could it hurt?

The more she rationalized the situation, the less it sounded like such a bad idea. Maybe her parents would let her go. She thought about just asking them. Then if they said no she would go anyway, and that would be worse. No, she would just go. She had made up her mind.

From the moment Amber was awake Friday morning she had a funny feeling in her stomach; like she knew something was going to happen, she just didn't know what. It was obvious to her though. She knew the jitters were because of her decision to deceive her parents and go out with a boy.

Everything was so exciting. She would have never thought

herself capable of something like this before. Amber headed out the door with a casual good-bye to her mother and the usual kiss on her brother's soft, chubby cheek.

She was more than a little surprised to see Dave at school. He walked right up to her and put his arm around her so casually that she didn't notice for a minute, and it felt nice to get some attention.

"So, babe, we still on for tonight?"

Amber blushed deep red. No one had ever spoken to her so brazenly in all her life. She hid her face in her locker, hoping no one would notice them, which only egged Dave on.

"Amber, you're blushing. You weren't this red last night when I was in your room." He had gone too far. Amber blushed even deeper. She had to say something. "One more word like that out of you, and I won't go with you anywhere, ever."

"Chill, baby. I was just teasing. I didn't know you blushed so easily." He paused for a moment and tugged gently on one of Amber's long curls, and then he looked into her eyes. He said nothing for a moment. She began to feel uncomfortable. When she looked away, he said confidently, "You look so beautiful." He winked at her and walked away. The bell rang shortly, leaving Amber with butterflies in her stomach and a smile she couldn't wipe off her face.

After school Amber looked around expectantly, hoping to see Dave somewhere. She had anticipated him waiting for her, but she couldn't find him anywhere. She was disappointed. She hoped he hadn't forgotten her. She boarded the bus for the ride home.

She took a seat at the back. She wanted to be alone; she needed to think. This was all happening so fast. Did she really think a guy like Dave was a good thing? And what if he really liked her? But what if he didn't? The bus slowed to a stop near her house.

There he was. He was so cool in his faded, baggy jeans. He wore a black hoodie with the small red logo of a skateboarder on the left side. He walked up to her as she stepped from the bus; she had already begun to blush. He grinned in response. Amber shifted her eyes to the ground. He stopped right in front of her and waited for her to raise her head. When she did, there he was again, looking directly into her eyes. He took a casual step closer. He whispered in her ear, "So I'll meet you right here, in this exact spot, at ten thirty, okay?"

Amber's eyes were huge as she thought for a second that he might try to kiss her in front of her house in the middle of the day when anyone could be watching.

Dave turned and walked toward his house without so much as an over-the-shoulder glance. She walked in the house and went straight upstairs to her room. She was not ready to see her parents. The giddy feeling in her stomach made her feel sure she was making the right choice.

At the dinner table Amber wiggled and twitched in her chair; only Linc seemed to notice, and he quipped, "Amber, you're supposed to sit still, ya know?" She smiled.

Her body vibrated with anticipation, whether from nerves or from excitement, she couldn't be sure. Forcing herself to breathe deeply, she finally managed what she hoped to be a casual glance at her parents. Were they suspicious?

They both made momentary eye contact with her, smiled slightly, and started eating. Her father began his usual, "How was school today?"

She answered calmly, "Fine, Dad. We get to dissect a fetal pig at school next week. Mr. Scott told all the girls that we're responsible for our own vomit." She smiled at her casual non-chalance. Her parents both chuckled, and they continued to make small talk throughout the rest of the evening meal.

After dinner Amber started clearing the dishes from the table; it was her usual chore. Her mother followed her into the kitchen carrying an armload of dishes.

"Is everything okay, Amber? You know your father and I are both here if you need to talk."

"I'm fine."

"It's just that since the accident—"

"Really, Mom, I'm fine. Stop worrying."

"I'm your mother. Worrying is what I do."

"I didn't ask you to worry about me. That's your hangup. It's not like I do anything anyway. I don't go anywhere. I don't have friends anymore. So really, what do you have to worry about?" Amber knew her tone bordered on reprimandable, but she didn't care. She was tired of the same questions every day, the underlying accusations that she wasn't fine, the continuous talk that she needed to see a shrink. Suddenly, she felt justified. She looked her mother straight in the face and allowed a fleeting happiness for the knowledge of what she was planning.

Catherine met her daughter's gaze. A strange chill ran up her spine. It left her tingling. "What exactly is going on?"

Was there wisdom in the question, or was it random?

"I told you, nothing. Stop harassing me. I need to be left alone, that's all."

"Do not take that tone with me, Amber."

"Or what?" She felt belligerent now. No one was going to accuse her. She hadn't done anything ... *yet*. What was her problem anyway? Compared to other kids at her school, her parents really had nothing to complain about.

Catherine looked so angry. "I have had it with this attitude of yours. Every time anyone around here tries to talk to you, you get irrational."

"No one around here talks to me. In case you hadn't noticed, everyone just accuses me. 'What's wrong with you, Amber?' 'You really need to see a shrink.' It's so fake! You're just worried that all your church friends are going to find out your daughter's a freak and your little family isn't perfect. Oh, what do they fill your mind with, Mother? I can just hear them, 'I bet she does drugs, Catherine. Check her school bag for drugs. No, I bet she smokes cigarettes. My cousin's daughter saw her hanging around with—"

Smack! Amber had not been struck on her face ever. Both she and her mother wore matching shocked expressions, only Amber's was colored with the red imprint of a hand on her left cheek.

Without a word Amber turned, fixed her eyes, and slowly walked away. She clenched her teeth, refusing any tears that threatened to fall. A storm brewed in her mind. A battle raged in her heart brought on by the intense self-pity she felt and a new feeling of justification. *You will not get away with that,* she told herself over and over.

Catherine was shocked. It had happened so fast. She, unlike her daughter, had no compunction for allowing tears to show, and hers slowly made their way down her tired face. The closer she tried to get to her daughter, the further away she seemed. Amber's accusations had been harsh. She hadn't realized that their preoccupation with fear for their daughter had led her to the conclusion that they expected her to be perfect.

It was eight thirty when Michael knocked on the door. "Amber, let me in." It was not posed as a question; it was a command. She made a point of only allowing herself to make a moment of eye contact as she reluctantly let him in. "I'm not going to ask you any questions or make any accusations. I just came up to kiss you goodnight and tell you that I love you." He spoke sincerely. Why did her dad always know what to say? She felt a lump rise in her throat. She wanted to be a little girl and throw herself into his arms and sob, but that just wouldn't do, not anymore. She was too close. She needed desperately to hang on to the anger. The anger made her strong and absolved the guilt. She would not allow him to weaken her resolve after his wife had been the one to start the battle.

"Goodnight." She leaned in to allow her father his kiss. He didn't say anything else for a moment. He just stared at her.

Then, in a husky voice full of emotion, he said, "You have grown into such a beautiful young lady." He paused for a moment, then continued. "You are so much like her." Amber forgot her decision to not look at him and stole a glance.

"Yes. Two of you. God must be punishing me." Amber heard the soft laughter in his voice. The deep smile lines around his mouth reached up into his moustache. The gentle lines around his eyes pulled back. He was so handsome. Even if Amber was mad at him for pointing out how alike she and her mother were, she could never really be mad at him. It was true, and he had always pointed it out. She shut her eyes. He kissed her on top of her bowed head and softly said, "Goodnight. I love you."

"I know."

Amber was completely dressed under her covers. Waiting. Staring at the clock. Ten thirty came around, but there was no sign of Dave. Ten thirty-five, nothing. Ten forty-five, nothing. She was beginning to feel relieved. She didn't really want to deceive her dad. He didn't deserve that. He couldn't possibly know what it had been like for her lately. And her mother, why had she taken it upon herself to try to fix her? She wasn't broken. She needed time and some space. She would be okay if they just left her alone.

That was what Amber had thought back then. *Leave me alone. I'll be okay.* As she looked back now, she wondered if that were true. There had just been too many other protagonists.

As the clock ticked, she continued to stew over her life and the preceding events. Michael was the balancer. She and her mother were too much alike. They clashed, and, of course, Daddy seemed to have the exact percentage of a father-husband ratio to keep peace in the family.

It was eleven when Amber finally heard the tick of a pebble on the windowpane. Excitement quickly returned. She leapt out of the bed and ran to the window. She waved at Dave, then climbed out the window and lowered herself onto the trellis to finish the climb down. She was greeted enthusiastically by her friend.

"I really thought you'd jam. I am impressed," he stated, giving her a onceover. And she did the same. She had chosen to stick with casual—jeans and a T-shirt. She had thrown on a soft pink woolly; it clung to her soft curves, and the color accentuated the healthy hue of her skin. Amber still felt a bit of a chill.

Dave also wore jeans. They were faded and hung off his hips; he wore a black waffle shirt that emphasized his youthful frame and a tan down-filled jacket that he left open.

Dave walked up to Amber, looped his arm around her waist, and let it rest gently on her hip. "Thanks for coming out with me tonight," he said in a way that made Amber believe he meant exactly that, nothing else. She smiled, relieved that she couldn't smell alcohol on his breath. He gently kissed her cheek. They walked the rest of the way to Amy's huddled together, trying to shut out the cold. It was odd at first to have her arm around him, but it quickly felt like the most natural thing in the world.

As they walked, Dave talked up a storm, telling story after story. He was charming and full of complements, something she wasn't used to.

He is so funny, she thought to herself. *Why haven't I noticed that before?*

The walk to Amy's was twenty minutes; after fifteen they could hear the music. It was booming. People were dancing everywhere. Amber had never in her life seen so much alcohol. Her wide-eyed expression must have said it all, and Dave set to the task of easing her mind. He grabbed her a drink. At first she refused; she felt so out of place.

Dave led her, making their way through the house. Amber stayed close to his side. There must have been over a hundred people crammed into the house. Amber found it intimidating; she had a death grip on Dave's arm. He couldn't have gotten away from her if he tried.

Dave finished his second drink and pulled Amber out onto

the living room floor, which had been cleared as a dance floor. A strobe light pulsed from the ceiling fan in the middle of the room. The music boomed out of six enormous floor speakers. Amber felt awkward; she knew she didn't fit in a place like this. She tried to pull Dave off the dance floor. He wouldn't budge, and he knew she wasn't going anywhere without him.

Finally, she leaned into Dave and shouted in his ear, "I'd really like that drink now!" He looked at her, tilted his chin, and raised the side of his mouth, a peculiar expression. Then he smiled, grabbed her hand, and led her to the kitchen. "Do you like beer? Coolers? Or maybe something harder? Jack Daniels, maybe?"

Amber, shocked at being so naive, had no idea. She didn't know what any of those things were except beer. "You choose."

Again, the quirky expression.

He poured a couple of different bottles into one glass and handed it to her. She lifted it up to her nose; it burned. How could she possibly drink it? Just as she was ready to brave her first taste, Amy, the hostess walked in. "Hey, guys, glad you could make it," she announced to the small crowd gathered in the kitchen area. That's when Amy noticed Amber. She stared hard and asked, "What are you doing here, Christian chick? Heard about your boyfriend. Killed right in front of you. That sucks. Who brought you here?"

Dave spoke up immediately. "I did. She's cool, Amy. Lighten up."

The tone in Amy's voice made Amber aware of how unwelcome she was. She started fidgeting with her glass, nervously swirling the dark liquid around. Absentmindedly, Amber took a big swig of the drink. She was unprepared for how harsh it would be. It burned her throat. It was scorching a hole in her stomach. If that wasn't enough, she started to choke.

She noticed the look of disgust on Amy's face. "If she pukes, Dave, she's your problem." She paused at the kitchen door and then turned back to finish her verbal assault. "I don't appreciate you bringing that hypocritical, 'you must repent' Christian to my party, and then you give her my booze to drink." Amy stalked out, leaving everyone to wonder why she hated Amber so much.

Though her comment was pointed to Dave, her eyes had been fixated on Amber. Amber desperately wanted to get out of the house. She grabbed Dave's arm forcefully. "I want to go home," she begged.

"Oh, come on. Amy's like that to everyone."

"No, Dave, she's right. I have no business being here." Amber contemplated telling Dave what she knew about Amy. There was no way he was going anywhere, so Amber began. "Our dads used to work together. My dad kept trying to convince her dad that he should come to our church. They actually started coming for a while. Amy never came, but two months after her parents started coming, her mother began having an affair. I heard it was with someone from the church. Her mother took off with the guy. Her father never blamed us, but he did blame the church. I think Amy blames our family for that. She must." Amber paused, then said quietly, "I would blame us too. The family fell apart after that." She needed him to understand.

Dave, in his own reality, happily retorted, "Her family hasn't fallen apart, Amber. Amy and her dad are doing just fine. As a matter of fact, he's probably here somewhere. He's always at Amy's parties. He's really cool. And I doubt Amy blames you for her mom leaving. She probably blames the church. I would. Anyway, you're not into that anymore, right? Forget it. Have some fun."

That should have been enough to send Amber running home. A shiver ran down her spine. She thought about what Dave had said: *You're not into that anymore, right?* She hadn't answered. Instead, she pleaded with Dave one more time to take her home.

"Why don't we sit outside on the lawn chairs? We can relax there. Finish your drink, and by the time you're done, if you still want to go, I promise I will take you. Deal?"

Foolishly, Amber agreed.

Amber's body was not used to alcohol. In the short time it took them to walk to the place where the lawn chairs were lined up, Amber had pounded her drink. She was in a hurry to finish it so they could leave quickly. It wasn't long before she felt dizzy. She looked up at Dave. He smiled, obviously aware of the effects the alcohol was having on her. She forgot that she had been in a hurry to leave and was giggling while being entertained with stories; whether they were true or false she didn't know. They were just funny.

Amber looked down at her own hand; it looked rubbery, and that made her laugh. She looked at Dave; she tried to touch his face with her wobbly hand. His skin felt so different under her numb fingertips. He reached up and held her hand on his cheek for a minute. He looked at her questioningly. He leaned over and kissed her full on the mouth, opening his, then sucked on her lower lip. He brought his hand up and cupped the back of her neck. She really had not expected that. Dave continued to kiss her. Her stomach flip-flopped. No one had ever kissed her with such skill. She was drowning in it. She needed air. She drew back for a moment to catch her breath. Her chest heaved as she gulped the air.

Perhaps it was the way she clung to the front of his shirt as she dragged in a long breath that encouraged him; he only gave her a moment. His mouth came down on hers again, and his expression said it all, but he rasped, "I want you." In that moment it seemed flattering to Amber. Such unflattering words, yet in this moment they seemed to Amber to be exactly that. His aggression made her feel as though she was somehow responsible for his reckless passion. It never crossed her mind that he could be insincere.

When Dave reached under her shirt, Amber made another attempt to pull back. Uncomfortable, she fully intended to say something, but again he only gave her a gulp of air before pressing his mouth down on hers. He removed his hand, so she felt safe to continue. All they were doing was kissing. There was nothing wrong with that. Amber was so naive to the dangers of passion.

Dave made another attempt to get his hand up Amber's shirt. She denied him two more times before finally giving in. Her decision-making ability was numbed by the effects of the alcohol, and it was all too easy to see where the innocent encounter could wind up.

There is no way he's getting into my pants. That will be my boundary. This is far enough, Amber thought to herself. Dave gently lowered Amber's chair until it was completely reclined. She felt the full weight of his body on hers as he tried to position himself between her legs.

"I don't feel comfortable with this, Dave. I want to stop." She was impressed with the assuredness in her voice. Dave, looking down at her, knew all the right things to say. "I'm sorry, Amber. I thought you were in to me."

"I am, Dave. I really like you. I'm just not ready—"

"I just lost myself for a minute. It won't happen again I promise. I-I hope you're not upset."

"No." She knew she sounded too emphatic. "I just—"

"It's okay. You don't have to explain. I respect you. You're so beautiful."

Amber's heart was still pounding from their passionate encounter. Dave had awakened feelings in her that she hadn't known she was capable of. It had been so hard to stop. She was glad she had though. He respected her. He had said so!

"I would be happy just staring at your beautiful face. You don't ever have to kiss me again. I'll just stare at you."

"No … " Amber wasn't sure how to respond, so she smiled and laughed awkwardly. "Don't say that." She blushed at her own eagerness.

"You like being kissed then?"

Amber chewed on her bottom lip nervously.

"Well, I like kissing you," Dave said. "I only slightly prefer it to staring at you."

Dave kissed her again. Her grin was so broad that all he got were teeth. They both laughed. He became more serious and asked, "If you still want to go home, I'll take you."

"No. It's okay. I owed you. I better stay till the deadline. Midnight."

Dave's expression turned serious. "If that's the only reason you're here, Amber, I would really rather take you home. I just wanted you to come so we could get to know each other, you know. But if you're not here to be with me ... " He looked her straight in the eye. To anyone less naive, the hidden agenda and the deceit in those words would have been all too apparent, but to Amber they were flattery, the answer to all the loneliness she had felt lately. She probably should have known not to trust him, but she really wanted to.

"I was only kidding," she tried explaining, but his expression showed disappointment.

"I'm going to go in and get another drink. I'll be back." He walked off before Amber could say anything else. She looked around and noticed they had been the only two outside. She sat there by herself, contemplating. She hoped she hadn't offended him. So far the evening had been much better than she had anticipated. She really didn't want to mess it up. Amber could see in the house. The party was still hoppin'. She was glad to be outside, away from all the noise. She was pleasantly surprised with her date. Dave really was a gentleman. She liked him more than she could have thought possible. And Dave's obvious adulation of her only amplified those feelings. It was a while longer then she had expected before Dave returned. She was beginning to wonder what to do. There was no way she was going back in *that* house, but how long was she supposed to wait? She wondered if she had truly offended him and he wasn't planning on coming back out.

When he finally came back, Dave brought two drinks and

a blanket draped over his shoulder. Amber watched intently as he swaggered across the lawn to her. She took one of the drinks from his hand. She didn't hesitate this time; she sipped it quickly. The first one made her feel like laughing a lot, so what could be the harm in a second? Dave moved them to a more secluded spot.

Only three short months ago there would have been no possible way Amber would have allowed herself to partake in such actions, but there had been a bump in her road, and now here she was. She took a large swig from her glass. As she did, warning thoughts came into her mind. Something felt so wrong about what she was doing, but what real harm could come from just one night out? Dave gently bumped the edge of their glasses, interrupting her musings. "To new relationships." He smiled.

Relationships? she questioned. *When had that been decided?*

Dave seemed different somehow, a lot more intoxicated then when he had left. Amber had no idea how many drinks he had slammed while in the house. They finished their drinks together. Soon Dave was all over Amber. She was nervous for a moment, as he seemed stronger somehow, less aware of who she was and the previously set boundaries. Those boundaries were somewhat hazy for her as well. Dave's new motivation was getting Amber's pants off. It felt good to her too, but Amber wasn't willing to give it all up in one night.

"I'm not ready for this, Dave. Slow down." The effects of alcohol had lowered her inhibitions, and to a pro like Dave, he knew it was only a matter of wearing her down and exhausting her resolve.

Amber lay on the blanket, feeling so vulnerable. She was unsure of how things had gone so far so fast. Dave finished with her and pulled his pants up. He was either completely unaware of Amber's ambivalence, or he didn't care. Amber put her hands up to her face, trying to hide. She didn't want him to see her in case he looked over, he didn't.

Silent tears had escaped during her half-hearted ordeal to

preserve herself. She hadn't tried hard enough. Dave didn't look at her; he casually recommended she finish putting her clothes back on.

"What time is it?" Her voice came out just above a whisper

"I don't know," Dave replied impatiently, "but it was already midnight when I went back in for our drinks. Let's go." Dave was standing above Amber. She quickly finished dressing and started walking. It was so uncomfortable. Her body felt different. She wondered how she could have let this happen. She consoled herself with the memory of Dave reassuring her that this was the beginning of a new relationship. Maybe it would be okay. She tried to convince herself. When Dave put his arm around her waist and tenderly kissed her cheek, she believed it would be.

When Amber climbed in her window, the first thing she did was look at her clock. It was 1:40. She had even more trouble sleeping than she had ever experienced before. Now that sobriety was creeping in, the realization of what she had just allowed to happen penetrated her heart, sinking deep, bringing with it a hollow sensation.

She was no stranger to depression, but this was different. It went deeper than the loss of her best friend. It permeated her soul. She felt the shame. Though clothed, she felt naked. No matter how many comforting lies she told herself, they couldn't ease the disquiet. She went into the bathroom and ran a bath. Surely the cure for being dirty was a bath. Amber often ran herself a bath when she couldn't sleep. She had since the accident. She hoped it would relieve something different tonight. But a child has no way of knowing that this kind of uncleanliness cannot be washed away with water. Nor would time erase its efforts to destroy the mind and harden the heart.

Monday at school was yet another matter. Dave walked up to Amber and kissed her. He tried touching her affectionately. When she felt uncomfortable and refused to let him touch her, he walked away, not saying a word. He pulled the same stuff a few more times during the day. Amber felt everyone's eyes on her. She was sure she heard whispering, which immediately ceased every time she was within earshot. She hadn't considered that Dave would come to school and tell everyone about that night. She refused to believe it. It must all be in her head, she tried to convince herself. By the end of the day, though, it was clear.

She knew other girls her age were having sex and not discreetly. There was even a girl who used to be in her homcroom that had gotten pregnant. She had attended school right up until the end of her third trimester. No one seemed to say anything about that, so why had this one lapse of judgment on her part made her the object of such scorn by the other girls?

After the last bell of the school day had sounded, Amber approached Dave outside the school. As she came within earshot, he exclaimed in a voice that was not meant to be discreet, "I don't think things are going to work out between us. I really thought you were a different person." With his final words, she felt the sting of the wound that had begun two nights ago: "I really didn't expect you to be so easy." Amber stared in disbelief. She could feel the heat seeping into her cheeks. She felt the stares of all her peers, and anger surged in her heart. She wanted to scream, "Take it back!" Amber knew tears were much more likely to come than the words she wanted to say. She looked at him helplessly. Her eyes pleaded for him to recant his lie. The returned expression bore only distaste. It was as if she had left the bad taste in his mouth and not the other way around. Her skin felt like it was crawling within itself, seeking an escape. There was none. The tears filling her eyes were going to fall any second. She lowered her head and walked away. She had not uttered a single word in her defense. What could she say? She pressed on toward home. Tears spilled down her cheeks as she walked.

Amber tormented herself further by reliving the experience in her mind. She would not make such a mistake again. She went over every detail that had taken place. Amy had said she was the Christian one. It provided even more ammunition for those out to destroy her.

How could she have been so foolish,? So naive? She wondered if Dave had planned it this way from the beginning. Why would anyone do that? It was so cruel. She knew him … a little; she had actually felt sorry for him. That was the only reason she went with him, wasn't it?

Amber rationalized another thought. Maybe if she had let him be more affectionate with her, as he had tried to be, maybe this wouldn't have happened. Maybe they would be sitting arm in arm on the bus right now, and she wouldn't be the one walking home alone, red nosed, puffy eyed, and sobbing. She caught herself wondering if it was too late. Maybe she should talk to him, apologize. She was confused. She didn't know what to feel about Dave. She had really thought he was great. Amber had been so flattered by his attention and his compliments.

Then she remembered all the other things that had happened. The whispers. The lie. The look of disgust on Dave's face. Only two nights ago he had looked into her eyes and said how much he liked her, how beautiful she was. *"This is the beginning of a new relationship,"* he had said. He had lied; he hadn't just changed his mind. The realization that he probably never meant any of those things hit Amber hard. No one had ever spoken to her like that before. She should have known it was all deceit. A man would say anything, she had been told that. She was a fool.

Amber got home and went straight into the bathroom without saying a word to anyone. She pondered revenge; she could cry rape. Who wouldn't believe her, a good Christian girl? Just the thought made her sick to her stomach. It never crossed her mind that the horrible accusation could actually be true. How could it? She knew she could have fought harder, she could have struggled more. It hadn't been like that—not violent, just persuasive. If only she hadn't had those drinks. Her mind would have been stronger, her choice clear.

What could she do? The damage was done. She felt so violated, and she couldn't begin to explain how empty she felt—like a crucial part of her had shrivelled so small that it no longer existed, yet she remained aware of its echo.

Amber knew in her gut she could never say anything about that night, to anyone. The only thing that would come of her saying anything would be that everyone would know.

Her family would know. They would know she had snuck out and deceived them. Worse still, they would know what *she* had done. Feeling defeated, knowing it had not been her choice to have sex that night, had she done enough to prevent it? Was that considered rape, or would that be a vindictive accusation?

She sat on the shower floor, feeling the cascading water down her back. It didn't make her feel any cleaner. Much like the bath she had tried only two nights ago, she scrubbed with soap until her skin turned red and her flesh burned. She had to make the feeling go away. The filth stuck to her. From the very beginning she hadn't known how to feel about it or how to act. It was too much to take on. She was only sixteen. All the scrubbing didn't help. She was dirty, she knew it. No amount of soap and water could wash away what had begun to accumulate in the pit of her being.

By the end of her shower, Amber had come to a few conclusions. The events from the party were better off forgotten, and she would do her best to do exactly that. She would never subject herself to that type of humiliation again. She would forget Dave. She refused to waste another thought of any kind on such a creep.

As Amber lay there in her cell, recalling the event in minute detail, she realized that night had changed her, maybe even more than the accident. After the accident, she still had hope.

Hidden Truth

"For you died , and your life is now hidden with Christ in God. And when Christ who is your real life appears then you also will appear with him in all his glory."

Colossians 3:3, 4

Jake Liddell was sitting in the cruiser right next to the sheriff when he got the call on his radio phone. He had a pickup at the courthouse two hours earlier than he was booked. Apparently, the inmate had fainted, adjourning court until the following day.

When Jake heard about Amber fainting, he wondered if maybe it had been a "put on," especially considering the encounters he had had with that girl.

Jake was a police aide. He got to do ride-alongs with some of the cops. That was how he had met Charlie Johnson. Charlie was the guy who escorted the prisoners from jail to court and back.

Charlie took a liking to Jake, though he heard that was rare. Charlie "didn't like nobody," or so he had been told. Jake applied to be an aide and took the short training. After his experience with Sofia, he wanted to test the waters, see if he might want to train to be an officer. He loved the ride-alongs. It gave a clear picture of what he would be in for in the field.

Jake smiled derisively as he remembered the events that had

brought him to this place. He was nineteen. He thought he would be in love with Sofia forever. However, she would not be in love with him for as long. He had left the East Coast, traveling across the country, searching for her after she'd left their hometown. She claimed she was searching for something, but she didn't know what. For six months she wrote, she called, she begged him to be patient. Suddenly, the contact stopped. Had she found someone else? Was she dead? Not even her parents had heard from her. Eventually, he put out a missing person's file with the police. Nothing turned up. He was told to discard any hope of finding her. If she didn't want to be found, he wouldn't be able to find her. If she was dead, well, she was gone then too.

Two months later, out of the blue, a letter came. It simply stated, "I am doing well. Please don't worry. Tell Mom and Dad I'm okay. Sorry, Jake, I've found someone." The pain he felt was like dropping a stone into the middle of the ocean; it just kept sinking. He believed for a while that the pain would never go away, which is why he decided that he needed to come look for her. Maybe she was in trouble. Maybe someone had forced her to write that letter. He followed the postmark on the envelope and set out to find his love.

Upon his arrival he located a police station. He showed a constable the letter with the address and zip code. They gave him a general idea of where he could start looking. That information came with a strong warning to be careful not to walk the streets alone. Jake was shocked. He was alone, so he picked up a can of mace from a corner store to be his sidekick, then he jumped in a cab and headed to the place he hoped would lead him to Sofia. Lovely Sofia. Gentle features. Graceful and slender. Long, dark hair accented her tiny waistline. Rosy lips. Hazel eyes. He loved it when they glowed green. He inhaled deeply, remembering her sweet fragrance.

He remembered how she stroked his chest when they lay together, watching television, smiling at him, eyes sparkling.

THIS ROAD I WALK

He was consumed with memories of her. Jake remembered the disappointment at not finding her that first night. He had envisioned their reunion. She would be so glad to see him as he rescued her from peril. They would be on their way home by morning.

Day two brought no further luck. The officer's advice from back home tormented him. He pondered the effectiveness of pursuing day three. He decided to go down to the station again. He brought a picture of Sofia with him. He planned to leave it with the cops there. That was when he met Matthew. Matthew took one look at that picture, glanced at Jake, then lowered his head. Instinct told Jake he would not like what the older man had to tell him.

"Come on," he said and led Jake to his patrol car. Jake noticed him moving his lips all the way out to the cruiser. Matthew unlocked the door, and they both got in. Matthew didn't say anything, but his lips kept moving. Jake knew now that he had been praying. Back then he thought maybe the guy was "a weirdy."

It was three years ago now, and Jake remembered like it was yesterday. Pulling up to the entrance of the back alley, walking along the heavily littered back street, the strong stench of urine assaulted his nostrils. His stomach churned; he wanted to vomit. They approached a small alcove where a few people loitered.

This man has the wrong girl. There is no way this can be where my Sofia is, Jake thought to himself. But there she was on the steps. A crack pipe held between her knees. She was strung out and almost unrecognizable.

How had this lovely woman gone from such a beautiful person to the wretch in front of him? A person he barely recognized. She was gaunt, and her skin was gray. Her clothes and her hair were unkempt; he could see dirt under her fingernails.

Jake felt guilt grip his heart. He should have come looking for her sooner. He should have come with her. This never would have happened. He tried talking to her but could get no discernable answers. Soon after that Sofia's parents tried bringing her back home, but she ditched them at the airport. They got on the plane and, as far as he knew, never looked back.

Matthew took Jake out for coffee that morning;, he didn't say much. Matthew must have said more than nothing though, because the next thing Jake knew he was out of the hotel and renting an apartment. He got a job right away thanks to his new friend. He was hired in a convalescent home. It was a job similar to the one he had back home. In the beginning Jake would head downtown to visit Sofia every day after work and on his days off. He began to spiral downward. He was depressed. He knew it but felt powerless against it. Everything was hopeless.

It had been during this dark time in his life that he had found Jesus, or rather Jesus found him. He needed something to help him get through the pain and the guilt. Matthew continued to spend time with him, chatting over coffee. One particular evening Matthew noticed how grief stricken Jake was. He invited him over for dinner, and dinner turned into church the next morning with Matthew and his family. He went a few other Sundays. Then there was the Sunday they had the altar call. He was certain it had not been his own feet that did the walking. His spirit was stirred. That was what had moved him, and he found himself up at the front, face moist, sins forgiven—free. He knew immediately because the feeling was so amazing. He felt perfect and whole, yet unworthy all at once. It was as though he had never committed a sin in his whole life, not because he hadn't, but because, as the Bible says, "Therefore if anyone is in Christ he is a new creation, the old is gone, the new has come," he was new.

Anytime Jake had doubts about his newfound faith, he would look back on that moment and relive that feeling of freedom and weightlessness. Then he knew undoubtedly there was a loving and awesome God whose forgiveness was boundless. He revelled in that knowledge. It brought him through many hard times, and it would continue to do so. Pain and guilt could get him down, but they could not overtake him. He was protected by the propitiating blood of Jesus Christ, the one who stood in his place.

Over the next couple of years Jake would go occasionally to see Sofia. He brought food and clothes. He made sure she had blankets in winter. Sometimes he just wanted to make sure she was still alive. As long as she was, he would pray for her and never stop hoping. He often wondered what it was that had changed her.

Anytime Jake saw Sofia, if she was even remotely lucid he would attempt to offer her hope. Tell her of Jesus' love for her. She had begged him to stay away the last time, and so he had for way too long.

She was deteriorating rapidly. If he was honest with himself, he stayed away to save himself the pain of watching her die slowly. Yet the Spirit of God, who wishes for none to die in their sins, prodded him. Through that next year he continued to pray for her and all the other young women who had abandoned hope and taken to the streets with no homes to go to and no families who missed them.

One girl told him the story of how her mother's boyfriend had raped her. When her mother found out, she went into a fit of rage and beat her daughter up, accusing her of "seducing her man." She kicked the helpless fourteen-year-old out into the street. Jake felt her shame at that admission. He saw her pain. It showed in the hollowness of her eyes. She had been the one to tell Sofia, "You don't know how lucky you are that someone wants to love you. You should run away with him while he still wants you." The drug was powerful though and Sofia's drive low. Again she stayed and refused Jake's help.

Finally, he came to terms with the fact that Sofia may never want what he had: Salvation. That troubled him deeply. Neither of them were saved when she had left the home they shared. It didn't seem right that through her demise he found salvation.

It had helped him rid himself of the empty ache she had left him with.

He would never understand how or why such tragedies happened, and he no longer asked the question. He knew God had a purpose for him. Right now that purpose was to encourage young street people into going home, for those who could go home. For those who couldn't, all he could offer was an occasional meal and warmth. He hoped to see a few saved. Not many people had the unfortunate opportunity to know the pain and suffering of the streets as personally as he did. His presence became accepted by the other street kids, so if that was God's purpose for him, he would give it all he had.

Three months ago Jake finally went back. The time since he had last been down that familiar alley seemed to be swallowed in the stench, and the sight before him as if it were only yesterday. Matthew pulled his car over and turned it off. Jake got out. He approached the small alcove that housed the numerous homeless addicts. He checked the ground as he walked, watching for needles and used condoms.

There she was, in the exact same spot where he had left her. She looked so much worse. Her skin was sallow; she was strung out. Jake crouched down beside her and spoke gently to her. Whatever she tried to say was mostly unintelligible. He wondered if she recognized him, if she remembered him, if she ever thought of the happy times when they were a couple.

Her body was full of track marks. She couldn't have weighed more than ninety pounds—barely a shadow of the woman she once was. He touched her cheek gently. She was skittish, and she jerked at the feel of his warm touch. Her skin was so cold. Jake walked back to the car. He grabbed a blanket from the trunk and wrapped it around her. He said a prayer over her and headed home.

Jake went to see Sofia a few more times while she was in such a state. He had gone too long without seeing her. Now it was apparent she didn't have much life left. He tried again to convince her to check herself into a dryout or a hospital so her last days could be peaceful. She had agreed, though he wasn't sure if she really knew where they were going. They did random HIV testing at the dryout, but Jake felt that he already knew the outcome. While there, Sofia had a bout of clarity. She confessed to Jake, if he chose to believe her story, what happened to her those long three years ago.

She slurred and jerked her story through a twisting jaw, a side effect from her drug abuse. She told how she had gotten accepted for a part in a movie. That was what she had come here hoping for. She was told there were low-key love scenes with a guy. When she showed up, she found out that she would have to do more than that, much more. She wanted no part in it. She went back to her apartment. Again and again she got the same offers. Some filmmakers were honest about what they were filming and exactly what she would have to do. She turned them all down. Then her money ran out, but there was no way she was coming home. She would never go back to her parents' house, and Jake, well, she didn't want to face him after how she had left.

She refused to come home with her tail between her legs. She had no money to get there anyway. In that moment she decided she was a survivor; she would do what it took, and she took a small role. She hoped that it would be a way for her to get noticed. She hoped that it would get her foot in the door for a real acting job. It was a sacrifice she chose to make. That didn't happen, but that was when it began. And this is where it would finally end.

Another week went by before Jake saw Sofia again. She was transferred to a hospital room with five other terminally ill patients. He walked into the room she occupied. The room smelled like death, and it would only be a matter of time before she would be gone. He prayed for her every time she entered his thoughts. He didn't pray for her to recover, just that she would be comfortable, free from the pain. He prayed that she would get one more chance to accept God's gift of salvation. He had not had the chance to explain things to her. He wanted her to go peacefully into her death, and he knew that without salvation she would fight death.

Jake got the chance when she had an episode of clarity. Her thoughts were obscure, and it was difficult to have a meaningful conversation. Still Jake talked, then he prayed with her. He spoke to her of God's love.

"John 3:16, 'For God so loved the world that he gave his only son that whoever believes in him will not die, but have eternal life.'"

Her eyes widened.

Then he spoke of hope, "First Corinthians 2:9, 'It is written no eye has seen no ear has heard, no mind has conceived what God has prepared for those that love him.'" She sucked in a deep breath. Then finally he touched on faith. "Ephesians 2:8, 'For it is by grace you have been saved through faith, and this not from yourselves. It is the gift of God, not by works so that no one can boast." And finally repentance, "First John 1:9, 'If we confess our sins, he is faithful and just and will forgive us our sins, and purify us from all unrighteousness.'" She closed her eyes. It was too good to believe, too easy.

Reading her expressions, Jake thought she understood. She nodded her head when he asked if she believed that Jesus died for her sins and that he had conquered death when he rose from the grave. She drifted off for several minutes after that.

A lump caught in Jake's throat at the memory of it.

When she opened her eyes, they were clear. She looked at Jake and said, "I understand your love," she said while reaching for his hand. He squeezed bony fingers gently in his firm grasp. Sofia breathed her last breath. Her eyes were wide open.

That was two months ago. Every night since Jake had wondered about that last day with Sofia. Had she truly understood? Was it enough? Was she in heaven now with her renewed body, a bright mind, living in the Spirit? He would not know until his time came.

Jake noticed Charlie staring at him. "Still having a hard time with it?"

He was surprised his feelings were so transparent, but the wound was still fresh and his emotions raw. It was frustrating to see all these young people with so much to live for on a daily basis. There was hope, if only they would grasp it.

"I'm okay,"

"You keep telling yourself that and it will be true."

Jake smiled at his friend and said, "Thanks."

"Is that sarcasm with your superior?"

"I'm a volunteer. I didn't know I had a 'superior.'" Jake smiled as he said it. The two men were silent a moment, then Charlie spoke up, saying, "That girl didn't faint. It was all a put-on. I just know it. Ya gotta like her spirit though."

Jake smiled. "That was the very first thought I had when they made the announcement over the radio." It was true. Jake enjoyed her liveliness. She wasn't mean spirited like a lot of the girls the cops picked up or talked to on rounds. She was just feisty.

They were nearing the courthouse now, and Charlie got out of the cruiser. Jake was right behind him.

"Uh uh, you stay in the car and wait for me."

"Come on. Let me go with you. I need the practice for when I take over your job one day."

Charlie smiled, and Jake knew the older man had already given in. Charlie waited at the desk to sign out Amber. Jake made his way to the room where she was being held. Charlie tossed him the cuffs. She would have to wear them to leave the building. Jake knocked lightly on her door before walking in.

"Ms. White, we have to take you back now. You'll try again tomorrow."

Forsaken

"The Lord is with you when you are with him, if you seek him he will be found by you, but if you forsake him, he will forsake you."

2 Chronicles 15:2

Amber sat on the edge of the cot; she was taken to this room after fainting in the courtroom a few short hours ago. It was clean and smelled of Pine Sol, just like her mother's bathroom. Amber waited for the officer who would pick her up and take her back to Klahanee. She heard the approaching footsteps, then the light knock, warning that someone would be entering. She was surprised when it was Jake Liddell who opened the door. She knew he wasn't a police officer. He was way too young.

Jake smiled at her. Amber returned the smile, recalling her first meeting with him roughly a year ago. There was an abandoned warehouse that she and a few other runaways had found. It was the same warehouse where she and some others had witnessed Stan's death. It had no running water or bathroom. No electricity. The windows that weren't bloodstained were broken. The roof leaked, giving the place a dank, musty smell.

When Jake walked into the room, Amber's round eyes widened in surprise. He was so handsome and young. Dark hair, cut short, messy on top. His eyes were deep brown, almost black.

His natural tan was appealing to her. Even then she noticed his eyes sparkle when he smiled. His hands were tucked into his faded Levi's. So unsuspecting, so unaware.

Matthew was the arresting officer on the scene that night. He walked into the warehouse, hands on his holster, prepared for anything. Amber had tried unnerving Jake's calm demeanor.

"Aren't you out a little late for a school night? Does your mother know where you are? Maybe you should give her a call."

"My mother knows where I am. Does yours?" Jake returned her cheeky comment. The smile in his voice could be heard. Amber wouldn't let him off that easily.

"My mother doesn't know where I am; why would she care where you are?"

"What? Your mother doesn't know where you are? What's your number? I'll give her a call. I am sure she would love to know where her daughter is." Jake was still smiling. He hadn't meant anything by it, but his words affected her. Her mother, unbidden, popped into her thoughts. Did her mother think about her? Had she given up on her? Maybe her mother was glad she was gone; she had been so difficult before taking off.

The other girls brought Amber back into the conversation. They were waiting expectantly for her response.

"Ooh, you gonna let him get away with that?" the girls jibed.

Not to be outdone, Amber began the nonexistent area code, "555—"

"Yeah, I already got that number," he interrupted, laughing. Even Matthew laughed.

Officer Matthew Benson began reading Amber her rights. This was Amber's second arrest, and she had enough cocaine on her to carry a heavy charge.

Amber looked at Jake, taking in his features. He looked back at her intently. What was he thinking about her? She wondered what it would have been like to meet him under different circumstances. She realized what she must look like to him. She felt ashamed and dropped her eyes. When she looked up, he was still looking at her, but his expression had changed. There was intensity in his face. A half-smile crossed his mouth. He had seen what she would never have allowed. Doubt. Worry. Sadness. Amber quickly wiped the expression from her face, forcing an awkward smile in return. She liked him. He had a hearty laugh. His heart was pure. She smiled at her own thought. He wasn't above laughing at himself.

Amber continued to taunt him; they carried on in playful banter all the way to the precinct. By the end of that night Amber wished she had met Jake a long time ago. He stirred her heart, not an easy task.

That was Jake's first ride-along. Each time their paths crossed he continued to be of good humor and was never judgmental. He never spoke down to her or anyone else. The more Amber got to know the handsome young man who bore a sweet resemblance to a boy she had once adored, the more she understood why.

"I'm ready, Mr. Liddell. Where is your sidekick?"

"Actually, I am his sidekick. He's downstairs signing you out." They walked in silence. Amber roamed her memories. She recalled another run in with Jake. She and a couple of friends were hanging around the back alleys, about to get high. He had come out with Officer Benson. The two men stopped and talked to the girls. Jake began to tell stories about a man named Jesus, a man who loved and never condemned.

"There was a woman. She was unmarried but living with a man who was not her husband," he began. "The religious leaders wanted to stone her. That was what they did to unfaithful women in those days. The men brought her out to Jesus. They were already picking up their stones.

"'Teacher?' one of them asked, 'the law says we are to stone this woman; she is full of sin.' Jesus didn't even look up from what he was doing. He just replied calmly, 'Let him who is without sin be the first to cast the stone.'

"One by one the people dropped their stones and walked away. The woman looked up, for the men had tossed her at Jesus' feet. Heart full of emotion, she touched his sandals. She was so grateful, yet terrified.

"'You, in fact, have lived with five men, none of whom were your husband,' Jesus spoke. She kept her head down. 'Go in peace. Sin no more.' The woman was overcome with joy and relief. She went all over her town, telling of the Jesus who knew all she had done and had still forgiven her."

How Amber's heart had ached. She wanted to hold on to that so badly. Guilt kept her from embracing it. The other girls had commented about the "story." If only they knew she was a believer once. She had belonged to Jesus herself, but she had been abandoned, left to defend herself. She had lost too many battles.

"Jesus only loves who he chooses. Maybe you get lucky and he chooses you. Maybe you don't," she said flatly, trying to keep emotion from her voice. That was all she had said. Jake read everything into that simple statement. She saw it in his expression. He looked at her like he knew. Her face flushed with shame.

Jake used the comment as an invitation to, in her words, "preach" to her. She quietly heard him out. He had an element of innocence. It reminded her of childhood, of keeping hope alive. Sometimes it got her through another night

"You're sick?" Jake brought her out of her reverie.

"I've been better," she said honestly. She hoped he wouldn't take it as an invitation to preach. He surprised her by saying nothing. It was usually Jake who did all the talking.

"How are you?" he would ask. He really wanted to know. "What are you thinking about? What gives you hope?" *If* only he knew how painful it was for her to be reminded of hope. But being around him did that. She couldn't allow herself to hope.

Uncomfortable with the prolonged silence, Amber began talking. "So how's the weather out there?"

He looked over at her and raised his brow. He was waiting, perhaps hoping for something deeper. She knew Jake would already know what had happened in the courtroom. Still, he said nothing. Was he waiting her out? The silence was getting to Amber. They reached Charlie, and all three of them headed out the door, making their way to the cruiser. Charlie walked ahead. Amber could see the cruiser—fifty feet to go. Jake stopped; he turned and looked at her.

Last chance. He didn't say it, but it was written all over his face. She wasn't ready, he wasn't ready, only he was too naive to know it. She would spare him but not let him go empty.

"You're a man of the law, Mr. Liddell. What do you think my future holds?"

"Your father in heaven knows. You ask him, and the outcome will be exactly what it's supposed to be."

Amber looked squarely at Jake Liddell. Her eyes pleaded, *For once, please, you know that's not what I'm asking you. I want a real answer.*

"Only Jesus knows what the future holds—"

"Forget it. Forget I asked," she spit out the words and then walked away. She was relieved to have an excuse to feel angry.

"Why do you fight him, Amber?"

He had never called her by her first name before. Never had he felt so familiar. It caught her off guard. She liked the way it sounded.

She pondered a moment before replying. Her answer was a surprise to both of them. "'Be sure of this the wicked will not go unpunished but those who are righteous will go free.' Which am I, Jake Liddell?"

Jake looked at the young woman in front of him. They had reached the car. The quotation she had recited was from Proverbs. Only the Good Lord could have known how shocked he was to hear the forlorn girl quote Scripture. He understood that

Amber was seeking hope. A simple question, but there was no simple answer. He remained silent.

Gesturing to the open car door, he waited for her to get in. He got in next to her and undid her cuffs. He stared at her, trying to maintain composure. Gently turning her face toward him, he faced the woman beside him. Amber cringed, preparing herself for anything.

How could he know all the things she had been through? How could he possibly have known that the first thought that came into her head was, *What sexual favor is he going to want from me? What is he going to do to me?*

For a moment she felt a stab of pain. She desperately needed to believe that he wasn't like everyone else, that he was genuine, but when he smiled and did nothing else, she felt hope.

Charlie started the cruiser and they took off. His smile was so innocent. She realized she had miscalculated his gesture. An enormous grin spread across her own face. She felt the shine in her eyes, a shine she thought was long gone.

Jake looked at Amber. He had always thought her to be beautiful, but somehow, in that moment, she was more than that—she was radiant. He found himself looking deeply into her eyes, forgetting momentarily that he was supposed to be offering her hope, not ogling her the way he had seen so many others do. Jake lifted a nervous hand and placed it gently on Amber's. He noticed her surprised expression. He didn't allow it to deter him. He closed his eyes and began to pray. "Thank you, Lord, for this moment. Renew our hope in you."

Charlie continued on the scenic route back to Klahanee. Jake silently waited upon the Lord. Amber was grateful for the momentary peace.

She adored him for giving her this moment. She wasn't a delinquent; this time she was on the good guy's team. It felt good. Her spirits lifted.

"Pass me the radio transmitter," she demanded with a smile. Charlie passed it through the thick-wired grill that separated the front and back. He said nothing, but his expression was quizzical. She was careful not to press any buttons, and she spoke sternly into the transmitter, "Officer Liddell, please report. We have a 411 in progress. Please state your coordinates." Pleased with herself, she grinned broadly at the unsuspecting man beside her; even Charlie grinned. Jake laughed and then took the radio from her hand and asked Charlie to turn it on.

"I hope I'm not getting in any trouble 'cause of you two?"

"Hey, Matthew, pick up. We got anything happening on our busy streets tonight? Over."

"Yeah. We had another robbery at Garland Pharmacy. Just users lookin' for a fix. I'm bringin' 'em in. Over."

Jake pulled a gutsy move; he couldn't resist the huge grin on Amber's face. She was beaming, and like a high school boy, it egged him on. He handed her the radio and coaxed her to say something. For the first time in a long time, Amber was able to forget, not push it out of her mind, but actually forget her circumstances. She felt human. She took full enjoyment from the situation.

"Uh, Matthew, you out there? We got us a situation. Seems a truckload of pigs toppled over. We got pigs everywhere, pig poop all over the highway, and, not to mention, the pileup of vehicles crashed from skidding in all that pig poop."

Jake could barely contain his laughter as he let out a whoop so exuberant Amber herself couldn't hold in the laughter.

"Over." She was still laughing when the voice came back across the radio.

Charlie just shook his head but said nothing.

"Hey, Jake you're not supposed to be sharing my 'the reason I'm late' excuses with people. My wife's going to find out that I made that up if they keep happening." Laughter filled the cruiser. Even Charlie gave in. Jake explained to Amber that Officer Matthew Campbell was his old ride-along partner. Matt had used that same story with his wife after he'd returned home excessively late from a football game one evening.

Too soon they arrived at the prison. Amber was jolted back to reality; the agony of it gnawed at her insides.

Jake noticed the immediate change in her as they waited for Charlie to let them out of the cruiser. He took the moment to pray silently for the comfort he knew she desperately needed. He had no idea what had brought her to this point in her life. The "what" didn't matter to Jesus, and it didn't matter to him, but the more he got to know her, the more he wanted to help her. Facing the broken child in front of him, he recognized wide-eyed fear, yet tonight she had glimpsed hope. They were both aware of it.

Jake took her hand, helping her out of the cruiser; she leaned against the door. Looking at Jake, pleading with her eyes, she quietly asked, "Can we just stay here a minute, please? I know I shouldn't even ask. You have already been more than kind." She was so vulnerable. Jake looked over at Charlie, who nodded his approval. Jake inwardly rejoiced at the tenderness displayed in her hardened young heart. "Of course. Enjoy the fresh air."

Hands in his pockets and carelessly kicking at a clump of dirt, too nervous to look into the deep sea of Amber's green eyes, Jake looked at the ground. He felt the words of the Spirit prompt him; he had asked for the guidance, so he obeyed. Looking up, Amber met his gaze; she seemed to know he had to say something. She stared with anticipation.

Jake quoted Lamentations 3:21–23, "Yet this I call to mind therefore I have hope. Because of the Lord's great love we are not consumed, for His compassions never fail. They are new every morning." His eyes demanded that she understand. "God hasn't forsaken you, Amber. Not you, not me, not anyone, ever. You know that he's waiting for you to trust him so he can—"

She cut him off, unable to let him finish. The tears were on the surface; one more word and they would spill, and she wasn't willing to let this Jesus freak see what he could reduce her to. "I have had enough fresh air. Charlie, please return me to my cell now." The words were meant to be harsh, reminding the "holier than thou" man exactly whom he was dealing with. Like he could forget.

Instead of being dejected and upset, Jake separated the distance between Amber and himself and offered her his arm. She surprised herself as much as him, burrowing into him briefly. He could not know how intensely she whished to grasp his offer of hope. Jake held her as long as she allowed. Amber walked over to Charlie and held out her wrists. Jake knew not to take it personally, but her sudden coolness toward him caused a stab of pain in his heart.

Charlie and Amber approached the entrance, unaware Jake had followed them. Once inside, Amber's usual rough exterior resurfaced. She smoothly sauntered away. Jake tried not to let his disappointment show. It didn't matter; Amber didn't give him another glance. She hurried toward her cell as though she were glad to get away from him. Turning to go, Jake wondered how long he would have to wait until the next encounter with the woman who so badly needed him ... or did he need her?

Charlie wondered what had happened in the backseat of his cruiser. Jake was soft. A woman like Amber could devour him with no compunction. He, unlike his naive ride-along, had not been fooled by her camaraderie. He prayed silently for his friend's gentle heart. He hoped his interest in her would remain platonic.

Charlie got in the cruiser and waited patiently as Jake walked slowly back. Looking around, it suddenly hit Jake. Amber was looking at this place, the jail, as her home for an indeterminate amount of time. The thick barbed fence surrounding Klahanee was already intimidating, as were the guards bearing their weapons like army commanders, ready to shoot at a moment's notice. Here, her life was at the mercy of others. Once inside no one could protect her. Worry shot into his heart as he realized the worst of her circumstances lay inside those cement walls. She had to be hard, for her survival counted on it.

Every moment was spent looking over her shoulder, listening for any sound that could be threatening. A shiver ran through Jake's body as he realized what this woman, whom he was beginning to care very much for, was facing.

No wonder she was angry with him; he had treated her heartfelt question like a Bible quiz. He gave her intellect; what she needed was understanding. She had needed him to comfort her.

"Let the words of the Spirit fall on fertile ground." He murmured a prayer, "Lord, weren't they the words you gave me? Your Word does not go out and return empty. Protect her, Lord. Surround her with your angels." He knew Amber was reachable. His arm hair prickled with the message that followed that thought. "She's so much more than that."

Amber was somewhat grateful to be back inside her cell. What were these irrational hopes being conjured in the void of her soul? She was better off feeling dull, which enabled her to deal with the reality of her situation. Jake had no right to create false hope. Little did she know the harsh dose of reality she sought was only moments away.

"Hey, sweetie," Lauryn cooed. "How was the trial?" Lauryn often spoke to Amber that way, reminding her that as inmates she was a superior, and Amber was considered fresh. She could handle herself, she thought, with arrogance, though the events of one year ago were evidence of the contrary. Only three years ago Amber had no idea what drugs were. She had learned quickly though and became a master mixologist.

Amber studied chemistry and dedicated the next two years of her life to creating cheaper methods to get longer-lasting highs while making a profit. Some of the items she used were common household and kitchen supplies. Unfortunately, when the

other dealers found out their supply was getting cut and someone else was making a profit, they felt ripped off. There were
some serious repercussions.

Stan bought an eight ball, cocaine, off Dennis. Dennis had
been given orders by his top dog to cut the stuff with strychnine.
Stan, the main supplier for the "downtowners," took a sample.
The purity of the supply was how Amber gauged how much
she could cut the stash without raising any eyebrows. She could
make their people happy and keep the others from being suspicious, meanwhile lining their own pockets. She made quite a
name for herself. It made her feel good to know she had respect
among these people.

They had a run going down; all that went down that night
was Stan. The whole scene played out in real time was maybe
fifteen minutes, but to the onlookers it seemed like hours, never
ending. Stan's body twisted and thrashed. No one else moved,
watching in horrified silence. A resounding thud let everyone
know the ordeal was over. Stan lay lifeless on the cold concrete
floor. Sixty seconds passed, then they all looked expectantly at
Amber. She was terrified. The room of hardcore junkies looked
at her like she had just killed their next fix. They wanted to
know what she was going to do to get them all high.

She mixed a small amount of cocaine she had left in her
dirty old jacket. She cut it with more ephedrine than she had
ever used before. She looked around the old warehouse. There
had been plenty of dealing that had gone on in the building
over the years. She came across some old crystal meth lab bottles. She scraped the resin out of those. *Good and potent,* she
thought. She cut all of it together. Hopefully there would be
enough to go around. She had no idea what the effects of the
mixture would be. She had never done such a mix before. She
turned on the mini burner, put the concoction in a metal pot,
and held it over the burner. She poured in some ammonia and
proceeded to cook it down. The mixture crystallized; she separated the potent and possibly lethal rocks. She broke them up

and handed them out. They were all eager to get high and forget what they had just witnessed. She left quickly, not sticking around for a fix.

Amber knew Stan better than anyone else in that room. He was her friend. She didn't know what to feel. She went to a phone booth and placed an anonymous call to the police. Then she went home.

No one she knew returned to the warehouse. No one mentioned what happened either. As far as she knew, no one was ever questioned about Stan's death. No one really cared when junkies bit it. It was swept under the carpet like it had never happened, a service done to society. The media would write their blurb, but no one would know the story. No one would ever know that Stan had been born a crack addict, that he got his first taste of the drug from his own mother, that she had pleaded with him to start selling drugs so he could support her habit. No one would know how he had struggled to stay in school but always failed. His head was delayed from the day he was born. No, if any of them died, no one would ever know their stories. No one would care. But a voice soft and gentle that sent chills up her spine whispered, "I care, my child. I care so much."

She tortured herself further by recalling more details from the sordid life she had chosen. No one even went to Stan's funeral. She made a brief stop herself. She didn't stay long enough to see who was there. She kept the column that was printed in the paper in her special spot; right next to it was the letter her dad had written her after Adam's death. She was sure her parents knew about it, but both parties pretended the secret place and all its hidden secrets didn't exist.

All of that seemed pretty mild compared to some of the hardcore criminals in Klahanee. She hoped her association with the Deas brothers would ensure some safety. They ran a good

portion of the drug trade in their town. They supplied to runners who went into nearby cities and Canada. The Canadian
dealers had the weed, the American dealers had the powder
brought in from Mexico. And did they have stories. Amber
remembered them clearly.

The boys who did the border runs would fill their back-
packs with the merchandise, walk through some dense forest,
and arrive at a park. From there all they had to do was scale a
fence and they were in Canada. They would meet the driver,
who was waiting for them on the other side.

That particular story ended with the scaling of the wall.
Damian got his pants caught on the barbed wire. Suddenly, he
heard the sirens. Then the police dogs. He couldn't get more
caught than that. He hadn't even had the sense to drop the bag.
They had laughed hysterically.

There were other rumors about border crossings, like police
dogs and shots fired. Runners running through fields with
police dogs hot on their heels. Amber asked to go once but
was relieved when she was turned down. She would stick to
mixing. It supported her dime-a-day habit, which was quickly
increasing.

Upon her arrest she had detoxed quickly and painfully. It
almost felt good to have control over her mind again. But those
first six nights behind bars she thought, even hoped that she
would die. Lucidity wasn't all it was cracked up to be. It enabled
her memories to surface. Her goal had been to bury them too
deep to ever retrieve.

This thought brought Amber back to the present. She hoped
none of the inmates knew about her fainting in the courthouse
today. That would be weakness, providing reason to devour her.
With that vivid thought, shivers of unthinkable evil ran up her
spine. She thought up a lie to Lauryn's question and hoped not
to have to use it. She knew that in order to be convincing, she
would have to let the story roll. No hesitation, or she would
arouse suspicion.

THIS ROAD I WALK

"How was the trial, Amber?" Lauryn asked the question again, her tone demanding. Amber felt the hair on the back of her neck prickle. Her insides went cold.

"One of the State's supposed 'star witnesses' was called to another court hearing. It was apparently more high-profile than mine, so I get to wait. But guess who drove me home?" Amber used a suave voice and answered her own question. "The totally hot young saver of us all, Jake Liddell." She giggled and fully expected the giggle to be infectious, as it usually was with Lauryn, but she didn't make a sound.

All the girls joked about how hot Jake Liddell was. Some of the girls shared lewd fantasies. Amber never took part in those. She felt as though it was betraying him. He would have been appalled by such salacious talk. She smiled as she thought that he would probably blush.

"No sense of humor today, Lauryn? What's up?" Amber tried to sound indignant, hiding the uncertainty she felt. Lauryn remained solemn, eyes narrowed, arms folded. Amber felt the hatred emanating from her stare, like visible shadows ebbing into her profile. It caused her stomach to flip-flop. Instinct told her to scream. Call a guard. Act fast. She couldn't.

Neither girl spoke. They sat on their cots waiting. Amber knew that whatever it was she was waiting for wouldn't be good. Lauryn hoped the plans had changed and that her cellmate wasn't in for the worst night of her life. Lauryn had been warned as well as threatened. If she didn't keep her mouth shut, she knew what would happen. She was helpless. Both girls knew that to interfere was to invoke a fate far worse than anything else one would suffer in prison.

Hope Lost

"If I speak in the languages of men and of angels but have not love, I am a resounding gong, or clanging symbol. If I have the gift of prophecy and can fathom all mysteries, and all knowledge, and if I have faith that can move mountains but have not love I am nothing. If I give all I posses to the poor, and surrender my body to the flame but have not love I gain nothing."

1 Corinthians 13:1–3

Lauryn nor Amber had spoken a word since that first inter-action following Amber's return from court. Both were aware that something was going to happen. Amber knew to be afraid; she just didn't know what and she didn't know when, but she felt into the marrow of her bones it would be soon.

Shortly after returning from the mess hall, the billy club began its ritual—*clang, clang*—on every bar. The guard's rough voice echoed through the long, narrow hall.

"Open 120, open 121, open 122." He continued all the way up to 129. One by one the doors whined and squeaked as they lazily opened, allowing two girls from each cell to emerge. It was shower time. There were two shower rooms, and the inmates went twenty at a time, ten to each room. Seven minutes was the allotted time for showering. Dignity absent, the girls stripped, grabbed their soap, received their squirt of shampoo, and got busy.

Two guards were assigned to each shower room. Chief guard Tyler Porter was stationed in Amber's shower room. She held out her hand for her soap. Tyler slowly placed it in her hands, looking at her intently as he did. She felt discomfort rise in her gut as she muttered an expletive while walking away.

There were unspoken rules about the shower: don't look left, and don't look right. Keep your eyes on your own business. Anything else would be considered an invitation. Amber was doing just that when a blur of curly red hair crossed her path. Instinctively, uneasiness crept into Amber's gut.

Before she could think of what she should do, someone took a hold of her long, thick hair and yanked her head back, tilting her throat upwards.

Amber got an up-close glance at her assailant, a skinny, wiry, freckle-faced redhead who was as psycho as they come. As far as Amber knew, she didn't go by a name; she was appropriately nicknamed Candy. The name could apply to her candy red hair or the way she infused drugs into her body like they were candy.

A second assailant grabbed Amber's arms. Amber recognized the dark-skinned Amazon from cell block C. Amber remembered hearing that she was in solitaire for stabbing some girl in the face with a fork for making some "colored" remark. Beth put her knee into the back of Amber's legs, dropping her to her knees. Each girl held one arm. Beth let go of her hair. Now they had some control of her. She was hefted back to her feet. Finally, the figure from the shadows emerged. Amber was overcome with loathing at who she saw. Her heart pounded; she was going to vomit.

Chief Guard Tyler Porter, known to the inmates as "Tyler, sir," moved close enough for Amber to see the evil glean in his eyes, like a man possessed. His arrogance and distaste for the female inmates were always present, leaving Amber with no doubts as to how this night was to end.

In a moment of panic she head butted the guard; blood sprayed. The broken nose did not deter the blood thirst of her attackers. She would not be taken easily. Amber felt the jolt of a right hook across her jaw. As her body spun and wielded from the blow, she caught a glimpse of Lauryn. She knew better than to hope for help. Everyone knew, no one gets involved in a jump-in.

The six other girls in the shower room continued as though nothing were going on. Lauryn huddled in a corner of the shower, hoping something would happen, anything to end the attack. The fear from the night she was jumped in came unbidden into Lauryn's mind, bringing with it fresh fear. Amber's face hit the ceramic wall, and the two girls jumped on her, grabbing her arms again. This time as Tyler neared, he grabbed Amber's thick locks and forced her neck back. He pulled back harder and harder till Amber thought her throat would rip open, spilling the blood they all seemed eager for.

"Beg me. I may have mercy on you." The prison guard gloated his power. Pride and hate brought forth the answer, but it lacked wisdom.

"Go to hell." Tyler pulled tighter and taunted, "Wrong answer." He thrust a fist straight into her gut. "You don't make things easy, do ya?" He sneered and touched her in a way that made her nauseous. Gathering her wits, Amber used the opportunity to raise her knee. She connected, dead center, between his legs. Tyler went down, struggling for air and holding himself. Something wasn't right. That wasn't just "him" in his baggy pants. She heard a cracking sound when her knee connected. Regardless, she hoped the dead-on shot had foiled his plans at least for tonight. As he clutched himself and struggled to regain domination over the situation, he smiled at her. It wasn't going to end that easily.

Tyler slowly stood and slugged her again. The second shot to the face sent her reeling. She could feel consciousness slipping. It fed her hate. Beth and Candy held her face flat to the wall, gripping her at the shoulders, and each had a hand on the back of her head. She couldn't move at all. Tyler was touching her again, trying to hurt her. She felt a surge of repulsion and a need for retribution. She refused the tears that wanted to fall. Instead, she fed herself hate and thoughts of revenge. The assault was brutal. The guard's insatiable appetite for perversion was more than even his hardened accomplices were willing to deal with.

"Ty, enough," Beth finally said. The massive woman was stunned by the slap across the face.

"I say when it's enough." Evil shined in his eyes, reflecting through the white tiled wall. Beth and Candy simultaneously let go of the girl. As her head cracked against the wall, she crumpled to the floor; both inmates realized she was unconscious, Looking down, they noticed the blood. Beth grabbed Candy's arm and both girls quietly retreated, slowly heading back to their cells, stopping briefly to grab their clean prison wardrobes.

Tyler stood and dropped the bottle he was holding; the tip was jagged. Amber had busted it when she kicked him. Amber's kick had only succeeded in infuriating Tyler. Using his forearm, Tyler slowly wiped the sweat off his face. That's when he noticed the blood. At the same time he heard his partner approaching. In a panic-stricken tone, he called his partner.

"Jared. Hey, Jared, get over here, man. I need help." Hearing the panic in Tyler's voice, Jared rushed into the open shower stall. Jared was repulsed. One look at the girl on the floor and his stomach lurched; he had never seen such a sight. Blood flowed rapidly from her body as well as her mouth and somewhere on her head he couldn't tell from where.

Jared touched the young girl's shoulder. She barely stirred.

"Go get help," he demanded of his partner. Jared grabbed a towel. That's when he noticed Lauryn shivering in the corner, tears streaming down her face; he had never seen that before. These women didn't cry.

Jared gently laid the blanket over Amber then gently asked Lauryn, "Did you see who did this?"

Lauryn's eyes were huge. What could she say? Tyler gave her a cold look before leaving to get help, mouthing a few expletives. She realized she was the only one left in the shower room. Lauryn knew to keep her mouth shut. Who would believe her over a guard if she did tell? He took an oath to protect people. Tyler's eyes had flashed, leaving no room for misinterpretation. She shut up, or she was next.

Lauryn looked up at Jared. He was new. He had only been at the prison for three months. In the two years she had been at Klahanee, she had seen lots of wide-eyed young men caught off guard by the brutality that went on. It didn't take them long to harden then begin taking their pleasures for themselves. Few of the good ones ever stayed. Even those refused to risk their jobs over protecting criminals. They offered advice and comfort. Never hope. Lauryn was sure Jared would be no different. Jared looked at her, hoping for something. Lauryn defiantly clamped her mouth shut, grabbed her towel, and attempted to leave. Jared wouldn't give up that easily; he would try to get her alone. He knew she had witnessed the whole thing. She knew who did this.

The on-duty nurse came quickly, pulling a gurney and leaving Tyler behind her. They got Amber strapped on and began making their way to the infirmary. All the commotion roused the other inmates. They started getting rowdy. Tyler yelled for them to shut up. Jared thought someone might be willing to talk. There was no better way to quiet down a rowdy prison block than to start asking questions.

Amber was beginning to stir. The pain was intolerable. Her stomach felt like the insides had been ripped out. Why did she hurt so much? The nurse quickly explained that she was losing a lot of blood and needed to be taken to the onsite hospital area.

"Who did this to you?" she demanded. "Did you see them? Do you suspect you may have been pregnant?"

Pregnant? That last word reverberated in Amber's mind.

The pain and emptiness those words word invoked were intense. She tried to push it away, but it remained and tormented.

"Please, just make the pain go away! Please." She clutched her stomach and moaned. Her eyes welled with tears that her hardened heart could never let fall. They would not destroy her. She was strong. She swallowed the pain, and her heart got a little colder. As she choked back the tears, her hate grew.

She glimpsed Tyler out of the corner of her eye; he had wanted her dead, she was sure of it. She knew to be terrified. The intravenous drip the nurse had stuck in her arm began to have an effect. The pain was subsiding; she was getting drowsy. Still she noticed Tyler's fixed glare. One word, that's all it would take and her life would cease. He had the propensity to do it. She needed out of her hellish existence. She closed her eyes and entered the false security of a drug-induced sleep.

When Amber finally roused, she felt stiff and sore everywhere. The aching between her legs and the stench of old blood was a quick and painful reminder of the events that had taken place only hours ago. She looked around the sterile room. Turning her head, she could see Jared talking in hushed tones to the nurse. She strained to hear what they were saying.

"I need to speak to someone I can trust. Any suggestions?"

Chloe, a heavy lady with sassy auburn curls and dimpled cheeks, answered Jared, "The best person to speak to is someone from the precinct. Don't even bother with anyone from here. Except maybe Eddie. He's the warden." She paused before continuing thoughtfully. "You could try talking to the sheriff. He and his assistant are good people. They drive Amber to the courthouse. Should be able to trust them. I hear the assistant is soft on Amber."

Grinning openly, Jared retorted, "I'm sure it wouldn't be hard to find a man with a soft spot for her!" He glanced toward Amber.

Chloe returned his grin and replied matter-of-factly, "Good. That should make doing the right thing easy for you." Chloe made her way over to Amber. "Well, Sleeping Beauty, how are you feeling this morning?" She kept talking, not waiting for an answer. "Can I get you anything? You still in a lot of pain?"

Amber opened her mouth to answer, but her throat was dry and tight. An inaudible rasp escaped.

Chloe knowingly held up her hand and rushed to the fridge to get her some water. "Here you are, drink slow. It's the effect of the medication I gave you earlier." She waited for Amber to respond.

Amber had two words on her mind: pregnant and Tyler. Revenge began wrapping long tentacles around her heart. He would not get away with this, not while there was air in her lungs or life in her body. Pregnant. Despite the effective drugs distributed by Chloe, that word was bold.

Chloe noticed Amber struggling and encouraged her to speak. "Do you want to talk about last night?"

Amber shook her head, remaining silent.

"Do you have pain anywhere?" Chloe's question gave Amber the opportunity to ask the question unrelentingly niggling her brain. "Yes. My stomach aches. I know these aren't period cramps. I remember last night you said something about a pregnancy." She paused—did she want to know? "Was I pregnant?" Her question was void of emotion.

Chloe held Amber's gaze. Amber saw empathy in the nurse's eyes as she nodded then quietly said, "Do you know how far along you may have been?" Amber shook her head, not paying attention anymore, lost once again in her jungle of memories. It was true. She had been pregnant. The irony was ludicrous. Oh, yes! She knew exactly how far and whose.

That baby was the one chance she had to prove that the scumbag psychiatrist she was forced to see was the evil person she claimed he was. The long-awaited moment to reveal the truth to her parents, to the courts, and to him was destroyed along with the pregnancy. She had envisioned the moment since the inception of the idea. Vengeful thoughts got her through

THIS ROAD I WALK

the sexual act. Oh, the gloating she would do. By the time she was through with Gordon Forbes, she vowed, he would beg her for mercy. Now it was all for nothing. Her already disquieted soul filled with inconsolable grief at the memory of her words, echoing in her mind as she descriptively recalled the encounter. "No one else will ever suffer at your perverted hands again. I'll make sure of that." And so she thought she had.

It was after Amber's last arrest that the judge declared herself compassionate, assigning Amber to six months of meetings with Dr. Forbes instead of jail time, along with community service. Her stomach had knotted and twisted at the mention of his name. It made her nauseated to know she would once again be forced into psychiatric bondage. At first, she thought she would fight him. Fight the system. She started by telling her parents. She had been foolish, thinking they would believe her.

Dr. Forbes told her what would happen. Who would believe a dope whore? The doctor "fixed" her urine specimens in return, a mandated subclause in her conditional release. The fact that he could do such a thing made Amber very aware of the power he had over her. That knowledge left her vulnerable, with no one to trust, breaking her down further. Still so naive, she believed he was doing her a favor. She soon discovered it was easier to force oneself on someone who's doped up. Doped-up victims don't talk.

Dr. Gordon Forbes made it very clear what it would take for Amber to get a quick pass out of his program. He would get it eventually. She could give in and be done with it, or she could fight him until he wore her down, like a cat catching a mouse.

After an exceptionally sordid incident with the doctor, Amber was, without explanation, handed a "pass" out of the program. She walked out of the office undignified, defiled, but free. Freedom did not hold all Amber had expected and hoped for. Her desire to get high grew at an alarming rate. She could no longer tolerate sobriety. Whenever she was straight, the good doctor's face would make an appearance, taunting her. She could smell his filth, always at the forefront of her sober mind, gloating that he had won.

Amber was arrested again, the same reason as the last time. She was sent back to Dr. Forbes for a new program. It was the second time things got really bad. He stated emphatically, and the words would never leave her mind, "Amber, passing my course the first time was easy compared to what you are about to go through. By the time I am finished with you, you will have a much stronger desire to stay out of trouble." She coldly recalled how he had groped her, adding, "Unless you like this and just keep coming back for more of me." A shiver still ran up her spine at the memory of those words.

He pulled out all the stops, destroying all she could hope for—her worth. She was aware that he had every intention to make good on all his threats. He preyed on the only value she had left—her freedom. He threatened to have her committed. Her freedom hung in the balance of a psycho instead of a psychiatrist. She knew he would do it. He probably already had. He had the ear of the judges and no conscience. He would lock her up and forget her. No one would ask questions. He knew how to win. At what point does one give in and stop fighting? That's where Amber was after that first appointment back. Appointment after appointment he wanted more from her. Between the drugs she was reliant on and the doctor's head games. As he dangled freedom like a piece of meat over her head, Amber was becoming a shell of her previous self. She deserved his depraved treatment. Attempting to salvage whatever remained of herself, she summoned all the sanity and all the soul she had left and devised a plan. One thing the doctor hadn't considered was her determination. He underestimated her will to win. Her plan was simple: she would conceive his child.

The smell of brylle cream in his hair. The taste of his dirty mouth as he kissed her—a repugnant mixture of sweat and salt. His coarse facial hair chaffed against her neck. He breathed rampantly. Maybe he would have a heart attack. How she hoped for that. He squeezed and rubbed her body so hard that she would later see bruises. She quivered with anxious malice as she took a small pin and poked it through the condom he would eagerly put on. Her heart beat wildly in her chest. He would get what he deserved. She was making sure of it. It would cost her the remnants of her soul, but it would be worth it when she could reap the reward of his demise.

Today she discovered her plan had worked; she had gotten pregnant. Revenge was so close to her lips that she could taste it. Just like the life she once knew, both were whisked away in a heartbeat; only a remnant of either remained. Life was cruel. She would never be able to prove she had been the person telling the truth. Gone were the dreams of apologies owed to her. Oh, for the shred of her soul that might have still been redeemable. She should have known redemption wouldn't come through vengeance. She had no backup plan, just dismay. Dark thoughts eroded her mind. She needed something. She needed a way out.

Her carefully planned vengeance lay in a pool of blood on a white-clothed table. A stain, just a bloody stain.

Seeking

"Where is another God like you, who pardons the sins of the survivors among his people? You cannot stay angry with your people forever because you delight in them."

Micah 7:18

Catherine was exhausted by the time they finally got home. She was eager to get her son to sleep so she could do the same. She looked adoringly at Lincoln; he had been asking a lot of questions lately. It was hard to know how much to tell him. Just then Michael looked over at her from the kitchen, where he was preparing a pot of tea. He gave her a cockeyed look and lopsided grin. Oh, how she loved him. She felt her face stretch into a full grin. She tried to return his suave expression with one of her own. Just then Lincoln came back into the living room with a book in hand. He noticed his mother's strange expression and asked, "Mom, what are you doing? Do you have something in your eye?"

Catherine and Michael laughed heartily. How corny they must look to a little boy. She took the book from Linc, snuggled him up to her chest on the couch she had been reclined on, and began reading.

After having finished the very long book her son had picked out, Catherine brought Linc upstairs and tucked him into bed. Turning back for the stairs, she stole a glance at Amber's shut door. Closing her eyes and gritting her teeth, she turned the knob. An incessant urge overwhelmed her as she entered the forsaken room. After the arrest the police had gone through everything. Catherine put it back together the way it had been and hadn't opened it since. She turned on the light and looked around, unsure of what she was looking for.

She walked to her daughter's bed, sat down, and waited. The room brought back memories of happier times, the exuberant person her daughter used to be. She hugged her daughter's pillow, inhaling the familiar scent of her hair and perfume. Looking around the room, she noticed the night stand; there used to be a picture of Adam there. It had been replaced with one of people Catherine didn't recognize. Lincoln's picture was all that was unchanged. It was taken the summer before the accident. Catherine remembered Amber borrowing the camera to take the shot as she and Linc ran through the sprinkler. His curly hair was wet and tousled, his skin was bronzed. A huge grin emphasized his dimple. She smiled wistfully.

Catherine casually scanned the room. That's how she noticed the piece of corkboard in the ceiling. It didn't look right. Her hands started sweating, and her stomach knotted. *It's just ceiling boards,* she told herself. Compelled, she moved closer. She could see that the piece was definitely misplaced. She grabbed the stool from Amber's vanity, moving clothing strewn over it. She stood on the stool but couldn't move the board. It hit something sturdy; she pushed it the other direction and it slid easily. Cautiously, she felt around with her fingertips. She brushed against the solid object. She knew immediately it was the doll cradle. She groped around, hoping to find something to grasp. She struggled to pull it through the opening but lost her grip. It slammed onto the floor, scattering papers and pictures everywhere.

Catherine started aimlessly looking at the papers and pictures that lay at her feet. A shiver ran through her spine. "Do you trust me?" She felt the words. Her immediate thought was,

Of course I trust you, Lord. She shook it off as her subconscious seeking solace and continued with the task at hand. She browsed the mess. An old picture of Linc in the tub caught her eye. Pictures of Amber's old friends, then pictures of ones she couldn't name. Friends they were never meant to know. Catherine shuffled loosely through the pile. Another picture caught her attention. She held it up and examined it closely. Amber looked so happy in the picture. Arm in arm with Adam, people would have thought they were a couple. Catherine and Michael, as well as the Farrells, had hoped they would be. Lots had changed since then. She looked wistfully at that picture; a tear ran down her cheek as she wondered how different life would have been if not for that one moment that night.

"God, please, by your grace, get us through this."

"Do you trust me?"

The hair on the back of her neck prickled. She shoved all the things back into the cradle and put it in the closet. She didn't notice the lone paper that had fallen to the floor. Catherine purposefully headed to her room, relieved to be out of the place that held the memories that bore such pain.

She took out her Bible and began to pray out loud. As she did, she flipped the pages of the Psalms then read, "Though my enemies slay me yet I will put my trust in Him." Her mind was brought back to the two times in the bedroom. *"Do you trust me?"* She meditated on those words.

Michael strode into the room and sat beside his wife. Taking hold of her hands, he spoke playfully, "Do you know what I would like to do?"

"What?" she dared to ask.

"I want to go on a very long vacation, all of us, or just some of us, preferably just us. We could drive south, head to California, spend some time on the beach. We could head east, check out those Idahoan potatoes we hear so much about, or south, south is nice."

"Are you insane?"

"All right, what do you suggest?" he wagered.

"I'm thinking airplanes, and far." She played along. Still holding hands, they lay back on the bed and stared at the ceiling, contemplating the make-believe journeys they would like to take. Michael rose up on one elbow and looked at his wife's face. Adoringly, he leaned over and kissed her. She had too much on her mind to enjoy the moment.

"Michael—" she started to protest.

He interrupted her with his mouth, placing it firmly over hers with a possessiveness she had not felt in a while. It was a relief to give in to. She eagerly put her arms around her husband, welcoming the opportunity for intimacy. He lowered himself onto her body. Their breathing became rhythmical, entwining their bodies in passion.

Catherine was thankful for her creator, who knew what she needed more than she did, and for an understanding husband. She was thankful for a partner who shared her feelings and emotions. Most of all, she was grateful for the strength she extracted. Exhausted, she fell asleep.

———

The morning brought with it the reality of her world once again. Catherine needed to be careful, or she would end up losing her mind. Depression ached to creep in. She got out of the shower and dressed in attire fitting for a courtroom. Downstairs, she began making her family breakfast. Michael came up behind her wrapped his arms lovingly around her.

"You okay?"

She nodded. "Michael" ... She paused, looking at him. "Last night before you came up" ... She paused and smiled. "I was in Amber's room, and I found something."

"What did you find?"

"Amber's old doll cradle. She keeps stuff in it."

He looked up from the steaming coffee he was sipping, eyebrows arched, and waited for her to finish.

"She still has that letter you wrote her after Adam died."

He smiled but said nothing. He nodded his head in feigned indifference. Catherine shook her head; she did not understand the man before her.

"I couldn't get the cradle back into the opening in the ceiling, so I was hoping you could"... She didn't get a chance to finish. He headed upstairs. She smiled inwardly to herself.

Lincoln scrambled into the kitchen gleefully and full of anticipation. "What will we do today?" His joy lifted her spirits.

"Well, mister, you have school. Then Grandma will pick you up." Catherine tried to sound enthusiastic.

"Aw, Mom, Grandma's again? If I go to Grandma's, I can't have any friends over."

"Sorry, buddy. Hopefully we won't have to keep this schedule for long." Before the boy could protest, Michael re-entered the kitchen. His expression was not what Catherine had anticipated. His eyes looked glazed. Lincoln didn't notice as he chattered excitedly to him.

"Michael, your son is waiting for an answer."

Still distracted, he replied, "What?" and forced himself to look at his son.

"When this schedule is over, is that when Amber will come home?"

Michael looked at Catherine, forgetting momentarily what he had encountered upstairs. In the silence of hesitation, Lincoln spoke up in a very soft voice. "I know where Amber is. She's in a jail, 'cause she did something really bad. The kids at school say she killed someone." His eyes were sorrowful; he bowed his head, waiting. Michael was paying attention now.

"Your sister has been accused of things," Catherine said. "We have to wait for the judge to decide if she believes that Amber did those things or not."

"Do you believe them?" he asked.

Suddenly, their baby seemed so grown up. Catherine bit her lip; she tasted blood, and it kept her from crying. Her son was asking for adult answers to adult questions, and she had none.

"What exactly did you hear?" Michael asked gently.

Lincoln hung his head, saying nothing for a moment. Then, with all the somberness that a seven-year-old could muster, he spoke shocking words, "I think she did it."

Michael and Catherine exchanged brief but confused expressions. Unconsciously, they moved closer together, reaching for each other.

"Why would you think that?" Michael asked cautiously.

The boy started fumbling with his buttons, looking down again, scuffing his feet.

"Linc, do you want to tell us something about Amber? You know you never get in trouble if you tell the truth, right? It's okay, whatever you want to tell us, but just tell the truth."

The reluctant child gave in to coaxing and spilled his truth with the energy of a penned bull. His story had been held in far too long. "One night when Amber was home, and she hadn't been home for a lot of nights, I went in her bed to sleep with her … "

"Go on."

"Well, Amber thought I was sleeping … "

"And … "

"And I heard her talking on the phone."

Catherine's mind quickly filled with all the horrific things her son may have overheard. Michael comfortingly placed his calloused hands on his wife's shoulders, then he released her and knelt in front of his son. "What did you hear, son?" Into the silence, he breathed a prayer while awaiting the confession. A story popped into his mind, the story of Job. How much did he suffer? Yet he remained faithful. And yet another of Abraham with his only son, Isaac, tied to an altar to be sacrificed. *Forgive me, Jesus,* he prayed. *I am just flesh, and I am weak, but through you I can do all things. Strengthen me.* But even as the words left his heart, he wasn't sure he could uphold them.

"Lincoln, what did you hear?"

Now their son talked, alleviating himself of the long-held burden.

"I heard Amber talking to her friend Jersey. I heard her tell her that 'if that pig doctor tries to touch me again, I will kill him,' then she said it's better that he suffers instead of her. She didn't care anymore." His eyes became huge as he continued. "Then she said, 'I mean it. If I get the chance, I will *destroy* him.'" Michael and Catherine were both speechless.

Lincoln broke the silence. "Doesn't that mean Amber did the bad thing they think she did?"

Catherine wept; she had tried so hard to keep it together in front of Lincoln. He didn't need to see his mother crying all the time. More realization began to sink in. The pieces of the puzzle that had led to their daughter's destruction were beginning to fit.

If Lincoln was accurate in his recollection of the phone call, which he seemed very sure of, they had to re-examine how they had dealt with Amber's problems from the beginning. She had been telling the truth about Dr. Forbes. The awakening brought with it nausea. Suddenly, Catherine knew she was going to throw up. She barely made it to the bathroom; her head was pounding, her heart broken. They had forced their daughter to spend appointment after appointment with that cruel man, paying for her to be in his care. Finally, she understood why Amber hated them.

What purpose could God possibly have in this? Why was it happening to their family? The more memories that came, flooding her mind, the more nauseated she became. Her head reeled; she grabbed the side of the toilet as she heaved. Through the vomit and amid the turmoil she cried out, "What have we done, God? What have we done? She's your child too." Then Catherine cast the final accusation, the one she had pondered but never dared speak aloud, "Why did you bother saving her from the truck? For a life of torture and abuse? I don't understand you." Dissipated and weak, she slouched beside the toilet and sobbed.

Michael looked from his distraught son to his wife, who seemed on the brink of an emotional breakdown. He picked up Lincoln and said, "I am very glad you told us the truth, son. That must have been so hard for you. It was extremely brave, and know what?" His smile was superficial, but it was all his son needed.

"What?"

"This might help your sister, and that doctor you heard your sister talking about is not the man who died. A different man died, do you understand?"

The boy slowly nodded his head, truly contemplating the information. Could it be that he had actually helped his sister? He was proud of himself. He truly was brave.

The putrid stench of vomit stuck in his throat, and his stomach tightened. The sight of his wife crumpled on the floor, face buried in her hands, filled him with compassion. Her legs were drawn up to her chest; she spoke between whimpers, "We forced her to go. She told us, but we wouldn't believe her. We questioned but did nothing. We can't undo it, and our daughter is the one left bearing the punishment for our mistakes. It's not supposed to be that way, Michael. Parents don't send their children helpless to the slaughter, but we did, we did." There were no words of comfort to console such grief, so he held his wife like a child.

"Catherine, we have to go now or we will be late," he gently reminded. "As soon as we get to the courthouse, we will tell Nina what Lincoln told us."

"We have to take responsibility for our part in this, Michael. We perpetuated the problem." Admitting to that caused the tears to spill again.

"No good comes from tossing blame or throwing guilt. We

have the benefit of knowledge now. We can use that. Hopefully, it will open up a doorway of communication with our daughter. Something good will come out of this yet. We have to believe that. God promises that 'all things work together for good—'"

"Can you so easily absolve yourself of any wrongdoing?" She was angry, and she had every right to be. They should have protected her; did he truly feel no guilt?

"That's not what I mean, and you know it. You're just emotional right now."

"Emotional!" Her voice rose. "Only a callous, arrogant … " She struggled for a word to describe exactly what she thought of his choice of words, but he interjected, "This is not about you, Catherine. Whatever feelings you have, get them in check. We have to be on the same team when we see our daughter. Divided, we all fall."

His words infuriated her.

"So you blame me?"

"I never said that. You are being irrational." She knew he was right about that. She could feel it, but she didn't care. She was tired of sadness, tired of complacency, accepting questionable answers. How could he not feel outrage?

Michael read the frustration on his wife's face. She had dark circles under her eyes. Her emotions were plucked raw. Regardless, no amount of guilt would change their situation. She had to put things in perspective.

Catherine responded cynically to his rationale, "Maybe that is what I am now. Irrational. Insane. You can have your daughter in jail and your wife in a nuthouse." She tried his patience. He worked his jaw. She was glad. She wanted to anger him; wasn't that what he was doing to her, only more subtly?

"We are leaving now." He headed for the door. Catherine remained there, arms crossed. Michael reached the front door, and there, in the adjacent doorway, was his son. Michael let out an cxaspcratcd brcath and slumped his shoulders in defeat. His son had witnessed the horrible display.

She can just be so ... He caught the trick, the master of disguise attacking his marriage. He looked back. *God, please soften her heart,* he prayed silently as he walked over to her. She already had. He hugged her, holding her tightly. She wrapped her arms around him. Both were eager for forgiveness.

"We will get through this. Things will work out."

The drive to Ruth's to drop off Lincoln was quiet. Catherine's mother had been so helpful through the turmoil. At sixty-four she was retired and for the past eleven years a widow. Bill had died at the young age of fifty-five after a heart attack. It was a devastating shock to everyone. Ruth mourned her husband for a long time.

She was an attractive older woman. She had long hair that she pulled up into a proper bun. She colored her gray, stating, "You don't need to be vain, but you should look your best." Ruth was the only family member they had around. They were thankful for her help.

Catherine had two sisters. One had married a man from Honduras. Miguel and Debbie had felt they could do God's work there, so two years into the marriage they made the move. They had two girls, only fourteen months apart. They were four and five now.

Darlene and her husband lived in Savannah, Georgia. Paul's job moved them a lot, usually every two years, and, thankfully, she was finally pregnant

Michael's family was quite different. His father had moved into a home just two years ago, and his mother lived in a convalescent hospital. They were both in their seventies now, and Michael and Catherine decided not to burden them with the things that had been going on. Michael had only one brother, Trevor. He was eleven years older than Michael. They hadn't seen him in five years, and Paula, his ex-wife, had divorced him several years back but not before having two children. Trevor hadn't seen them in five years. They lived with their mother.

Michael and Catherine took the kids faithfully for two weeks every summer. This summer was the first time they hadn't. The kids had stopped asking about their dad a while ago. No one had heard from him for a long time. Michael initially went to see him a few times, but he was always drunk and usually hostile. Michael decided to leave the next move up to him. He was still waiting.

Ruth answered the door in her usual joyful manner and offered hugs and kisses to her adorable grandson. He was more interested in the fresh cookies he saw on the table.

"We are late, Mom. We have to rush," Catherine said as she ushered Lincoln inside.

"You don't have to stay for cookies, but I would like to pray with you before you leave."

"Thanks, Mom." Catherine immediately felt encouraged and stronger.

Driving in silence, Catherine and Michael were deep in their own thoughts. Catherine looked longingly at her husband. Did he feel what she was feeling? He had to be strong, for her and for their son. If only she wasn't so weak, she could shoulder more of the burdens. She said nothing but gripped his hands and looked intently at him.

Michael was remembering back to the morning.

"When you were up in Amber's room last night..." He paused, wondering if his wife could take anymore. "Do you know what was on that paper, Catherine?"

Her stomach knotted, remembering the strange experience she'd had in her daughter's room. She couldn't speak. Her tongue was thick. She just shook her head. As Michael spoke, she saw the pain in his eyes.

"It was a recipe card containing a list of ingredients to make drugs. How much ephedrine you need to add to cocaine to achieve a high that will last six hours, and how if you buy Sudafed you can soak it in water, add Drano and iodine, and come up with crystal meth. Did you know that? Each rock our daughter sells makes her ten dollars. It terrifies me. I keep stumbling around in the dark, hoping to find answers. That helplessness is a reminder that's it's not in our hands. It never was." He inhaled deeply. "No matter what we do, the end result is in God's hands, where it has always been. 'In his heart a man plans his course, but the Lord determines his steps,'" he quoted from the Bible.

"'When times are good be happy, but when times are bad consider that God has made them both,'" Catherine added. "'I can do all things through Christ who strengthens me.'" Smiling weakly at each other, they drove on in silence.

Arriving at the courthouse, Michael parked the car then took his wife's hand. Michael prayed, "Jesus, lift us up. We are weary. Give us strength. You know all things. Nothing is hidden from you, yet you hold us in your loving hands if we but surrender to you. Thank you, Jesus, for all you have done and are yet to do. Amen."

Peace swept over both of them like a gentle breeze—peace that passes understanding. That is what Jesus promised.

The moment belonged to God. If it lasted five minutes, they would be thankful for those five minutes. If they stumbled, they would give it back to God. They would be thankful for every moment they remained faithful. God's mercies were new every morning, as were their struggles. As for now, they would wait upon the Lord and pray without ceasing.

When Michael and Catherine reached the inside of the courthouse, they were sent home. The trial had been postponed until

Friday, a full week away. No explanation was given. They hurried home, anxious to contact Nina, their lawyer. She would have more information and would know what to do about Linc's story.

They were dismayed to learn that evidence given by a child under the age of eight was inadmissible. Further, the "story," as she called it, had no specific pertinence to Amber's particular case. They could proceed with filing a formal complaint through the court, but testimony given by a seven-year-old wasn't likely to be taken too seriously. Amber would have to admit to the accusations. Then Nina would present it to the judge. If they really wanted to see something come of the allegations, they would need to do some detective work, find other clients of Dr. Gordon Forbes, and see if anyone else was willing to come forward, *if* there was anyone else. Most important, she concluded, Amber would have to agree to testify, and a State prosecutor would rake her over the coals for any and everything from her past.

Catherine quickly pointed out that Amber knew nothing about this yet.

"How do you think she will react?" She looked at Michael while talking to Nina.

"I was wondering the same thing. You will have to deal with that when you see her. How is Amber doing?" Catherine got the feeling Nina didn't expect the answer to be good.

"She's doing okay. She doesn't really tell us much, but—"

"I mean, since the attack?"

Catherine felt the blood drain from her body. Michael noticed her changed appearance; she was ghostly. Catherine grasped Michael's hand firmly. "What attack?" She stared straight into her husband's eyes, needing his succour.

Nina's voice was full of annoyance but devoid of concern. "You mean, no one told you?"

"Told us what?" Catherine did her best to brace herself for the answer she knew was going to knock her down again.

"You need to go to the prison now. Someone should have called you. Amber's in the infirmary."

Jake sat in Matilda Anderson's room. The elderly lady was near passing. The head nurse had already made the call to the family; they would be in shortly. Jake was sitting at "Ducky's" bedside, as she liked to be called. Her breathing was shallow; he knew from experience that she would soon be gone. Ducky was one of his favorite patients. She spoke with a thick English accent and had the dry humor to match.

"You comfortable, Ducky?" he asked gently. She could see the shine in his eyes and knew that it mattered to him that she was. She nodded slowly. It was all the strength she had. Jake gently stroked the paper-thin skin of her hand and then carefully rested his large hand on top of hers. It was cool and bony. It felt like death. Ducky was one of few ladies at the convalescent home where he worked that he knew would pass peacefully. She knew Jesus. She knew him well. She spoke of him in such a personal manner. He had learned from her. Her emphasis had often been on God's blessed mercy. If he had not loved God before meeting Ducky, he was certain he would by now. She was ninety-three, and as friends and family members had passed on before her, she would sometimes become discouraged. In between pills and swallows of water before breakfast, she would commonly say, "God's forgotten me. Can ya remind him about me?"

Jake did not want to remind God of Ducky. He adored her, and he needed the wise woman around a little longer. He was thankful that her passing would come during his shift. It was an honor to hold her hand.

Jake remembered telling Ducky about his ride-along with Charlie. He had told Ducky about Amber. How she had smiled and laughed. She felt Amber was reachable.

"Isn't that the same girl you told me about several months ago? You said she was the meanest, nastiest, rudest lady, if you could even call her that."

He had thanked her sarcastically for her memory of his exact words. Her memory seemed to work much better about his life than hers.

Regardless, he continued to share the rest of his story about Amber with Ducky, how she had changed instantaneously the minute they reached the prison grounds. The old lady had actually suggested that God put Amber in his life for a personal reason.

"No more personal than any of the other people we try to help," he had explained.

"Humph," she retorted.

A couple days later Ducky asked him about Amber again. This time she was bolder. "That girl has affected you, not the other way around."

He hadn't replied. He didn't want her to know that her comment bothered him. He was supposed to leave an impression on her. He had too much work to do, too many people who needed reaching. He couldn't afford to dote on just one.

Jake looked at Ducky now. Her cold had progressed into pneumonia. Fluid gurgled in her chest with every breath. Her eyes were open partway. She searched for Jake's hand, pleading with her expression. It was time for her to go. She would finally "be this day in her Father's house."

"Hold on," he coaxed. Her family would be there any minute. They would want to say their good-byes.

Ducky rasped a prayer, "Loving God … I thank you for the care … of this young man … As surely as I come unto you … I am confident … of this. You show the path … where we are to walk … You point the right direction … for us to follow … You lead by truth … and teach us … for you are God … who saves … All day long … my hope is in you."

Jake understood. God would lead if he allowed him too.

His part was obedience. God's will, not his. Jake bent down and kissed Ducky's cheek. She breathed twice then no more. Jake sucked in a deep breath and brushed away a tear that had begun to make its way down his cheek. He had seen a lot of death in this place, but this lady was special to him, and her passing would be hard. He had comfort in knowing she had lived a full life and they would meet again.

Ducky's family got there shortly after, but she was already gone. As they came in to say their goodbyes, Jake made his way to the lunchroom; he would wash up, get his things, and then head home.

His shift had ended twenty minutes earlier. The next shift had just finished getting their pre-shift report. He stopped at the nurse's station to give his then made his way to the lunchroom. Jena, one of his colleagues, was outside the door when he walked out; she had been waiting for him. "I guess Matilda passed tonight?"

He nodded.

"You want to grab a coffee or something down the hill? We could walk. It's nice out."

"Maybe another time. I don't have a change of clothes, and I know I smell." He looked down at a splatter of vomit that had gotten on his uniform earlier.

"Doesn't matter to me."

"Thanks, Jena, but I want to get home. I have another thing I am supposed to do tonight."

"Are you going on another ride-along?" she asked excitedly, eyes wide. It had been exciting to him in the beginning too; now it was morose. Every time before heading out, he prayed that God would lead them to someone who really wanted help, someone who wanted out of the life they were in rather than just someone wanting justification.

"Yeah, I am supposed to."

"Well, let's make it another night then. What days do you have off?"

"Sunday, Monday, Tuesday."

"I'm off Tuesday. I'll meet you at the Bombay Grill on Seventh Avenue at six." She flipped him a business card from her backpack. He read it and smiled.

"Another moonlighter?"

"I can't do this forever." She gestured at the building. He smiled at her.

"But you could do this *forever?*" he said the last word with fake enthusiasm.

She grinned. "Jake, are you making fun of me?"

"I would never make fun of … " He read the title on the card again, "Jena's Cakes Made Just for You, for children or adults. Adults?"

"I have a talent. I can decorate cakes, and you would be surprised how some adults want those cakes decorated. It's made me blush," she said defensively, touching his arm. "So I'll see you at six on Tuesday? Don't leave me hangin'." She walked to her car.

He walked to the bus stop. He thought a lot about Jena on the ride home. He knew she liked him, because she had never tried to hide it. She had asked him out before. He usually found excuses. He hadn't been interested in dating anyone after Sofia had died. Jena had remained friendly but stopped asking him out. She gave him time. Apparently, time was up.

He hadn't agreed this time either; she hadn't given him the opportunity to accept or decline. It might be nice. He looked at Jena's card again and wondered, *How many kinds of cakes can you make?*

———

Jake walked through the front door of his apartment. He lacked both the energy and the drive to go on the ride-along tonight. He was thinking about Ducky and the things she had said to him. He turned his agitation into a prayer. As he prayed, he felt an urgency to pray more. He felt the power of his spirit being restored. He recognized it from the day he had first dedicated his life.

Jake went to the freezer and pulled out a TV dinner. He popped it in the microwave and sat at the small drop-leaf table in the kitchen. He pulled his Bible from the drawer meant for cutlery. Ducky's last words reverberated in his mind. He opened the Bible and began to read from Psalm 25, where Ducky had gotten her prayer. "Forgive the rebellious sins of my youth," he read, "look instead through the eyes of your unfailing love." Tears began to well up in his eyes. He was struck that even to her last breath, Ducky encouraged him, and, in her wisdom, she knew what it was that he struggled with.

Jake made it to the precinct by ten. Matthew was waiting for him. They headed out into the downtown core. They were greeted by sullen faces, people who never really looked at you but through you. One girl couldn't have been more than fifteen and was dressed in almost nothing. She noticed the patrol car. She smiled cunningly. Jake looked at Matthew; he wondered if it still tore at his heart to see so many hurting people. A young kid, obviously selling something, stood on the corner, eyes on the car till they drove by.

Who, Lord? Direct us. Who needs you tonight? Jake prayed in his head. He noticed an older woman; it was hard to tell how old she really was. This life added years that were never lived. She wore a thin nightgown, but it was the lump of fur and sullen face that caused Jake to notice her. It wasn't uncommon for the homeless to have pets. They shared fifty-fifty whatever food they got with that pet. Jake had come to realize that a pet supplied the unconditional love they craved. It never rejected them, never turned on them. It just loved with no expectations. He understood. He looked at the woman intently. Her unconditional love, her only love, lay in a heap on her lap, dead.

Matthew pulled the patrol car over. She looked suspiciously at the car. He could see she was too forlorn to take off. Jake got out and approached her slowly. Matthew came up beside him but stayed a few feet back as not to be intimidating. Jake got closer and was hit with a putrid stench. He put his sleeve up to his nose to keep from gagging. The pet must have been dead for several days. When he was not more than a foot away from the woman, he saw something so disturbing that his knees nearly gave out. Maggots. Her love was crawling with maggots.

"God," he breathed a prayer, "strengthen my weak stomach. I don't want to offend her." He looked back at Matthew for some help. He smiled back reassuringly at the rookie. Jake knew he was on his own.

He got down on his haunches. He turned his nose into his shoulder and took a breath.

"What have you got there?" he asked gently, motioning toward the dog. She looked up at him, eyes glazed. "Is he friendly?" Jake asked.

She narrowed her eyes and spoke harshly, "He's dead."

Suddenly, it was he who was the pitied one. He saw it in her eyes, *You can't tell he's dead.*

"Was he friendly?" he tried to recover.

"Not to cops."

He knew instinctively that Matthew was laughing at his foul-ups.

"I'm not really a cop."

She leaned closer to him and whispered, "What are ya doin' with 'em if you're not one of 'em?"

No answer was safe, so he tried diversion. "What was your pet's name?"

"Scruffy. Doesn't he look like a Scruffy?"

"Yeah, he does. What about you? What is your name?"

She appeared to be thinking. Maybe she would give him an alias. "Barb," she finally said.

"Barb, can we go for a walk? There is a small garden area

one block over. We could give Scruffy a proper burial. Maybe you could say a few words about him." He could see she liked the idea. He held out his hand to help her up. Instead, she gestured to pass him Scruffy.

"Oh!" he exclaimed before he could suppress his shock. "My friend will wait here with you. I will be right back." He looked at Matthew, who gave him a strange look that said, *What do you intend to do?* Jake didn't answer. He ran into the corner store.

Once inside, he looked around quickly. *What will work?* He saw boxes of granola bars. *No, Scruffy is bigger than that.* Boxes of cereal, they seemed awkward. There it was, the perfect box. Soda crackers. Jake paid for his purchase and hurried back to Barb and Matthew. As he approached, his senses were assailed by the offensive odor. His eyes began to water. Barb noticed. She reached up and touched his hand gently, affected by his obvious sadness over the loss of Scruffy. Jake wiped at his eyes and proceeded quickly with his plan for fear that Barb would try to pass him Scruffy again.

Jake opened up the box and handed Barb the crackers. "Can you gently slide Scruffy into the box?" he coaxed. Barb wiped a tear from her cheek. Jake barely held in a gag as Barb bent to kiss Scruffy before placing her beloved into the box. That done, Jake let out a huge breath. They began to walk together to the place Jake had mentioned.

"What are you doing?" Matthew asked.

"I am going to help her bury Scruffy."

"No!" was Matthew's shocked reply.

"We have to," argued Jake. "I promised."

"No! Where do you think it will be okay to bury a dead animal in the city?"

"You follow in the patrol car. I'll show you."

Matthew knew it was not going to be good, but he went back to the car, got in, and followed Jake. He didn't go far. By the time Matthew got out of the car, Jake had already started digging a hole with his bare hands in a city flowerbed.

"What in the world are you doing?" his voice startled them both.

While they had been walking, some of the maggots had started squirming their way out of the box. One had touched Jake's hand. He had nearly dropped Scruffy right then but managed to control himself. Now he dug hurriedly and did not bother answering Matthew's question. Besides, it was self-explanatory.

"Seriously, you can't do this. It's against the law, and we are the upholders."

"It's already partly decomposed," Jake reasoned with the senior officer.

"Leave him be," Barb reproached.

"There." Jake laid the box in the hole and began covering it. He patted down the fresh earth and then looked at Barb. "Would you like to say a few words about Scruffy?"

"Nope. He already knows everything I got to say. I told him every day."

Jake smiled. He wondered if someone had told Barb something good every day, she might not be in this place at all. Jake walked Barb back to her corner. "Are you going to be okay now, Barb?"

"Yeah. Maybe Scruffy did like cops. I don't know, he didn't talk much."

Jake smiled, knowing the woman was complementing him.

The Next Corner

"Many are the plans in a man's heart but it is the Lord's purpose that prevails."

Proverbs 19:21

The night staff was off, and Amber's new nurse was a young and seemingly inexperienced girl by the name of Emma-Jean. Amber smiled as she read her tag. Amber had tried several times to convince her that she needed more narcotics for her pain. Emma-Jean had relented easily, giving Amber an extra shot of morphine.

She was in her sweet, dreamy place when she heard a distant, familiar voice. It sounded more like an echo to Amber. She knew that voice. Where did she know that voice from? Oh, it didn't matter. She let her mind drift and float. She was weightless and worry free. She was almost certain she was flying. Yes! It was bliss.

"Amber." The voice held profound grief. She strained her eyes to focus on the face. She cursed under her breath as she began to recognize Jake Liddell. Why was he looking at her like that? The effects of the drugs were too strong, and she was pulled back to her wonderland. A broad smile reached across her face, and she looked up at the young man. He was disturbed about something. The young guard who had found Amber last night had given the precinct a call. As soon as Matthew got the report, he called Jake. Jake came in as soon as he got clearance. Matthew tried to prepare him, giving him a few details. Jake felt confident that he had seen a lot and could handle it.

Jake was not just in shock at seeing Amber, he was absolutely furious. How had it happened? He had been with her two nights ago. She seemed so hopeful then, so alive. Now she was doped up and completely unable to form a complete sentence. She had a large bruise on her left cheek. More bruising was on her arms. A rectangular-shaped bruise ran along her forehead. Her cheek was swollen into her nose, causing her to appear disfigured. Her lip was split. Dried, caked-on blood trailed from her lip to her chin. He could not have prepared himself for the sight before him. Adding to the appal of the situation was the stench of old blood.

Regardless, Jake was thankful for the call from Matthew. He needed to be here for Amber right now.

"Nurse, I think you are giving her too much morphine," was all he could think to say. *You have got to toughen up,* he mocked himself silently.

"She's in a lot of pain, and she keeps having nightmares. What would you have me do?"

"Well, she's not competent to answer any questions. The warden and Harris are both going to be here soon to question her. Do you have any of the details on what happened here? She won't be able to give any." He had to focus, but all he felt was anger.

"I don't disclose that information to you without a senior officer present." Seeing his annoyance, she added, "You're welcome to wait."

When Senior Officer Harris Metcalf and the warden came in, they had a lot of questions. Jake felt sorry for Amber at first. She was completely uncooperative though, and shortly he began to feel annoyed. Why wouldn't she tell them what they needed to know? Finally, Emma-Jean got the file from the end of Amber's bed.

"Jumped in by two inmates, both in solitaire for the attack. Hmm. It says here too that she was pregnant. She'll have to have a D 'n' C."

Jake looked puzzled. The other two men knew.

"Scraping the uterine lining to remove anything left over from the miscarriage," Emma-Jean elaborated. Jake was working his jaw, trying to maintain calm. He was anything but.

Emma looked up from her file, speaking directly to Jake. "She must like you." Emma-Jean smiled warmly.

Jake looked puzzled.

"You wouldn't have been allowed in here without her consent."

He blushed. "She would have said no if you didn't have her so doped up."

Emma was still smiling.

Amber was somewhat aware of what was being said about her. She knew the last thing she wanted was for Jake to know all that information about her. He already knew all her other crimes; did he really need to know she had been pregnant? He would never know by whom, and that was the most humiliating part of all. She closed her eyes and willed them all to go away, especially him. They did go, with the exception of him. Amber was in no mood to deal with his preaching and perfection right now. If she just closed her eyes a bit longer, maybe he would leave as well. Then she could continue to enjoy the high she had finally managed to get.

"Amber," he lowered his face and talked just above a whisper. She could smell his breath. It was sweet, a hint of spearmint, mixed with his cologne; he smelled good, much better than she did. Amber wondered to herself without opening her eyes, *How close is his face? If I stuck out my tongue, could I lick it?* Her own foolish thought caused her to laugh out loud. The noise surprised Jake, who had innocently thought her to have fallen asleep. What could she do now? All shreds of dignity had been cast. She opened her eyes as best she could and took in the look of shock on Jake's surprised face. She continued to snicker as he stared at her, unsure of what to do next.

Taking in Amber's altered features, Jake remembered why he was there and started to question her. He hoped that without the other men present, she might reveal something, anything to him. They had really connected the other night. He hoped she would trust him and be cooperative. It didn't take long for him to realize that the morphine in her body was still way too high to get any real answers to his questions.

He gently told her that he would return later in the evening with his partner, Matthew. He expected her to be in a state that would enable her to answer some of their questions then. As he turned to go, he hesitated and kindly added, "Amber, you will have to tell someone what happened here. I had hoped it would make it easier for you if it was me." He reached down and softly touched a curl that had strayed off the pillow.

She squeezed her eyes shut again, either to keep herself from seeing him or to keep him from seeing her, she wasn't sure which. She knew she couldn't deal with looking deep into those all-too-understanding dark eyes. She just couldn't, not in her state. She was relieved at the sound of receding footsteps and chanced opening just one eye to peek. No luck. The nurse was walking away. Jake knew he had very little time; he needed to ask his questions quickly.

"Amber, please try to focus. Look at me." He paused and waited for her to respond. She didn't, so he continued. "I know. I already know. The nurses know. The cops know. They just need the name of the third attacker. Listen to me, I know it was a guard. You might think no one will believe you, but they will. We will. We already know." He looked at her urgently, willing her to look at him.

Amber could feel his stare boring a hole into her thoughts. She let out an exaggerated breath and opened her eyes. She tried to look aloof and gave the always-kind and unsuspecting gentleman "the voice." It was well practiced. "Well, Jake, it seems you know more about what happened here than I do. I really don't remember anything. Perhaps whoever you got your information from could fill us both in on some more details. Personally, though, I'm quite happy to forget the whole thing." Amber made sure her expression remained emotionless. She wished he would just go home. It was too draining.

She wanted to feel the euphoric high she had been enjoying and never come out of it. He was ruining the first high she had gotten in ages.

Jake was not done at all. He spoke harsh words, cutting into her pity trip.

"Amber, your silence doesn't just hurt you. This is happening to other new girls as well. It has to be stopped. No one ever wants to talk about it. But you, you know to do the right thing. You have support. It would be so much easier for you." Maybe he was being presumptuous, but he was sure she should be able to talk openly with him. He kept thinking about the other night when they had dropped her off after picking her up from the courthouse. He was reaching her. He knew he was. So did she. Why couldn't she just admit it and let him help her?

She didn't respond, so he continued. "With you they made a mistake. Whoever did this doesn't realize how strong you are. This is a perfect opportunity for you to use your strength to do some good."

The candor with which he used to accuse her succeeded only in making her feel defensive. While she had pretended to be annoyed initially, she felt the trueness of those emotions now.

"Jake, what good do you expect from me? I have enough problems of my own. It seems to me that if it was a uniformed man who did this to me, the last person I need to be talking to is a uniformed man." Amber raised her brow, a clear indication to Jake that while it served her purpose, she was including him as one of them.

Maybe it was true what people said about her. She probably didn't feel anything for him. She had just been playing him the other night. His own pride began to swell as he judged her harshly. A gentle voice prodded, "Tenderly. Look at her, look into her. See what I see." He was annoyed and convicted at the same time. He took a deep breath and looked deeper. It was easy for the gentle to come at taking in her wounds.

He saw the hardness for what it was: survival. As Jake often did, he surprised Amber with his retort. He didn't accuse; he didn't get mad. He spoke softly and from his heart. "Amber, I didn't come here on the job as part of a team to get information from you. I came here for you. I thought you would trust me." He caught the shift in her expression and waited, hopeful again of an altruistic response.

His kindness added to her guilt, and though she desperately needed to trust him, she allowed frustration in the guise of anger to rule her emotions. She lashed out at him verbally. "You expect too much from me. I'm not this saveable person you seem to think I am. I have no desire to do good deeds, so you and your cop buddies can come in here and arrest some evil guard and walk away with a hero badge for my humiliation. Stop thinking you know me!" She refused the urge to look at him to see if her words had struck. She waited, arms folded rigidly, jaw held tight, eyes glaring, heart cold and full of bitterness, armed for any counterattack he may have.

There would be no attack from Jake, just sadness. She had succeeded in deflating his ego. Good! *Who does this guy think he is anyway?* she thought. She turned her head and looked away, a sure sign she was done with the interrogation, though he didn't seem too big on picking up on signals. He moved but not away. He got closer. He leaned close, and she held her breath for a moment. Shocked. She hoped he wasn't going to hurt her. He took her hand gently and said, "I am truly sorry." He released her hand and softly touched the rigidly folded arm with the back of his hand. Then he left. She exhaled heavily.

Jake was barely out the door when Amber jumped up and made her way as best she could to the bathroom, ignoring the pain that was shooting through her body. She locked herself in, and the battle of her emotions began. She was softening, yet she refused to shed a single tear. She looked at the poor reflection in the mirror. She forced herself to remember. It was easy. The anger and bitterness were always there, always on the surface. They were easy to arouse.

"Who protected you? Who sacrificed for you?" she asked. As she did, the anger got stronger, and the echo responded in her head, the answer she felt. "No one."

There was another answer though, but she refused to hear it. "I did."

Her arms shook. She gripped the sink with all her strength. Her legs throbbed. "Control yourself," she demanded. "You are all you have." She convinced herself of more untruths. Amber sucked in a deep breath and then did exactly that. She unlocked the door and slowly made her way back to her bed, feeling victorious. Exhausted, she fell asleep.

Emma-Jean, still smiling exactly as she had been that morning, brought Amber her lunch. She tried to make small talk with her and really hit a tender spot by mentioning Jake. She referred to him as "that hot young thing." She continued, "You know, not very many men who don't have to come down here do." She paused and thought a moment then continued. "Actually, unless it's a conjugal visit, none do." She winked at her and arched her brow, hoping to get a response. Amber had long since come down from her high; all she felt now was groggy, and she had no desire to reply to the remark.

Amber remained silent, so Emma-Jean switched topics. "The doctor is going to be in at one o'clock. I will prep you after lunch."

Amber snapped her head around, staring at the nurse as though she had announced the end of the world. "What doctor?"

Emma-Jean was shocked by the dramatic reaction. Amber softened her expression, realizing Emma would have no idea how crazy "doctors" made her. She smoothly blanketed her emotions, allowing the vacant expression to take over. Her eyes remained hard, focused expectantly on the nurse. Emma-Jean saw the change in Amber's disposition.

"The doctor will do a rape kit. It's a mandatory procedure after a rape. Do you want me to go over the details so you will know what to expect?" Amber could feel the heat rising in her cheeks, both from embarrassment and anger. She wasn't sure which she despised more. For the second time that day Amber felt a lump rising in her throat. Why did she have to endure so much? Hadn't she been punished enough for one day?

There it was, the source of her weakness: self-pity. Amber shook her head and smirked to herself. "Go ahead, Emma-Jean. Tell me what I'm in for. Is it going to be fun?" Before she could respond, the doctor came in.

"You're early. The patient hasn't had her lunch yet, nor is she prepared."

"I just got a page. I have ten minutes, then I have a court appearance, so I do this now, not later." He paused then added, "Evidence is time sensitive." He wasn't rude, just matter-of-fact. He tossed Amber a gown. "You will need to get this on. If you want, you may have one person present in the room during your exam. I will be back in one minute. Be ready when I get back." With that, he walked out. He left no room for discussion or argument.

Amber stared at the gown on her bed. Emma-Jean picked it up. Picking up on Amber's discomfort, she held up the gown for her. She held out the armholes so it would be easy for her to slip her arms. Amber cooperated and started to remove her clothes.

"It's regulation. Someone must be present during the exam."

Emma was familiar with people like Amber. She already knew the feisty girl enough to know she would be too proud to admit needing support. "I can stay, unless there is someone else you would prefer. Let me know."

"No. You will do," she answered, defeated. Emma-Jean tied the strings in back of the gown, and Amber reluctantly removed her underclothes. It was humiliating. She was still bleeding from the miscarriage. She was in excruciating pain from the assault. Now she was going to have to be poked and prodded in those same places for science.

Amber held the gown shut at the back and climbed back on the bed, pulling up the covers. Her legs were bruised and her arms had distinguished finger-imprinted bruises, all screaming of evidence that there had been a third assailant. The doctor walked in, cutting into her private thoughts.

"Remove those blankets and slide to the end of the bed." Amber did as she was told.

As the doctor spoke, he dropped the lower half of the bed she had been lying on. The doctor snapped on his sterile gloves, pulled up a chair, and began the "examination." He carelessly flipped up the already-revealing gown. He reached for a surgical box. It was stainless steel and full of stainless steel equipment. He placed the box on her bedside table, grabbed a long tweezers, and began his exam. Tears glistened in Amber's eyes. None would fall. She refused the weakness, emotional or physical. Emma-Jean did not hide her emotions; her expression bore all the pity she felt and the pain she knew Amber must feel.

She held Amber's hand firmly. The doctor put down the tweezers and grabbed another object from the stainless steel box. This was , one with a long, circular handle. On the end of it was a circular blade. He scraped the edges of Amber's labia, hoping to get a trace of semen or some fragment that could be used to get provide a DNA sample. Emma continued to alternately look away and into Amber's eyes. The hardness was all that was evident. Her face held no expression. The doctor followed up this the last procedure with the internal exam. The long metal probe was extremely cold. He inserted it, and her abdomen cramped, resisting the internal intrusion. The doctor clamped the apparatus, and again scraping followed.

The doctor was rough as he rushed through the exam. Amber could no longer bite her tongue. "Do you have any idea what you are doing? I was accosted by two women who are already in solitaire for this? There is no semen, because there was no semen. You won't find hair samples either. I hope you are about done down there."

The doctor was an elderly man, probably in his early sixties, totally gray, and balding at the front. He had perfectly smooth skin. Perched on his pointy nose were round-framed glasses that looked as though they had always been there. Amber noticed the abundance of hair on his forearms, scrutinising, *He should take the stuff from his arms and transplant it to his head.*

Amber began to feel a bit more at ease as she sized up the old man. She could take him down if she needed to. The doctor looked knowingly over his glasses at his patient and calmly replied to her accusations, "Your story is just 'a story' that will be revealed for what it is. You can 'say' there were only two people involved in this assault, but I know otherwise. I can assure you, I will be exhaustive in my endeavors to extract any evidence that will help uncover the facts and reveal what really took place. Give up the name or don't give it up. The evidence will do all the talking even if you refuse. I am done here."

Amber was shocked by the doctor's abrasiveness, but, not to be outdone, she quipped, "Thanks for the 411, Dr. Tips." The doctor grabbed his tools and wrapped them up. He snapped off the bloody gloves, threw them in the trash, and headed for the exit. As he was walking out, he paused in the door long enough to give Amber an unnerving retort, "We already know who is responsible. Now I have collected the evidence. Thank you for your cooperation." He walked out.

Enraged, Amber shouted after him, "What, no kiss good-bye? Call me," followed by myriad expletives, leaving no need to guess how she felt about the doctor.

Emma-Jean interrupted her vocal outburst. "Hey, let it go. He is a doctor. They can get the best of anyone." The girls exchanged knowing looks.

"Thank you for staying in here with me. I know that wasn't a regulation," Amber said honestly.

"Why don't you want to tell the truth about what happened? These things happen in places like this. The one working both sides is the one who never seems to get caught. The dirty guard. It's so cliché! You're lucky the guard who spoke to the officer isn't callous yet. He took the details of your attack to the right people, not even worrying about his job or his back. Do you get how important that is? Something is going to be done this time." Emma sounded so sure. She paused and thought a moment. *How many young, unsuspecting girls have been in Amber's shoes? Only no one told. No one wants to get involved.* "You have angels watching over you, girl," she said with a smile.

Amber listened quietly to Emma's rationale. She liked talking to her, but her last statement hit a nerve. It was saturated with stupidity.

"I was attacked and beaten by two disgusting and enormous women. I was further assaulted with the use of objects by a man so evil Satan asks him for tips. I lost the baby that would have proven my shrink was using his professional position to have sex with me, as well as anything else that came into his perverse mind. I take little comfort in knowing that it wasn't just me he violated but any other disturbed female who had the misfortune of walking through his professional doors." Amber's words were laced with venom, entwining any foul word she could think of.

"Oh! Did I mention that I am in jail on trial for a murder that, had it been anyone else, would have been an obvious case of self-defense? But for me it just happens to be a police officer's son. Did I forget anything? And I have an angel? Where? When? He's not doing a very good job. You want him?" Amber wasn't yelling, but she was frustrated. What was wrong with people? Analyzing her like a festering cyst. People would see what they were looking for. That didn't make it the truth. That is one thing she could attest to.

Emma-Jean realized that in Amber's forthcoming speech,

she had divulged a lot of information. She remained silent, suddenly feeling insignificant in the face of all Amber had endured. She had no right to speak.

Amber's voice was weak, barely breaking the silence. "Guess that was more than you needed to know."

"Well, you still didn't give a name. Am I pushing it?"

"Completely?"

"I am sorry for all you have endured, but honestly, just saying a name seems like such a small thing in the scope of everything else."

"It's not just a name, it is a name that has power. Get someone else to be the snitch, risk their skin. As you say, I have endured enough. Would it help if I said it with a few more adjectives?"

"I get the picture."

Amber hadn't meant to hurt her feelings. Emma was kind. She quickly added, "But if I did decide to be rat, I'd rat to you. I could use some more morphine." She said the last comment with a smile.

Emma returned the smile. "I'll see what I can do about that. I know you're in pain. Whether you are prepared to admit it or not, what happened to you hurts the inside and the outside. I want to help you. I know it's rough."

Amber didn't say anything. It was the gentle way Emma had spoken that caused the familiar lump in her throat. If she did have an angel, maybe it was Emma-Jean. She knew that with all the things she had done, the last person God would send to protect would be her.

She tried to think about something else, anything else. Relentlessly, God kept intercepting her thoughts. She finally gave in closed her eyes. He shone like the sun in her imagination, warming her on the inside. Clouds began rolling in, covering the glory of the sun. It was going to pour on her. She cleared her mind. God was not watching over her. He hadn't for a long time. God would have no reason to have any interest in her.

THIS ROAD I WALK

She was the thorn that pricked when one reached out to touch a rose. Her thoughts tried to recede to that place again, where they grew darker and crept deeper until her soul felt raw. She dwelt on them in the silence.

Emma-Jean was paged. When she came back from the call, she had, according to Amber, even worse news, worse than the previous news of the doctor. Emma delivered her news cheerily. "Amber, your parents are on their way up to see you. You better go in the bathroom and make yourself a little more presentable."

"What? No! Tell them not to come. Send them home. This is the last thing they need. They can't see me like this. They won't be able to handle it."

"They might surprise you. Give them the benefit of doubt."

"You don't know them. My mother will freak. She'll start crying. No! I can't take this."

"They have already been through a lot. What makes you think they can't handle this?"

Amber continued as though she hadn't heard Emma-Jean. "And my father? He won't know how to act. He'll be all weird. Oh no. No." Amber's anxiety escalated as she spoke.

Emma-Jean held up her hand to quiet Amber. She walked away, leaving Amber alone with her thoughts. She went quickly toward the nursing station. Amber watched until she was out of sight. Emma came back quickly. Her black leather purse was tucked under her arm. "Come on, we only have about three minutes. Let's pretty you up. I have some cover-up in here and some concealing powder and a few other things that might help us. We'll cover up the dark bruising, make it easier on Ma and Pa, okay?" Emma didn't wait for an answer. She knowingly helped Amber out of bed and to the bathroom where the girls began their makeover.

Amber looked in the mirror. Emma-Jean was quite good with cosmetics. She had to admit, she wasn't quite as shocking to see. Amber was just climbing back into bed when she heard footsteps. Her built-in radar picked up her parents' specific walking rhythm. Emma-Jean gave Amber a reassuring glance and headed out of the room.

Michael and Catherine had been briefed about Amber's condition. They were told she had been assaulted. They were spared the details. They had an idea of what to expect when they saw their daughter.

Amber immediately realized significant change in her parents when she was the one who had to start the conversation. "So how's my little bro doing?" Michael and Catherine both knew that would be Amber's first question, perfectly guiding the conversation to where they needed it to be.

"He's doing all right. He misses you, of course. He mentioned some things, Amber." Her mother no longer wore the constipated expression that had become her usual facial canvas. She was focused. "If you don't feel comfortable discussing it with us, we have made Nina aware and she will discuss it with you. We just wanted you to hear it from us. Lincoln was pretty upset, but—"

"Hold on," Amber interjected. What could her little brother have told them that required a legal discussion? "What did Linc say? What have you said? You promised not to tell him what is going on here." Her voice escalated at the uneasy thought of her innocent brother knowing the things his stupid big sister had gotten involved in. She would never forgive herself. She would never forgive them. They had promised.

Still not reacting in the typical way for either of her parents, Michael spoke up. "A few nights ago, Linc … " Michael paused for a moment, choosing his words carefully. He wanted to make sure Amber wouldn't interpret what he was going to say as them blaming her. "You must have thought your brother was sleeping, but he wasn't, and he overheard a telephone conversation. You were very upset. He heard you say you would kill Dr. Forbes if he ever touched you again." Seeing the horrified expression on his daughter's face, he hurried on. "Some kid at school said you killed someone, so Lincoln put two and two together. He thought you must have really killed the doctor." Silence engulfed the room like storm clouds awaiting thunder. Michael and Catherine remained calm, standing side by side, awaiting the eruption that was typical of their daughter.

Amber finally spoke, but it wasn't the outburst they expected. "What did you tell him?" Regret filled her voice. Michael sat at the foot of the bed, watching her expression as he retold of the conversation with Linc. "In the end, he believed his information would help his big sister. You know, he knows what's going on. Why don't we bring him in on the weekend to see you?"

"No! Daddy, please, no! It's not right. He shouldn't ever have to come here, ever."

"We understand, but your brother really misses you. You're missing out on him growing up. Be honest; it's not him that can't handle this, it's you. What if you are here for a long time, Amber? Will you ever see him again? Your relationship will end if you refuse to let him see you."

Amber contemplated her father's words. Catherine stood quietly, hoping there would be some reasoning on their daughter's part. Amber sucked in a breath, readying to say something. Neither parent could tell from her expression what would come out of her mouth. Michael didn't give her the chance. He spoke up, switching topics, "In your own words, please tell us what happened both that night with Duncan when he was killed and, if you are willing, what happened with Dr Forbes. We want the truth, and we want to hear it from you. We will believe you."

Michael could see that somewhere in what he had just said he had lost her again. For a moment she had seemed pliant. Now her face hardened, and he awaited yet another verbal assault, which, through Amber's expression, was sure to come.

"What? You want to believe me now? You had the chance to help me. You turned your backs on me when I needed you. Now your precious son speaks a few words and you call a lawyer? Do you really think that helps me to know this? You believe your son and not me. Am I not your daughter? Did I not deserve your trust then? What about last night? Will you believe me about that? I was pregnant. They killed my baby! The baby growing inside my body. Dr. Forbes' baby! Do you know how his baby got inside my body? That's one thing you might know. Now you can suffer, and I will tell you why."

Amber finally paused, drawing a deep breath. When she spoke, her voice was laced with pain, tangible, that no gauze could heal. Her eyes revealed the light had gone out behind them, leaving only a void lined with suffering. She finished her accusation. "So I could prove to my parents that I was telling the truth!" Tears silently rolled down Catherine's face; her chin trembled. Michael struggled for control.

Their reaction gave her power; she would make them sorry. "So, no, I will not discuss this with you. No, don't bring my brother to see me. You don't get the privilege of making decisions for me anymore. You lost. Go away. Leave." Her voice was low, quiet, an aural display of the intensity of her emotions. Her mother did not pull one of her usual "what happened to you?" or "think positive" trips on her. They just stood side by side, hand in hand, unified.

Michael spoke into the silence. "We can't change the past any more than you can. We are all guilty of making bad choices. Your mother and I can't be the only ones with regrets. We will do whatever it takes for this family to survive this. Together, preferably. It's up to you." He paused, holding his daughter's eyes, and in a trembling voice he spoke words he hadn't said in way too long. He needed her to believe him. "I love you, Amber. I always have, and I will never stop. No words you say, no things you do will ever make me stop loving you. My daughter. My gift."

"That would have been a nice speech, but you're about two years too late," she said solemnly. Now they knew, they knew everything, and they knew they played a huge part. No more secrets, nothing to hide. They would go home and talk about her, and they would show their love like they always had. They would go to church and ask everyone to pray for their prodigal daughter. Would they ask for prayer for themselves? Would they confess their part in her turmoil? Would they be so willing to talk about her now that they knew everything? Maybe they would forget they had a daughter.

Michael and Catherine recognized the accusations for what they were; in part, they were their daughter's rightful anger at them for not protecting her. It was consequential truth; they chose not to believe her when they had the chance. Partially, she was frustrated about her predicament. The hardest thing was, it was too late for "I'm sorry." It didn't matter what they knew or what they thought they could prove. The damage was done, and through a series of sordid circumstances someone was dead, and their daughter was the one being blamed. No immediate restoration, for the wrong and the unjust events that had unfolded in Amber's life were plausible.

Each held on to the hope of divine healing for their daughter's oozing spiritual wounds. They would work hard at restoring their relationship with her. It would be foolish to think it would be easy. Amber had a strong mind, and she would make them work for her forgiveness.

Michael got up from the edge of the bed. He searched her face for some emotion, something in her eyes to say how she felt, but she appeared vacant. Michael's words bespoke all the love and grief he was feeling. "I can see in your eyes that we have failed you. I see the pain, but you still have a choice to make. You had a choice when all this was happening to you. You had the choice of how you wanted to deal with your circumstances. You still have choices to make. We all do, every day."

"A choice? When did I have a choice? I begged God to take me and leave Adam. He was the faithful one. Do you think if God had taken me, as I begged him to, that Adam would have let his life get messed up like this? And that doctor, did I have a choice about that? I haven't had any choices." Amber lowered her head, and her voice softened for a moment at the flashback. "The few I did have I really messed up on." What could anyone say to that? Catherine and Michael were relieved at the slight acceptance on Amber's part.

All Amber felt was the downward spiral pulling her to a place she knew she couldn't get out of. She preferred having something over her parents. She found solace in knowing they were guilty. Why had she gone and told them everything? Oh, her stupid mouth. What must they be thinking about her? Why did it affect her? She had turned that off a long time ago, or so she had thought.

Catherine spoke into the silence, her anguish audible. Her daughter would see her emotion as weakness; she didn't care. "I am truly sorry that I let you down. I don't expect your forgiveness. I hope for it. That choice is yours. We need to start trusting each other again. By that, I mean us trusting you, but you need to start talking to us. Amber, I hope at some point in your life you come to forgive me for the role I unwittingly played in this. Please don't let pride or anger keep you from us. We are a family. No matter what, we are the only family you have. There has to be a way to heal and repair this family."

There was a part of Amber that screamed to accept their offer. Reality told her it was too late and that her mother was wrong. Besides, she would always have Linc; he would never turn against her. Caught in her thoughts, she didn't have the chance to avoid her father as he bent down and kissed her forehead. Without another word, they left.

Michael had tears in his eyes as he bent to kiss her. Amber winced at the painful memory of the night she was arrested. There were no tears then. How could there have been? He had been humbled before all their neighbors. He had to consider what the church people would say. There was no arrogance today, just an undeniable calm laced with humility. Both her parents seemed protected by it. She couldn't figure out what "it" was.

Amber hated the way she felt. She vied for something to remind her of the anger; it gave her power. She knew how to be angry. The reasoning she longed for came; she enabled rage to fill the spaces left empty in her soul. Recalling her mother's words, using the term "role" like a character in a made-for-television drama instead of her life. She used self-righteousness to drown out the voice that accused, *What part did you play?* She struggled to shut out the thoughts. She needed the anger. She needed to cast blame.

Emma-Jean was at the front desk. She looked up to see the Whites leaving. She noted their faces. They lacked the beaten expression so many other families wore when leaving. She continued with her paperwork. When she looked up again, she noticed they were talking to a guard.

"Mr. White, Mrs. White, hello. I am one of the chief guards here at Klahanee. I was on duty the night Amber was accosted. Do you mind if I ask a few questions?"

"Regarding?" Mr. White answered, eyebrows arched questioningly.

"Regarding your daughter's attack. She hasn't exactly been forthcoming with what happened. I thought maybe she would speak to her family."

"So what's your question?"

"Did Amber give you any information regarding what happened to her?"

They hadn't asked her about last night. The only mention of it had come in a whirlwind of accusations.

"Jesus." He breathed the name that brought him comfort. "We did not get a chance to discuss Amber's trauma. She is a strong-minded young woman. If her mind is set, you will not drag it out of her." He was about to say more, but something held him back. He could see Catherine in his peripheral vision. She looked as uncomfortable as he felt. He knew they were sharing a thought. The guard looked from Catherine to Michael then back to Catherine. His face was hard. The man did not like their daughter. Something warned them, something in Michael's gut. "I am sorry, I didn't get your name."

Emma-Jean was approaching. The guard nodded and

walked away. Michael looked after him. When he turned to face the approaching nurse, he caught her expression and his heart jumped. Michael waited for the nurse to say something. He hoped it would ease the apprehension he felt.

"Hi, I am Emma-Jean. I have been Amber's nurse during her recuperation." She paused only a moment and then gestured with her chin to the retreating guard. "What did he want?" Her question was deeper than the simple words she chose.

"He was asking about Amber. The attack. He wondered if we knew anything."

"What did you tell him?" The Whites were both surprised by the intensity of the nurse's voice.

"Nothing. We don't really know anything."

"You should keep all discussion about your daughter's attack strictly with the police." Emma-Jean looked as though she wanted to say more but didn't. Michael and Catherine were too involved in their own thoughts.

"Thank you," Michael said as he took his wife's hand, indicating they were leaving. Before they could go, Emma-Jean began talking again.

"There is a full investigation going on. The warden is doing everything he can to help catch Amber's assailants. The attack on your daughter may have been an inside job, not just between inmates."

Michael felt his blood run cold. He thought about running after that guard and throttling him. What was going on? They were so completely helpless. Did Emma know what she was talking about? It was insanity to comprehend what the nurse was insinuating.

"Do you want to know what happened?" she asked. Terrified of what they would hear, but not wanting to cower to that fear, they nodded. If their daughter had lived through it, the least they could do was hear about it. Emma began, avoiding too much detail. Enough. They understood. Emma went on to tell of what she knew from Jared and the nurse's reports. When she was nearly finished, she asked, "Is this too hard for you to hear? You seem able to take it."

Catherine nodded, and Michael spoke up, "Please."

"Please tell us. We want to know," Catherine added. She was honest. "Amber doesn't tell us anything. Even if there was something she wanted us to know, she wouldn't tell."

Emma-Jean reminded herself to be gentle in her choice of words as she finished telling them what she knew.

"Two inmates were caught. The problem is that no one will talk. The other inmates are terrified. None of the guards are talking. The one person who did come forward has remained anonymous.

"The two inmates are being held in solitaire until they disclose the name of the third party involved. They haven't given in. Neither has Amber. Today Amber did admit, in a state of rage, that there were three people who accosted her, but there is no one who is willing to give up the name. If it is a guard, she would be offered protection in exchange for revealing the attacker. The cops want to make sure they have sufficient evidence to put the person away for a long time." Emma reiterated her point, "She needs to give up a name, preferably to someone astute."

Don't Look Back

"As soon as they had been brought out, one of the angels said 'flee for your lives, and don't look back, don't stop anywhere flee to the plains. Flee to the mountains or you will be swept away.' But Lot's wife looked back and she became a pillar of salt."

Genesis 19:17, 26

Amber was in a daze as she lay in the silence. Why had her parents come? Their presence aroused old emotions, adding salt to festering wounds. It caused her to remember the events that brought her to this place. Her heart ached with the memories she couldn't escape. They were who she was.

Her first visit with Dr. Gordon Forbes had been in March, shortly after the incident with that snake, Dave. She would never admit it, but he had broken her. It was after Dave that she began ditching school. Her parents found out, and they thought it was because of the accident with Adam that she wasn't coping.

Mrs. Humphrey, the school principal, looked at Mr. and Mrs. White, waiting for a reply.

"Dr. Forbes comes highly recommended. If your child is experiencing problems with the law, Dr. Forbes is a court-appointed psychiatrist. His knowledge is valuable." The high school counsellor who sat in on the meeting was trying to be helpful. Following a long pause, Mr. Kelly chose to add more of his thoughts and concerns. "We already know Amber is experimenting with drugs. She just hasn't been caught. Her new friends have no compunction about drug use."

Amber sat in her chair as the four talked about her as though she were not there. No one asked her any questions. No one even spoke to her. They were all too smart, sitting smugly in judgment of her.

They had the perfect plan to fix her their way. None of the people in that room needed any information from her. She crossed her arms across her chest, shutting out her accusers. Why didn't her parents defend her?

Go ahead, Dad, tell them this is garbage. We don't need to be here.

But Michael kept listening.

Come on, Mom, show them some of your annoying, overly positive attitude.

Amber kept her thoughts to herself. Catherine and Michael chose to play their sympathy cards.

"She wasn't like this before. It's just that since the accident, Amber hasn't been herself… "

She tuned it out. She was sixteen years old, and she would not have the stigma of "needs psychiatric help" attached to her. One week later, however, she found herself in the good doctor's office. When she returned, she had a fit.

"I am never going to see that pig again. You can't make me. He's sick."

"Amber, calm down. You will see him again."

"He's vulgar. He smells. He has bad breath. Know how I know? He was sitting way too close to me."

"Amber! That is enough nonsense. If not for agreeing to these appointments, you would have been expelled. Do you want to make sure you have no future?"

"Dad, please talk to her! She is so unreasonable."

"Amber, I agree with your mother. Avoiding your behavior seems to be enabling it to get worse."

"I won't ditch school anymore. I promise. Let me switch schools." Amber could see neither of her parents were softening on the issue. "Mom, he makes me feel … uncomfortable."

Michael and Catherine both looked at Amber. Catherine's eyes were huge, her mouth agape.

Michael clenched his jaw. "What do you mean?"

Amber analyzed her parents' expressions. They didn't appear to be able to deal with the truth. She was probably overreacting. "Never mind. Maybe all therapists touch their patients that way."

Perhaps it was the lack of emotion in the way she said it. Michael and Catherine exchanged knowing expressions.

"That is a very serious thing to say about someone, Amber." Her father sounded disgusted with her.

"Yeah! It is." She walked toward the stairs. No one came after her. No one asked any more questions.

Amber continued seeing Forbes. The worse he got, the worse she got. She would ditch the appointments with the doctor and school. Eventually, she would add home to the list of things she ditched. She met some new friends from the downtown area. She began staying out all night. It had been so gradual. Initially, Michael and Catherine fought with her about it. They tried grounding her, like that would work. They both worked, so they couldn't keep their eyes on her all the time. Her father had on many occasions, after long hours of work, driven around looking for her. Sometimes he would find her. He would watch her, make sure she was safe. Sometimes he would force her into the pickup and drag her home. Sometimes she would be gone again by morning.

Then there were the scary times when they didn't find her at all, the times she didn't see the truck following her.

In another attempt to regain control of their wayward daughter, Michael and Catherine stooped to putting her under the care of her grandmother, knowing her adoration for the woman would encourage her to be more cooperative. That may have worked in the beginning, but as Amber continued on the path she was on, her hatred grew. Her heart hardened. Her conscience seared. Her friends got worse. The drugs got harder, and everything else mattered less. Even Grandma eventually felt the sting of Amber's ruthlessness.

"Maybe we should cancel the appointments with the doctor."

Amber had just slammed the door on her way out, following yet another yelling match.

"Michael, if we give in, then what? She won't get any help."

"She ditches the appointments. She's not getting any help now." He was matter-of-fact.

"Let her stop for a while. If things improve, then maybe there is something wrong."

"You didn't actually fall for that, did you? Please, Catherine, he's a doctor. Sometimes you really surprise me."

"Don't do that to me."

"Do what?"

"You are belittling me just because I don't have the same opinion as you."

"You certainly don't."

"There it is again." She threw her hands up and walked away.

Michael called after her, "So shall we tell our daughter the good news tonight or whenever she decides to return?"

Catherine turned around, anger blazing in her stare. Did he really think she was so foolish? "Not just like that, Michael."

"Please, tell me your plan to rescue our daughter."

Catherine narrowed her eyes. There was that tone again. She took in a long breath then let it out quickly. *God, grant me patience.* She was walking back toward her husband. She had a few words on the tip of her tongue, but she would keep them to herself today. "We could try to make a deal with her."

He didn't say anything, so she continued. "Like if you stop cutting school, we will cancel the appointments. For now."

"And if she agrees and doesn't follow through, what is our recourse?"

"Look, I don't have all the answers. I am just trying to work with what we have."

Amber didn't come home that night. She came out of her room that morning though, just five minutes before her bus would come.

"Amber, I will drive you to school today."

"No thanks."

"It is not an option. Your father and I were discussing some things yesterday. I want to talk to you about them. I think you will actually like what we decided."

Amber rolled her eyes. "Fine." She sat at the table and drummed her fingers impatiently.

On the drive Catherine spoke to her daughter. Amber was surprised at what her mother offered. Did her parents finally believe her? She was relieved. Then disappointed. Nothing in what her mother said gave any indication that her accusations against the doctor were the reason for dropping the appointments. Amber agreed to the terms set out in the deal. And for a while she held true to them.

Amber couldn't believe how hard school was. She had missed the last thirty of ninety days.

Her friends weren't there to learn; they were there because they had no choice. The people she hung out with attended the majority of their classes stoned. The other people she hung out with were her downtown friends. Most of them were dropouts and druggies. Their only purpose was to sell enough drugs to make enough money to buy their next fix.

Amber did have one friend from school, Stan. He would, on occasion, remind Amber that she was smart. She should study more. Stan hung out with the street kids as well. He continued at school like Amber. Unlike Amber, he struggled with learning. He knew one day an education would be the difference between the life he had with his crack-addicted mother and the life he hoped to have, which included a job and a car and no drugs.

"Nice to see you back." Stan smiled. She hadn't seen him in a while.

"Yeah."

"I got some happy sticks on me. It looks like you could use one."

"I'll meet you at lunch." She could hardly wait until then.

Finally, the bell rang. Amber made her way down the trail. She knew that was where Stan would meet her.

"What ya got for me?" she asked eagerly.

"What happened to the Amber I used to know?" he asked with mock sadness. He shook his head at her. "When we used to hang out, you were the girl who took my doobie and threw it away. Now you're the girl who takes my doobie and smokes it before I get any."

Amber didn't think he was funny; besides, pot wasn't cutting it anymore. She needed something harder. Stan knew who, how, and what to fix her up with. They smoked the happy sticks, cocaine-laced joints, and when the bell rang they went back to class.

Michael and Catherine knew something horrible was happening to their daughter. Her decline was picking up momentum again.

She had been arrested the week she ran away. She was given more sessions with a psychiatrist. She could take it or end up in juvie. She took it. The judge appointed Dr. Gordon Forbes. She knew where she was going if she ditched, so she went. Something happened to their daughter after that. Something visible behind her eyes—lost innocence.

Michael and Catherine felt more and more helpless. They interfered less. They were just happy to know where she was. Any attempts they made to enforce rules were met with rage and accusations. Two or three days would pass before they would see her at all.

One night, after a particularly nasty confrontation that included accusations of knowing Amber was using drugs, they told their daughter they would turn her over to the police if they had to.

"It is time for some tough love. We will do what we have to."

"Tough love." Amber mocked her father. "That is the only kind I have ever gotten. I didn't know there was any other kind." She stayed away a whole week. That was when she got arrested.

She had stayed with some friends in the warehouse. Stan came around, checking on her. He brought with him an assortment of things to try. Amber was always eager to try something new. Stan brought cartoon acid, magic mushrooms, and anything else he could get a hold of. Everyone else was huffing, but Amber really wasn't interested in dying. She knew that stuff could kill her. That week was Amber's initiation into a whole new world. And there was still plenty out there she hadn't tried yet.

As Amber delved into her memories, she convinced herself that those experiences had made her strong. They were the reason she had been able to endure everything. The more things she hardened herself against, the more impenetrable she became. That, in fact, had become her goal.

Before the week was up, Amber's worried parents did what they said they would; they phoned the cops and filed a report.

Wednesday afternoon, as she dragged her malnourished body home, a patrol car pulled in front of her. The officer put Amber in the back and closed the door. She begged him to let her go home.

"My house is right there. Please, let me go." The officer didn't answer. Enraged, Amber gave in to screaming. "Let me out! Help! Let me out of here! I'm gonna be sick! Ahh!" She kicked the Plexiglas, to no avail. She continued to scream. She hissed and she spat. Arms and legs flailed in desperation.

Amber smiled at the memory. Comforting herself, she had not gone down easy. Yes, that was how she rationalized the events. They could take her, but she would go kicking and screaming, fighting the whole way.

Still enraged, she used the ride to nourish bitterness caused by the injustice she felt. Her parents got the call at eight o'clock that night to come pick her up. They were told she was high when the cops picked her up. And so the life of trials, lawyers, and judges began for Michael and Catherine White. It was two days short of one year since the car accident.

At the first trial the family lawyer, Nina, pled for leniency based on it being Amber's first charge. Nina pulled out school records, her honor roll certificate, and details of the accident. The judge did not deny that the accident had been the catalyst leading to the present problems. Leniency was granted. She was handed a suspended sentence of three months in juvie with six months probation. She was ordered to reconvene appointments with Dr. Forbes. Her only alternative was juvenile, so she agreed.

In the days that followed, Amber stayed locked in her room, overwhelmed by what awaited her at the appointments. He was repulsive, and she could pass his class or go to jail. The judge ordered her back to school, which she did, but at a different school. She may as well go somewhere that no one would know her or her baggage. Everyone seemed to have renewed hope, including her.

Stan, her only friend from County High, dropped out of school shortly after that. He had tried so hard. He just couldn't do it. He began selling dope full time then. It was only a short time after that Stan had his mishap in the warehouse.

The new school, Maple High, was where she met and became acquainted with the Deas brothers. Initially, Amber decided she would try to graduate. She wasn't sure why, but her teachers from the previous school had passed her to grade twelve. If she could keep it together for one more year, everything would work out and maybe she would be okay. She hadn't worked Dr. Forbes into the equation. He was more unbearable than she could handle.

It became definitive in the first meeting what a degenerate she was facing; when she saw him before he was perverse. His statements were laced with double meaning. He would brush up against her breasts and constantly look her up and down. He made no attempts to hide how he perused her body with his eyes. Being appointed by a judge to see him increased his power; the evil intensified.

His first statement upon her return was haughty. "So you need my signature on this piece of paper, verifying completion of my course for a judge. Mommy and Daddy can't just pull you out this time, and you can't quit, or it's off to jail. That means while you have your one-hour session with me, I am God to you." He hesitated to make sure she was paying close attention.

He closed the distance between them and put his lips to her ears. "Right?"

Amber could feel the hair on her skin stand straight up. Her body went cold, and for a moment she couldn't feel her feet underneath her. She stumbled slightly. Feeling with her hands behind her, she grabbed the doorknob. Her parents were still in the waiting area; why didn't they save her from this raving lunatic? She pulled hard on the door, but the moment's hesitation was enough for the doctor to get his foot in front of the door, and it wouldn't budge.

"Go ahead, Amber. Open that door. Tell your lies. Who will believe you? A street girl with a drug problem. I'm a doctor. No one will believe you over me. I bet your own parents wouldn't believe you."

Amber knew he was right. She had already told her parents about what had happened the last time she was forced to see him. She was less messed up then, and they had chosen to believe Dr. Forbes over her.

Dr. Forbes continued with his contemptuous speech. His voice softened slightly, and he backed his foot away from the door. "I can make it real easy for you to pass this."

She met his gaze, still a bit naïve, wondering if it was with any kindness that he spoke; it was not. The look in his eyes, to someone more experienced, would have given away his intentions completely. Amber did not say a word.

Dr. Forbes looked toward the couch. He gestured with his hand. Amber did as she was expected. She sat down, feeling even more vulnerable. What choice did she have? She refused to meet his gaze, though she could feel his eyes burning into the top of her head. It was weird then how he started acting like a normal psychiatric doctor. He asked her questions. He wrote stuff down. Half the session was already over. Amber felt her protective wall ebb ever so slightly. Then he asked a strange question. She wasn't sure if it was part of his normal line of inquiry or if there was a malevolent reason for his question.

"Are you currently sexually active?"

She quickly tried to recall what she had told him so far. Why would he ask that? When she didn't answer right away, he calmly added, "Drugs are often a problem for young women who are sexually active. Their minds have a hard time coping with all the emotions they didn't expect to play a role in their daily lives. Guilt, abandonment if the relationship doesn't work out. This leads to depression, even to suicide."

She looked at him uncertainly. How could she answer that question? She decided to be truthful. "No. I'm not."

"Not what?"

"No, Dr. , I am not currently sexually active."

Dr. Forbes took out a separate notebook from his desk and wrote a note.

"What are you writing?"

"I will tell you any information you need to know, and I ask the questions." Dr. Forbes narrowed his eyes.

Amber pursed her lips together and waited. He said nothing. He wrote something else down then he got up, walked over to Amber, and handed her the Post-It. As he handed it to her, he brushed his hand up against her breast and smiled at her.

"Until next time."

His smile was not a kind smile. It was meant to be unnerving. He clearly intended to intimidate her. Amber felt it, but she didn't care. She snatched the paper from his hand and stood up quickly.

She made her way to the door, not looking back. She hated that man; she despised him. If there was a hell, it was clearly intended for pigs like that arrogant, self-absorbed, disgusting freak who called himself a doctor. His every word had hidden meaning; his every suggestion was reviling. She read the paper she held in her hand. She had exactly one week until her next appointment. With that thought, she shuddered.

Amber started the week in her new school as planned. She made a few new acquaintances. On a particular Wednesday she was in chem class. The class was an 11/12 split, so Wyatt and his twin brothers, Kyle and Cody, found a lab bottle with some liquid still in it. They added it to the experiment they were presently working on. There was a loud explosion, and smoke filled the room. Everyone was evacuated.

When the smoke had cleared and everyone was called to go back to class, Amber, Cody, Wyatt, and Kyle were nowhere to be found. They were out behind the school, through the field, and heading down to the river. They were laughing and reliving the moment when Kyle pulled out his little sheet of paper. They all took one of the little squares and placed the acid under their tongues. Ten minutes passed before they started to feel the effects. The four teenagers held hands, forming a chain, and started running through the woods. They ran through the river, getting soaked. Stumbling, falling.

They got back up and ran around until they fell in the water again. They stayed where they fell, laughing, making no sense for hours. It seemed like no time at all. It must have been getting close to dinnertime. Cody felt the hunger in his belly. Kyle's stomach growled aloud. Everyone laughed. The effects of the potent hallucinogen were wearing off. They relaxed, leaving their legs dangling in the river and their bodies up on the pebbly edge.

Wyatt was the first one to speak. "What's your story, Amber? We know you were transferred here from a different school. There are different rumors why."

"Were you really in that car—?"

"He was my best friend." She found herself confessing. She didn't feel the reluctance she usually did at the mention of the accident. "His name was Adam, and yeah, I was there." She looked at the faces in front of her. Wyatt was empathetic. Cody wouldn't look her in the eye. Kyle was just curious. "No one has really asked me about that. Not even at my old school. It's weird, ya know? It's been two years, and no matter what I do people pull out this 'Amber's excuse card,' and I don't really get in trouble. I can get away with just about anything. Even the judge was lenient."

"Cool," all three boys said in unison.

"Was it gory?" Kyle wanted to know.

Wyatt elbowed him hard enough that he caught his breath.

"It's okay," Amber replied candidly. "It's okay to talk about it now. I haven't been able to erase the picture from my memory. It's weird. I remember the blood. I remember perfectly where the truck flipped over. But Adam's face … " She paused and closed her eyes for a moment. She already knew. She tried to remember him, but his face was vague, like when she tried on Nan's reading glasses and her focus distorted. That was how she remembered Adam now. "I can't really picture him in my mind anymore."

Kyle spoke up, offering his own understanding. "That's how I remember my dad. It's foggy, like in the fall, when the fog rises up from the streams and you can't make out anything unless it's right in front of you."

Wyatt looked at his younger brother, furrowed his brow, and shook his head gently, trying to deter his brother from relinquishing family secrets.

No one said anything for a moment. Amber truly hoped he would continue.

"Our dad came home from work one day. He just snapped. No one knew why. He wasn't fired from his job like some of the stories you hear about psychos. He just came home, got the gun from the shed, loaded it, and shot our mom. She was pregnant. Then he turned the gun on himself. We were told it was lucky we weren't home, or he probably would have shot us too. There were three more bullets loaded in the gun. We had stayed late after school playing basketball. Know what's weird, though? I don't really remember either of their faces. Me and Cody were eleven, Wyatt was twelve. I always wondered if that was a baby sister my mom was carrying."

"That's enough, Kyle."

"What? Just because you don't like to talk about it, Wyatt?"
"I said shut up."
"We always wonder if one of us will be like our dad and just lose it one day. Ya know, snap for no reason and kill the people we love. Freaky, eh?"
"You just don't learn, little brother. I said shut—"
"No, you always do that. Take over, make us hold it in. The therapist said we should talk about it if we want. Well, I want to talk about it. If you don't, then don't."

Wyatt was up in lightning speed. The right hook to his brother's head cracked, connecting with his jaw. His neck twisted sharply, knocking him flat into the water they were still sitting in. Amber watched wide-eyed in disbelief. Kyle was not down long. He lunged at his brother, and a fistfight ensued. Amber glanced at Cody; the look on his face was so sad. How did any of them cope with this life? At seventeen and eighteen, the boys were emancipated, and Amber couldn't help wondering if this was normal for them.

The boys stayed in school regardless of how hard it was, because the courts required they did or they would lose their emancipation. Children's services threatened that the younger two would go back to foster care, so no matter how the younger two got beat by Wyatt, no one was going to say anything. What mattered was staying together.

Cody calmly walked up to his duelling siblings. "That's enough!" He said it loudly, not yelling, but with confidence. "You're not making a very good impression on our lady friend."

Kyle wiped the blood trickling from his lip. Wyatt grabbed his shoulder.

"Forget it," he said. His distaste for his brother's actions clung to every word.

Everyone had long since come down from their high. As Amber's high receded, reality tugged at her memory. It was already Wednesday, and Friday loomed heavily over her head, filling her thoughts. All the acid in the world wouldn't stop Friday from coming. Amber realized she was gradually ebbing into unredeemable places. She was powerless, struggling like a fawn in the coils of a boa slowly squeezing out her life. Every time she tried to take a breath, the snake's muscled torso tightened. As Friday got closer, the snake's grip tightened, and breathing was more constricted.

"It's getting late. I need to get home." The boys walked her most of the way. She approached her house and turned back to see them standing on the corner, watching her. They waited until she stepped into her house before they turned to walk away.

Amber stepped inside, greeted with yelling and accusations. Lincoln walked up to her and wrapped his arms around her. She bent down to return his affections and then bolted past her parents and ran upstairs to her room. It wasn't long till she heard the knock. It was her father who entered.

"I thought we were done with this erratic behavior. I thought you were going to make an effort this time." He sounded desperate, not like he believed what he was saying, but like he needed to. "What can we do, Amber? How do we make these problems go away?"

"You can't. I just have to get through them on my own. There's nothing you can do. So there, I'm not your problem anymore, okay. You are absolved. I'm my own problem. You can stop looking at me like that."

"I am your father. Your problems are always going to be my problems—"

"Stop, just stop!" Amber yelled. The guilt was eating her. Why did her parents have to make it their problem? "If you really want to help me, you would let me stop seeing that stupid freak doctor. He's sick, really sick, and you won't believe me. Why won't you ever believe me?"

"We've been over this, Amber." Michael was exasperated with her accusations. "You're going to continue with those sessions, and you can thank yourself for that. It's completely out of our hands now. It's appointments with that doctor or jail for you."

Amber bowed her head in defeat. Would he relent if he could see her eyes brimming with tears? There had been a time, she could remember, when that was all she had to do: shed a tear and Daddy would make it better. That seemed like a long time ago.

"Then I guess there's nothing you can do for me." She spoke somberly and then turned her back to her father to let him know she was finished with the conversation.

Michael walked out of his daughter's room frustrated and bone weary. Once in the hallway, he allowed his calm demeanor to slip. He was on the brink of insantiy. He knew it would have to be Amber who made the decisions. He couldn't make them for her; she had been right about that. It was hard to believe that not so long ago she thought her daddy was the strongest man in the world, a man she so proudly proclaimed, "This is my daddy." But now was different.

Catherine was just coming up the stairs. Seeing Michael in the hallway, she moved to embrace him. Was he comforting her, or was she comforting him? It didn't matter. They just felt better in each other's arms.

Amber sat at her vanity brushing her waist-length hair, waiting impatiently until all the lights were out and her parents were in bed. Then she would perform her usual trick of climbing down the trellis outside her bedroom window.

She reached the ground and noticed a light on in the living room. She poked her head up a bit and watched the scene unfold before her. Lincoln was snuggled up on their mother's lap, his body shaking with sobs. Catherine tried to console him. Amber could see clearly, but she was thankful she couldn't hear him crying. She knew he was trying hard to hold it in. Boys seemed conditioned that way. She took in the sorrow etched into both faces. The little boy she so deeply adored let something slip from his fingers. It was a picture.

Amber knew exactly which one it was. It was the one from the fridge held by a magnet that read:

"Do you love me, Lord," and the Lord
answered, "Yes, my child."

"How much?" I asked.

He replied, "This much," and he stretched
out his arms and died."

Recalling the quote struck a chord. *God,* she thought, *how do I stop this?* She didn't listen for the answer, but it came. *Ask. I will provide the way.*

The picture hit the floor, and Amber felt her heart break. She knew. She was the cause of Linc's pain. It was for her that he cried. She couldn't bear it. She bolted across the lawn, blinded by the tears that stung her eyes. Why? Why did she have to see that? Amber rounded the corner. She couldn't go any farther. Her lungs burned; her heart ached. She battled the sobs that begged to be released. The lump in her throat was hard; she thought it might burst if she didn't give in to it.

There is no giving in to weakness now, she rationalized. She would survive better without tears, acts of self-pity. Shutting her eyes tightly, she forced herself to think of something else, anything. She brought forth the memory of the loathsome doctor. Amber got up wearily, drained from the battle that raged within her. She sought anger; it was her ally. She needed to be a lot tougher than this to face the doctor on Friday, which was only a day away. She clenched her jaw and hardened her resolve, determined.

She succeeded in shifting her emotions and came up with a plan. She consoled herself with the thought all the way to Stan's, where she hoped to get high awhile and not have to think about anything.

Stan's house was situated at the back of their property, nestled between some enormous old trees. The scene was daunting in the moonlight. She was relieved to see Stan coming out. She had been to his house on two other occasions. His mom really freaked her out.

"Hey, can we hang out?"

"What happened to you?" he asked the minute he could see her face.

"Nothing. You wanna hang out or what?"

"I guess."

There was something desperate in her expression. He hoped she hadn't been binging. He knew she came to get high, and while that was fun, he didn't want any part in surpassing anyone's limits. Still, he wasn't one to let a friend suffer alone.

"I got busted last week, so I have to stick close by, all right? We can hang out here."

They sat on the hood of the beat-up Pacer at the back of the house. All four tires were missing, huge pieces had rusted away, and it remained propped up on cinder blocks. It had been that way since Stan's dad had run off five years ago. He left to get away from Cynthia's drug habit. He couldn't take it anymore. It was too bad he hadn't thought to take his then twelve-year-old son with him. He might have turned out completely different.

Stan always had something on him. He pulled out a little piece of folded newspaper.

"You want to sample?" he asked, taking out another plastic bag.

Amber wrinkled her nose. "Got anything—"

"You wait and see how I doctor this up for you." He took the white powder from the newspaper and rolled it up in the joint.

A broad grin swept across Amber's face. "Nice," she complimented.

He lit it and passed it to her. "Now you want to tell me what this is all about?"

They lay back against the windshield of the car and talked. They talked until the sun began to rise. By then the effects of the narcotic were wearing off.

"I gotta go. Thanks, Stan." She jumped up to go. Before he could say anything, she was gone.

Amber boldly walked through the kitchen when she arrived

home. She went straight to Lincoln, who was sitting at the table. She picked him up, kissed him, then swung him around.

"Want to do something fun with me today? I'll take you on the bus. We can go to the mall, or maybe a trip to the pet store. Would you like that? We can do anything you want."

His face shone with delight. "Can we go to the ice-cream store? No, the fish store?" Then he gasped. "I know. We can go to the zoo. Can we, Amber? Can we?" His joy was infectious.

"Anything your heart desires, precious." She snuggled her nose into the nape of his neck and kissed him.

Catherine was coming down the stairs. Lincoln was so excited; he began to run to his mother to reveal his news, but Amber quickly turned him around and put her finger up to her lips, firmly shaking her head. He looked quizzically at his big sister. Was this to be another empty promise? He began to shrink inside, but Amber quickly reassured him. Leaning over, she whispered, "If you tell Mom, she won't let you go. It has to be our secret, okay? I'll pick you up from Nan's house. Nan will say yes, so it will be okay."

He looked at her, eyes wide as saucers, reeling with anticipation. The thought didn't occur to him that his sister had just taught him how to lie, but Amber felt it. She felt the twinge in her gut. She felt the remainders of her conscience slipping away. She shoved the guilt down into the pit of her stomach, forcing it away. *We will have so much fun,* she kept telling herself. *This is for Lincoln.*

Catherine entered the kitchen. She didn't say a word, nor did Amber. She walked right past her and headed upstairs. She needed to shower and change. While she did these things, she contemplated a plan. She had no money. How was she going to get into the zoo?

Amber dressed in casual jeans and a T-shirt and then made her way back downstairs. She made a couple of sandwiches for her and Linc, packing them in her duffle bag. She added some drinks and an apple each.

"It's great to see you in such a good mood," Catherine commented kindly.

Amber did not take note of her mother's condition: the dark circles around her eyes from lack of sleep, the loss of weight from endless worry, and lack of appetite. She only noticed the infringement on her privacy by her mother's accusations. What was she implying? *Good to see me in a good mood.* She always started the day in a good mood, but people constantly said and did things to change her mood. Before she blurted out any nasty remarks, she caught her brother out of the corner of her eye. She smiled, deciding she would not put him through another fight this morning.

Amber chose a cordial response to her mother. "I want to go to Nan's today, if that's okay?"

Catherine was going to protest. Amber looked over at Linc and gave him a little wink. He giggled, and Catherine was left peacefully speechless with a smile of her own.

"I think that's a great idea. I am proud of you, Amber. You're really making an effort."

Once at Nan's, Amber began to feel the effects of sleep depravation from last night.

"I am going to have a nap, okay, Nan? Please wake me before lunch." She bent down to kiss Linc and reassured him, "I will have a short rest, then we will go, okay?"

"That's what Mommy says sometimes. Then she puts on a movie, and even when the movie is over she is still sleeping." Amber was shocked for a moment. Why would her mother need to nap in the middle of the day? She shook her head, not giving it anymore thought, and replied, "If I'm asleep when the movie is over, make sure you wake me up. Okay?"

"Okay," he promised.

When Lincoln woke Amber, it was already one o'clock.

"Linc, I told you to wake me," she accused harshly.

"Nan told me I had to let you sleep, Amber. I'm sorry. Are you mad at me?"

"No. Of course I'm not mad. Come on, let's tell Nan. We will leave right now. Okay?"

"For real? Right now?"

Amber approached their grandma. "Nan, I promised Lincoln I would take him to the zoo today. That was mostly the reason I was able to skip school. We are going to go now."

"Sure, dear. Have you got enough money?"

"Don't worry, Nan, I'll manage."

"Nonsense. You can't have fun at the zoo without money." She dug a ten-dollar bill out of the side of her black leather purse and shoved it into her granddaughter's hand. Amber accepted graciously, and as she grabbed her brother's hand to head out the door, she called, "Thanks, Nan. I love you. We will go straight home from the zoo, so don't expect us back here."

They exchanged waves and were gone.

Lincoln chattered all the way to the bus stop. Once on the bus, Amber asked him, "So what did you and Nan do while I napped?"

"She stayed in her room a lot. I watched a movie and some cartoons."

What's the matter with that old woman? Amber thought angrily. *Why does she babysit if she's not going to take care of him?*

"What does she do in there all day?" she asked with concern.

"She prays," he said honestly.

"What the heck was she praying for all that time?" she said it out loud, not expecting an answer.

"She prays for a lot of things. But mostly for you. Just like Mommy and Daddy, and the people from the Bible study who come to our house. They all pray for you, Amber." He continued with childlike innocence. "Know who else comes over and prays for you? Adam's mom and dad do. I remember Adam, do you?"

"Hmm." She nodded. It was too much. She wanted to yell

and scream at him. She didn't need reminding. They should just get off the bus and forget the zoo. She looked at Linc; it was all she could handle. He was just a little boy. He couldn't know how his words stung. The lump in her throat was so hard, she thought it might rip her throat open. She kept swallowing, but it wouldn't go away.

Make the memories go away, she commanded herself. *Toughen up, Amber.*

She forced her thoughts to her appointment tomorrow with the evil doctor. That was enough to squelch any weakened emotion. She swallowed again. This time she defeated the lump, and again she got a little harder.

"Want an adventure, Linc?" Amber spoke with mock excitement. They had reached the zoo.

"Sure," he replied enthusiastically.

"Let's play pretend," Amber coerced. "We are monkeys, and we have to climb this fence to get into the zoo. Then we can find our monkey mommy and daddy, okay?"

"Can't we just play 'monkey' once were inside? There is barbed wire on this fence. It will be easier to get in through the front gate."

"Easier, yes. But funner? No."

"What if I fall, Amber?"

"Don't you trust me, Linc? I won't let you fall."

The boy relented and let his sister help him over the fence. The hard part for him was getting over the barbed wire. Amber cut her hand holding it down for him. He quickly scurried down the other side.

"Amber, we have to go this way." He pointed right.

"No. Let's go this way," she insisted.

"But we have to go this way to pay." He was equally insistent.

"We'll pay when we leave, okay? Right now we have to find the monkeys, remember?"

Averting his attention back to the animals, he quickly forgot about paying and they began their day.

It was nearly eight when Amber and Linc climbed off the bus. He had fallen asleep in her arms. It was a feeling she hadn't had for a while, and she cherished it. She was still carrying him in her arms when she reached the front door. She made a poignant effort to be happy upon entering her home. It didn't matter. She was greeted the way she always was, with questions and accusations.

"We were worried sick. Where have you been?"

"I told Nan where we were. What's the big deal? I'm seventeen, I can handle it."

"That's not the point."

"What, you don't even trust me with Lincoln? I would die before I let anything happen to him."

The yelling had begun. Tempers flew. The boy who had fallen into such a peaceful sleep was woken by what had become the usual chaos in his home. He clung to Amber. Why did Mom and Dad always yell at her? He didn't understand. They had just been having fun, that was all.

Amber walked past both her parents. "I'm putting my little brother to bed, if that's okay. Unless anyone's worried I might stick him with a needle." Her words were meant to hurt, and they stung. She walked upstairs and tucked her brother in.

"Say my prayers, Amber?" he asked sweetly.

"You say them. I'll listen."

"Thank you, God," he began, "for my mommy and daddy. Thank you for my sister. I pray you will help everyone get along, God. And help Mommy and Daddy not be mad at Amber anymore. Thank you for my wonderful day at the zoo. Amen."

He was so pleased with himself. He was so proud his big sister had heard his heartfelt prayer offered up to his heavenly Father. He hoped now she knew that he prayed for her too. Maybe she would be like the old Amber, happy and attentive.

Amber went straight downstairs and right out the front

door, without saying a word. Michael had had enough of her behavior. He went into the street after her.

"Get back here right now!" he bellowed from behind her.

"No!" she hollered back.

"If you're not back in this house in five seconds, I am going to call the police." Michael could see neighbors lifting the edges of their blinds discreetly, not wanting to get caught snooping but not wanting to miss the peril either.

She turned around and challenged him. "Call them. Go ahead. Why don't you call the church while you're at it? Get everyone to pray for your wicked, wayward daughter." Amber finished screaming and then turned and ran.

Michael got in his truck and started looking for her. He felt helpless and angry, driving around for hours, accomplishing nothing.

He finally spotted her coming out of a long alley. He pulled the truck over and turned out the lights. He watched with anticipation. What if he caught her doing something he just couldn't deal with? But what if God had put him in this spot for a reason? He watched and he prayed. Amber just walked, ambivalent to the chaos she had caused. He slipped the truck into neutral and let it silently coast, staying behind her.

He could see the exhausted gait in her walk, the bow of defeat in her back. His heart went out to his daughter. He wanted to carry the burden she felt, lift it from her shoulders, but only God could do that.

Once she was within a few blocks of home, Michael pulled the truck down a side street and quickly drove home. He was upstairs and had just lain down beside Catherine when they heard the front door open quietly and Amber crept in. They heard her make her way up the stairs and into her room. Finally, they could sleep. It was 1:40 in the morning.

Amber could not sleep. She was haunted by the daunting appointment with Dr. Forbes. She decided that if her parents weren't going to help her, she would have to help herself. She had walked all the way out to the Deas' place. She hadn't been sure she would be able to find it. She was so high when they told her where they lived. She bought some pills from Wyatt. She didn't know how else to deal with the doctor. Her head ached with the thought. Sometimes she felt like she was going to go schitzo. She was too exhausted. She didn't know what else to do.

Amber tossed and turned most of the night, a problem she wouldn't have to experience if it weren't for that stupid doctor. She got out of bed feeling as though she hadn't slept at all and got ready for school. Amber was up and ready for school. Catherine set some toast in front of her, but she had no appetite. Without a word she got up, kissed Lincoln, and headed out the door. Catherine let out a sigh. The tension immediately left the moment Amber walked out the door. The events that had taken place last night consumed her. How had Amber actually thought it was okay to just take her brother like that? Sure, her daughter was seventeen, but she was more trustworthy and responsible at twelve than she was now. Michael had stayed up most of the night, unable to sleep even after she was home. Catherine finished getting her son ready for Nan's house. She grabbed a banana and some yogurt from the fridge for her lunch and headed out the door.

"You want to hang at our place after school?" Cody asked Amber at lunch.

"I can't. Not today. Maybe I can hook up with you guys tomorrow."

"If you want." He tried to be nonchalant. "What have you got going on today? You got a job?" Kyle always wanted to know more information than one gave.

"No. My parents make me see a shrink," she answered honestly. She wasn't usually so forthcoming with her personal life, but after all Kyle had told her it didn't bother her. She knew they had no expectations.

"Whoa," all three brothers said in unison.

"The judge in our case wanted to make us go as a condition of our emancipation. We went to a couple of sessions, but it was just too weird. Some man trying to make you talk to him about all your personal stuff. 'How do you feel about that?' 'Was that difficult for you?' It's too weird. The only thing we have to do is stay in school. Otherwise, the counsellor could have me and Cody put back into foster care. Wyatt's too old," Kyle said.

"There goes the bell. We better get to class. See you guys."

Amber rolled over on her cot; it was so easy to bring up the memories. It was like everything had happened yesterday. She could recall it so vividly. That yesterday was over a year ago. She began to wonder what those days would feel like if she ended up convicted of Duncan's murder. They would probably feel like forever. She looked at the big clock on the wall. It was late, after ten. She hoped the nurse would come in soon to dope her up some more. Alone with her thoughts memories proved to be depressing. Her entire life over the past two years consisted primarily of her getting high and avoiding her own memories. In the last six weeks those thoughts and memories were what made the time go by. She gave a self-depreciating smile at the irony. She could dwell on other things, like the trial. She found it much safer to revert to memories. There was comfort in knowing how everything turned out.

Walking In Shadows

"The time is coming when everything will be revealed, all that is secret will be made public, whatever you have said in the dark will be heard in the light, and what you have whispered behind closed doors will be shouted from the housetops for all to hear."

Luke 12:2–3

"You in any pain?" Chloe asked Amber.

"Yes," she said. Chloe unlocked the med room and opened the cabinet. She took out the small vile with the narcotic she wanted. She took a syringe from the box on the medical tray and filled the tube. She walked back to Amber, who held out her arm. Chloe injected the potent serum. It would take a while to have an effect. While she waited for sweet sleep to come, she allowed her memory to pick up where it had left off.

After school Amber made her way to the double aluminum doors that led to the outside. She walked slowly, fingering the small plastic baggie in her pocket, the one she had bought off Wyatt last night. When she had arrived at their dimly lit house, all three boys were so high they could barely move off the couch. The tiny living room was thick with blue smoke. She could get high off the fumes. She didn't plan to stay long enough for that to happen.

She had told Wyatt at school she would come by. She needed something that would help her relax. Wyatt slowly made his way over to the table. Amber looked at the table; she quickly masked her expression. There was dried up, crusty food. A pizza box had flies darting in and out of it, and bits of tobacco were strewn all over. It appeared the boys did a lot of rolling on the table. She noticed a small mirror with a white powder substance that she knew right away to be cocaine. There was a set of small scales for measuring things in grams. Then she noticed the baggies. There were about a hundred baggies filled with anything from powder to pills to tiny crack rocks. She tried not to stare too hard; she didn't want her shock to be insulting.

Once at the table, Wyatt reached an unsteady hand down to the table, picked up one of the small baggies, and handed it to her.

"This'll do it. You wanna stay awhile with us?"

Amber shook her head, examining her baggie. How could he know what he gave her? What if he gave her the wrong pills? Her baggie contained four purple pills. They looked like gel caps. She put the baggie in her pocket and handed Wyatt the money. Not another word was spoken. None of them said anything when she left.

Amber had felt anxious all day. It was the day of her appointment, the thing she had dreaded all week. She thumbed the small baggie in her pocket; it gave her a false security. Being high meant being numb, and feeling nothing was exactly what she needed.

Amber walked out the doors and headed toward the path all the kids used to smoke, toke, and the like. She stopped in her tracks when she heard her mother's voice call her name.

"Talk about stopping you dead in your tracks." Amber muttered some expletives to herself and turned to face her quickly approaching mother.

"Did you forget your appointment?" She was so eager to have shown up just in time to save the day.

"No, Mother," Amber hissed in agitation. "I can get there myself. I don't need you to hold my hand."

"It's too far to walk. I'll drive you."

"I want to walk. Leave me alone. This is so embarrassing." Amber could see her friends out of her peripheral vision. Wyatt had a huge grin on his face. She wanted to scream.

"Amber, enough! Just get in the car." The fake sweetness was gone from Catherine's voice and her impatience showed.

"Whatever."

The drive couldn't go by quickly enough for either. Amber kept fingering the little bag of relaxation in her pocket. Catherine walked her up the three flights of stairs to the office.

"Are you going to be waiting for me when I get out too?" Amber asked sarcastically.

"No," she answered flatly. "You can call if you want to be picked up."

"Would you stop?" Amber made every effort to emphasize her annoyance.

"Whatever," she muttered and walked away. Then she turned, presumably not having annoyed her daughter enough. She spoke quietly and earnestly to her daughter. "You know, if you let him, Dr. Forbes could really help you. You need to give him a chance."

"Sure, anything for you, Mother," she said sarcastically as she glared at her mother. Amber wanted to scream. She wanted to reach out her arms and choke her. How could she be so stupid?

Catherine simply turned and walked away. Amber looked after her, still wondering what it took to be so foolish. It was willed. No one was that naive without trying.

Amber looked up at the small clock on the wall. She was fifteen minutes early for her appointment. Her mother was gone, and she still had enough time to go for a short walk and do her deed. As she was about to leave, the door opened. Dr. Forbes came out, followed by a young girl. Amber figured her to be a few years younger than herself. Amber immediately noticed the girl's shirt. It was open too far for a young girl. Her mascara was slightly smudged. Amber tried looking into her eyes. She wanted to make sure of what she already knew. The young girl's head was bowed low. Too low. Amber knew.

A sickening realization hit Amber; she wasn't the only person preyed on by Dr. Forbes. Well, not her, not today.

"I will see you same time next week, Candace," Dr. Forbes said quietly. The girl did not reply. Amber tried to catch a glimpse of her face; she barely made eye contact as she walked by.

Amber made an effort to remember that name, Candace. She wasn't sure how or when, but she knew that girl would be indispensable. Dr. Forbes called Amber into his office, and for a moment he seemed like any normal professional.

He gestured to the chair, and Amber willingly took a seat. She was ready, anticipating his moves. Gordon Forbes' line of questioning that afternoon was proper and professional till near the end of her session. If he had not already shown Amber his true nature, it would have been easy for her to believe that he was a typical psychiatrist.

"What's in your pocket?" Dr. Forbes demanded suddenly. Amber went cold. She held her breath, staring him straight in the eye. She was unaware of his ability to analyze and dissect every expression. He knew he had latched onto something.

"Nothing," she answered defensively.

"Don't lie to me. How long do you want to be in this program? Put whatever it is on my desk. Now."

She hesitated a moment, and then she apprehensively pulled the baggie out of her pocket. As she did, she tried to use her thumb and index finger to open the small bag, hoping to let the contents spill out before exposing them. She couldn't do it. All she could do was reveal the small bag with the pills in it.

Dr. Forbes looked at the baggie, then at Amber. She could see the devil reflected in his evil eyes. A grin spread across his face. Amber knew to be terrified.

"Swallow them," he ordered

"There're four in there. That's too many," she protested, frightened. She didn't even know what they were. Wyatt had said they were ludes … *"Take one before each visit."*

"Take them all now."

"No. You're crazy." She attempted to stand up for herself. "I thought you already got your fill for the day from Candace. Leave me alone." She tried to sound confident.

Amber had revealed way too much in that statement. She could see the anger overshadow the confidence for a brief moment. The doctor slowly walked around his desk and stood behind Amber. Her body shook within itself. Gordon Forbes clasped his hand tightly over Amber's mouth. He grabbed all four pills and shoved them into her mouth. He continued to keep his hand firmly clasped over her mouth, making certain she would have to swallow to get air.

Amber writhed and struggled. She was on the verge of hysteria. Then she let her mind go somewhere else. She stopped struggling and swallowed. She was finally allowed to breath. She inhaled deeply, took a long-overdue breath, then panted a moment, replenishing her body of much-needed oxygen. Amber glowered at the doctor. He would not get away with this, she vowed to herself.

Shortly, everything started changing. She felt her reality altering. She was losing control and, in present company, that was very bad. Her body began to slouch until she sagged in the chair. She felt calm, relaxed. Her mind was in a transient state of peace; her anger was gone. Amber tried to look angry, but it felt weird on her face and that made her smile. She wondered if she was dreaming.

Dr. Forbes turned her chair around. He unbuttoned her blouse. He was smiling that same insipid grin. It didn't matter to Amber right now; nothing did.

"You should come to all of your appointments like this. Who knows what we could accomplish."

"I had planned to, but you made me take them all at once," Amber said, giggling.

Gordon Forbes undid the zipper of his pants, and then he undid Amber's. He probed and violated her. He was vile and rough, but she felt nothing. Her senses were numb, and she didn't care. The whole act lasted five minutes. When he was done, he got up and went to wash his hands.

"I think we can be done early today."

Amber felt nauseated. The drug was picking up momentum; she was getting farther and farther from reality. The doctor continued to speak, but she was losing her clarity.

"You know, Amber, I think you are getting very close to completing this program. Most of my clients don't get to pass so quickly, but you catch on fast."

Amber made no comment. She appeared too out of it to fix her clothes. Dr. Forbes was gentle as he zipped up her pants and straightened her shirt.

"Time to go, sweetie. We'll see you Tuesday," he said and rubbed her shoulder. Then he pushed gently, helping her sedated body out of the chair.

"What? No thank-you?" Barely on her feet but still caustic, that was Amber.

Not to be outdone, the doctor replied, "You didn't do anything, honey." He helped her to the door.

She would have hit him if she could have, but she could barely walk. She staggered; her equilibrium was off. The drugs were powerful. She continued her struggle to stay erect long enough to get into the elevator. She needed to sleep; she was so tired. There was no way she could make it home.

Amber ambled in the direction she believed was home. She went as far as she could. When she couldn't take another step, she walked onto the grass, found a shaded spot under a bush, and lay down. She didn't know where she was or how far she had yet to go. She just had to sleep.

Amber was woken up by a friendly dog licking her face,

followed by the distant sound of childish laughter. She sat up quickly, surprised at how drugged she still felt. She rubbed her eyes, forcing herself to see more clearly, then stood up. It took so much effort. She needed to go before the children saw her. Amber willed herself to continue her plight for home.

She crossed the road. Her mind was beginning to work, and she was struck by a memory of the doctor with his hand in her pants. She began to remember more of the events. Nausea gripped her stomach. She wrapped her arms around herself, as if that could stop her from vomiting, but it didn't. Her body purged and heaved, attempting to rid itself of all the vile things it had ingested. Amber squatted, trying to regain her balance. Aware that someone was watching her, she lifted her head slightly to see three small children looking absolutely astonished and one disgusted mother staring at her. Disgusted with herself, Amber forced herself up. Still off kilter, she ambled home as best she could.

The minute Amber walked through the door, Lincoln ran up to her and threw his arms around her. He was wearing his flannel Spider-Man pajamas. He was so soft. As she hugged her brother and felt his small arms wrapped around her, another memory assaulted her conscience. A vivid, grotesque picture of herself flashed unwelcomed into her head. She was placid as the doctor had touched her. She had not even attempted to stop him. She could smell his cheap cologne. It clung to her clothes. She hadn't smelled it then. She knew it though; that smell was unmistakable.

Amber started to feel sick again. Looking into her brother's eyes caused an awareness of the innocence she lacked. That reality compounded her nausea. She dropped Linc and ran for the door. She didn't make it outside before throwing up. Her fingers clutched at the door frame, and she continued to retch. She allowed her body to melt till she was sitting on her haunches. Lincoln was staring at her.

"I'm so sorry." Her eyes pleaded with him for understanding. She got up, wiped the remaining vomit from her mouth with one hand, brushed the other one over Linc's head, and took off. He stared after her, imprinting the moment to memory.

Amber had no intentions of going back home, not ever. She would not taint her little brother with her screwed-up life.

Catherine came downstairs to find Lincoln on the couch watching a cartoon, exactly where she had left him before she went upstairs to shower. She made her way into the kitchen. That's when she noticed the vomit on the floor.

"Are you all right, Linc?" she asked, peeking her head into the living room. "Are you sick, honey?"

"Not me, Mommy, Amber. She barfed everywhere. It's smelly." He wrinkled up his nose as he spoke.

"Hmm…" Catherine was thoughtful. "Where is Amber now? Is she in her room?"

"No, Mommy, she ran away. She puked everywhere. Then she looked sad and ran away."

Catherine chewed on her lip. She felt anxious; something felt very wrong. She had left her daughter several hours ago at the doctor's office. She picked up the phone and called the police.

Amber had immediately hopped on the bus. She rode it downtown. When she got off, she went straight to the abandoned warehouse. Lots of street kids hung out there; it supplied shelter and a false sense of security. The drugs hadn't worn off yet, and Amber curled up in a corner and went straight to sleep. She slept through to the next day. Waking up near noon, Amber headed straight for Wyatt's place. The boys were all home. They took one look at her and could tell something was up. They could see and smell the street on her.

It was obvious she had not changed her clothes or showered. There was vomit on her sleeve. Wyatt pointed out a chunk in her hair. They offered her their shower and some food. Once she was cleaned up and her hunger sated, she proposed a plan to the brothers.

"I have nowhere to live anymore," she confided. "I need to make some money. I can sell for you, and don't try to pretend you don't know what I'm talking about."

Wyatt was immediate to respond. "No way. No chicks and no addicts. Chicks pick up the habit too quickly, and they smoke all the profit. Then they make stupid mistakes. *No way.*"

"Come on, you guys." Amber knew Cody had a bit of a soft spot for her, so she worked him. "What am I going to do? There's only one other way for a girl to support herself on the streets. You wouldn't let that happen to me, would you?" She walked over to where Cody was sitting and looked him in the eye. She said his name in a way that only a woman can, a way that draws a man's immediate attention. "Cody?"

He had to answer. She was in his face. He couldn't escape her pleading eyes. There was so much emotion as she said his name.

Cody looked pleadingly at his older brother. "Come on, Wyatt. What harm could she do?"

"I'm smart, I could help you guys count, weigh—"

"What?" Wyatt interrupted, insulted. "You think we're stupid? I can't count? Ten purple pills, three blue pills."

"I didn't mean it like that. I meant you just wouldn't have to." She quickly covered her tracks. "I could do it for you, and other stuff too. Whatever you need."

"Look," Wyatt replied, looking more at Cody, who he knew was hoping his older brother would soften, "the best we can offer you is you can stay here awhile, but that's it." He was trying to sound definite, but Amber could tell he was softening. By the time she left their place, she had a backpack with enough stuff to get her on her way.

When she got back to the warehouse, the usual faces were there. A couple of girls who were more experienced with drugs than she was told Amber about household items they used to get high. They planned to mix and add those things to what Amber already had and make some money. Amber agreed.

That night, the girls, mostly Amber, figured out different mixtures; one in particular could really rock someone. The other girls tried out each concoction. Amber did not. She remembered Wyatt's words: *"Chicks pick up the habit too quickly."* She would not open that doorway. Amber was impressed with herself. She was getting stronger and wiser. She would survive on her own.

Despite her initial enthusiasm, Amber couldn't get herself to do it. She couldn't hustle drugs. It went against everything she believed in. As night approached on the fifth day, hungry and restless, Amber ventured out. She was starving and easily convinced herself she had no choice. She needed money to survive, and this was better than the alternative. She gathered up all her courage and headed out into the city streets. A black Acura slowly pulled up behind her. She turned anxiously and was horrified to see Dr. Forbes. She recognized him immediately. She wondered if he recognized her. He slowed to a stop, and for a minute Amber's legs turned to jelly and her stomach flip-flopped. *Toughen up,* she commanded herself. *You'll need to be able to stomach a lot more than that pig if you're going to survive on your own.* She fought the nausea that wanted to overtake her stomach. She bent over the open window of the car. She didn't say a word, she couldn't. She allowed all the loathing she felt for the man to be evident in her glare.

Gordon Forbes felt the hatred in her stare; it permeated his arrogance. He sensed vulnerability though. He knew he still held the power.

"Get in." They drove into a back alley.

Panic gripped at Amber's heart. *Why did you get in this car? Idiot! Why did you get in this car?*

Forbes wasted no time telling Amber what he expected. She would not allow him to think of her as weak. She hardened herself to his request, fighting the disquiet in her heart, ignoring the pleading in her soul, shutting out the voice that begged for recognisance, and did exactly as she was asked.

When she was done, she made a point of staring him boldly in the eye. She was ready to tell him, "That better be my pass," but as she glared into his vacant eyes, she saw nothing that indicated he even recognized her. She was shocked when he flipped her eighty dollars. Did he think she was a prostitute? She snatched the money from his hands and walked away. Nausea rose up from her core; she shoved it down; she refused its dominance. She was a survivor. This is what she was forced to do.

Once the doctor's car was out of sight, she searched the duffle bag.

Just this time, she told herself. She took out the little rolled-up baggie that carried the concoction she had made. She felt an urgency, a panic to get something into her body to override her guilt and shame, realizing the detestable thing she had done.

She folded the paper carefully, ensuring a thin line. She laid it flat on the concrete and rolled up the fifty-dollar bill Forbes had just flipped her. Crouched low on her hands and knees, she put her nose to the bill and her face to the ground. Finding the thin white line, she sucked the powder in deep, the way she had seen in the movies. At first it stung. She rubbed at her nose and squeezed it tight. In a moment she entered a world she would have never known possible. It was bliss. The land of "Forget It All." It was a powerful place at a time like this. She did not go back to the warehouse with her tail between her legs. She headed for the main street. She was ready to sell her new brand of "forget all your troubles," and she did it well.

Michael came home to a distraught wife. The problems with Amber were escalating, not getting better. Michael once again headed out in his pickup. He drove around for several hours.

His daughter was nowhere to be found. When he returned home, he checked in with the police.

"Any word on my daughter?" he asked the sergeant on the other end of the line optimistically.

"Not yet, sir," came the disconsolate reply. "We will let you know as soon as we have any leads or if we find her."

That was not good enough for Michael. It was his daughter they were talking about, and how dare he say *if.* Of course they would find her. Why would he say *if?*

Feeling desperate, Michael went out again in search of Amber. The endless searching and driving around, looking for Amber continued for three days. Catherine took sick leave from her part-time job. She stayed home with their son, though she barely made it out of bed to feed them. The house was a disaster; neither of the Whites had slept in days. Every time the phone rang, they jumped, afraid of who it might be or what the message would be.

By the fifth day they both realized it was too much for the one child they still had. They were encouraged after consulting their pastor; the church was praying for them. Amber was in God's hands. They didn't know where she was, but God did. That had to be good enough. That night at the Bible study they held in their home, friends, the people who loved and cared for them, gathered round them and prayed, each in turn, heartfelt prayers to a gracious and loving God.

Once everyone had left, Catherine went up to her room. She got down on her knees in front of her bed, palms raised heavenward, head bowed in submission. She cried out to God.

In my time. The hushed answer sent a chill up her spine.

"We can't go on living like we only have one child." She knew she had allowed the situation to sap the life out her; they both had. It wasn't fair to Lincoln.

"God protected Daniel in the lions' den," Michael encouraged. "Surely he can save a young woman from the lions."

"Different kind of lions, dear."

Michael looked earnestly at his wife, all kidding aside.

"Pray with me," he said quietly. He took her hand, and they knelt together, shoulder to shoulder. Catherine smiled at her husband. It was a warm, encouraging smile that was vacant of sadness.

Jake and Matt had been watching the action unfold on the main drag when they spotted Jersey making a deal. She hadn't noticed the officer who tagged her, and she led them right to the hideaway. Initially, they both thought Jersey was the missing girl. All five girls they pulled out were charged with drug possession. Court dates were pending. Only Amber had parents waiting to take her home. Jake remembered well that second encounter with Amber. She had changed so much in the short time that had passed since their first meeting.

Jake Liddell smiled down at the pretty young girl. He bent down and gently pulled her up by her elbows. They found her asleep on the floor. Unlike some runaways, she had parents who were worried sick about her. They had called the precinct every day, sometimes several times a day. Her father would leave reports of where he had driven looking for her. He found himself wondering, *How did she end up here?*

Asleep, she appeared angelic. Upon waking he was quickly brought to reality, confronted with bitterness, hard eyes, and a mouth that would make a trucker blush. Jake remained effortlessly kind. Taking off his jacket, he placed it around Amber's shoulders. It was the earliest hours of morning, and he knew she was cold. To her it was just part of an annoying act, and she treated him as such.

"I don't need your charity," she accused, flipping off the jacket and throwing it. Jake gently pulled Amber to her feet. Jake walked over and picked up the jacket. There was no hint of annoyance. She continued to try his patience all the way out of the warehouse, into the car, and through the drive downtown to the police station. When the usual search was done, Matt found enough drugs on Amber to make a serious charge.

While the other girls arrested along with Amber waited to be fingerprinted, they passed the time by flirting with Jake. Jody glanced at Amber, giving her dirty looks, annoyed at her belligerence toward Jake.

"What's your problem?" Jody muttered along with a few expletives. Then she smiled at Jake. "Sorry about the language, Matthew. Who's your new partner?"

"He's not that new," Amber fumed. "This is the second time he's arrested me,"—she glanced at Jake—"isn't it?" Wisely, he said nothing.

It made Amber sick. She thought she knew the girls. Disgusted, she glared at Jody. *Sellouts,* she thought. Jody stuck out her elbow as Matt led her past Amber; she caught her in the ribs. Amber lunged at her, but Jake had a firm grip on her arms.

She was infuriated. "Let me go!" she demanded, pulling and fighting.

The brawny six-foot man holding her didn't listen. She glared at him. He was unfazed. He could see the wild in her eyes, like a caged animal. He knew if he let up on his grip, she would attack whoever was closest, and that was him, so he kept his grip secure.

Once charges were laid, Catherine and Michael got the call to come pick up their daughter. They didn't talk all the way to the police station. Both were angry and unsure of what to expect. They walked into the police station, and the minute they saw Amber, the anger evaporated. Catherine gasped, unable to keep the sound in. Amber snarled at her mother's innocence.

"What? Should I have requested a shower before you got here so I wouldn't be so offensive?"

"I just didn't expect this."

"You knew I wasn't staying at the Ritz."

"Is that vomit on your sweater? Dear Lord, she hasn't washed since she left?"

"Toughen up, Mother." Amber was indignant.

It wasn't just that she was dirty; she looked thinner, and her complexion was sallow. Something else had changed, something more eternal. Her eyes were not blank; that would have been better than what they saw. They were hard and full of hate, hate for them, hate for the world. Not a remnant of innocence remained. It had only been a week.

Monday morning Amber was back at school. She had her meeting with the school counsellor explaining her absence. She simply said she had been away; basically, that was the truth. The Deas brothers laughed at her.

"Amber got busted, ha ha! That's why we don't work with girls," Kyle joked.

Wyatt chimed in, "See, the oldest is always right. I knew better." Then, of course, the paranoid drug dealer in him asked, "You didn't say where you got the stuff, did ya?"

Amber was insulted. "Of course not. Then I wouldn't have a job to return to, right?" She was testing. The boys laughed, and so did she.

"No way," Wyatt pretended to sound firm, but she winked and flirted.

"Oh, come on. You'll give me another chance. I'll come over after school and clean your house for free."

Wyatt raised his brows. "Now that would depend on what you would be wearing."

Amber was shocked at the sexual innuendo, but she found it tantalizing.

She was about to answer when Cody, who remained silent until now, interrupted, "It's not gonna be like that." He looked at Amber; she looked back at him, smiling in a way that let him know she had noticed him. Amber felt a little leap in her tummy at the way he looked at her. It had been a long time since she had been taken in by flattery. She would not be foolish enough to think it genuine, but she would certainly play along.

Michael and Catherine never got their daughter back. When she came home, she would play with her brother, but she remained distant from them. Michael could not believe that just two short years ago he still tucked her in and kissed her goodnight; now he couldn't remember the last time his daughter's arms were around him.

Friday approached. The day of Amber's doctor appointment came without a hitch. No outbursts, no protests; they found hope in that. Neither wanted to find themselves in the middle of one of Amber's tirades. They had gotten through the week by avoiding eye contact. Now they hoped the doctor could help them get their daughter back. They prayed for that. Neither of them were surprised on Friday when, once again, she didn't come home.

Amber had made it, thanks to the Deas brothers, through the whole week of school. After school she would read to Linc or play with him, whatever he wanted, until dinnertime. She would go downstairs and set the table when she was supposed to, avoiding any confrontation. It was obvious her parents were doing the same thing. In the evening she stayed up in her room, often going right to sleep, depending on what drugs she had taken.

When Friday had come, it was time for another appointment with the doctor. Amber walked into the lobby right on time. She was called into his office, and her heart automatically leapt. She cursed herself for being so weak and then walked in as bold as could be.

"I see we have made great progress," the doctor offered. "My recommendation is that you are ready to move out of these sessions. I think you are doing well enough that a school counsellor will be sufficient."

Amber was in shock; she did not see it coming. She was so excited; the first thing she did was go straight to see Cody and his brothers. She needed to celebrate.

Amber walked straight to Cody. She was suddenly very aware of her feminine power. She put her hand on the back of his head and, with force, kissed him full on the mouth. She hesitated only a moment before pulling away. The poor boy was stunned. She did not give him a chance to consider what had just happened.

"I'm done. Look, this is my release. I'm done with that sick doctor." She whooped and hollered shrieks of delight. The boys shared in her joy, though they had no idea of the root of her enthusiasm. She caught a glimpse of Cody out of the corner of her eye; she wouldn't allow it to affect her right now, but something in his expression gave away that he understood more than she had admitted.

The four of them celebrated by getting high. Wyatt had some acid, his hallucinogen of choice, which he shared. It was five in the morning before anyone started to feel normal again. Amber crashed on the couch; she would go home when she was able. She felt the burden removed like a weight from around her neck. She knew she would be okay now. She had to be. Her obstacle was removed.

Amber roused first. The boys were all still sleeping. She quietly got herself out of the house and headed home. As she approached the house, she noticed the driveway full of cars. She looked at the Honda. Was that Pastor Michael's car? And the blue Ford, wasn't that the Farrells'? She was getting that feeling again. Her body went cold; her legs did not want to move. Her stomach flipped and her heart pounded. She was so familiar with the scenario. She knew it meant that something wasn't right. She walked up to the front door. Hesitantly, she thought, *Everyone is probably in the living room. If I go through the side door into the kitchen, I may be able to slip in undetected.*

The last thing she needed was to see those people, and she believed that might actually be something her parents would thank her for. She couldn't imagine them being happy about her appearing on a Saturday at three in the afternoon in front of all those church people after not being home for the night.

She quietly walked in ... so far, so good. She took off her shoes to make less noise. She was so focussed on being quiet that it took a moment to realize what was taking place in her house. She was shocked, horrified, and then embarrassed

They were all in her living room taking turns praying for her, for her return, for her safety, for spiritual healing, and then for her redemption. How dare they say such things. Who did they think they were? She was ready to blast into their prayers with a rude awakening when Linc spotted her from the top of the stairs.

"Look! Your prayers worked. Amber's here! Look she's here!"

Every bloodshot eye, tearstained face, and even those who held their emotions in turned to look in amazement.

They were all thrilled to see how quickly their God had answered their prayers. She could see the joy in their faces, but to Amber it was humiliating. She didn't know which way she should run. She didn't want to go out; she was tired. She ran upstairs, past her brother, not looking at a single person in that living room. She ran into her room and shut the door. She grabbed her pillow and her blanket and threw herself into her closet. There she curled up on the floor and forced herself to think of something other than all those people downstairs praying for a miracle. She was so angry.

Why had they gotten their miracle? Why did she have to come home right then, of all the timing? One more unjust in a line of many. She allowed herself to wallow in self-pity. It felt good to mull over the past; it fed her anger, heating the rage. It gave reason for the bitterness she kept closer than a friend. As she looked back, she remembered things she had forgotten, blame she had neglected to pass. How could she have possibly thought her circumstances were her fault? No, there were people who needed to pay. There was definite blame to be hurled. She would not go down alone. Yet one thing, one moment kept niggling in the back of her brain: Why had she gotten into Gordon Forbes' car?

She could not escape the question, nor could she answer it.

Temptations

"I do not understand the things I do. I do not do what I want to do, and I do the things I hate. And if I do not want to do the hated things I do that means I agree the law is good, I am not really the one doing these hated things; it is sin living in me that does them."

Romans 7:15–17

I t was four o'clock. Jake had been doing his devotions, reading God's Word, and praying. It was already Tuesday; he was supposed to meet Jena in two hours at Bombay Grill. His heart wasn't in it. As he read, he kept thinking of Amber. He prayed for her. He hoped for her. He felt God's message on his heart. It encouraged him.

"Love her."

He could almost hear the voice.

"Yes," he agreed with the voice in his heart and repeated the verse from his devotion in the book of John. "So now I am giving you this commandment, love one another. As I have loved you, love one another."

No, love her as Solomon loved the Shulamite, Jake thought for a moment. He reread the passage about Jesus washing the disciples' feet before his crucifixion. *Lord, I will love her as you loved your disciples, as I love Matthew and Charlie.*

"No," was the answer. He did not understand. He flipped in his Bible to Song of Solomon, a book he had never paid much attention to. He was shocked by what he read. "May your kisses be as exciting as the best wine, smooth and sweet, flowing gently over lips and teeth." He read on, feeling slightly embarrassed by the passion revealed in the text. Then, catching on to the message God was giving him, he felt embarrassed.

I am in no hurry, Lord. I can wait.

"Love her." There it was again. Jake closed his Bible, still shocked and a little uncomfortable at the realization that God truly knew even his private thoughts. He had felt something for Amber; he believed it was hope. Why would God want him to love her like that? He must be mistaken. It had been a long time since he was in the company of a woman, he reasoned.

Jake jumped into the shower. He was going to be late. He looked for the card Jena had given him; her phone number was on it. He could call and let her know he was going to be late. He found it crumpled up in his uniform pocket; he had washed it. *Jena's Cakes* was all that was readable. He threw on his jeans and found a blue cotton shirt. It was a little wrinkled, but he smelled it and it was okay. If he had wheels, he could make it on time. He ran to the bus. If he missed it, he would be at least thirty minutes late. If he caught it, he would only be about four minutes late.

Jake was getting off the bus when he noticed Jena pulling around the corner to park her little red Miata. *Chick car,* he thought to himself. *No way Amber would ever be seen in a car like that. Where did that thought come from?*

Jake waited at the front door. When he saw Jena rounding the corner, he caught his breath. She wore a short, tight, red halter dress that left very little to the imagination. Her legs were long and smooth. She walked purposefully toward him, hips swaying gently. She wore her short, dark hair flipped up. Her features were dark. Black liner emphasized her large, saucer-shaped eyes. Her mouth was embellished with shiny gloss. He couldn't keep from staring at that mouth. Her grin was broad as she looped her arm through his. Her hair smelled like fresh air. Her skin was so soft on his arm. His senses had not been titillated in a long time. He took in all of her as he returned her smile and led the way inside.

They were ushered to a small circular table in a corner. There was a floor-length window overlooking the bay.

"I wasn't sure if you would show." She was truthful but still smiling.

"I see you daily at work. I had to show." Jake returned her smile.

Jake forced himself to keep his eyes away from Jena's mouth. *Look at her eyes,* he reminded himself several times. She smiled at him constantly. He felt so at ease in her presence. He caught himself toying with the thought, *God, if you want me tied down, this is more of what I would have in mind. She is beautiful. She's funny. An entrepreneur. And she has no baggage.*

She was smiling again. He hadn't heard what she said. He smiled back. She was full of life; she certainly had a lot to say. Jake looked at the menu. Their waiter came, and Jena ordered a salad. He furrowed his brow. *A salad eater. Where's the protein?* Jake ordered a steak cooked rare.

Jena had noticed his expression. "I like to stay fit," she defended. Jake shrugged his shoulders and offered a casual smile. Eager to change the subject, Jake asked about her cake business.

"You would be surprised, I get pretty busy." Jena took one question and made it a full conversation piece.

She appeared delightful. Her legs crossed, she swung one back and forth as she talked. Her smile engaged him. She flirted coyly, dropping little innuendos as she spoke. His eyes widened as he was taken in by her flattery when she told him she had been attracted to him immediately.

"You have the most stunning eyes," she complemented.

Jake began to feel the effects of her wantonness.

"Do you work out? I would love to do a workout with you. I love to sweat." She made it apparent she would like nothing more than to be available to him. It was so easy to be taken in. He hadn't even realized it. She made him feel like a schoolboy. Part of him wanted to blush; another part of him was all too familiar with her intentions. It had been a long time since he'd been with a woman. This one wanted to make sure he would not have to wait any longer.

Jake straightened in his seat. Had she really just said that? He was trying to pay attention, but she talked so fast. And again her crass words. He was near embarrassment as she described in detail certain pictures she had been requested to replicate on her cakes.

"You don't ever just say no?" He was serious; she laughed.

"Why would I say no? It's hilarious. I enjoy that part of my job the most. I am very creative."

Jake looked at Jena again. Had he missed something? The feelings that had begun to stir in his body were quickly being turned off. Outwardly beautiful Jena. As she continued to talk, her conversation became more lewd and suggestive. If not for hunger, Jake considered leaving.

It had been brief, but Jake was surprised how easy it was to forget where his heart was supposed to be. He had travelled from zero to sixty and back to zero in a very short time. Had God had him on this date just to teach him that? He got it. Then he wondered, *If this educated woman can be so vulgar, how much worse would the speech of a criminal be?* But when he thought of Amber for a brief moment, he pictured her genuine smile, her hearty laugh, the way she had been the night they went on the joyride. Yet something in him cried against it. *Lord, she is in prison. How long will she be there? Is there no one better suited for me?*

The waiter came by. "Would anyone like to order dessert?"

Before Jena could answer, Jake requested the bill. He was anxious to leave.

Jena realized that somewhere in the conversation she had lost Jake's interest. She couldn't figure him out. He really seemed to adore all those old people, and he spent his spare time with degenerates. There was something about him though. It wasn't just that he was handsome. He was genuine, rare. It both bothered her and intrigued her that he hadn't succumbed to her wiles. Well, she had given it a try.

———————

Jake lay on the top of his bed, hands folded under his head, still disturbed by his date. Two years ago he would not have had a second thought as to what to do with a woman like that.

———————

Morning came too early for Amber. She had found great comfort in the infirmary. She had managed to stay there for the past five days. She was back at trial this morning though, as a result she was sure she would be back in the cage. That possibility brought with it other irrational thoughts. Her paranoid mind taunted her with possibilities of scams and covert agendas, racing through myriad scenarios.

Amber was ready to go by eight. Her escort would arrive shortly. She caught herself hoping Jake would be along. She imagined with a grin what she might say to him as she checked herself out in the tiny mirror. Realization hit her; she remembered the way she had treated him the last time she had seen him, the vulgar facts that Emma-Jean had revealed to him from her medical file. She closed her eyes and winced at the harshest memory of that last meeting, his face. He had looked as though he literally hurt *for* her.

In her present state of mind, she decided she would actually be relieved if there was someone else to drive her today. She heard the approaching walk and knew instinctively that it wasn't Charlie or his partner. She held her breath in anticipation. The approaching officer was very old. She couldn't help but smile to herself.

This will definitely be better, she thought malevolently. *This guy has to be close to seventy, far past retirement.* She grinned broadly to herself. *Oh, this will indeed be a fun-filled drive.* She was already conjuring fabulous remarks she could make to the old-timer. *This will be fun.*

Sheriff Darryl Tate turned out to be no fun at all. Amber didn't even get a chance to burn him with one of her quick-witted comments. He shut down the lines of communication before she could open her mouth. Officer Tate helped her into the patrol car by putting his hand on the back of her head and shoving her in. She thought he had created an opportunity for her to say something, but upon her inhaling, preparing for her jibe, he said, "Save your comment, little girl. I heard 'em all. Nothing new. Nothing funny. If you ask me, you should save any intelligence you got for the courtroom. Better yet, you should say nothing.'" He glanced at her in the rear-view mirror. Amber's hair stood up all over. What did he know? She remained silent except for the wild beating of her heart.

"You the one causin' all the problems up there at the pen, eh? You drug addicts. You're all the same. Tryin' to cause decent folks a hard time. Ain't nobody up at that prison done things to ya that you didn't deserve or do to yerself." He glared at her through the rear-view mirror.

Amber stammered for a moment, searching for both words and a voice to defend herself, "I-I, uh, I haven't even ... "

Darryl was just pulling the cruiser into the law court's parking lot. He pulled into a designated spot. He undid his seatbelt, turned around, and pointed accusingly as he glared through narrowed black eyes at Amber. "I already know all the things ya done. I know yer whole rap sheet, and it's long. You aint gettin' out of Klahanee for a long time. You won't be causin' anyone anymore trouble. That's certain."

Amber's memories of the attack were fresh, and parts of

her body still ached. She kept her eyes forward. Terrified. She refused the urge to look away and resolved to harden herself against his threats. She would not give the old man the satisfaction of letting him know that she was intimidated. A foolish notion overtook Amber's senses. He truly was a very old man. What did she have to fear? In a moment of rage, she cursed back at the sheriff, "You can't threaten me. You have no idea the people I know. If you had anything to do with what happened, I pity you. I will see justice."

Darryl said nothing for the moment. He got out of the cruiser then calmly got into the backseat close to Amber. He clasped one hand to her throat, pressing firmly. "You try escaping again, ma'am, and I will use whatever force is necessary to bring you down. We understand each other?"

She understood perfectly. Darryl Tate was a psycho. What was his problem with her? She didn't recognize him from anywhere, yet the vendetta was definitely personal.

Darryl had more to say, but he relaxed his grip on her throat before continuing. "Before you get any ideas 'bout talking to anyone 'bout this ride, let me give you an idea of what will be waiting for you back at yer cell. It won't be like last time. It will be worse." He grinned a loathsome grin, showing stained teeth. His lips were stretched tight, lifting up the corners of his nostrils, and his eyes glinted pure evil. Amber felt as though she had just had a personal encounter with the devil himself. She was relieved when he got out of the car and waited for her to follow him.

Resentment and anger fuelled her emotions; she would not give in to them. Instead, she crammed them down to the molten pot of hate that had begun a long time ago, growing and hardening with each experience, banishing hope, especially the hope of redemption.

They were at the huge double oak doors that would lead them into the courthouse. Darryl had one hand on Amber's cuffs; he leaned in to her and whispered, "One word, Amber, tha's all it's gonna take." Darryl Tate emanated his evil hope, looking Amber up and down lustfully before continuing. "Personally, I hope you can't keep those lips of yers shut."

The loathing she felt came through in her sincere retort. "Not a word. Count on it."

Jake looked over at his alarm. Seven was way too early to get up. He had only gotten off work at eleven and did not get home until midnight. He'd had a snack; he was starving. By the time he got to bed it was near two a.m. A sucker for punishment, that's what he was. He knew Amber had her hearing today, and he was going to be there to offer support. He hoped he would get a chance to talk to her; she had stayed on his mind night and day. The worst of it was that he was helpless to do much. He wanted to offer her hope, not that she would ever accept it.

Jake sat up and forced himself to get out of bed. He ran his fingers through his tousled, dirty blond locks and went straight into the bathroom. He turned on the faucet and splashed some cold water on his face. *That should help wake me up.* He lifted his square jaw and caught his reflection in the mirror. *Looking very tired,* he thought to himself. The beginnings of dark circles were forming under his dark brown eyes.

"It's that girl." Never leaving his conscience. He felt as though he had personally taken on Amber's burdens. He convinced himself that if he wasn't there for her, no one else would be. He winced at the memory of her recent attack.

The image of her that day pierced his heart. Even if she got out of this mess, if she was not found guilty of murder, would she ever be okay? Thoughts of the things her body had endured and her soul had survived erupted in his mind. He felt the heat of rage at the inhumanity. What animals did such things?

Lord, how can I love her when all I feel is deep sadness and pity?

He gripped the sink and lowered his head, willing the image

of Amber to leave his mind. It was replaced by one of Ducky. Her funeral had been a few days ago. He had never gone to a patient's funeral before. He went to hers. Now her words rung out in his mind, "You alone are God!"

Jake turned on the shower as hot as his skin could take. The cascading water and steam that rose were purifying, helping to clear his head and align his thoughts.

"Whatever is true, whatever is noble, whatever is right, whatever is pure, whatever is lovely, whatever is admirable, if anything is excellent or praiseworthy, think about such things." He repeated the verse over and over for the duration of his shower.

He got dressed quickly and began his devotions. The topic was convicting: "Knowing God's Will." It began with Romans 12:2, "Do not conform any longer to the pattern of this world, but be transformed by the renewing of your mind. Then you will be able to test and approve what God's will is—his good and perfect will." He read the verse a second time. "Test and approve God's will."

As Jake read, his mind wandered. He wondered at the amazing things God had done and had yet to do. He allowed himself to think about Amber. Long blonde tresses and deep sea-green eyes popped into his mind. By appearance Amber had quite an allure. He hadn't been so stricken by anyone since Sofia. It wasn't the same emotion; Amber needed him. He was well aware of the appeal to his masculinity. He prayed solemnly that he would be able to help her. He could not lose himself or his purpose by becoming a slave to her outward beauty. He prayed that any feelings other than those that were pure God would take away.

He didn't; in fact, they intensified. Jake fought against the idea. He did not believe it was pity that drove him, and he was cautious of lust. That would help no one. He had love for her, but that was not what God was asking of him. The fact remained; he would still have to make the choice.

Jake headed out. Amber remained on his mind. *Pray without*

ceasing, he reminded himself. As he walked out the front door of his apartment building, he noticed Matthew in his pickup.

"Want a lift?"

"How long you been waiting there?"

"Just pulled up. Jump in."

Jake nodded, though he had been looking forward to the solitude of the bus. Matthew was perceptive to Jake's demeanor and said little.

Amber took note of her parents sitting in the front row, waiting. They appeared relieved to see her. Michael walked over to his daughter and embraced her for an awkward moment. He remembered when Amber had first begun developing into a young woman. For a short time, he had become uncomfortable with affection. He didn't know how to react to his changing daughter. She had made it so easy. She hugged him tight every night. She kissed him every night. She said, "I love you, Daddy." Every night. Just like always. She had shown him how to deal with her. "Just love me like you always have." She had not shown hurt at his withdrawal of affection; instead, she guided. Now she was the one uncomfortable with him.

He had thought that after getting through that time he would kiss her goodnight until she had a husband. He realized again his shortcoming; he was the one who stopped, not her. How many hugs and tender touches and goodnight kisses had he missed that she wanted to share? His heart ached with the thought. Next time he saw her, he would hug her so hard she would have to ask him to stop.

Thank goodness her father didn't ask the usual lame question: "How are you?" Amber was surprised by his affection. He gently kissed her forehead and was reassuring simply by his presence. She was almost disappointed when he walked to his seat and took his place next to her mother. It took her by surprise. It was as relieving as it was peculiar.

He offered no prayers, quoted no Bible verses, and, strangest of all, her mother was void of her constipated expression. Amber almost preferred it when they acted weird. It gave her justification.

She was led to the seat beside her lawyer, who was ripe with questions for her.

"Amber, I am so sorry I didn't make it in to see you. Are you doing all right? Since the rape, I mean?"

Amber's reply revealed how absurd she thought the question. "I'm great, awesome actually—"

Nina cut her off; she had no patience or appreciation for sarcasm. "Once we are done here, we have some issues we need to discuss. I suggest you get yourself in the right frame of mind for dealing with what's ahead of you, Amber. Are you able to do this or not?"

"Discuss what?"

"Your parents called me. They told me all about Dr. Forbes. I need all the details. *From you.* I need to be able to present your accusations to the judge. We might get a plea bargain if I can establish a link between your offenses and you being victimized by a court-appointed psychiatrist. We will have to be able to prove your story. You would need to undergo a psych evaluation, but if a few little things go our way, you could be off and home by ... well, sooner than if you're convicted."

"What accusations are you talking about?"

"You being 'touched' by Dr. Forbes. If we can prove that you were, as you say, touched inappropriately, then we could either go for the insanity plea or mental trauma due to your frame of mind. You'll fit the profile. That's not a bad thing. You'll get a reduced sentence. It's the difference between life in prison and five years." She was talking too fast, and Amber was still back at her first statement.

"I made no claims against Dr. Forbes."

"Do you deny it happened? You need to cooperate with me. Do you know you could be entitled to a financial settlement if we prove your claims that a court-appointed doctor is using his position to manipulate court-appointed clients for sex?"

"I am confused now. Did he rape me or just touch me inappropriately?" Suddenly, the lights came on. Amber knew exactly where this was coming from: her parents.

The judge's gavel interrupted what would soon have been a verbal onslaught. She would "tear a strip" off Nina later. The bailiff spoke, and as Amber rose at his words, she had a hard time stifling a giggle as she remembered how difficult this simple task had been the last time she was in the courtroom.

Judge Delores Grace, not to miss a beat herself, couldn't resist pointing that out. "Miss White, having a much easier time with the menial tasks today, I see. Hopefully you can continue in such a constructive manner through the entire morning."

Before Amber knew, her lips were moving. She was answering the judge. Her tone was somber, and her words were true. "I miscarried the child I was carrying and no longer suffer from the dizziness and nausea." The two women held eye contact for a genuine moment. Briefly, something appeared to soften in the judge's hard face, then instantaneously the steely expression that seemed etched into the fine lines returned.

The trial began and the facts of the case came about. Upon being arrested, Amber tested positive to the following substances: cocaine, trace amounts of heroin, and a large amount of ephedrine. At the time of the arrest she still held the murder weapon, a hypodermic syringe containing pure heroin laced with strychnine. The substances were different from those found in her body. Her lawyer entered a plea of self-defense.

The rebuttal from the State prosecutor was that the person who was murdered was the son of a police officer with no previous record of drug use. Amber had three previous drug-elated offences, one of which was trafficking. The self-defense claim was fabricated. How could a 110-pound girl overpower a 190-pound man? The proposed defense was absurd. Amber sat there, expressionless. She had already relived the events of that evening so many times. Who would believe her? She wouldn't believe herself. She closed her eyes. The event played out frame by frame behind her eyelids, the one day she feared she could never forget.

Duncan, she had learned later was his name, came across the street and approached her. He was well dressed, but one look in his eyes and she knew he was a user. He needed to talk to her, that was all. She knew what that meant. He was looking, so she offered him to follow her to a room in a run-down building that her group rented and used to "fix." Needle users had lived there before. The landlord hadn't bothered to paint. There was blood spatter on the walls from people shooting up. The linoleum floor was covered with holes. The blue shag carpet was mostly gray with numerous stains. Sheets, or pieces of fabric, hung across every window. There was running water and a toilet. The room was cheap, and they split it between the five of them.

When Amber and Duncan entered the little room, sleeping bags were strewn all over the floor. Amber looked around. When she looked back at Duncan, she noticed a change had come over in his expression. His face was dark. His deep-set blue eyes glared. The hair on Amber's arms stood up. She felt anxiety creeping into her stomach. Evil emanated from him.

Offering him some coffee, she fumbled with the electric kettle, ran some water in it, put the teaspoons of instant in the cup ,then waited expectantly.

"What are you looking for?" she asked casually. He closed the ten-foot gap between them. He grabbed her and pulled her into his chest forcibly, holding her wrist. She was completely aware of his dominating power over her. His eyes narrowed.

"You, I was looking for you."

"I'm not a hooker. All I do is shoot candy to people." She hoped her fear didn't show. He laughed and then looked her up and down.

"Obviously. My uncle warned me about your kind." He paused for a minute, easing his grip on her. "You don't know who I am, do you?"

She shook her head.

"Does the name Stan mean anything to you?"

"No! I don't know what you're talking about. I don't know you, and I don't your uncle either."

"Liar, liar," he seethed with hatred. "You knew Stan!"

"Stan," she said the name quietly. "Stan." She recalled her friend with sadness. "Stan died. I knew him. He was my friend. He died about eight months ago. It was horrible—"

"Lies. My uncle told me you would lie. That's why you deserve what you get."

Amber walked over to the water that was boiling. She unplugged it, remaining silent as she poured the steaming liquid into the prepared mugs. She looked at Duncan, who was preparing a fix. He exuded pure evil.

Horror erupted in her gut; she knew he was planning to do something to her. She had to act fast; she needed a plan. Amber inconspicuously opened a drawer. She was so glad she had left a bottle in there. She found what she was looking for— Visine. She nervously removed the lid and emptied nearly half the bottle of the powerful toxin. She looked at Duncan; he did not seem to notice her attempts at self-preservation. She picked up the mugs and walked into the area where he was sitting on the floor. Amber's hands were shaking as she handed him the mug. He barely glanced at her as he took the coffee. His eyes were empty black pools. His pupils were so dilated, she could no longer see the blue. She was even more terrified.

Amber had been told about the effects of Visine from a street girl. *"You put the Visine in the coffee. The guy drinks it, then he passes out. You grab his wallet, there's your trick."* Amber had so far only used it to "get the red out." She had never had to use it for something like this before. She wasn't sure how long it would take to have its slumbering effects. She hoped soon, and she really hoped she had used enough. Her heart beat fast as he sucked back the hot liquid.

Duncan looked at her suspiciously. "So what kind of lies are on those lips of yours about my cousin?"

She tried to look deep into his eyes to appeal to some reality that may still be present. The fact was that if this lunatic was straight, he would have seen the sadness on her face.

"Stan was my friend. I was the only one of his friends who went to his funeral. I kept the clipping from the paper. "

Stan's death had been a horrible one.

I was there that night," she spoke quietly. "Stan picked up a stash of coke from the guys on Southside. They laced it. They had it planned to get rid of all of us, but Stan tested it before I doctored it up. We were all shocked."

"No," he was adamant. "You were the potion master. My uncle saw the police file. It mentioned a girl. That girl is you. You were at the funeral. Did it rid you of your guilt? You mixed it. You killed him." With that accusation, Duncan leapt to his feet. In one motion he lunged at her, syringe cocked. In that instant the Visine began to work. Duncan swayed and lumbered, still coming toward her. Amber took her chance. Using the leverage from his body as he slowly fell, Amber grabbed his arm and with all her might twisted the large forearm and jabbed the syringe into her attacker, plunging the potent needle straight into the thick skin of his belly.

He tried to grab her hand before her thumb could inject the poison into his veins, but she was quick. She knew she only had one shot. Duncan squeezed her hand, tightening it on the syringe. He pulled. She gripped it with all her might as she fled the scene.

The drug had already begun its voyage into Duncan's veins. Amber didn't look back, not for a second. She ran as fast as she could, her heart pounding. She had to get out of there. The police must have been alerted that something was going on. She was stopped and arrested right outside the building. She still had the syringe in her hand. In the terror-stricken moment she hadn't even released the weapon. No one yet knew that young Duncan lay dying on that hard, dirty, cold floor, a death meant for her.

She would learn later that Duncan was a police officer's son. Things couldn't get worse than that. It had been a while since she had allowed herself to go over that day in detail. She might as well, she reasoned; she was going to need to now.

Wide Road

"When you pass through the rivers they will not sweep you away. When you walk through the fire you will not be burned. The flames will not set you ablaze."

Isaiah 43:2

Court recessed for the judge to make her decision. When they were all called back into the courtroom, the bailiff requested, "Amber White, please rise." As she did, she felt nothing, as though she were in a dream or watching someone else's life unfold before her.

"I find there is sufficient evidence to take the allegations to trial. Court will resume in two weeks."

Reality began spreading her wings. Amber realized this was real. Nina White stood up and made her request to the judge, "Your Honor, permission to approach?"

"Speak from there," the judge demanded.

"I have just been informed of new circumstances surrounding my client's allegations. It puts into question her mental stability at the time of the incident."

"Are you changing your plea of not guilty to an insanity plea?" Judges hated that. They knew it was usually a ploy, especially for women facing a jury. It certainly upped her chances of getting off.

Nina avoided the question. "I honorably request a moment in your chambers to go over these new facts."

The judge, with her high-arched eyebrows and steely eyes, looked at Amber, then back to Nina before answering, still looking displeased. "Can you not speak freely in the courtroom?"

"Honorable Judge, I am sure you must be aware of what took place at the prison only three nights ago. It's still fresh in my client's mind. I hope to prove there is a link between these incidents. I see no reason in torturing my client with reliving the events so quickly after they have happened."

Amber felt her face go hot. Anger surged at the candid way Nina spoke.

"All right," the judge replied with a heavy sigh, making sure to let everyone know the private visit was a bother.

"Your Honor, I have not yet gotten all the details from my client."

The judge looked even more perturbed at Nina. Amber was irritated; she hadn't agreed to go through with the accusations. She nudged her well-intending lawyer and spoke through gritted teeth, "Just forget it, Nina. I am not going in to details about this."

Judge Grace looked directly at Amber. "Do you have something to add?"

"No, Your Honor."

"My client doesn't understand that without her testimony, the evidence we have is useless. The evidence brings in to question my client's state of mind at the time of the incident, proving undoubtedly that she is innocent of the alleged crimes." Nina glared at Amber as she spoke and then turned her attention back to the judge. "I request a moment to go over these details with my client. I can be in your chambers in ten minutes."

The judge nodded. Amber went cold inside, realizing Nina had stuck her neck out for her, and she would now want Amber's complete cooperation. Complete cooperation meant Amber spilling her guts. That would include her own evil contributions. It was up to Nina to discern what parts of the confession were useable.

Amber inhaled deeply, thinking about what she should say. The thoughts came in a flood of memories best forgotten. She could feel her stomach lurching as she remembered the incident, the one that she had planned. It should have aroused shame, but all she felt was empty.

She began to question as she struggled for words and pondered the reaction. Would others, the judge, see it as her fault? Would she say she had a choice, condemning her immediately? Dr. Forbes hadn't held a gun to her head to make her perform. Further, she knew perfectly well that she had intentionally seduced him in order to get pregnant.

She wanted to humiliate him and ruin him. She was once again feeling the sting of another's crimes. Oh, what a defense he would have. Her stomach knotted. What could she say? No one would see it her way. Her head was spinning; she was weak. The truth was, she had just given in. Lauryn would never have "just given in." As a matter of fact, she was sure that if Dr. Forbes had tried to manipulate Lauryn the way he had her, she would have stuck him with a needle the first time, and she wouldn't have had any more problems. That's what Lauryn told Amber when she had told her about the pig. And when she had told Jersey what happened, she retorted, "My stepdad tried that with me. I put Visine in his coffee, and when he passed out I stole his money, his credit cards, and the keys to his crappy car. It got me out of town, into the next state. He didn't get the chance to try that twice." She had laughed.

Amber could see the impatience on Nina's face. She closed her eyes; her mind raced. It seemed like every vile thing she had ever done felt free to roam her memory. She shook her head.

"I can't, Nina. I can't." She stood up to run, but as she turned, she saw her parents. They were looking at each other. They were so strong. She was amazed at how calm they looked. Was it because they believed in her? Did they finally believe she was innocent? Did they believe she was strong enough to tell all the shameful things she had done? She would rather make it seem like it was all someone else's fault. Hadn't it been? Could her story dissuade a judge bent on a conviction? Maybe they believed that confession would bring her vindication. She couldn't. She just couldn't.

Nina gently grabbed her arm. "Amber, you need to do this. This story could be the difference between you spending the rest of your life in prison or not. How can you even contemplate this?"

Amber opened her mouth to speak. It felt so dry. Her tongue stuck to the roof of her mouth. She wanted to scream. She felt panic rise. She closed her eyes, resigning herself to what she had to do.

"What do you want to know?" As she said it, she wasn't sure she could do it.

Nina let out a very relieved breath. "Everything."

"No, don't tell me that. Ask questions, I'll answer."

"Okay." Nina spoke gently, with empathy. "The name of the doctor you were assigned to? Who assigned that doctor? How many times did you see him? After how many sessions did he begin to make sexual advances toward you?"

Amber remained emotionless through most of the questioning and diligently answered all she was asked. Nina stood up when she had finished her interrogation and thanked Amber. She reassured her that she was doing the right thing. A good thing. The information would not only help her case but others as well.

"If there were others, would that help?" Amber asked softly.

"If what?"

"One time when I was leaving I noticed a young girl much younger than myself. She came out of his office, and it was obvious she had been crying, and whatever, that wasn't what I noticed. This thirteen-, maybe fourteen-year-old girl came out with the buttons on her blouse done up wrong." She didn't say the rest of what was on her mind, that she recognized the beaten look in the young girl's eyes, the way her head hung down. She made no eye contact. They were all signs screaming out, "I am dirty! I am unworthy!" Amber was still haunted by those same fears.

"I need a lot more time with you on this, Amber, but for right now this will hopefully be enough for the judge to assign you to a psych exam. We will need to subpoena a list of all the doctor's patients. Hopefully someone else will be willing to testify." Nina was pleased with herself; she stood to relay the information to the judge.

"Don't you want to know about the baby?"

Nina appeared not to have a clue. "What baby?"

"I was pregnant with Dr. Forbes' child. I lost the baby during the attack Monday night. How could you not know that? You told the judge the incidents were related."

"Amber, how could I?" The eager lawyer became empathetic to her client.

"You're my lawyer. I was attacked in my cell. I was in the prison infirmary for five days. Court was postponed until I could heal. Look at my face. I still have bruises. I have had police officers in to ask me innumerable questions. I had a rape exam done. How could you possibly have missed all of that?!" Amber didn't realize that her voice had escalated to a tone just shy of yelling. Every person in the courtroom would know her secrets now. Well, so what. What kind of Mickey Mouse lawyer had her parents hired anyway? How was it possible that she didn't know this stuff? Amber muttered a few expletives at the even more shocked and newly informed lawyer, grabbed her jacket, and as she turned to go, she felt the shock that had permeated through the courtroom. She didn't care. She knew the judge would be staring at her too. She refused to care. She turned and faced the steely-eyed judge, glaring, daring her. She was shocked to see an almost pitiful expression. She didn't need the old bag's pity. She walked out toward the thick oak doors that led into the hallway, leaving behind a speechless lawyer, inquisitive parents, a pitiful judge, and a handful of shocked accusers.

Nina wasted no time in approaching the judge. "Can we please take this into your chambers now?"

"Mmm hmm." She motioned to the court security to fetch the accused.

Once in the judge's chambers, Nina was in a hurry to defend her client, which proved unnecessary. Compassion forced out the usual steel in Judge Delores Grace's face. She held up a hand to her and said, "I heard all she had to say. You can go on out there and find your client. She will be in trouble neither of us can help her with if she runs off."

"Are you going to tell me your decision?" she asked, but she already knew.

Amber reached the doors, still unsure of what she was going to do. Security guards were right behind her. She thrust open the double doors. She needed a moment to clear her head; her emotions seared. She couldn't breathe; her throat ached. The security guard grabbed her, ready to put on the handcuffs.

Amber recognized the tan faux suede shoes in front of her immediately. She looked up into the sweetest face. She caught her breath; a small gasp escaped.

"Jake."

Amber was relieved he hadn't arrived any sooner. The last time he had seen her, she was lashing out at him, and to have witnessed this outburst, well, she was really glad he hadn't. What would he think of her? Not that he could think any worse than he must already.

Regardless of what he thought of her, she was relieved to see him. She hoped he was there to take her back to Klahanee, relieving her worry that Darryl Tate, the psycho, would not be driving her back.

Jake took a long look at Amber's face, reading her expression. He knew he had arrived at the right place at the right
time. She looked like someone who had been beaten so many
times, they were just waiting for the next blow, putting up no
defense. If he wasn't mistaken, it was the closest he had ever
seen her to tears and thought, *The hearing must have been very
hard on her.* Looking around, he realized court was over. He
gestured to the guard who removed her cuffs and remanded
her into Jake's custody. He hadn't arrived late after all, as he
had worried earlier when Matthew stopped at Seven-Eleven
for coffee. He had arrived at precisely the right time—God's
appointed time—when he was needed.

Jake was one of the few people from the precinct where
he volunteered who believed that Amber had been protecting
herself, as she claimed, and was innocent. Of course, the other
officers at the Third Precinct thought she was strung out and
guilty. How did she accidentally happen to have such a lethal
amount of drugs on her the night she was allegedly attacked?
Unless she was suicidal. To further complicate her story, the
man she had allegedly murdered was a former police officer's
son. The other officers defined this case as a "no-brainer." Why
would the victim have attacked a pretty girl like that? By what
hidden force could she have overcome his attack if he had? It all
seemed too unlikely. Would he buy drugs from her? Not from a
street vender. Yes, the other officers all believed she was guilty.
They figured the only way a person could see her as not guilty
was if one were a fool and was sucked in by the innocence in
those huge green eyes, causing one to lose all reasoning. They
all thought that Jake definitely had. Matthew attributed his
friend's feelings in the matter to divine meddling.

Jake had noticed on more than one occasion how people
stared at her. As young as she was when he first met her, he
could only imagine how predators would have taken advantage
of her. As time went on, he learned exactly what they did to her.

No, there was no doubt in his mind that she had been defending herself. She was a survivor; she would do what she had to.

He looked intently into her eyes. What he saw there made his heart ache. He wanted to hold her close, to tell her it would be okay. He knew that she would not accept that. He reached out his hand and gently placed it on her shoulder, a reassuring gesture.

Recognizing the pity she saw in Jake's eyes and knowing what he must be thinking about her, Amber stiffened her body, refusing to accept the invitation. Ashamed, prepared to bolt; she didn't need his pity. She just needed to be alone. She had been through enough.

Jake felt her tension. He slightly tightened his grip on Amber's shoulder, afraid of what would happen to her if she escaped. She struggled against him and pulled, pretending to put effort into her release, but that just made her feel foolish, adding to her humiliation.

Embarrassed, she hung her head, refusing to look at him. He spoke then, calmly and assuredly. "When are you going to give this up? Stop fighting me. I just want to make this more bearable for you." The honesty in his tone made Amber feel a pang of remorse on top of the shame. She bowed her head and slumped her shoulders in submission and waited for him to guide her wherever it was she was to go.

That wasn't good enough for him. He tipped her chin up, forcing her to look him in the eyes. What he saw jerked his heart; he recognized the features. She masked it immediately, but it was too late, he saw it. Regret, overshadowed with pain, outlined in misery. It hit him then; she hated this life. Too late, she was enslaved by it.

Jake wanted more than ever to hold her and comfort her. He knew this wasn't the time or place, so he draped his arm around her shoulder and directed her path back to the court-room. Charlie stood up from the bench he was sitting on and followed. The officers mentioned that the judge needed to see Amber before returning her to prison.

"Ms. White," the judge addressed her immediately, "it is not wise to attempt fleeing my courtroom!" Delores Grace wasted no time with her accusations and obvious disapproval.

"Forgive me, Your Honor," was Amber's emotionless response. "I need to get out of here." She spoke to anyone who was listening.

"Miss White, while you were out in the hall having your tantrum, I had the opportunity to speak with your attorney. Do you wish to hear my judgment on the matter?" The judge took her silence as yes and continued. "I have decided that what you need is to see a psychiatrist. You will undergo an analyzation, and the court will have the opportunity to base its decision of your future based on the findings of your completed psycho-analysis. Do you agree to this, Miss White?"

Amber had looked up at the mention of another court-appointed specialist. It was incredulous. Did the judge expect her to subject herself to further abuse at the hands of the judicial system? Once again, what choice did she have? And that is exactly the question she asked the judge.

The Honorable Judge replied, "Your other option is to deny this evaluation, and you will not be able to submit a plea of insanity. Your choice."

"I will agree to this, only...please make the referral to a female. That is all, and I beg of you, if you have any compassion—"

"Your Honor," Nina interjected, "I apologize for my client's insinuation."

"Miss White has articulated her wishes appropriately." Returning her attention to Amber, Judge Delores Grace continued. "Now, your request is certainly reasonable. I see no reason not to grant it." Then she wryly cocked her head to one side, arching a perfectly plucked brow. "However, in the future I would make it a practice to stay away from words with negative connotation aimed at the judge seated before you." She barely waited for Amber to nod her head and rattled off a name. Kimberly Alexander. The initial appointment was set for Tuesday. Court would resume in two weeks, giving the shrink time to do her analysis. Amber humbly thanked the judge, feeling slightly relieved.

Handcuffs firmly in place, Amber once again headed toward the front door of the huge courthouse with Jake a few steps behind her. He sensed her need for isolation, so he said nothing while walking quietly behind her. Charlie waited a moment before following. He hoped Jake could instil some hope in Amber. The weariness she wore cloaked her whole being, from her furrowed brow to the bow of her back and the gait of her stride.

Once in the parking lot, Jake silently went ahead of Amber, leading the way to the cruiser. They both waited for Charlie to catch up and unlock the doors. Jake opened the door for her.

"An otherwise gallant gesture," she quipped as she smiled up at him. "Where were you this morning? I thought you boys would drive me?" Her tone was casual, a significant change from only moments before. She had been near tears in the hallway, but back in the courtroom in front of the judge the facade of the cool, collected master of her emotions had reappeared. Once outside her true emotions took over.

Jake, frustrated by her feigned emotions, ignored her casual remark and asked the question on his mind. "Why do you do this to yourself?" She had set him off, his own emotions ran high. "Don't you ever get tired of pretending to feel things you don't, pretending to be someone you're not? When do you get to be you?" He knew that only in anger was she truthful. He hoped to incite a response but didn't expect one.

Amber looked at him a moment, and her expression said it all. Exasperated, he threw his arms up in the air.

Amber spoke presumptuously. "Don't you get tired of wanting something you can't have?"

He was embarrassed for a moment. What did she mean by that? He started to defend himself. "Amber, I have never—"

"Oh, Jake, I'm just havin' some fun with you," she jibed, the drastic change happening again. "Can we get going, or do you plan to stand there staring at me with your mouth wide open awhile longer?"

He was angry, he was shocked, and he felt sad for her all at once. In that moment he realized what she was doing. She was playing him like a puppet. She could be whoever he wanted her to be or whoever she needed to be. She was an expert. One could never know her true feelings unless she revealed them. Otherwise, you only saw the thin veil of what she intended you to see. Pride hurt and emotions on the surface, Jake shut his mouth and shut the door behind Amber. He did not like to be made a fool.

Amber sat in the back contemplating his words. Stealing a glance at him through the rear-view mirror, she smiled to herself. His expression was hilarious, like a child caught with a cookie in his hand. That thought brought out a true smile.

Jake noticed. "You're smiling. Could it be genuine?"

"Yes, actually." She contemplated telling him the truth but decided against it, not wanting to embarrass him further. "So what's on your schedule after dropping me off?"

"Work," he answered honestly. "Are you ever going to admit that Tyler was involved with your attack so he can be arrested?" His question caught her off guard. Her head shot up, and there was no hiding the shock on her face. Her heart pounded. He already knew the truth; all she had to do was tell it. She couldn't. She didn't know if it was fear that held her back or shame. Admitting to him what he needed to would, somehow, condemn her. She could never admit it to him. She needed his acceptance too much.

"Want to know what happened to me this morning?" she said, an obvious ploy to divert his attention.

"Amber, don't try to small talk me into appeasement, please."

He was angry, though he tried to hide it. "Nobody can do anything about this without some information from you. As far as the prison is concerned, the case is closed. They are not looking for a third person." His anger subsided as he continued. "You need to tell someone. The police need to know what happened that night. They need to know who else was there!" He spoke passionately, but it seemed in vain. Was she even listening, or was she tuning him out?

"Did you know one of the guards called Matthew at home? He was afraid *for* you. Afraid that the other person involved would come back and kill you. Doesn't that scare you? You have one guard on your side, willing to take a risk. All you have to do is talk." He was desperate for her to cooperate. "The other guard told me who it was."

Amber felt the heat rising in her face. Was he completely clueless? She had absolutely no desire to have such a conversation with him. The last thing she wanted was to discuss what happened that night with Jake Liddell. He had no idea of the emotional turmoil she had been through and the physical pain, the sheer humiliation. Where did he get the audacity to speak of her torment as though she held the silver thread to line that cloud? She wanted to scream. Amber interrupted his well-intended pep talk with a small dose of reality. "Well, Jake, now I know what you need. Let me tell you what I need. I need you to leave me alone." Her words were harsh and laced with expletives. Her tone icy, she did not yell or lose control like he had witnessed before. She wanted him to know she had specifically chosen each word.

Amber caught Jake's expression through the reflection in the mirror. It went from shocked to hurt. She felt a twinge of shame. She hadn't intended to make him feel bad. His motives were pure; he just didn't know when to give up. She had tried to change the subject, but he wouldn't let up. She had no choice but to be harsh, she rationalized. Sadly, she knew Jake would forgive her. She knew he had to, for his belief in an endlessly merciful God would force him to. How many times? She felt nervous. Had she gone too far?

His eyes were fixed on her. She tried to smile, afraid that she may have ended the one relationship she needed. She needed him; she needed his friendship. She knew he would take it away if he knew about her. He would think she was dirty, unclean, unworthy; he was so pure. She felt a twinge of guilt looking into his eyes. They revealed disappointment and sadness. He remained silent. She was too proud to say anything. She would rather have him upset with her than have one single word out of her mouth about that night and risk him never looking at her the way he often did … with value, not the way he did today with pity.

"Jake?" She would make a peace offering. "I do want to tell you about this morning." She paused but not long enough for him to answer. "The other sheriff who picked me up, Darryl Tate, what's his deal?"

Jake knew exactly who Darryl Tate was. The fact that Amber didn't confused him. He thought carefully before answering and looked over to Charlie for a reaction. "I can assure you Darryl Tate didn't pick you up this morning!"

"That freak brought me to the courthouse this morning, I assure you." She was careful not to use offensive language. "I never saw him before. He looked ninety years old, and he didn't look good for ninety." Jake chuckled at her comment, but Amber's story didn't make sense.

"Amber, you must be mistaken about the name. First, there's no way Darryl Tate could be anywhere around here. Second, he's retired, and third… " He hesitated then looked again at Charlie. Charlie nodded so he continued. "His grandson is the one you are on trial for … "

Before the sentence was out of his mouth, Amber knew. She felt it in the pit of her stomach. Jake looked intently at her, as if willing her to remember a different name. He was sure she was mistaken.

She closed her eyes and hung her head. That man's grandson was dead. No wonder he despised her.

Charlie spoke for the first time, "Innocent until proven guilty." He was solemn. She wanted to mock him for being so naive, but her usual caustic humor was quelled by guilt.

"Amber, what happened this morning?" Amber remained silent, so Jake continued. "Is this going to be another one of those things you don't elaborate on for me?"

Charlie shook his head. "If it was Tate, I have to file a report."

Fear arose in Amber's gut. What if Darryl made good on his threat? Her mind started playing tricks on her, and her heart beat wildly. Who else blamed her? Who else would seek revenge? She looked at Jake and Charlie with scrutiny. They were both way too nice, a probable front for a dark, nasty side. Everyone had one, didn't they? No one is that kind without some selfish motivation.

She reached her hands up to her head, locking the mass of hair in between her fingers, pulling. Maybe pain would stop the madness. She was on the brink of insanity. She needed to trust someone. She had to have someone. She looked at Charlie and then at Jake; her paranoia abated. Both men wore desolate expressions. They appeared to feel what she was going through. Amber knew it was her; she was the one with the evil mind. The two men wouldn't entertain such thoughts, let alone act on them. One dirty prison guard and a retired sheriff, both with personal vendettas against her and eager for vigilante justice ... that didn't make everyone dirty and self-seeking.

She understood Darryl's loathe for her. Maybe there was a similar reason why Tyler hated her. She just didn't know what it was that she had done to him.

"Jake, please, you guys can't say anything. Just leave it alone."

"Amber, we can't do that. If Darryl threatened you, it has to be reported. We can't just ignore it." Amber couldn't survive another attack. It had drained too much of her soul the last time, and she didn't have much left. In desperation, she gave in to trust. She had to.

"Jake … "

Hope shone in his eyes, encouraging her to continue.

"I need you to keep this to yourself. Trust me that it is better this way. You have to give me your word that you won't tell anyone what I told you about this morning, at least for now. You have to trust me … Promise me, no one else gets involved." She squeezed her eyes shut tightly. It had only been hours ago that she had assured the putrid man, "Not a word." Now here she had shot off her mouth to the sheriff and to Jake.

Jake and Charlie both heard as much as felt the torment in her request. Charlie understood, Jake did not. Both simultaneously obliged.

Amber looked from one to the other. That answer was fitting of Charlie, but Jake? She expected questions and prying from him.

"What do you mean, 'Okay?' Don't you mean, 'Okay, but … '?"

"No … okay. I am sure that you have a valid reason for this request." He tried to hold eye contact through the rear-view mirror so she could see his honest intention. "Maybe if you can trust me with this, you will learn to trust me more. You may even find yourself wanting to tell me the answers to other questions." He smiled at her. He was being cheeky. She didn't mind, and she grinned back.

Amber contemplated his offer. She wasn't sure she could ever go through with it and tell him those horrible things. What would he think of her? At this point in Amber's life, Jake Liddell was about the only person left who treated her with any respect. He was kind and understanding. She refused to risk losing him. She closed her eyes, drawing on yet another painful memory. After Adam died, she struggled with friends. How could anyone else possibly understand what she had been through? She stopped going to youth group. She did not want to deal with the invading stories or the unasked questions that showed on every face. She would rather busy herself with her studies and avoid confrontation. She wondered now, had she endured it for a time? Would she have ended up with better friends? Friends who would have stuck by her? Helped her through the dark days by means other than what she had found? Some of her closest friends had stopped talking to her.

Her mother had said they probably didn't know what to say. *"Give them time,"* she had encouraged. *"They'll come around,"* but they hadn't, and she deviated further. She wondered then about Linc. Her parents said he heard from the kids at school what she had done. Would she be the reason for her brother to stumble? Would he end up hating her?

Amber knew other people blamed her. One mutual friend had commented angrily, *"It should have been you."* Both girls knew she was right. Amber was the wild one. Yeah, she went to church on Sunday, and sure, her parents were strict, but she was always talking about what she was going to do to get out of town. Turned out people were actually listening. After the accident, everyone just knew it had all been her fault. It didn't matter that she loved Adam too. Eventually, she gave up on everyone else. That's when she switched schools and met Stan.

Stan Porter was shy. He always wore his hair over his eyes. He was probably the first person to tell Amber not to listen to what other people thought. He listened to her story of what had happened, and to him it was clearly the driver in the yellow car who was at fault. What did he know? He wasn't there. He didn't know how persuasive she could be and how she had manip-ulated Adam to drive up the hill instead of going home. He smiled at her as though she was a child then and told her how naive she was. Adam had allowed himself to be manipulated; after all, he was a guy. She defended Adam. He wasn't like that. Though she was not convinced by Stan's attempts to relieve her guilt, at least he didn't make her feel worse. They began hang-ing together then. She liked Stan. He was all she had, so she didn't mind his drug use. He always seemed to have something on him. One time he had pulled out this paper. It was wrapped up all neat and had tiny cartoon images on it. Curious, she had asked, "What is that?"

"Cartoon acid."

She laughed, thinking him funny, but she started to worry when she watched him take one of the little squares and place it under his tongue. He pushed his arm toward her, holding out the paper with the perfect little squares on it, each with a small cartoon character. Her eyes must have nearly popped out. She had good sense then. She shook her head and ran back to the school.

His favorite vice was his "wacky tabacky," as he called it. She watched, bemused, as he rolled it tight, sucking on the ends. He never offered her that. Then one day, a rather awful day, he did.

"What do you want that stuff for? It just kills your brain, and you can't afford for that to happen. I don't mean to be rude. It's just the truth. You smoke so much of that crap, you're perma-stupid." It was obvious no offense had been taken; he just held out his hand, offering it to her.

When she hadn't taken it, he challenged her. "Maybe you don't need to forget all the things I do, but I think you could use it. Besides, isn't it you who likes to say, 'Until you have walked a mile in someone else's shoes'? Well, walk a few steps. You've earned it."

She contemplated a moment. He really seemed to understand her. They had spent hours talking, especially about home life. Stan's life really sucked. She knew she had no right to complain when she heard his story, but he never criticised her for her minuscule complaining.

She had grabbed the joint then, hesitantly eyeing first the joint, then Stan. She took a hit and thought she would never breathe again. As the thick smoke filled her lungs, she gasped for air. It was crushing her chest. She couldn't get air. Surely she would die. Her eyeballs were starting to extrude. Then she saw Stan, stupid Stan in the corner, laughing at her. Who was really the stupid one? Two minutes later, when he passed it to her again, she took it with no hesitation, and this time she only coughed a little. *What a wonderful thing to be proud of,* she thought critically.

Amber focussed on Jake's face for a moment. It took all the control in his body to not stare back. She spoke, her voice quiet, barely cutting through the silence. "It should have been me. Just a few feet to the right, my skull would have been crushed instead of his. That's something that never leaves you."

Jake glanced at Amber and then quickly drew his attention back to the front of the car. He knew she detested pity, yet her head hung in hopelessness. He took a slow, deep breath, seriously considering an answer that was good enough. None were. He hoped she had more to say. He focused his eyes on the road and sent up a silent prayer, *Lord, I need your wisdom. I only want to say things that will encourage her. She needs your comfort. God, soften her heart to what you offer. She is reachable. You chose her. Help me help her. In your time, precious Lord.* Jake couldn't possibly have known he was further from reality than ever.

Moments passed, and Amber seemed to brighten. She wanted to smile at Jake, to see him smile back.

"You must have really upset someone to be put on duty with the likes of me."

He arched his brows. "Are you admitting to be like this on purpose?"

"Like what?" she retorted indignantly, still grinning. They looked at each other and laughed. He enjoyed her when she was like this. It seemed to Jake that this playfulness reflected who she really was. He was flirting with her, a criminal, though he had never thought of her as that. He wondered then at God's message to him. He knew that if he obeyed God, he would marry this woman. He smiled to himself.

"I like this arrangement. I act foolish. You make me laugh."

"Well, we all have our special jobs to do, Mr. Liddell. I am just doing my part." She kept up the charade of happiness all the way back to Klahanee. When they arrived, before getting out, Jake dared to reopen the topic they had touched on at the beginning of the drive.

"I am going to keep my word to you not to say anything to anyone about your visit from Darryl. I am sure Charlie will do the same. I want you to promise me that if he tries something like that again ..." He didn't finish. There was no need to.

"Thank you. I appreciate you doing this for me." Then Amber made a brave choice. "If you do this for me, keep your word, I promise ..." She shut her eyes for a moment, feeling the full weight of her words. "I will tell you the answers to any question you want."

He could tell she meant it. Amber would have no appreciation for empty words. Jake looked at her appreciatively; however, he would never understand how much that would cost her.

Charlie checked Amber in. Jake stood beside her, hoping he could think of something to say. He hated this part, dropping her off at the prison. It was easy to forget that she was on trial for murder when they were talking or driving. Back at this place, reality had a way of sinking in its teeth. A guard came and took her to her cell. She looked over her shoulder as she was being led away, taking one last glance at him. He smiled at her. She returned the smile. It was faint, but it was there. It was as though she were making sure he was all right. It should have been the other way around.

Jake walked out to the car. Charlie was right beside him. He knew his buddy had a lot on his mind. Jake should have felt like they had accomplished something. She had agreed to tell him the information he had pleaded for. He wondered if she would sign the confession. He felt hope again. "Charlie, you won't say anything will you, about Darryl, will you?"

"You're asking a little late, aren't you?" Charlie replied with a smile. His weathered face always had peace etched into every line. His eyes twinkled with joy. Jake hoped to grow to be half the man his mentor was, to have his wisdom, his godly knowledge, his ability to discern when to be quiet and when to talk, a trait Jake didn't believe he would ever possess.

"Yeah, but I trust her. She'll confess the name. That's all that's needed, right?"

As if reading his earlier thoughts, Charlie replied, "Well, it would be even better if she would put it in writing."

"I'm not asking her that. You ask."

"She likes you."

"You know the verbal abuse I put up with to get this far? You ask."

"She really likes you."

"Stop saying that. She likes you too."

"You better start learning how to deal with that girl, 'cause you're going to marry her."

Jake was puzzled. He didn't recall telling his friend that. How did he know?

Charlie laughed at the perplexed expression on his young companion's face. "God told me you needed some help."

Jake didn't know if he was serious or if he was testing him. Jake said nothing. Charlie smiled. He knew Jake well enough; he would do what was asked of him. The two men got into the cruiser and headed out.

Jake's thoughts reverted to Amber. He knew she was beginning to trust him. She was funny, and he liked that about her. She obviously thought he was funny, and that he really liked.

No one can pretend to laugh, he thought to himself. *That's just wrong.* He had witnessed God's sovereignty before. He knew in his head that God could make Amber into a bride. He had done it with the Israelites, though that was a constant work in progress. He had done it with Hosea when he was told to take a harlot for a wife. That didn't go over too well either. He wondered if God was putting something into his life that would be bigger than he could handle. He did not want to have a wife who was going to be unfaithful as the Israelites and the harlot. Still, the choice was his. He knew God would love him. He knew the forgiveness of Jesus would wash away his disobedience. He had to decide: Did *he* love enough to do what God asked of him?

Amber sat in her cell, preferring to stay there. She thought about Jake. She knew he would keep his word. She also knew he wouldn't leave it for long. Charlie had a standard to uphold. He might remain quiet for a time but not long. Amber was certain that within a few days' time he would be working to get to the bottom of what had happened. Jake would do anything he could in order to make sure the guard was caught and punished to the full extent of the law. Tyler would not go unpunished; Amber was glad of that. Jake would see to it that everything was done by the book.

Not her though; she no longer had the will. It was too hard. The road was getting harder, and it was only going to get worse. She was spent. If not for Linc, she would have given up a long time ago.

"What about Jake?" a faint whisper reminded. He knew she wasn't guilty. He would see her absolved of the crime she was charged with. That was enough.

Amber wondered if she would be a better person with a man like Jake at her side. *Any woman would be,* she answered her own question. Then Amber remembered the promise she had made him. She took out a pen and paper. There had been no stipulation that she had to answer his questions verbally. She would write down everything he needed to know to arrest Tyler. As she wrote, she felt the catharsis of her confession. She continued writing. Jake would do the right thing. No one would go unpunished. When she was done, she pondered where to put it to make sure someone would find it easily. Exhausted, she laid her head down on her bunk and started planning.

A Bitter Route

"Their mouths are full of cursing and bitterness, their feet are swift to shed blood. Ruin and misery mark their way. The way of peace they do not know. There is no fear of God before their eyes."

Romans 3:14–17

It was time to get up. Morning started early at Klahanee Women's Prison. Amber had been at the prison a little over two months. The six a.m. bell was starting to be less intrusive on her precious sleep.

Initially, she found it harder to sleep in the prison than it had been on the streets, where every sleep was drug-induced and easy to give in to. When she arrived at Klahanee, she was at the tail end of thwarting an addiction to one of her homemade narcotics. When one makes and sells it, it doesn't take long to end up with a habit. She clearly remembered Wyatt's words that day so long ago. She had scoffed then; only a short time later, she lived it. She had been trying to free herself before the arrest, but once inside there were no other options. The dependency ended quickly and, at times, painfully. Thinking back now, she knew there was no way she could ever return to that life. It was too painful. Yet when she thought about it logically, what choice would she have? What else could she do?

Powerful thoughts broke into Amber's reminiscence: her

mother's unexpected visit yesterday. The timing was perfect. It had been a long time since she'd had a decent visit with her. Yesterday was different.

Why hasn't she always been like that? she wondered. *It would have been a lot easier to talk to her about stuff.* She pondered that while coming to conclusions about the path of her life.

She thought about her family. She loved them so much. She hoped they would one day realize that her choices hadn't been about them. It wasn't all their fault. She may have accused them when she was angry or frustrated, but the truth was, she reacted to the situations she was dealt at a particular time. Sometimes that was by lashing out with angry words. When she ran, it was because she wanted to protect them, especially Linc, from the person she was becoming.

At some point she had to admit that she was responsible, at least in part, for her own choices. The fact was, her parents weren't entirely to blame; they bore the pain of her choices because they loved her. It had been their responsibility as parents to arm their child with the wisdom and spiritual strength needed to get safely through this life with a healthy fear and complete love of God, enabling her to cope with any situation.

Amber sat by herself at breakfast. She poked at the porridge in front of her. The orange juice was fresh, and she drank it, but the toast was soggy from too much butter. She didn't care; she had no appetite. She gently fingered the letter in her pocket—all her secrets so carefully written in detail on that piece of paper, the names of her attackers and what they had done to her, the doctor whose child she had been carrying, the name of another patient she had recalled who used to be treated by Dr. Forbes. She boldly wrote about her encounter with Darryl Tate.

She included her confession of what had gone on the night Duncan was killed. Her heart pounded at the feel of the paper in her pocket. It held so much knowledge, and in the right hands it could be very powerful and do a lot of damage to people who thought they were in secure places. Back at her cell Amber was restless. Her past crept into every crevice of her mind, bringing with it guilt and condemnation, the two reasons she had left home. Confronted with Lincoln's innocence all the time made her feel dirty and unworthy. He would try to kiss her, but she would turn her head, only letting him kiss her cheek, as memories of things that had touched her lips would spring into mind. He would want to pray with her, but she couldn't. Unable to cope, she would run away again. The last time she went to Cody's, she had talked him and his brothers into letting her stay there.

Wyatt didn't want her to have anything to do with the business after that first arrest. She tried wearing him down.

"Come on, Wyatt, I need to be able to earn my keep."

"Good." Wyatt had been firm. "Learn how to cook and keep this place clean. Chicks who sell are chicks who use. I decided you can tutor my brothers. That will keep your mind sharp since you don't plan on goin' back to school for yourself. They have to graduate, so you can earn your keep that way."

She was left no choice. Cody and Kyle worked diligently while Amber tutored them. They didn't goof around and act stupid, like adolescent boys often do. They did their work. One day she found out why.

The guys were taking a break from studying. Cody took the opportunity to get Amber's undivided attention. Kyle got jealous and told Wyatt the minute he came through the door. "Cody keeps buggin' Amber. She can't teach us nothing.'"

"That true?" He looked right at Amber. She had no idea what she was bringing down on Cody by admitting, "He's just goofing around a lit—" She didn't even get to finish her statement. Wyatt crossed the room and landed his fist straight into poor Cody's jaw. Amber gasped. She saw Kyle smirk out of the corner of her eye. That moment she decided she hated Kyle. As

Cody struggled to get himself up off the floor, Amber's heart grew compassionate for him.

That night after the boys went to bed, Amber went into Cody's room to apologize.

"I'm really sorry. If I had known your brother would react like that, I'da lied for ya." She sat on the edge of his bed, looking at his swollen jaw.

"It's not your fault. Kyle is just like that. He knows Wyatt takes the 'big brother' thing seriously." He rubbed his swollen jaw gently and then continued softly, "It's what has kept us out of foster care. Kyle freaks him out sometimes. It's not hard to do."

"You ever get even with him?" Amber smiled mischievously as she asked.

"No. It's already harder for Kyle."

"What's harder for him?" It seemed it would be harder for Cody.

"Well, he likes you … " He paused then playfully tugged at one of Amber's long curls. She still didn't get it. He smiled at her confused expression, then he cupped the back of her head, pulling her into him. "But I've got you," he said and then firmly pressed his mouth down on hers.

Amber hadn't realized how hungry she was for affection; she swam in that moment until she was drunk of it. Her heart pounded. She clutched Cody; she hadn't felt so safe in a long time. He pulled back, uncomfortable with her aggressiveness.

"Slow down," he gently reassured. "I'm not going anywhere." He looked at her. Amber melted, and she wanted him even more. She had never felt this before. He kissed her again, gently this time, before offering her his bed. She assumed he expected to join her, but then he left and slept on the couch.

At first glance Cody appeared plain. His hair was black and straight, and it hung loosely around his face. His eyes were almond shaped and deep black. He had tan skin and a soft, full mouth. She couldn't stop thinking about how he had kissed her.

He destroyed her theory that all men were scum. He had been gentlemanly and sweet.

Things at the house changed slightly after that. Cody and Amber spent what time they could together, talking, kissing, or doing nothing. They had to sneak around. Cody insisted it would be better that way. He would tell Wyatt, but not yet. Amber agreed. She had seen firsthand how Wyatt could be.

Their romance blossomed; they stayed up late after the other two went to bed. He would write her little notes while he was at school. She would leave him notes in his room. Amber would have dinner ready when the boys came home. Was this how love felt?

Wyatt bought an old Datsun pickup to get him to and from his legitimate job. Amber would give him a list of necessities, and he would get what they needed. They played house, and it was working.

In the evenings they sat around getting high in between drug runs in the Datsun. As far as Amber and Cody knew, their relationship was a secret. She was becoming concerned that Cody still hadn't told Wyatt. She was worried that the longer he put it off, the more likely he was to find out.

Six weeks into the relationship, her fear materialized. Wyatt drove to a drop-off. Cody was doing one as well. He walked, for it was close by. Kyle was supposed to go with Wyatt, but he made up an excuse about homework, which left Kyle alone with Amber. She felt uncomfortable, recalling her dislike for him and the reason behind it. They had all gotten high before the two boys left. Amber decided to avoid Kyle, but he insisted she help him study.

"I'm totally ripped, Kyle. I can't help you with anything,"

"Don't be like that, Amber. You would help Cody."

Shocked, Amber wondered if Kyle was implying something. She tried hard to think before answering. In her state, all she came up with was, "Why would you say that?"

Kyle walked up to her. He was too close, and it made her

uncomfortable. The expression on her face told Kyle he was on to something.

"Well, you would, wouldn't you? You would do anything … " He let the statement hang; she could fill in the blanks.

It was a shot in the dark, but Kyle couldn't resist an opportunity to start something. Shocked by Kyle's ardent remarks, Amber took a step back. Kyle stepped closer. His cavernous eyes revealed the darkness of his soul. He felt her weakness, and it empowered him. She backed up until she reached the wall. Kyle put his hand on the wall behind her. She looked into his deep black eyes, appealing to something that just wasn't there. Fear seeped into her heart.

He leaned closer. "Why do you look so afraid of me?"

"I'm not afraid of you," she lied. "I'm just wondering what it is you're doing and what Wyatt is going to say about it when he gets back."

"He won't say anything to me. He is going to be smacking that dumb brother of mine around for not telling him about the two of you, carrying on in my dead parents' house."

"What are you talking about? There hasn't been any 'carrying on' in your parents' house." She was telling the truth.

He let out a deep sigh and noticeably changed his demeanor. "I'm sorry, Amber. I guess I just got a little jealous." He sounded sincere. "I thought you and Cody had something going on, and I really like you. He knows that, and he would do anything to keep you from me." Kyle seemed done with his strange attempt at getting her attention. Amber let her guard down. She reached up and put her hand on Kyle's shoulder, gently trying to push her way out of the corner he had backed her into.

"Don't worry about it, Kyle. I won't say anything, okay?" She felt like she had narrowly escaped an encounter with Satan, but he wasn't finished with her.

Kyle was so calculated. He heard the footsteps coming up the path, and he knew who it was. He smiled at Amber. She moved to go around him, but he blocked her path and then forced her back using his hips and pressing her against the wall. He kissed her firmly, holding her locked in place. She was shocked, too shocked. That was when the door opened.

Cody's face filled with rage. He lunged at Kyle, knocking him onto the floor. He didn't attack him, he didn't yell, he just went straight to Amber and asked, "Are you okay?"

"I'm okay. I—" She wanted to explain, but he held his finger up to her lips and shook his head. Amber threw her arms around him and held on with all she had. He held her tightly.

Kyle was furious. "When Wyatt finds out about the two of you ... " he threatened. Cody didn't bother answering. He draped his arm over Amber's shoulder and guided her to the bedroom. He sat her down on the bed and sat beside her.

"Are you sure you're okay?"

"Yes," she tried to sound certain.

"I am going to wait for Wyatt. I can't let Kyle get his whole side of the story in first." He stood up and then kissed her on her forehead. She watched as he walked out. Her mind was racing. For a moment she had thought the rage on Cody's face was because of her. She had felt so afraid, not of his rage, but of losing him. She was quickly growing to love him. She was sure he loved her. Their relationship was so pure. They clung to each other for support, for friendship. They made each other laugh. They had fun together. That was how a high school romance should be. It got too complicated when sex was involved. That's how she knew how lucky she was; Cody wasn't like that. He didn't expect that from her.

Kyle waited by the door; he was determined to get his side of the story in first. Headlights were coming up the driveway. Cody remained calm as he sat on the couch.

Wyatt entered the house. He already looked enraged. Kyle was intimidated by his look, and when the moment came to speak he couldn't find his voice. Wyatt noticed the expectant look on his face and addressed it. "What? You got somethin' ta say? Spit it out!" He was gruff. Cody remained on the couch.

Kyle took a few steps back and then blurted, "Cody and Amber are sleepin' together in Mom and Dad's house!" There, he had said it.

Wyatt glared at Cody. "That true?"

"Nope," was his secure answer.

"You're lyin', you and that slut."

Cody's eyes narrowed. He would take that up with him on a separate meeting. He remained silent.

"What makes you think somethin's goin' on with those two?" Wyatt was accusing Kyle.

"Ask him where she is right now. She's in his bedroom, waiting for him."

"That true?"

Cody was still calm. "She's in my room, but she's there because Kyle terrified her half to death. When I walked through the door just ten minutes before you got home, he had her pinned and was forcing himself on her."

Wyatt was in a rage immediately. "That true? Is that true?!" The lack of an answer angered him further. Wyatt thrust his forearm against Kyle's chest and forcefully moved him backwards until he was the one pinned against the wall. "You better answer!"

Then Kyle did the unexpected. "No," he declared. The boys had a strict rule: No one lies. Cody's chin dropped. He was shocked. Wyatt noted the expression on Cody's face and knew whom to believe, but he took it further.

"She's in the bedroom?"

Cody nodded.

"Let's ask her." Wyatt marched to the bedroom, Kyle and Cody on his heels. Amber was trembling. She heard the yelling, and she didn't want to be part of anyone getting beat.

"Amber, be honest with me," Wyatt started. He spoke almost gently. "What is your relationship with Cody?"

She looked at Cody and then back at Wyatt.

"Look at me," he demanded gently. Then he repeated the question.

"We have been sort of seeing each other."

"Sort of?"

"We aren't having sex." She blushed and momentarily made eye contact with Cody. "But we do spend time together, we talk." She looked up before continuing, "We have kissed, but that's it."

Now Wyatt looked at Cody and then back at Amber. "Has my brother been a gentleman?"

She was shocked by the question, but she answered truthfully. "Always."

"What about Kyle?"

Amber looked at Wyatt. She pleaded with her eyes; she did not want to answer.

He got it, but he asked again anyway. "Amber, what about Kyle? Has he acted properly with you?"

"Until tonight." She answered so quietly, Wyatt took a moment to calculate her answer. The room was silent.

The moment between the answer and the reaction stretched out. Breaking the silence came the torrent lunge. Wyatt thrust Kyle onto the ground, jumping on top of him. He hit him once and then began choking him. Cody grabbed at Wyatt, pulling him off.

"Run, Kyle! Leave! Don't come back!"

Kyle got up and ran. Wyatt tried shaking Cody off him. Kyle was still dazed as he staggered to the door, waiting for his equilibrium to return.

"Bro, you have to check that melting point." Cody was concerned for Wyatt. "He's gonna end up with a concussion. How will you explain that to the school counselor? This is not good."

Wyatt knew Cody spoke the truth; his rage had been escalating. Maybe it was a side effect of the drugs. He had been ripped when he came home, and now he couldn't feel anything from the coke he had snorted. His hand was scraped and his knuckles were bloody, he couldn't feel them either. Maybe he did need help.

"So what about you two? There is no disrespecting our mom's house." He looked each of them in the eye. They nodded simultaneously. He went into his room and closed the door. Amber stared at Cody, unsure of what to say or do. Cody grabbed the extra blanket from the couch and guided Amber back into the bedroom. "I'll sleep on the floor beside you tonight."

Amber and Cody lay on the bed talking. She was also concerned about Wyatt. He was not how he used to be. He was getting worse. He was going to end up killing someone. She wondered if she should be afraid. Cody comforted and reassured her.

Cody slept peacefully on the floor. Amber was still awake when the bedroom door slowly squeaked open. A thin line of light shone in, and Amber closed her eyes. Terrified, she wasn't sure who it was, but she was relieved to have Cody between her and the person at the door.

The next morning, it was like nothing happened—for the boys at least. Kyle was back. Amber knew instinctively that it had been him who peered into the room last night. She hated him even more. She knew he sought ammunition to get revenge on her and Cody. Despicable snake, he deserved every wound that would fit on his big head. She could not understand how this family functioned. The three boys laughed and joked around as usual, like nothing had happened. Wyatt got ready for his job. Kyle and Cody got ready for school. Amber seemed to be the only one who felt uncomfortable. Cody noticed.

Everyone left and Amber went back to bed. It was getting crazy around the house. She missed Linc so much. She began to wonder if it would be better for everyone if she went home. Somehow she knew she was to blame for the chaos.

At noon Amber got up. She began weighing and getting the narc orders put together: three grams of cocaine mixed with three grams phen, two boxes of Sudafed tabs crushed then mixed, folded in small pieces of newspaper, and bagged.

Some of the regular people they sold drugs to made Amber sick. Wyatt took her to a house just a couple nights ago. A husband and wife sat at their dinner table smoking crack with their glass pipe; only ten feet away their babies, just one and two years old, were lying on the couch. It knotted her stomach; her comforting thought was that people like that would get their fix somewhere; it may as well be them. They did what they were supposed to do and walked away. Amber was sure Wyatt had picked that house to deter her from drugs, but he had been wrong; it just hardened her more. She swallowed it down just like she always did.

Amber waited anxiously for Cody to come home from school. He walked up to her and hugged her tightly; she hugged him back. They could openly show affection now that their relationship was approved by Wyatt.

"Cody, I need to talk to you."

He looked inquisitively at her and waited patiently. "I need to go back home. I'm causing tension around here. I'm sorry. I hope you understand."

"No," he said. She was puzzled, and she looked at him, waiting for more. He caressed her cheek gently. He was looking into her soul, then she realized he didn't understand. "We will still be together. We will see each other all the time. Whenever we can. Every night." She buried her face in his neck, wrapping her arms around him. He held her in return. When she looked up, he answered her unspoken wish—he kissed her. He kissed her as if they had already been apart. It was a passionate kiss, yet pure.

When Cody finally spoke, he relented. "If this is what you want, you should do it. We will see each other whenever we can."

"Thank you for understanding." She went on to explain to him about being arrested and being on probation. If they were going to have a future together, she needed to take care of that stuff. It wasn't fair to leave her parents wondering. They probably thought she was dead somewhere. She went home that night.

Catherine burst into tears the moment she saw Amber. She hugged her, and though Amber allowed it, she didn't return it. She was glad Lincoln was sleeping. She would surprise him in the morning. Michael stared at his daughter as if she were a stranger. He felt as though she had been unfaithful to him, unfaithful to all that he had invested in her, his love for her, and his stomach lurched at the thought of the things his precious daughter had probably defiled herself with.

Amber noticed her father's distance. "What's the matter, Daddy? Aren't you happy to see me?"

"Of course I'm happy to see you. What kind of a question is that?"

"Don't start with her, Michael," Catherine scolded.

"Are you hungry?" he asked, changing the subject.

"I'm fine, Daddy. I am going to bed. I am very tired."

Catherine tried to hide her disappointment but agreed sweetly. "Lincoln will be excited to see you." She tried to remain positive.

"Good night," Amber said in return.

Amber got up early and made a pancake breakfast. That didn't go well; there was no syrup. Lincoln was excited to see his big sister, but it was obvious something had changed.

"Aren't you excited to see me?" she asked.

"Yeah," he replied casually.

"You don't look it," she accused.

"Last time you came back, I got excited, but then you ran away again and everyone has been sad since." His words hurt. Guilt clutched her heart. She was quickly reminded of why she had left last time.

Amber wanted to scream. She contemplated running again but decided against it. She was stronger now. Funny, the streets couldn't destroy her, but in twenty minutes a six-year-old had her wanting to run.

She needed a plan of survival. When she came up with one, she went downstairs and announced it. She would finish her grade twelve by correspondence and graduate. They didn't see that one coming. She congratulated herself.

Catherine was quick to be encouraging. "That's wonderful. We can order the material on the Internet. My friend Anna, you remember Anna, don't you, Amber? Well, she just started taking her GED through this school and it's going very well."

"I don't need a GED. I need to graduate. I want to take real grade twelve courses by correspondence. But good for Anna. I hope she does well." Amber's sarcasm was evident.

Amber began seeking information. Correspondence, Amber found, would cost her two hundred eighty dollars and some change. Was there any chance her parents would help her out? Probably not. She would try that night at dinner anyway.

She was turned down gently.

"Amber, maybe once you have had some stability for a little while. We would love to help you out, but right now there are more important things for you to do."

"What could be more important than my education?"

Then came the truth.

"Well, you haven't been that reliable lately. You need to earn the privilege of our trust again. You can't just walk in here after being gone for six weeks and expect—"

"Expect what? My parents to help me out?"

"You don't want our help, you want handouts."

Amber was furious. "Pay for my schooling with the money you saved by not supporting me the last couple months."

Their expressions spoke their thoughts. Amber huffed off to her room without finishing dinner. She comforted herself that at least she hadn't run.

The next day Amber took the bus downtown. There was a high school that was for alternate learning. It ran on semesters. She hoped they would let her take second semester and then she could graduate. She made an appointment with the principal.

The principal, a dishevelled woman, approached Amber. She had dark circles under her eyes and a deep creased brow. She reminded Amber of a rubber band stretched beyond its limits.

"Please sit down." She gestured. "What can our school do for you?"

Amber was intrigued. "Accept me as a student."

"Do you have a referral from a counselor or the principal of your last school?"

"No." Amber wondered what angle to work the woman. She decided on persistence.

As it turned out, she didn't need to persist. Principal Carry Shaw informed Amber that she would need to request the transcripts from her previous school. If all went well, she would start second semester in January. It had been too easy.

Two days after her visit to the school, Ms. Shaw called and left a message. Amber was welcome to register at her school, but based on her file she would need proof that she was continuing with her psychiatry appointments, which would include a signed letter from the psychiatrist. Amber hardened herself. She was much stronger now, she told herself. That man could never get to her again. She would make him feel vulnerable. By the time she had made up her mind, she relished the idea of going back to see him. She announced this to her parents. They were both shocked and pleased by her initiative and her decision.

Amber excitedly told Cody. He was relieved she wouldn't be stuck in this way of life, just like they would have options too. Selling drugs was just to get them through this time in their lives, see them through to better days.

Thursday afternoon arrived. Amber would have her first visit to see Dr. Forbes tomorrow. Her stomach turned. She contemplated backing out. She needed Cody, her strength, her love. He would encourage her. She met with him after school. They walked along the old familiar trails.

"What's up?" He noticed her mood right away.

"I'm just nervous, that's all."

Cody didn't know about the things that had happened with the doctor. The words wouldn't come out. She felt so ashamed. He would probably never kiss her again if he knew. She decided that if she told him what the doctor had done to her, she would have to tell what she had willingly done to him in the car, and there was no one she could blame for that, so she would rather pretend none of it had ever happened.

"I am impressed you're going through with this. Kyle said you would back out."

That settled it for her; she was going.

"Are you going to be okay?" He was concerned.

She smiled assuredly. "Yes, thanks to you."

He bent over to kiss her. She let him kiss her the first time, but when he moved in closer to kiss her more fully, she laughed and pulled away from him. She ran into the wooded area surrounding the well-used trail. He followed her curiously. She giggled as she freely ran through the forest. She got far ahead of him. He couldn't hear her footsteps for a moment. He thought she must have eluded him. Then he heard her purposeful laugh; it was meant to guide him to her. As soon as he got close, she would run again. Being the nature of man, he quickly gained on her. He was close to catching her. His heart was pounding, and it drowned out the sound of Amber's feet making their trail through the autumn leaves. She zigzagged through the trees, crouching to miss branches, cutting sharp around the huge trunks. Cody was getting close enough that she could hear him breathing. Her heart quickened; she was going to scream from the sheer exhilaration.

Just before he could grab her, she turned around, eyes ablaze with passion, passion for him, for his love. She would return that feeling to him. She clutched his shirt in her grasp; she kissed him, barely able to catch her breath. He kissed her in return; they clung to one another. They made love in the woods, amongst the trees. Amber believed she would love this man forever. He believed the same.

Friday arrived. Amber continued to swim in the delirium of passion that she and Cody had shared. It would get her through the horrible event she was about to undergo. He would be on her mind, strengthening her. She underestimated the anxiety; it was strong, overshadowing, and drowning out the good feelings. She walked into the office, forcing confidence she didn't feel, a palpable disguise. Gordon knew his patient too well.

If she appeared confident, she was probably high. He gladly accepted her into his office.

"Welcome back, Amber. What brings you here?" he said with a kind grin. It was his depraved way; everything had double meaning.

"I am registered to go back to school, and so I have to be here to graduate." She was honest.

"Let's see how quickly you can get a pass out of my class this time."

"No." She was proud of how emphatic she sounded; there was no mistaking that answer.

"Have a seat, Amber. Don't be so tense." He was all business. He continued the session that way. Amber couldn't believe how easy it had been. She had said no many times before to no avail. Not as confidently, she reasoned. Amber would once again prove to still be naive. She found that out at her next appointment.

Amber sat in the patient chair. She poured herself a glass of water while waiting for Dr. Forbes. The last appointment had been so casual, she hadn't given this one a second thought. He entered shortly and again began the session in a professional manner. Shortly, she began to feel groggy. She wasn't high, but she felt it.

"I feel strange," she confessed.

"It's probably your body purging itself of excessive drug use over the past year, Amber. Do you recall the last time we saw each other? You were using hard drugs on a regular basis."

"I don't think that's it." She wanted to explain, but it was so hard to think.

"And then there was the time in my car, do you remember that?"

Amber looked up. Had he really said that, or was her mind tricking her? His grin was disdainful. Speaking softly, he reiterated the encounter in detail. Amber felt sick, and she knew without a doubt that he had done this to her with purpose. What was he going to do to her? She was going to be sick.

"No," she whispered. How had she gotten herself into this mess again? She had thought she was in control.

Amber regained her senses. She was in the back of a police car. They were parked in the front of her house. Her head was spinning. The officers in the front seat were Matthew, whom she recognized as the one who had arrested her in the warehouse with his partner, and Jake. She looked in the rear-view mirror. Matthew's lips were moving, his eyes were closed. What was he doing? Was he praying? Here? And Jake? Was he praying? Why? Jake opened his eyes and nudged Matthew. Jake smiled. She knew then it was for her they prayed.

Matthew got out of the patrol car and helped her out. He led her to the front door, knocked, and handed her into the custody of her mother. Catherine had received a call from Dr. Forbes stating that Amber showed up to today's meeting on drugs. He would reschedule her appointment for Wednesday. He was having her escorted home by an officer.

When Amber woke up, it was near eleven Saturday morning. Her memory was fuzzy as she tried to remember what had happened the previous day. It was vague, like it had been a dream. She was uncertain of reality. She rolled over in her bed. She ached in all her private places; it made the dream that much more realistic. She tried to remember.

Amber went into the shower. She scrubbed herself with soap until her flesh was red, trying to cleanse the inside from the outside. That is when she noticed the bruising on her inner thighs. Now she knew for certain that the doctor had, as she thought, raped her while she was drugged. He had somehow gotten her that way. That was the proof she wanted. She should go to the police with this and have him committed.

That was exactly what she intended to do. Then she heard it again. That inner voice. The one that always showed up to destroy her, to tear her down. "Who will believe you? Not even your own parents. You could have stopped this. This is what you deserve for the way you have chosen to live your life."

She could not deny the voice, so she submitted to it. Amber remembered something else in the wake of her realization. Only the day before she had made love with Cody. Oh, Cody, what would she tell him? He didn't deserve this. She couldn't tell him; she would deal with this on her own. She needed a plan.

At her next appointment the doctor remained professional. Amber couldn't execute her plan. Her next appointment was the same. He made his innuendos and comments, nothing else. The following appointment was on a Friday. Somehow, in the pit of her stomach, Amber knew this was the day. She fought the waves of nausea in her stomach. She refused the urge to get high. That was what he would hope for. The trick would be to fool him into thinking she was.

She tried to mentally prepare herself, but Cody kept interfering with her thoughts. She felt guilty. She pushed him out of her mind. It was time to make the devil pay.

"I am going to my appointment now," she called into the air.

Catherine hurried around the corner. "Amber, should I pick you up?"

"No, I'll catch the bus." She was not rude, just matter-of-fact.

"But when you go there ... " Was her mother finally showing some concern for the appointments? Maybe she should tell her again, tell her what really went on. She looked expectantly at her mother, waiting for her to find the courage to finish her derogatory sentence. She just stared pleadingly at her daughter.

"I won't come home in a squad car this time. Is that what you need to hear? I was okay last time and the time before that." Hope dissipated. She was stuck facing the doctor on her own. Her mother would never get it; she would never take her side. If only she knew how that alone destroyed her. It didn't matter that she may deserve a bit of that mistrust. Parents are supposed to keep on trusting, keep on forgiving; they aren't supposed to give up on their children.

Amber was prepared for the degenerate. She entered the waiting area, let the receptionist know she was there, and then took her seat. Gordon Forbes opened his office door. A woman Amber's mother's age came out smiling. She shook the doctor's hand and paid lip service to his wonderful treatment. It was enough to make her sick. Amber noted the grin on his receptionist's face also. Was it possible she had no idea what went on behind those doors? As soon as Gordon spotted Amber, he looked to the receptionist. "Give me a minute before sending in the next one, please, Ellie."

Ellie nodded and then smiled over to Amber. "He'll just be a moment." It took all of Amber's self-control not to mock her.

Palms sweaty, Amber rubbed her eyes one more time. She thought herself clever. She had a small piece of soap in her pocket. She rubbed her hands on it and then touched it to her eyes. That would make them bloodshot. She popped some ephedrine while still at home; that would make her pulse and her pupils irregular without altering her mind. Hopefully the doctor would think she was high. If he thought she was messed up, he was certain to try something, and then she would nail him.

The intercom buzzed.

"You can go in now." Ellie's voice cut into Amber's vengeful thoughts. She shuffled her feet as she walked, lowering her head, avoiding eye contact. She walked directly to the chair in front of the desk and sat down, head still bowed. She began fidgeting.

The doctor took the bait. He reached for Amber's chin, tilting her head up. One look at those bloodshot rims and he was fired up. She could practically see the evil forming. He began talking. Amber smiled complacently, saying nothing. He groped her. Hatred burned in Amber's heart; it was only for a moment. He would find out today why he shouldn't have messed with her. Gordon continued to bring up Amber's past, her troubles, problems she must be dealing with, all the while getting closer and closer to Amber's trap. He removed her shirt and just kept on talking, then pausing, giving Amber time to answer. He pulled her up by her arm and removed her pants. Amber felt really sick. She wasn't sure she could go through with it. It would be too humiliating. She had not thought about that. She hadn't really been present the last time.

Be strong, she kept telling herself. *No one will ever have to endure this pig again. Just be strong. You can do this.*

The doctor kept talking casually. He pushed Amber gently onto his patient couch; he undid his pants; he was ready to get on top of her.

How much longer should I wait?

When she felt his skin touch her bare flesh, she couldn't take it any longer. She couldn't do it. Amber let out the most bloodcurdling scream she could. She dredged it up from her soul. It held the pain of every encounter with this pervert; it had power. The people in the next building should have come running. She screamed until her throat burned. In between her screams she uttered her threats, how he would not get away with this. She cursed him. Swore at him and then screamed louder. She contemplated gouging out his eyes, but that might give him cause to say she was delusional.

No one came. No one even tried to open the door. No voice asked, "Are you all right?" Nothing. He was right; no one would care about her.

"*No, no.*" She refused to believe that. "*Someone has to care about what happens to me.*" Dr. Forbes was growing tired of her charade, and his ears were beginning to hurt.

"Are you done?" His eyes shone the evil she knew his heart contained. He squeezed her breast so hard it brought tears to her eyes. Why was it she suddenly felt afraid again? He had stolen all her valour. Amber looked down, defeated before she began. Her eyes caught a glimpse of something. He held a condom between his fingers. Where had he gotten it?

Think hard, she commanded herself.

"I am finished." She answered his question with all the hatred she could amass. She had a new plan. This one would take more evil than she possessed, but she would find it, she would dig deep into her vault of bitterness, and she would unleash it on him.

"Good. Then let's finish up."

Amber was true to her word. She made it home without the escort of a police officer. She ran straight upstairs. Once again, she counted on the shower to purge her of her guilt and feelings of dirtiness. It seemed to leave her less and less clean. She fought tears, and she forced herself to plan perfectly what she had to do. There would be no room for error. She promised herself she would be the last to suffer. Her deed would save many young women from what she had endured. Maybe others in her predicament would get real help and not end up on an eternal path of destruction. Finally, maybe someone would believe her.

Cody would find out about it eventually; she would need to tell him. Amber convinced herself that he would understand. She had an appointment with the doctor for the following Friday. She would see Cody tonight; she needed to replenish her stash. By now the boys probably had some mixing for her to do as well.

"I have to go out for a while. I will be home before Linc goes to bed, so I can tuck him in. I'll see you later," Amber called as she headed out the door, not awaiting a reply. She headed to Cody's.

Catherine watched helplessly as her daughter walked toward the bus stop.

Will she return? she wondered. She hoped. She turned the worry into a prayer and begged, "Please, Lord, please bring her back." She couldn't help but think, *How long this time?* She put her head in her hands and sobbed. What was it that kept pulling her away? Whatever it was she was running from must have caught up with her once again. She needed to pray for her daughter, pray without ceasing. She would pray and fast from now until Amber returned. She would beseech God in a new way; he would hear her. Her prayer would be answered. Her daughter would return, she was sure of it.

It had been a week since Amber last saw Cody. She hadn't realized how much she missed him until she saw him. They hugged and kissed like two people who had been separated for years.

Amber quickly got into her chemistry, cutting all the right ingredients together, the right amounts and the right selection. Her task complete, she collected some money from Wyatt and then Cody led her into the bedroom.

"Can we go for a walk or something? Get out of this house?" Amber asked.

"I need to do a quick run with Wyatt, then we can go for a walk." Cody replied.

"Can I come with?"

"Sure, we should all fit comfortably for a short ride."

Cody offered her a "treat" before leaving. She surprised herself by turning it down. When Cody rolled the white concoction into a joint, Amber looked at him; she knew her disappointment showed. He shoved it into a plastic bag. He would have it later and spend this time with his love. That was obviously what she wanted, and he was cordial.

The drop was ten minutes away, the perfect distance for a walk back. Cody ran into the shoddy apartment building and returned shortly. Wyatt dropped them off with his blessing and warned against them "messin'" around. "No one better come home pregnant," which made them both laugh, knowing that would never happen.

They walked along holding hands, each waiting for the other to start talking. They turned and walked partway down an alley. There were no streetlights close; it was pitch black. Amber was relieved to hide behind the dark. She took Cody's other hand in hers, facing him, searching for the words, where to begin.

The lust of a teenager's heart is strong and desires release; he misunderstood her gesture. Cody had something else on his mind for the moment. It was awkward and uncomfortable, but Amber relinquished to his momentary passion. It was weird for a moment after that. They began walking again. The closer they were to home, the more anxious Amber felt. She had to tell him. She had to say something. Finally, she just blurted it out. "I think the doctor drugged me and raped me."

"What? What doctor?"

"The one I've been seeing—"

"What do you mean, 'you think'? That's a strong accusation, Amber. You need to know."

"I do know. I just can't prove it."

"Do you want to talk about it?" Cody led Amber down a sidestreet with no exit. He began to feel guilty, recalling how he had taken his pleasures. She was willing. She should have said something. He didn't know how to feel or what to say. He remembered in tenth grade, a young girl had started a rumor about Kyle. She accused him of date rape. It was never proven. It had only been after the incident with Amber a couple weeks ago that Cody had given more thought to those allegations.

At the end of the alley there was a narrow walking path dimly lit by neighboring houses. To the side stood a quaint wooden bench with wrought-iron legs cemented to the earth. To the right of the path was a circular flower garden; the buds would be vibrant shortly. They sat there for a moment, Cody trying to see through the night into the depths of Amber's eyes, Amber trying to avoid his.

She cut into the silence in a thin voice marked with pain. "It began the first time I had to see him. I told my parents. They didn't believe me. No one believed me. He started with small things. Then last week, he drugged me and raped me."

"I'll have him killed. You know I can. Why didn't you say something? We just—"

"Stop!"

"I'll take care of it. I see him Friday. It will end then."

It occurred to Cody that Amber wasn't sad; she was furious. She had already hardened herself to the reoccurrence of it. He would not let it happen again. He would kill him himself.

"He won't touch you again. I can have it arranged, Amber, you know I can." Even as she declined his offer again, he started thinking of a plan.

"He's a prominent doctor. The law would track both of us down, and then we'd be in jail. What good can come of that? The only reason I am seeing him is for us, for our future."

"This is not worth it, Amber. Forget about it. Come back. Live with me again. Skip school. How can you even contemplate this?"

"It's not just school. I will go to jail. Will you wait around? And after I get out, then what?"

"I'll take care of you." He reached up and gently pushed her hair back. "Just don't do it. It's not worth it." He wondered if she was rational. Did she know how insane she sounded?

It wasn't worth it to him because he didn't have anything taken from him. He didn't understand. She needed revenge. She had to do it. Maliciously, she revealed the plan.

"I know how I will get him, Cody. I will bring him to his knees. He will beg me before I am done ... " She paused, waiting for his reaction. He waited apprehensively, pain growing in his stomach.

"The only way to beat him is to prove what he's doing, right?"

Cody felt nauseated. This was going somewhere he didn't like, he could feel it.

"I am going to conceive his child."

"How?" Cody asked naively.

"It's the only way," Amber insisted before Cody fully grasped what she was saying.

"No way." He was vehement. Amber had never seen his eyes so hard. "Listen to yourself, Amber. What are you asking me? You want my permission to have sex with another man and get pregnant with his child? You couldn't have possibly thought I would think that was okay."

"I've thought about it, Cody. I've seen other young girls come out of there before. Younger than me, crying. I saw one girl come out with her blouse undone. I think his secretary knows. I tried to fight him at my last appointment. I screamed and screamed. No one knocked on the door to see what was happening, no one came in, and on my way out I wasn't even questioned. Whoever gets sent to this guy is like human waste. Nobody cares about what happens to you. He has to be stopped. Cody, with you, I'm strong enough to do it."

"I forbid it."

Amber was caught off guard. He sounded so much like Wyatt. He spit the words out as if they were vile in his mouth.

She had thought it would be so easy to make Cody understand. She was reasoning and losing. He wasn't giving in.

"I told my parents, they didn't believe me. He drugged me last time. What am I supposed to do? As long as I keep seeing him, he is going to take sex from me, that's just the way it is. He has to be stopped. The only thing I need is your support and your love to get me through this." Then, as if actually pondering the idea, Cody sadly asked, "And what if you do conceive this hate child, 'cause that is what it will be, Amber. Then what?"

"Once I prove it's his child, that's it, he's done. The judges are going to look so stupid. He'll be locked up. Throw away the key." Cody was sickened by the evil gleam in Amber's eyes as she savored the idea. How could she be so foolish? It was still going to be her who got hurt.

"You still didn't answer my question. What about the baby?"

"I did answer. It will prove I was right. It will—"

"What are you going to do with your child? The child that you will have from your vengeful encounter? You will have started a life, Amber. Think about that. It's not going to go away when the doctor does." He was losing his patience.

Amber sat in perplexed silence; she hadn't even thought of that. "I don't know, raise it I guess."

"Amber, I have grown up without parents. You don't just 'guess' you're going to raise a child. It takes a lot, and I don't want…no, I won't raise some other man's child, especially a child that's the result of something as evil as what you're planning."

Amber was indignant. Had he accused her of being the evil one? She opened her mouth to address his calloused remarks, but he wasn't finished taking her down.

"You have parents. You totally take them for granted. You are nothing but spoiled. I am having a hard time even believing you could be serious about this. I thought you were much better than this. My mind is made up. No way will I support you or love you through this." There it was, the words that drew blood. Her heart pounded in her ears. She refused to believe this.

"So I should just continue letting him rape me and anyone else he chooses? That's how you suggest I deal with this?"

"No, Amber, use some backbone. Fight him. That's the person I thought you were. A fighter. Tell someone. If they won't listen, tell someone else."

"And in between all this telling, what's happening to me?"

"There is one other way to take care of him. Just tell me his name and where his office is."

"No, I won't let you do that for me. I won't put you at risk."

"Oh, but I would put you at risk by letting you carry out this crazy scheme?"

"I didn't say that. And if I'm crazy it is because of that doctor."

"The only thing more evil than that doctor is this idea." The conversation wasn't going anywhere. Amber was getting more upset. Cody was becoming more determined. She had been the stupid one. She thought this would be easy. He just didn't understand; if she could just get him to understand.

"Fine," she finally agreed, but they both knew she didn't mean it. Cody got up and walked away; he didn't say another word. Amber hopped on the next bus. As she had promised, she was home in time to tuck in her brother. It was eight o'clock when she walked through the door.

"'Night, Mom," she said casually.

Catherine wanted to weep with joy.

Amber had her appointment as scheduled. She carried out her plan. She only had one shot; unknown to her at the time, it was successful. Cody refused to have anything to do with her after that night. She knew it was because he was hurt, but so was she. That hurt the most. He had been her tourniquet. When she thought she would bleed to death, he saved her. She hadn't thought it would be temporal. They were supposed to heal each other, but she had lost. Festering wounds unbound, and once again she was left to bleed, alone.

After the encounter with the doctor, she ended up back on the streets. She ran into Kyle one night. He told her Wyatt was in jail for nearly beating a man to death. Charges were laid, jail time was pending. Kyle had no compunction about a girl selling drugs. He hooked her up. Between that week and the next three months until her arrest for Duncan's murder, Amber had a full-on guilt-induced habit. She thought that was the reason her periods had stopped.

Amber wondered if Cody knew what had happened to her. She wondered if he would feel any guilt or, at the least, empathy for her. Maybe he would come visit her if he knew. She had definitely travelled a long, hard road, and there was no hope at the end. She had demolished everything good that came into her path. Now, no good came to her. She lay on her prison cot. It didn't make her angry like her other memories. When she remembered Cody, it was always with a deep sadness and the knowledge of something worthy lost. She had earned this end. Depression was a dark and lonely beast, and right now it hovered over her where angels once had been.

Forbidden

"You are slaves to the one you obey. Whether you are slaves to sin which leads to death, or to obedience which leads to righteousness."

Romans 6:16

L auryn entered the cell. It was the first time she had been alone with Amber since the attacks. She truly felt bad for the girl; she hoped she understood. It was nothing personal, but really, what could she have done?

"How are you?" she asked genuinely.

Amber, never one to play games, just came right out with it. "Look, Lauryn, if you're worried about … well, I don't blame you. There isn't anything you could have done."

"Ya know, the next night, while you were in the infirmary, that loser Tyler had the nerve to come out here again and threaten all of us. I've been in this jail nearly two years. I have seen a lot of scary things, but I have never seen such a vengeful act as what Tyler did to you. So I started thinking, what did you do? How'd you get him in such a rage?"

"I don't know. I wish I knew. I can't be the only person who ever fought back."

"I don't know, girl, but you need to watch your back."

"Why? Lauryn, do you know something? Tell me, tell me if you know something," she insisted.

"I don't know anything more than what I saw here last week, but you need to find out his beef with you before—"

"Before what? What do you know?" Amber tried to squelch the fear that scoured her sanity, refusing its dominance.

"All I'm sayin' is, watch your back. You need to be more aware. Ya know these crooked professionals go all the way to the top. You can pay off a judge if you know the right one."

"Yeah, I think that's the one working my case."

"Something isn't right about this. You shouldn't even be here."

"I'm here because Duncan was a cop's kid. No leniency for me."

"Even that story is messed up. His autopsy should prove he was high. Isn't that good for you?"

"Guess not." Amber was tired of talking about it; she already knew her luck was bad. People just seemed to hate her.

"Open your eyes, girl, or you're gonna be dead before your trial's even over."

A chill ran down Amber's spine. It wasn't doing her any good to hear this; she was powerless to change anything. Why were they discussing *her* life? Recalling Lauryn's words, she recalled feeling the same way. Tyler must have something personal against her. Maybe he fit in with Duncan and Stan somehow. That family would blame her for two deaths. She wished she had thought of that sooner and put it in her letter for Jake.

She took a deep, shaky breath at the memory of that letter and its intensive purposes. That family hated her. They wanted her dead. Blood for blood. Her body went cold. Druggies died every day. Common people hardly ever paid attention.

It was near lights-out time. Amber lay on her cot, thinking, fearing, hopeless. Her fate was sealed. Since that night with Adam, death had been nipping at her heels. It was finally closing in. Sleep was evasive.

Adding to Amber's anxiety was the terror of anticipation. When would Tyler be working nights again? Would he try to kill her? Would he terrorize her again? She was defenseless either way. All she could do was wait. Lauryn was right; she had to pay attention to every detail of things going on around her. If Tyler wanted her, there would be nothing she could do to stop him.

She decided then she would sooner die by her own hand than ever be under his savage brutality again, giving him the satisfaction of knowing he had beaten her, that he could violate her whenever he felt like it with no remorse, no worries of getting caught, or ever having to pay for the evil he inflicted. No, she would make sure she was in charge; she would win. By early morning, out of thoughts, with no ideas, she resigned herself. Somehow she had known it would come to this. And that plan she already had.

The days and nights monotonously ran together. Every day Amber lived terrified of the next time Tyler would come walking down her aisle. The lack of sleep she incurred over the next few days had her near delirium, and that night she heard him. As she lay awake in her cell, there was no mistaking the arrogant walk, the annoyance of an agitated guard thumping his billy club on every bar of every cell, as if to remind every woman in the joint they were indeed behind bars, and he, the true criminal, was free. She hoped for him a fate of hell more excruciating than her mind could fathom.

He walked up to the cell and put his face close to the bars and smiled at her. Though her better senses warned her not to look at his face, she had to. She couldn't let him think she was cowardice by not meeting his stare. He tapped his club continuously on the bar—*clang, clang*—and stared. Amber knew he was hoping she would open her mouth and give him an excuse to use the club on her. She smiled back at him, biting her tongue until she could taste the blood. He was getting impatient; she kept smiling, thinking every malevolent thought she could, wishing and hoping every evil on him that she knew, using every foul word she knew.

Finally, he broke the silence. "Keep smiling, whore. I can't make you scream tonight. My new partner wouldn't understand our relationship."

Amber envisioned herself leaping up, grabbing his face through the bars, and gouging out his eyes, tearing his flesh from his face with her nails. Yes, that thought made smiling easier; she just kept smiling.

Tyler kept digging, hoping for the comment that would send her over the edge. When he mentioned her baby and how it had been ripped out of her body, she blinked hard a few times. She hoped he hadn't noticed that his words had struck. He hoped for anger. One could always count on anger to cause someone to do something stupid.

She responded to his comment in a quiet, deep voice, quoting Proverb 29:11, "A fool gives full vent to his anger, but a wise man keeps himself under control."

Now he was the one who was fury ready. She had the shallow peace of knowing she was safe tonight. Jared, sweet Jared was on, and he wasn't going to let Tyler out of his sight for a moment. With Jared only a few cells over, Tyler risked pushing his face into the bars, contorting his expression to seethe a retort. "You may be safe tonight, but I hardly think you'll have such a righteous attitude tomorrow."

Amber kept the pasted half smile on her face, refusing him any satisfaction. Jared walked over. As the two guards walked away, Jared gave Amber a concerned look. She turned her face. He was a nice man with good intentions, but she doubted the baby-faced man could handle much.

Let him save someone else, she conceded.

Jake walked into his apartment; it was early, and he was already very tired. He sat on his couch and put his feet up. He was too tired to cook anything. He had too much on his mind. He relaxed and leaned his head back. Deep green eyes and long blonde hair occupied his thoughts. With his eyes closed he could hear her laughing at his jokes. He could stare at her this way. He focussed on her face. A smile crossed his mouth.

He sighed heavily and got up to start his dinner. Usually he grabbed a bite on the run, but he actually had an evening off. He began sautéing some vegetables; he would make a beef stir-fry. He poured a tall glass of milk; before he could take a sip, the phone rang. It was Jena. He didn't remember giving her his home number. She made small talk. Growing impatient from hunger, Jake blurted out, "Do you want something in particular?"

"Oh! Am I bothering you?" She sounded hurt.

"Not bothering. I just haven't had dinner yet, and I'm starving." He was apologetic.

"I'll cook you dinner. I'll be right over. What is your buzzer number?"

The last thing he wanted was company. "You don't have to come cook for me. I have been on my own for a while now. Besides, my food is just about done."

"Great, I'll be right over. I haven't had dinner either." He looked at the meager portion in the skillet; he only had enough for one. He was hungry, and he didn't want to share. Again, he commented, "Tonight's not a good night. I work tomorrow. I have to be up early."

She was silent. Had he deterred her? She remained silent. "Hello?"

"I'm still here."

"All right. I'll see you at work?" Jake was relieved he had gotten out of it.

Twenty minutes later his intercom buzzed. He knew who it was.

"Hello?"

"Can I come up?"

Jake buzzed her up then went back to his dishes.

"Hello."

He didn't say anything, but he arched his brow and smiled.

"I know you didn't want me over tonight. I promise I won't stay long. It's just, my ex keeps phoning me." She was still talking. Jake wasn't paying attention. Girls were like that. Always having some problem, some drama in their lives that ended up requiring some man's assistance. Five minutes later they were furious about some sexist remark someone made that women needed men.

"Jake?"

"Pardon?"

She smiled. He hadn't been paying attention. She went into the bag she had brought over and said, "I'll pick." She opened a few of the cupboards, found the corkscrew, and opened the bottle. She poured a glass of red wine for each of them. "Anyway, I thought if I hung out with you for a while, it would keep my mind off him."

Jake looked at Jena for the first time since she had arrived. She was dressed nicely, not as provocatively as last time. He relaxed, sitting back on his couch, sipping his wine slowly. They talked a bit, casually. Jena got up and turned on Jake's old stereo. He had the Christian station tuned in. She tuned it to one that played soothing music. She began to dance. Jake opened his eyes wide. He looked into his glass. It was nearly empty. Jena noticed. She danced her way into the kitchen and grabbed the bottle off the counter. She topped off both their glasses.

"Oh, no more for me," Jake protested. The glass was already full. He would finish it and then no more. He watched Jena as she moved smoothly to the music, swaying her hips, a sultry smile aimed at him. Had he been wiser, he would have known cats play before they pounce.

Jena walked over to the couch and tugged playfully at Jake.

"Dance with me." He was quite happy to watch her. His head was getting fuzzy; his second drink was gone. Jake shook his head.

"Come on. One dance and I'll leave you to your boring, lonely self."

Jake smiled, liking the attention. Her persistence fed his ego. She bugged him a couple more times to dance, but he still refused. She finally sat back down. She sat very close to him. He was talking about a patient. She wasn't paying attention to his words, despite the fact that she was looking right at him.

Jake got up from the couch and put his glass in the kitchen. When he turned around, Jena was right behind him, glass in hand. She poured herself another. Jake feared the woman would become intoxicated and never leave; he tried to remove the glass from her hand. She let him have it. She came on to him strong. He was shocked.

"What are you doing?"

She smiled seductively, toying with the buttons on her blouse. His eyes widened. He knew what she offered. Jena kissed him. He brought his hands up and caressed her bare shoulders. A gentle moan escaped her throat. His passions were running high. He kissed her more possessively. He kissed the pulse on her throat. It beat rapidly—evidence of her desire for him. Jena began to remove her blouse. Jake stepped backed, gazing at her soft curves. He looked at her, and he suddenly became very aware of what he was about to do.

"You have to leave," he rasped.

She looked confused.

"Now." He blamed her for the moment. She came there with every intent of seducing him. The gentle voice that still had power reminded him, "You knew that while you were talking on the phone."

Jena was putting her shirt on. Jake looked away.

"What is wrong with you?" Jena was mad.

"Just go." He was angrier.

"It's not her fault," the voice gently cautioned. He hung his head. In Jena's world there was nothing wrong with what she wanted to do. He had been the weak one. He had allowed it to get that far.

"I'm sorry." It hurt his pride to say that. He wasn't ready to accept any blame. Two years ago he would have thought he was the luckiest guy on earth. He knew the pleasure of sating his sexual desires. He also knew the emptiness it left in its wake.

Jake jammed his fingers through his hair. Jena could see he was distraught. She didn't understand the man in front of her. Most of them were so simple.

"Do you have a girlfriend or something?" That would explain his behavior.

"According to God I do." He mocked himself, *She is sitting in a prison cell right now.*

Jena looked at him oddly then smiled. "Well, if your God ever decides that you're single, call me."

"Last I heard, I think I am engaged." He was pathetic. Jena grabbed her stuff, and with a wave of her hand and a casual "See ya," she left. Jake went into the bathroom. He splashed cold water on his face. He had been very close. A verse came to mind: "The only temptation that has come to you is that which everyone has. But you can trust God, who will not permit you to be tempted more than you can stand. But when you are tempted he will also give you a way to escape so that you will be able to stand it." He prayed, thanking God that he had made a way for him to escape. He went to bed suffering the effects of his wantonness.

Catherine began her day as usual, praying, seeking God. It was hard to watch her child go through so much pain. If only she could take the burden for her.

Love overflowed in the whisper, "I can."

Silent tears ran lovingly down her face. She answered out loud, "I know you can, but how can I get her to let you?"

Ruth was coming over that evening for dinner. Catherine began preparations. Lincoln was excited when he came home from school to learn that Nan would be coming over.

"Will she play my new video game with me?"

"Doesn't she always?"

Lincoln ran off to his room, excited about the evening.

When Ruth arrived, she went straight to play with her grandson. He beat her at a few rounds of "Tony Hawk Elite Skateboarding." They played until dinner was ready. After dinner was cleaned up and dessert was served, the adults had their time to talk while Lincoln had his bath.

"You know, we've been saying God's will be done, but I think we meant what we wanted," Catherine began. She told her mother the story Lincoln had told them.

"That man will have his day before God," Ruth proclaimed, "and you can be very sure your daughter will get her justice."

"I have to confess," Catherine responded, "it's only been since I found out what happened to Amber at the hands of that evil doctor that I have begun to believe she was innocent." She breathed a heavy sigh; that was a truth she had not ever revealed. What kind of mother was she believing that her daughter, her flesh and blood, was capable of murder? In her defense, Amber hadn't told them much. She didn't deny what happened, and the only details they got were from the police. Catherine liked believing with all her heart that her daughter was innocent. That in itself gave her strength.

Michael smiled at his wife. "And I thought you were the optimist. You sure had me fooled." He winked at her. There was still a long way to go, but somehow believing in their daughter made whatever else they would have to endure a little bit easier. For that they were both grateful. Before leaving, as always, they joined hands around the table and took turns saying a prayer. Then Ruth was on her way, and it was just the two of them.

"So you really thought Amber did it?" Michael wore a shocked expression.

"It wasn't like that, Michael." Catherine wanted to defend herself. "I just believed her to be guilty. I know it was in self-defense, but you had to have wondered how she got herself into that situation. And with everything that had been going on." She didn't like him bringing it back up; it left her vulnerable and it was unfair. "I didn't hear you offering any confessions," she accused.

"I kept mine to myself. So while you may be the optimist, I am the intellect."

She gave him a playful nudge. "Come on, confess."

The smile left his face, and he looked at his wife as she had looked at him earlier, pleading for understanding. "I wished she wasn't my child."

Neither spoke; they just lay on the couch holding each other.

Having had no sleep for yet another night, Amber was up early and ready to be escorted to her appointment with her new shrink. The meeting would be was on the fourth floor, a place Amber had only been to once. Her stomach twisted with anticipation. The meeting meant a lot to her future. She wasn't sure if she should risk acting absolutely nuts, and, aside from a nomination for the Golden Globes, she would hopefully get approved for an insanity plea. That would entitle her to more years of counselling, she thought sarcastically, being that the first year had done so much good. She had to admit, faced with the alternative, that wouldn't be the worst thing that could happen.

At least I can see a female shrink this time. Why didn't they do that in the first place? Just like here, why are there male gaurds in a women's prison? And male shrinks for screwed-up young girls? She wondered, *Are people so naive? Or are people so corrupt? Maybe it is some sort of job-security tactic to keep people messed up and ensure they need shrinks and prisons.*

The guard led Amber to the room where her interviews would take place. The moment Amber was introduced to Kimberly Alexander, she wanted to run. The woman was at least fifty, wearing a micro-short skirt. She conceded that the woman did have nice legs. She could deal with the stiletto heels, but what was going on with the woman's gray and purple hair?

Pick a color, she thought.

The gray and purple was spiked out on one side and nearly shaved on the other. A lovely pair of original sixties cat-framed lenses finished the look. Was she supposed to take the freakish-looking woman seriously? It had to be a joke. She cautiously looked around and decided, *No joke.* Kimberly looked like she could pull off the "I'm the crazy one" facade a lot better than Amber could. How was she supposed to keep a straight face? Never mind her tongue; that in itself posed a huge challenge. It was going to be difficult.

Kimberly Alexander introduced herself to Amber as "Just Kimberly will do. No need for titles with me."

Amber, trying her best to maintain the repertoire, responded aptly, "I am Amber. Just Amber will do fine for me also."

Kimberly wrinkled her nose and forehead simultaneously, obviously thinking, *What else would I call you?*

Amber smiled back innocently, to which her smile was returned. The meeting started off well enough. The line of questioning was as Amber had expected, about her childhood. Then she asked about Adam's death. She asked whether or not she was still using drugs. Amber raised her eyebrows at the question.

"If only I could get some … something for the pain."

Kimberly noted the sarcasm, then she jotted down some notes in her little book. The questions went on, and Amber was beginning to think that "Madam Crazy Hair" wasn't so bad, when from out of the blue she asked a question so inappropriate and vulgar, it caught Amber completely off guard.

The one thing the question would accomplish was that her answer would be unprotected and true to her soul. Kimberly whispered, "Amber, there's a place we can go. All you have to do is … " She was calculated. She looked directly into Amber's eyes, searching for the answer. " … have sex with me, and I will write whatever you want on this report."

The sentence was barely out of Kimberly's mouth. Amber leapt across the small surface that separated the two women. She grabbed the pen out of the astonished woman's hand and stabbed it into the hand that was still laying on the table. Blood spewed, as did Amber's venom.

"Never! Never!" she screamed. "Never!"

It was happening; she was truly losing her mind. Crawling backwards off the table, Amber was horrified by what she had done.

The guards rushed at her.

"No, please." She began to whimper, edging herself slowly into a corner. "Please, no more. This is more than one person should have to bear." Her heart broke; it tore and cried out. In that instant, delusion crept in. Tears tried to force their way out, but they had been pent up too long. Her sanity ebbed.

Kimberly was bleeding. She accepted medical attention for her puncture wound. She wouldn't allow them to touch Amber.

"This is a breakthrough. She needs to work through these emotions." She spoke quietly and firmly, and so they all stood around watching, witnesses to her so-called "breakthrough."

Amber clutched at her heart. It ached, true physical pain, and then it stopped, and she was laughing, giggling hysterically, crumpled on the floor, curled up in a ball, escaping to the only place she could: inside herself. She laughed until she was taken away. Amber was sedated and taken back to her cell. The doctor had her answer.

It was three a.m. Jake was finally winding down. He would soon be asleep. Suddenly, he sat up, terrified. It was so real, it clutched at him. He prayed.

"Pray for Amber." The calm voice was insistent. Jake made a call to the prison. Both Jared and Tyler were on duty. Believing this was the cause of the urgency he felt, he decided to go to the prison himself. He called up Charlie and told him what had happened. Charlie headed right over.

As the two men neared the prison, Jake felt an urgency. "Hurry," he coaxed. His palms were sweaty. His heart was pounding in his throat. He prayed continuously. He prayed for Amber. He prayed for safety and strength. He prayed for wisdom. Then he thanked God for all he would do. Jake was soon to be enlightened. He would soon realize the necessity he felt was a precursor for what he was about to witness.

Dark Places

"For the Lord your God is the one who goes with you. To fight for you against your enemies. To save you."

Deuteronomy 20:4

It was three a.m. Ruth looked at her clock. Why had she suddenly bolted upright in bed? What was this menagerie of dreams, if one could call them that? They were more like messages.

"Pray, pray," every message pleaded. Again, she looked at her clock: 3:07.

"Lord, what is this message your spirit has put on my heart?" she asked, but the insistence to pray clouded any answer she may have hoped to get. Ruth grabbed the quilt from on top of her bed and kneeled at her bedside. She began to pray. The longer she prayed, the more urgent the demand was. She prayed harder. Tears began to run down her face; her plea grew stronger. She prayed on. Her knees began to ache, yet her praying did not cease.

It was three a.m. Catherine tossed and turned in her bed. She rolled over to look at the clock on her night table yet again. The bright red numbers showed that only six minutes had passed.

She rolled back over to snuggle up to her husband. She tried to go back to sleep, but sleep would not come.

"Are you awake too?" came Michael's voice, just above a whisper.

"I can't get back to sleep."

"Me either," he replied. "What's on your mind?"

"Amber."

"Me too."

"I really feel a need to pray for her."

"So do I."

"Join me."

Michael and Catherine crawled out of the bed. They held each other as they kneeled at the side of their bed, and they prayed. It was three twenty when they heard a small noise. They looked toward the door. There stood Lincoln.

"Mommy, I can't sleep. I keep dreaming about Amber."

Michael and Catherine both felt the rush. Goose bumps overcame their bodies. Without hesitation, they invited their young son to come over and join them in their prayer mission. Even Lincoln made known to God his concerns and his commission for his sister. And God heard the child.

It was three a.m., time for Amber to put her plan into motion. The day's events had left her heart numb and her mind certain of the path that she had to take. She knew she had no choice. All that lay before her life was endlessly spiralling downhill, and the momentum was rapidly increasing. The future was hopeless. With her head in her hands, she beckoned the memories instead of shutting them out. She envisioned faces. She reached under the pillow and grabbed the syringe she had snuck from the infirmary. Amber thought it fitting to end it in the same manner it had all began. One had to appreciate the irony. Having witnessed Stan's death this way, she wasn't sure she would have the courage. She had to go for it; there would be no thinking about it.

Walking over to the cell door, she slid it open. The paper she had jammed inside the lock just before lockdown had held. She looked around, making sure no one had noticed her. Clinging to the wall, she walked nervously past the other inmates' cells. She reached the end of the row and turned to go down the hall toward the infirmary. Once there, she peeked in the window. Just as she had hoped, no one was there. From her five-day ordeal there, she recalled the night shift took unusually long breaks. She opened the door. She was sure that even if no one heard the door, they could definitely hear the pounding of her heart.

She needed a liquid base. Lauryn had gotten her some morphine. She knew what it was like to need to forget sometimes, to pretend all those things had never happened. She knew Amber did too, so she didn't hesitate to help her out.

Amber remembered when she was first experimenting with drugs. She convinced herself it was okay; it wasn't like she had a problem or anything. Lots of kids did it. It had all seemed so harmless. That had proven to be a very destructive thought.

The deeper she got, the more haunting every memory, every moment became. She had been proud of one fact: she had never used needles. No matter how badly she wanted to get high, she had never done needles. She had supplied many other people. *Many people's children*, she thought. A shiver ran down her spine.

Yes, she had personally been responsible for making it easier and cheaper for kids to get drugs. Now this would be her end. It was a horrible life. She had been lying to herself, making believe that the good times outweighed the bad. The reality of that lie came crashing into her mind as she found what she was looking for. She reached for the box of strychnine.

The cabinet was not locked. Prisons were breeding grounds for rats, rodents, and all kinds of creatures of the night requiring immediate extermination. It was easy to find in a lone cupboard on the floor of the infirmary bathroom. She picked up the small box with trembling hands.

Once back in the main hallway, Amber made her way to a long tunnel, the one the guards used. It always remained locked. She peered out the small opening in the door window. No one was around. It was too perfect that Tyler was on again tonight. She hoped he would be the one to find her. She wanted nothing more than to have her death on his head. Maybe no one else would know, but he would. She wondered if a pig like Tyler would even care. She encouraged herself with the one thing she had to hope for. He would be found guilty of all his crimes.

Amber sat down in a small alcove at the end of the hallway. She mixed up her deadly concoction and then took a hair elastic and placed it just above her bicep. Taking the syringe, she sucked up the lethal fluid. She mimicked the actions she had seen used by other needle users. She tapped on the vein until she could see it throbbing beneath the pressure of the blood flow. It seemed to be waiting, pleading for the salve. Amber closed her eyes and took a deep breath. "Oh, God." She breathed, full of trepidation. She pushed the needle into the vein that eagerly accepted the liquid it was offered. Amber laid her head back against the wall and waited for the eminent struggle her body would enter in its fight for the life it would not be able to attain.

Faint footsteps were approaching. She groggily opened her eyes, forcing the muscles in her neck to work. She looked; it was not Tyler. She was too weak to fight the drug. She had made sure to give herself a lethal dose. It would make her go quicker, she hoped. Now she just let her head flop back. Her skull made a sickening sound as it cracked against the cement wall.

There was no mistaking the submissive body as Jake, from the end of the hall, tried to make out who it was half sitting, half laying at the other end of the hall. The long curly hair and the too-thin frame defined her. He already knew. The groan escaped his gut before he knew he was pleading. He ran with apprehension, knowing full well what he would find. The once-ardent woman lay limp and lifeless.

"Get help! Help!" he bellowed. He could hear voices, but they were indiscernible. "Someone get help!" He may have heard someone respond, but he wasn't sure. Charlie immediately ran to find the nurse.

Jake reached Amber. His knees buckled, and he hit the ground off balance. He didn't notice the hot tears that made their way down his cheeks. He lifted Amber's pliant body and cradled her. She seemed so small in his arms, like the lost child she was. He noticed the syringe still in Amber's hands, clutched tightly in her white-knuckled grip. He pulled the hair band off her arm gently and with purpose, hoping that somehow by removing the band and prying the syringe from her grasp, he could undo this tragedy, forcing the blood to flow and drawing the poison out.

He looked down at her arm. The beautiful pale skin was so flawless. He closed his eyes. How many women would he have to watch die? Would God not intervene for one?

"You saved her in the truck accident, Lord," he accused. "For what? Was she right? Do you only help those you choose? What joy, what purpose can come from this? The dead can't praise you. Were you testing her to see how much one girl could withstand? Did you get what you hoped for? She is lost now. This is not what you promised."

Jake's body racked with deep, guttural sobs. He knew better than to question the wisdom of God. In this tragic moment he didn't care. It cost him years of hope. Both for Sofia, his lost love, and now Amber, the lifeless woman he held in his arms. For this brief moment he didn't care what God had in mind, nor about his so-called divine purpose. He continued his tangent of self-pity.

"You told me to love her. For this? What can save her now? Who can save the dead?"

"I can." The voice was vigilant, and though it was a whisper, it was powerful. He felt fear at the intensity of it. He was ashamed at his selfish outburst. Opening his eyes, he noticed a glow. Jake looked closer. Shivers ran up his spine, and his hair stood on end. His heart pounded in his ears. With his thumb he rubbed the spot where the needle had made its entry, allowing the toxin to do its primary job. He stared in amazement. What was he seeing?

He brushed away the tears with the back of his arm. He stared, waiting. The vein burned bright red. He continued watching in awe. The blood recoiled in the vein, a miracle transpiring before him. The small prick the needle had made healed over instantaneously. The lifeless body in his arms stirred. Jake began to weep, this time from sheer joy and amazement.

Despite his lack of faith, God allowed him to be part of his awesome work in a way he would never have fathomed.

"Yes, Lord," he confessed, "you *can* save the dead." He spoke with a grateful heart, tears streaming down his face.

It was the first time Jake had ever seen peace on Amber's face. For even in death, and he had seen her in death, her expression was a mixture of fear and discontent. Amber's eyes opened wide in childlike astonishment, as though the innocence lost over the last years had returned. Jake looked again at her arm; the needle mark was completely healed. She looked up at him then, her eyes shining and grinning widely. Jake pulled her into himself, hugging her. He held her tightly, cherishing the heaving of her chest, proving her life had not been extinguished, that air filled her lungs. Life had returned to her blood.

Just when Jake thought the trauma for the night was over, he heard the rushing footsteps. He looked up to see the nurse, followed by Charlie and Tyler and Jared.

"How do we explain this?" he asked quietly with a chuckle.

Suddenly, it was as though Amber remembered everything and her face filled with horror.

"What have you done to me?" she accused.

"If you're referring to bringing you back from the dead, it wasn't me. I was just the blessed individual who witnessed it," he whispered to her firmly. He looked deep into her eyes, willing her to fathom what had taken place. "It was a miracle, Amber. It was …" No words could describe the phenomenon he had witnessed. By the look on her face, she didn't care what he had witnessed. She was supposed to be dead.

People were approaching them. What was he going to say to them? Charlie would understand divine intervention. The other three were another story. He'd believed he needed to be here to protect Amber from one of the men who would soon be standing in front of him. How was he supposed to explain that?

He stared at each man individually, trying to withhold the hatred he felt for Tyler. He didn't want him to know that he had him figured out … yet. He would be patient. God would provide the right moment. His timing was perfect; evidence of that was still very fresh. Emma-Jean was on duty. She and Jared wore looks of concern. Only Tyler was expressionless.

"Help me get her up on the gurney," Emma ordered. She shone a flashlight into the docile girl's eyes. "Reactive pupils, a good sign." Emma looked compassionately at Amber. What force kept driving the girl over the edge?

Jake grabbed Charlie by the arm. The two men walked up to Emma-Jean, and Jake spoke just above a whisper, "I need you to run some tests. Specifically, run a search for strychnine." Jake thought for a moment and then added, "Is there strychnine or any other pesticides kept on hand here?"

Emma didn't hesitate before answering. "Of course. We have as many rodents as we do inmates. Why?" She looked from Amber to Jake then raised her eyebrows with understanding. He veered his chin downward, encouraging her to look toward his hand. He inconspicuously held out the syringe. She nodded and gave Jake a look of empathy.

Aside from the needle, she really wasn't sure what he could be getting at. If the girl managed to get strychnine in that syringe, she would undoubtedly be a dead girl, not just the subdued one before them now. Emma-Jean was sensitive to the situation and agreed to do the testing anyway and asked no questions.

As soon as Jared and Tyler signed Amber into the medical room, they continued with their rounds. Jake took the opportunity to go into further detail with Emma and Charlie. Emma listened carefully while drawing a vile of Amber's blood. Jake reached for it quickly. "I'll take that vial, Emma. Fill up another one for yourself. I will get this one tested elsewhere." He passed the vial to Charlie.

Emma knew the two men knew more than they were letting on.

"Either of you want to tell me what this is all about?"

Charlie shrugged his shoulder.

Jake smiled and asked, "Are you a spiritual woman, Emma-Jean?" He paused a moment, waiting for her answer. She nodded apprehensively. He could tell she didn't want to commit to an answer. She figured any question like that was a trick question.

"Well," he paused, looking around the room speculatively, adding drama to an event that required no dramatization, "I saw something tonight. I saw a track mark in a young girl's arm. I found a syringe in that girl's hand. The syringe was full of poison. I found her lifeless body." He was looking from face to face, making sure they were paying attention. "The girl hoped to die. But God was waiting. He waited until the perfect time, until she had already breathed her last breath. Then he breathed the breath of life back into her nostrils, giving her back her life. Know what that is? It's a parting of the sea, 'Lazarus, rise up and walk,' Old Testament-type miracle." He proclaimed the last phrase with so much hushed enthusiasm that neither were sure whether they should take him seriously or not.

"Seriously? What's going on?" Emma asked.

Jake pulled the syringe out of his pocket. Again he told Emma and Charlie what he had witnessed. He was certain they would find strychnine in that syringe.

Emma's mouth gaped. Her eyes went wide, and she drew in a long breath, held it for a second, and then, as if suddenly realizing she was the victim of a cruel prank, she playfully slapped Jake's arm. "Now, Jake, that's not funny. You be serious. Tell me what the heck is going on."

The look on his face grew serious, and Emma knew he was being completely honest. Charlie stared in amazement.

Jake left Klahanee with a renewed feeling of awe for his Savior, realizing that in an all-consuming way God was sovereign. As the Holy Bible says in Lamentations, "Yet this I call to mind and therefore I have hope. Because of the Lord's great love we are not consumed. His compassions never fail. They are refreshed every morning. Great is Your faithfulness." He was relieved that God, who was in control, was a God of love and a God with boundless mercy. He smiled at the thought of having a fabulous story to pass on.

Neither man had much to say on the drive home. Words were empty in the afterglow of the occasion.

Emma couldn't help but stare in wonderment at the wild young woman before her. Would there be no end to the trauma in her life? She thought over the events as Jake had suggested they had happened. She was alarmed when she realized he hadn't even mentioned the word "suicide." Had he been aware of that? This was a suicide attempt, not a miracle attempt. Based on the conversation they had, he didn't, and that worried her.

He obviously liked her, making denial very dangerous, especially with a girl like Amber. She needed help. She had already been assessed. Rumor had it she was going to be moved soon, following the events that had taken place with the psychiatrist only yesterday. Emma continued to look at Amber. What had driven her to the edge? She wanted to ask her so many questions, but now was not the time. She needed to concentrate on her patient, not on fulfilling her own selfish curiosity.

Amber was sleeping peacefully on the medical bed.

"What were you thinking, honey?" Emma whispered out loud, if only to herself. She walked over and examined the tortured young woman. Jake must be mistaken. Where on earth was he coming up with his idea? This girl didn't have a single track mark. There was no point of entry anywhere on her body. She sighed deeply. She would run those blood tests anyway. She put the vile of blood in her pocket. She would have it tested elsewhere, definitely not through this place. If both test results came back the same, Jake would have confirmation of his miracle.

Jake was too excited to sleep. He raised his arms jubilantly, praising God for his awesome power. He could feel it. He felt like a child. He prayed that night in a way he hadn't for a while. He knelt down, his face turned upwards, arms outstretched, reaching toward heaven, toward his Savior. Resplendent joy glowed on a grateful face, his a heart was so full it wanted to burst. It had been too long.

He prayed with renewed hope. He prayed for Amber, that this would be her turning point. Then he waited. He stayed that way and waited ... for an answer? For confirmation? For anything. He wanted to hear God speak as he had so clearly earlier. He pictured Almighty God, Creator of all things, sitting on his throne and surrounded by angels, looking down from heaven at him. Jake knew he smiled at him.

God had known all along how the night would turn out. Jake had little faith. God hadn't held that against him. He remembered and envisioned the events. As he did, his core warmed and shivers covered his skin. A warm breeze caressed his cheek, and he knew undoubtedly that Jesus was with him. He had felt Jake's anguish at the sight of Amber. He had shared in his joy at her awakening. Jake went to bed savoring every shard of life.

Chloe was on duty when Amber awoke. When she noticed Amber's groggy eyes forcing themselves open, she came over.

"Well, you must have been having a great dream. You really didn't want to wake up this morning."

Amber looked quizzically at her. She appeared out of focus. She couldn't think or remember what had happened last night. Why was she back here? She was still tired, and she didn't remember dreaming at all.

"How did I get in here?" Even through Amber's half-closed eyes, she could see the question on Chloe's face.

"I was going to ask you that? There's no report. Nothing. I have no idea what you're doing here or who put you here. There is no information at all. When Emma-Jean gave reports last night, she never even mentioned you were here."

"So you just found me here?" It made Amber's head ache to think. Chloe narrowed her eyes and tried sizing up Amber's answer. Did she really not know how she got there? She appeared deep in thought, trying to remember.

"Well ... " She hesitated a moment then decided to tell her. "I was doing some cleaning and stocking the shelves. When I first saw you there, I thought you were dead. Scared me half to death. I supposed that would have been the reason Emma didn't report your admission. But I walked over closer to your body to see who you were, and you were breathing. Imagine my surprise."

As Chloe continued to talk, it brought back memories and realizations of the night. It seemed like it was all a dream. Then she got a flash picture. She was supposed to be dead. How could she be alive? Who did this to her? Then another picture flashed behind her eyes. She remembered Jake. He was running up to her. Had he done this? It couldn't have been anyone else. He must have had something to do with this. Even that didn't make sense.

She interrupted Chloe in the middle of her rambling. "Can rat poison go bad? Does it have, like a 'best before' date?"

Chloe stammered for a minute, thrown off by the odd question. "I, uh, I-I'm not sure. You would really need to ask Poison Control. I think we have some in the back though. I can check and see if there's any information on the box—"

"No! No, forget I asked. Never mind. If there is no reason why I'm here, can I go back to my cell?"

"I'll call a guard and have you taken back if that's what you want."

"Thanks," she muttered.

"Can I leave you alone in here? I have to finish stocking the shelves. You can wait here."

Amber nodded. The minute Chloe left the room, Amber sat up. She was taken aback by how unstable she felt. She grabbed onto the side bar of the bed. She waited a moment for the dizziness to pass before moving. She was blacking out, and she felt as though she may pass out. She grabbed the bedrail with both hands and gripped with all her might. She swayed. All sound was blocked out by humming in her ears. Then, as quickly as it had come, it passed.

Cautiously, she let go of the bedrail then straightened. She slowly began to move toward her destination. Looking around a moment, she checked to make sure Chloe couldn't see her. She knew she had to attempt to get that box back. Something very strange had gone on here.

She had personally witnessed two deaths already from the

very same chemical that was in that box. How was it that it hadn't worked on her? She looked around quickly before bending down and looking inside the cupboard for the box. She was shocked to find it gone. She stood up and made her way back toward the bed, awaiting the guard who would return her to her cell. The guard arrived shortly. Relief filled Amber's core when she saw she was female.

She led Amber down the hall to her cell. As they made the walk, she could feel the searing stares of the other inmates. Her head throbbed. Did any of them know what had happened last night? Did they know she had attempted the coward's way out? She would soon find out.

When she got to her cell, Lauryn wasn't there. An indescribable fear hit her. She felt it in her bones. She looked around the eight-by-ten-foot cell. She looked at the two cots. One on either far corner. Each with a mattress, a blanket, and a very flat, useless pillow. A small table was in one corner, and a toilet chamber with a four-foot wooden wall half encasing the area, apparently to make it private, or at least to allow one an artificial dignity.

Nothing in the room seemed out of the ordinary. Still, she couldn't make herself enter that room, not without Lauryn in it. She hadn't realized the comfort her familiar presence brought. Amber couldn't remember ever feeling so vulnerable. The guard waited patiently for a moment before asking, "What's the problem? Get in there!" She did not sound mean, just impatient.

Amber really didn't know what to say. "I can't." Her voice came out as a hoarse whisper. Her mind was racing. Every memory of what had already happened in this place were taunting her.

"Can't or won't?" The guard's patience was abating. Amber tried to turn around to look at her, to plead with her eyes, being that her voice had abandoned her. The guard, unsure of what Amber was doing, but also aware of her previous acts of hostility and her proclivity to violence, most recently to the therapist she had stabbed, took no chances.

Using the full weight of her body and her forearm, she propelled Amber into her cell, giving her no opportunity for a struggle. Amber spun around quickly, hoping to get out. The cell door was already closed behind her, and it locked.

"Please, I think I need to be taken back to the infirmary. I am not feeling well."

"You have a toilet in there. If you feel like you're going to be sick, use that. The infirmary is for serious injuries, not tummy aches."

Amber looked around. Everyone in the neighboring cells looked like cartoon characters. Their faces contorted, their large mouths gaping open, huge white teeth showing. They held their stomachs as they laughed at her. They laughed so hard, they were rocking back and forth. The sound reverberated off the walls. It echoed and returned. It was making her crazy. They wouldn't stop laughing. She brought her hands up to her ears.

"Make it stop," she begged, growing more hysterical. A lump was rising in her throat. Tightening. Straining. She screamed, "Stop! Stop!" They were never going to stop. She hurled herself to the floor and buried her head in a blanket. The sound was jumbled now. She knew they were still laughing, laughing at her, at how stupid she was. They were never going to stop laughing. Every muscle in her body was tense, rigid. She held the blanket tighter.

"Make them stop," she begged over and over. She stopped when she heard the footsteps.

They created an infraction in the chaos of sound in her head. It was the one sound she could separate from the rest.

Please, she thought, *let it be my savior. Let those shoes belong to Jake.* She dared to hope.

The cell door swung open. Her security blanket was ripped away from the tight ball it had become around her head. Two men grabbed her.

"Hold her still," one said. She could barely make out Chloe's face. She looked so scared. Scared of what? The meager amount of sanity that clung told Amber what she feared. She feared *for* her.

The strong hands that gripped her did a good job. She couldn't move. She felt the brief sting of the needle as Chloe pushed it into her shoulder. Her body slowly relaxed. She tried to fight it. This time the drugs would override her will.

Amber awoke in the infirmary. She immediately noticed the man sitting in a chair in the corner of the room. His head was in his hands, fingers digging deep into his scalp, as if that way he could locate and remove the pain. His shoulders drooped, and she felt a deep sorrow. She knew it was for her that he despaired. She had caused the pain; she didn't know how to make it better. Amber wanted to make him smile. She needed him to know she was okay.

"Jake," she started.

He immediately lifted his head and smiled adoringly at her. How peaceful his expression was. It completely belied his posture, telling her his expression was a front for what he truly felt, so that it would seem she wasn't the only one who masked her feelings.

"Have you been here very long?"

He didn't know what to say to her. Where to begin? He had so much he wanted to say, so many questions. He wondered if she remembered last night. He wondered if she remembered her promise to him. She was waiting for an answer, and the question wasn't a difficult one. As a matter of fact, at the present, when there were so many other things to talk about, it was mundane.

"No, not long at all. How are you?" There was great depth to that question.

"I'm okay." Then her mouth started moving. She felt like she wasn't the one controlling it, and her truth spilled. "I'm losing my mind, Jake. If I am convicted, there is no way I will survive in here. I'm on trial for murder. No one will believe a psycho acted in self-defense. I stabbed a pen into a psychiatrist's hand. Did you know that? I lost complete control." She was breathing erratically. The reality of all the things that hung over her head was defeating. She felt the thoughts trying to seduce her again. Sanity was so fragile.

"I tried to commit suicide." She stopped and looked at Jake. Some emotion had found its way back to her calloused heart. She could feel the burn of tears that wanted to fall and the lump that insisted on forming in her throat. It ached and pleaded to be released. She willed it away. Tears were self-pity. They only proved weakness. She took a deep, shaky breath and tried to think of something else for the moment, anything to keep those tears from falling. Amber had refused her tears for too long; she was good at it by now.

The lump softened, and she continued her confession. She opened her eyes wide, smiling faintly as she recalled, "But you, you came by at exactly the right moment. You saved me. You saved me from death. You always show up at exactly the right time and save me." She spoke with adoration.

The hurt and confusion on Jake's face were undeniable, but she didn't understand. She revered him. He was amazing. He should know that. Amber tried to talk again, but he interrupted her, adamant that she understand and know the truth.

"Amber, I was there," he stated emphatically. "I know what I witnessed." He got up from the chair and walked over to the bed that Amber occupied. He looked at her intensely, gripping the side of the bed. There was no mistaking the accuracy in his recollection. "I watched, Amber. I saw the mark where you put the needle in your arm."

She tried to look away. The last thing she wanted was to be reminded of the experience.

Jake gently tipped her chin, forcing her to look at him. He wanted to see her expression when he got to the best part. "The blood flowing in your veins began to glow bright red, and then it stopped flowing." He searched her face for any acknowledgement. "The blood changed color, and the poison that was injected into your bloodstream evaporated within your body. Then you began to breathe again. Look, look at your arm. The needle's point of entry completely healed before my eyes." He firmly grabbed her arm and turned it over, pointing to the area where the needle had gone in. She knew the spot; she had put the needle there herself.

"And you say 'I,' how could I have possibly had anything to do with that? It was a miracle. Give the glory to the one truly responsible, truly capable of such things. Your maker. The one who knows your innermost parts, who knit you together in your mother's womb. I will not allow you to say I did or could have done this. I will accept no glory."

He was emphatic in his declaration. "You need to remove the scales from your eyes so that you can see truth. Soften your heart to the will of God. He kept you alive twice. He wants you. So he will have you. Surrender to him. Put an end to this pain."

He finished quietly. "Put an end to the insanity."

Silence enveloped the room in the truthfulness of his last statement. Amber honestly contemplated all that he had said. He was so passionate.

"Twice." Amber reiterated the comment in her mind. She had escaped death three times, not twice. She looked up at Jake. He could tell she knew. For this moment her sea-green eyes hid nothing, and he recognized it immediately. She knew. He hoped that would be enough, but the expression was masked instantly and a blank stare was in its place. Jake recognized the change and wanted to scream. He was so close, she was so close.

No, she would not believe. Somewhere deep inside her gut she knew he was right. She would probably have to deal with that one day. For today she would not believe that God had anything to do with sparing her life. The ironic point was, she had intended to forgo her life. If he had saved her, it was just another slap in the face. She stared at Jake in wonderment. This is the one she would adore. It was he who was her savior. He always was.

Jake moved closer to her on the hospital bed. He had to make her understand. It wasn't him! How could a simple man bring back the dead? Didn't she understand that? He cupped Amber's face. He wanted her complete attention. Compassion burned in his heart. He looked deeply into her eyes, pleading for her to listen, not with her ears, but with her heart. He was ready to make another attempt, to make her understand. He would be gentler this time. Amber misread Jake's intensity and his gesture. She reached out her hands and dug them deep into the back of his head, pulling him down firmly and bringing their mouths together.

Jake could feel her heart pounding. He reached his arms upward. He was shocked at her strength. He removed her arms from around his neck and stepped back.

Amber was overcome. She had believed for a moment that he shared her passion. No one spoke for a moment. Amber wasn't sure of what to do. Overwhelmed with shame, she looked away. Every evil and horrible deed she had done flooded her mind, and the pain struck her soul. *Why would he want you?* she scolded herself. *Wasted and used. Look at yourself. Who would want you? Certainly not this righteous man before you.*

She bowed her head, feeling the full weight of her life's sin on top of her shoulders. She knew how she must look to him. He already knew most of the things she had done. He must be so disgusted. She was stupid. It was one thing to save her, but he couldn't possibly love her. Not like that. He was just kind. She was wretched and dirty. He deserved much better, and he would get it. Surely God would provide that for him.

Jake didn't know how to react. How had this gotten so off track? At that moment kissing Amber would have been the last thing on his mind. He looked at her: head bowed, shoulders slumped. He didn't want her to feel that way. He didn't want her to feel rejected. That wasn't why he had pulled away.

"Amber..." He waited for her to raise her eyes. She didn't. He reached out and tilted her chin. All he saw was remorse, a trail of regret and feelings of unworthiness etched deeply into every feature.

When she looked at him, all she could see was compassion. That just made it worse. She would always be pitiful to him, and she hated that.

"Please, don't say anything. You should go." She turned her face away from his gentle grip. She heard him drop his hand to his side. He didn't move. He would not go. They had been too close. She was good at hiding her feelings, but he had seen the awakening in her eyes. She knew the truth; there was no doubt in his mind. He wanted to stay, make her admit it. That was foolish pride talking, and it wouldn't help his plight.

He pondered explaining about the kiss, but he didn't know what to say without making it worse. She could be so difficult; he never knew how she would react. He wondered if she would always make things harder than they had to be.

Jake stood up, and Amber chanced a glance at him. She noticed that the hope had dissipated from his face. It was replaced with one of reality. She felt a twinge of guilt. She knew she had let him down again.

"Amber, don't you know how much you matter? 'Not a sparrow falls from the sky that God doesn't know about, he knows the number of hairs on your head...' He knows the number of tears you have cried, and he wants to let him wipe them away."

"Stop preaching at me! You're not the only one who can quote the Bible. I can recall many verses from my childhood, but they haven't helped me at all. Look at me. If God knew I would end up like this, then you can't say he cares, because if he's the God you're talking about, he would love me more than this. That makes you both wrong and contradictory."

He should have left when she asked him too. He was getting to her. He was under the surface. It was uncomfortable, so she lashed out. She would make him wish he had left when he had the chance.

"What would I see if I put your life under a microscope? Would you still look so perfect?" He ignored her comment too late; she caught the inflection.

"He loved you enough, Amber, that despite knowing all about you, *even the stuff that nobody else knows.* Even though he knew you would be in this place. He loves you enough to give you a choice. He loves you enough to wait for you, to continue to offer you hope, the hope of salvation. He wants better for you, but you have to believe it. You have to want it, and it's up to you to accept it."

"I will have better, but it will be by my hand, by what I do."

Jake worked his jaw; the muscle flexed, showing his irritation. She was obstinate. He dug deep this time and went to the core. Here was the truth. "Maybe, Amber, this is in God's plan for you. He knows how hard-headed, stubborn, uncompromising, and obstinate you are. He knew there would be no other way for you to attain salvation than by completely destroying the old you so he could start fresh with you." Feeling as though he had been a bit harsh, he added playfully, "Now tell me that's not love."

She softened at his humor and kept up the camaraderie. "If that's your idea of love, I would really hate to be your girlfriend." They both smiled.

"How many more chances do you think God is going to give you?"

Her answer made his heart skip, and he had to smile. "As

many as it takes." Amber had nearly succeeded in distracting Jake from the main reason he had come.

"Amber, I was hoping, if you are up to it, we could talk about Tyler." Jake believed wholeheartedly that Amber had tried to take her own life rather than live in fear of that dreadful guard. He wondered if she knew she was being transferred. He wanted the information before then. Somehow it lost validity from someone living in a psych ward.

Shivers ran up Amber's spine as she remembered the letter. Where was the letter? Who had found it? Had anyone found it? One thing was certain, when it was found, everyone would know. She hadn't planned on *telling* Jake anything. She should be off the hook. She should be dead; her end of the bargain would catch up with him in a letter.

"Is that why you're here? You came here to get information from me to help you out. So what? The new guy can be the hero? Forget that." Her pride was hurt. She thought he was there because he cared, because of her. She was such a fool.

Jake was insulted. She knew better than that. She was playing him, and he didn't like it.

"Amber, are you going to keep your end of the bargain or not?"

She felt the heat of shame seeping into her cheeks. Jake just didn't understand. The only reason she had agreed to that deal was because she wasn't supposed to be around to answer the questions.

"You ask too much. You want your information, but you don't care what it costs me."

He had to admit that he hadn't thought about what it would cost her. He wasn't sure he understood what she meant. He tried reasoning again. "Amber, I trusted you. I got Charlie to go along with you too. We could both get in a lot of trouble for not reporting Darryl."

She hardened herself against his gentle plea. He was truly the last person on earth she would have chosen to betray, but she had to look out for herself. No one else was going to. Her life was crazy enough. She already felt sanity slipping through her fingers, and it would take nothing to send her over the edge. She just wasn't capable of handling the weight of the truths about her life. Further, passing those truths onto the one man she actually cared about, the one person that it mattered what he thought of her.

"I don't remember what happened."

Jake had had enough of the insolent woman. He would get his answers another way. He stood up to go, and then he hesitated just a moment, waiting, giving her one last opportunity to be honorable. Amber was stubborn. She said nothing except, "Bye. Come see me again."

He was angry. She was determined. They would get nowhere like this. What would it take for her? He felt hope dissipate as he remembered reading how five hundred people had witnessed Jesus, after his persecution and death, rising into heaven. Yet some still didn't believe. Would Amber be one of those who saw and yet still refused to believe?

Jake was exhausted after his shift at the hospital. He had gone straight to work after his exacerbating visit with Amber. He got home and went straight to bed. His body craved sleep. Sleep was just taking over when the phone rang. Three rings, then four. He got up and answered it. It was Emma-Jean.

"I have that information you requested regarding tests. You're going to completely believe this. I have to admit, I'm having trouble with it. That syringe had enough strychnine to drop a herd of elephants. No human could survive that. I also ran the test on our lovely patient. There were traces of the drug found in her bloodstream and an abnormal white blood cell count. Nothing close to the readings that injecting this needle would have caused."

He already knew that. "Thanks for the call, Emma. Hey, has she mentioned anything to you about the attack?"

"Not since that first encounter."

"Can you pry a little?"

"I could try. You know she is being moved soon?"

"I did know. Thanks." If Amber was being moved, it would be safe to rat out Tyler. Maybe now she would sign a statement so an investigation could begin. Jake still had so much faith in the legal system.

Another attempt was made to put Amber in her cell. She noticed Lauryn right away. She thought it would be a relief, but the girl looked at her like she thought she was crazy.

"Lauryn, I looked for you yesterday. I couldn't find you."

"Stay away from me. You're a psycho." Her statement was laced with expletives.

Amber was hurt. She didn't try to defend herself; instead, she changed the subject. "I hear you're out soon?"

"Who says? Your cop friends? You're getting awfully chummy with the other side. Don't forget, they are still the reason we are in here. Your stud, Jake, may be hot, but he's still one of them."

"They didn't put us in here. We got ourselves in here. By whatever circumstances or excuse in our lives, they didn't make those choices. We did. I did."

Lauryn narrowed her eyes at Amber. Both girls were condemned by that statement; both were bothered by it for different reasons.

Amber looked quizzically at Lauryn. Why was she harassing her? Didn't she know she was struggling? They were supposed to be friends.

"You still aren't very smart, are you, girl? You think your boyfriend can get you out of here? You think he can protect you? You better stop talkin' trash. Everyone is already talkin' about you. People are asking me a lot of questions."

So that was it. Amber understood.

"I am losing my mind." She decided to be honest. "I can feel it. It's like I know what is happening, but I'm only watching it. I can't do anything about it."

"I don't want to know your problems."

"Stop it! You are my friend, Lauryn. I need to know I have someone."

"Shut up!" Suddenly, Lauryn was at Amber. She shoved her into the bars with all her strength. Amber just stood there. Lauryn came at her again. The other prisoners averted their attentions to the fight. They all began chanting, "Cat scrap! Cat scrap!" Amber yelled out as Lauryn tugged at a handful of her hair. The sound of the guards' feet thumped as they ran down the corridor. The girls stopped immediately.

"What's going on here?"

"Nothing," Lauryn spoke up. The guard looked from Lauryn to Amber. "There better not be anymore nothing going on or one of you is going to solitaire."

They both nodded; neither spoke. The guard walked away.

"And you say I'm nuts," Amber muttered under her breath.

"What?"

"There are enough people out there against us. I would never do anything to a friend. I may be a lot of things. The one thing I'm not is disloyal." Her words struck. Lauryn's expression softened. Amber pressed. "What got into you?"

Lauryn could never tell Amber what it was that had made her react the way she had. She had found Amber's incriminating letter pressed into a library book. That girl was either stupid or desperate. After reading it, Lauryn knew what to do. It infuriated her that she had to compromise herself for this girl. She requested a meeting with the warden; she would be moved to a different prison or to a different floor at the very least. If the other inmates found out she was a snitch, they'd get her good.

Lauryn knew that within a few days Amber was being moved to a different kind of facility. She truly was losing her mind.

Lauryn gave a deep sigh. "I don't know. This place. You. Why do you get all the attention?"

"It is not good attention. I could do without it."

Lauryn was trying to be cordial, but Amber knew something was different. Their conversation was drowned out. The other inmates started chanting, "Fresh, fresh." They must be have been bringing in a new girl.

Amber looked at her as a girl was ushered past their cell. She looked so defiant. That would change. Another inmate echoed her thought. "In a couple of nights, little girl, you'll be cryin' for your mama." The guard was talking to the girl. Seeing the new girl got Amber and Lauryn talking about when they had first arrived.

Amber recalled that she had an addiction; the withdrawal felt like it would kill her. Lauryn recalled fury. She got put away for trying to sneak a pound of heroin over the border by shoving small bags into her body. She had several other convictions. That one had been her last straw. Then Lauryn recalled something else. Amber's heart stopped. She felt the goose bumps. Her hair prickled all the way up to her neck.

"When I first got here a couple of years ago, all the talk was about Tyler. His son had died of an overdose. They called it foul play. He had been drugged. Come to think of it, I think he was injected with the same stuff as Duncan, you know the guy you—"

"I know, I know." Amber stopped paying attention after that. Lauryn was still talking, but Amber's head was cluttered with her own thoughts. Was Tyler the loser dad who left his poor kid with a crack whore, pursuing a better life for just himself? Regret must have fanned the flames of guilt into full-blown vengeance. That was why he hated her so much.

It all fit together. Amber closed her eyes. There was Tyler, standing by Cynthia with his arm around her as they watched their son lowered into the ground. She replayed the moment like a movie reel in her mind. Tyler was looking around. He noticed Amber off in the distance. She wore street clothes; he recognized her as one of them, the kids his son hung out with. He burned her face to memory. She remembered him now. Why hadn't she remembered before?

Tyler's stare had made her uncomfortable. When she left, he was still staring at her. She felt the power in that knowledge. When she saw Tyler next, she would deflate his ardor. Lauryn noticed the expression on Amber's face. Amber didn't trust Lauryn anymore; she wouldn't tell her what she knew. This was her gem. She would find opportunity to make it shine.

Wait On

"They that wait upon the Lord shall renew their strength. They shall mount up with wings as eagles. They shall run and not be weary. They shall fall and not faint."

Isaiah 30:41

Three days earlier

Catherine got up. The alarm wouldn't go off for a few minutes yet. She turned it off and began her day as she should, in prayer. As she prayed, she thought of the people God had put into her life. She prayed for each one. She prayed for her husband and her son. Fervently, she prayed for her daughter. She remembered her psych appointment with the new doctor today. Catherine prayed that this time their daughter would have a doctor who cared, who had knowledge as well as compassion. She prayed Amber would accept whatever help was offered. Then she prayed for her daughter's heart.

"Soften her heart with the oil of your love. Jesus, I pray for you to put godly people into her life. Let her remember you. May she seek your face, Faithful Lord. Let her yearn for you, Jesus. Love the Lord my God with all my heart, and with all my soul, and with all my strength, and all my mind." She repeated the verse, drawing strength from its very core.

She went downstairs repeating the most important of all the

commandments. That is what Jesus had told the Pharisees, the very people who would crucify him. He had continued, knowing they hated him. "The second is like it. Love your neighbor as yourself." She recalled the parable from Luke 10.

"Again a man of the Law of Moses asked Jesus another question meant to trick him. 'Teacher, who is my neighbor?' Jesus with wisdom and gentleness told of the Good Samaritan. 'A man was going down to Jerusalem to Jericho, when he fell into the hands of robbers. They stripped him of his clothes, beat him and went away, leaving him half dead. A priest happened to be going down the same road, and when he saw the man he passed by on the other side.

"So too a Levite, when he came to the place and saw him, passed by on the other side. But a Samaritan, or non-Jew (these two openly detested one another. Jesus specifically chose this story to illustrate that love had no bounds), as he travelled came to where the man was; when he saw him he took pity on him. He went to him and bandaged his wounds. Pouring on oil and wine. Then he put the man on his own donkey, took him to an inn, and took care of him. The next day he took out two denarii (two days' wages). He gave them to the innkeeper. 'Look after him,' he said, 'and when I get back I will reimburse you for any extra expense.' Which of these men was a neighbour?'"

Jesus always had an answer or a deed that projected his complete and perfect love. Oh, to have a heart like Jesus, to love like he did.

Catherine prepared to take Lincoln to school while still deep in her own thoughts. She put the last item in his lunch bag, took a final sip of her lukewarm coffee, and yelled for her son. "Get your jacket and your shoes on. It's time to go."

"Okay, Mom," came his agreeable response. That was how he had been the last few days, so unlike the weeks before when he had fought her about everything. It had helped, she assumed, that day that all the truths had come out. Having that burden removed from his small shoulders had made a noticeable difference in everything around home and at school too.

Catherine felt more confident in discussing things with him and answering his questions honestly now—something she had not done before. She was still contemplating those abating thoughts when she heard the door slam, telling her that Lincoln was already outside. Simultaneously, the phone rang. She looked out the kitchen window; she could see her son pulling on the car door.

"I can't answer you right now," she said to herself. "Sure hope you're not important." She half walked, half ran out the door.

Catherine rushed home from her grocery shopping. She chanced a glance at the phone; the light was blinking, indicating there were messages. She didn't want to hear them. She did the dutiful thing and walked over to the machine to press play. It was better to listen to them before Lincoln got home. He would be full of stories and wanting her attention. The first message was from her sister, Darlene. They would be moving again, possibly across the border. "Pray for me," she requested.

The second message was her beloved, her strength, her husband. He didn't just support her, he picked her up and carried her through many situations. He always had a verse on the tip of his tongue to uplift and give hope to them both. He credited her as the positive one, but she got the strength from him. The journeys had been together, but it was he who wrought the way. He called to say he loved her and, though he knew she didn't need the reminder, it was Amber's appointment today. He would pray for them both. The third call was from a Mr. Garret, the prison warden. His message simply stated that during Amber's psych evaluation there had been a situation.

"Please contact us as soon as possible so arrangements can be made for a consultation."

There were a fourth and a fifth message, but Catherine heard none of those. She blankly pulled out a chair, sat at the kitchen table, and buried her face in her arms.

How long, oh, God? she wondered. *How long will we have to endure the enemy's victory over us?* She was angry and repentant in the same instance. She prayed fervently. She didn't even know the words she was saying, and still she kept pleading. She didn't know what Mr. Garret was referring to, but one thing she had learned, a call was never good.

She kept praying. She knew God had already heard her prayers. Every one of them. As she prayed, her vials in heaven were filling. They would pour forth their content at the right time. She would remain diligent, praying without ceasing. In his infinite wisdom, in his time God would respond, and it would somehow all work together for good because that was what he promised to do for those who truly loved the Lord. She truly did with all her heart, all her mind, and all her strength. Catherine kept murmuring until the door opened.

In walked her son, so full of joy, so innocent. Linc was looking at the most beautiful woman in the world. She shone like an angel. Even when she was sad and her eyes were red from crying, she was lovely. She loved him despite the trouble he sometimes caused. He recognized in his pure way that she needed love. He walked up to her and put his arms around her. His gesture was tender and exactly what she needed. She gave him a reassuring squeeze and held him close.

Catherine phoned the warden and made the arrangement for a meeting the following evening. Mr. Garret was brief on the phone, stating that he thought it best for any discussion to take place in person with both Catherine and her husband present.

Catherine decided it was a good time to go have a visit with her daughter. Maybe she would tell her what the warden was calling about, maybe she wouldn't; she hoped either way the visit would be an opportunity for her to encourage Amber regardless of what had happened.

She visited the next day. They had a wonderful visit. Amber seemed relaxed and was very cordial. Catherine hadn't seen her like that for a long time. Neither brought up the past. They had already said everything there was to say about it. If Amber wanted to discuss anything, Catherine knew her daughter well enough to know she would bring it up. She didn't want to make every visit like a question-and-answer period.

Catherine reinforced her love for her daughter, reiterating that she and her father were standing with her. She wanted her to know that she had someone in her corner, that she wasn't alone. Amber was chatty, asking questions about family and adding quips about her roommate … like she was at summer camp. Catherine left with a peaceful feeling and renewed hope of a personal relationship with her daughter.

She got home and was gushing to Michael of the wonderful visit. How friendly and talkative their daughter had been. It had felt so good to see her smile and relax. He was happy, really he was, but something didn't seem to make sense. He knew their daughter as well as his wife did. It didn't make sense to him. How could it to her? Did she need to believe that things were better so badly that she would lie to herself?

"I really wish I could have been with you," he answered honestly.

It was eight the following morning while Michael was still home that another call came from the prison warden.

Mr. Garret was sorry to be phoning with such bad news, but their daughter had had another breakdown today. Her condition was psychologically unstable. He informed Michael he had already put in a request to the judge to have Amber transferred to a psych ward. He requested one in minimum security but would take any with room.

Mr. Garret continued talking. Michael tried to absorb all the information.

"How could this be?" he asked. "My wife visited yesterday and commented specifically on how uplifted she seemed." Michael questioned further, seeking an explanation that would suffice. None could. He wanted to know where the dramatic decision had come from. Was there something they were not telling them? Mr. Garret's only answer was that they were already scheduled for an appointment with him later in the afternoon. They could discuss their daughter's complete case file then. Further to that, by four o'clock he hoped Amber would already be moved. The place they were sending her was called Everbrook. Catherine watched Michael's face expectantly.

Michael hung up the phone and began the task of relaying the message he had just received. They would both find out more at their appointment that evening. In the meantime, Michael and Catherine thought it best to consult their lawyer. Maybe she would be privy to more information than they were.

The morning left negative anticipation hanging over their heads. Michael had taken the day off for the meeting with the warden. They used the time to talk, speculating over the cause of Amber's mental meltdown.

"Michael, this could be a good thing for Amber. Going to that home will ensure she gets the help she needs. She has suffered so much already. We can't even comprehend what she has been through. Jail time for a crime she committed in self-defense wouldn't be right."

Michael had a hard time feeling his wife's optimism.

"Amber needs to be aware of what she has done, Catherine. Another family out there has lost their son forever. He won't 'receive treatment' and return home."

"Are you saying our daughter deserves to spend her life in prison, paying for a mistake made in self-defense? I believe her wholeheartedly, Michael. Don't you?"

"Are you sure you're not just refusing to believe you raised a monster?" The comment was made to make her be realistic; it wasn't how he actually felt. The minute the words were out of his mouth, he regretted it. "Catherine," he started softly, "I am sorry. I didn't mean that."

She looked so hurt. She didn't respond, but he knew he had hurt her. His wife needed him to speak truth. She needed it delivered gently.

"If her sentence is too easy or her punishment too light, she won't have time to heal, to change, to realize." He took her hand from across the table. She allowed it but didn't reciprocate the gesture. Michael looked at his wife intensely. He willed her to understand his perspective. "She won't be made new. She will be released, and she will be the very same person who wound up in prison. That puts us, and her, right back where we are now. Only we will all be older and more tired," he said with a smile and then continued seriously. "She has to take responsibility for what has happened, self-defense or not. I have yet to see the slightest bit of remorse or regret in our daughter."

Catherine knew he spoke the truth, but they were her parents. Did it matter if her sentence was too light? They had prayed so faithfully for Amber. Why couldn't this just be God answering their prayers? She refused to be a cynic like Michael. She had faith in her daughter, and further, she had faith in the justice system. Most importantly, she had faith in what she had been praying for.

"I guess I am not like you." Her tone was condemning. "I cannot so easily objurgate my own flesh and blood." She was still sore from his earlier statement. Did a marriage always have to come down to a scorecard? What about forgiveness? He wasn't going to play. Not today.

Catherine pulled her hand away and got up from the table. She walked over to the counter. She lowered her head and rubbed her brow deeply, kneading it with her fingertips. No, the pain wasn't going to stop. She had known that taking a shot at her husband wouldn't make her feel better; it made her feel worse. Michael walked up to her and placed both hands on her shoulders. He whispered in her ear, "Repeat after me, I can do all things."

She forced a smile. "I can do all things through Christ who strengthens me," she finished. Catherine would repeat that verse most of the morning and all the way to the prison for their meeting with Mr. Garret.

Eyes to See

"I will lead the blind by ways they have not known, along unfamiliar paths I will guide them. I will turn the darkness into light before them and make the rough places smooth. These are the things I will do. I will not forsake them."

Isaiah 42:16

Nina had agreed to meet the Whites at the prison. She knew about the request to have Amber transferred. Kimberly had put in the requisition to the judge immediately. Nina had been informed of that today. Mr. Garret, as was written on the outside of his office door, stood at least six foot four and was around fifty-some years of age. He was distinguished in appearance.

Contrary to television portrayals of prison wardens, Mr. Garret neither smoked, nor did he look seedy and dirty. He was well dressed but not overly so. The furrow in his brow led one to believe he cared for his female inmates and his prison.

Nina arrived before the Whites. Catherine and Michael noted the expressions on both Nina's and Mr. Garret's faces. Following the introductions, Mr. Garret offered the Whites a seat. Michael gestured to a chair for his wife; he stood behind her—the pillar of strength: hands on her shoulders, bracing himself, protecting her. Catherine gripped the armrest of the chair nervously. She could feel the tension in the room. She had already experienced enough of the "punch in the gut" moments, and she mentally and physically prepared herself for this one. Catherine glanced at Nina; the prudent lawyer wouldn't look her in the eye.

Michael was the first to speak. "Let's get on with this. We already know most of what you have to say. We know it's not good, so just spit it out."

"Sometimes truth is more difficult to take than one would anticipate. What I have to tell you will be told in truth. It will not be easy for you to hear." Mr. Garret paused, looking momentarily at Nina. Did he expect support from her? They knew Amber was being moved to a criminal psych hospital, and they knew she was unstable mentally. Was there more?

Mr. Garret continued, speaking empathetically, but that didn't lighten the blow of the truth. "Amber suffered another breakdown yesterday. It appeared to be a panic attack. She attacked the guard who was putting her in her cell. She had spent the previous night in the infirmary ..." He paused, searching for words. "She was there because of a suicide attempt in the early hours of the morning." Mr. Garret looked from face to face, allowing the information he had dumped on them to absorb. The rest of what he had to say worried him most. A suicide attempt was a difficult pill for any parent to swallow. But the story just got weird after that. How was he, as a professional, supposed to explain the lab findings?

He had been transferred to Klahanee two years ago. He had heard rumors and gossip about the corruption there. He had vowed under his watch that would be different. He had plans to implement a lot of changes. For one, he was determined to find every male guard in the place a job at a men's facility. A man had no place being a guard in a women's jail. It hadn't made sense how that could have ever been allowed in the first place. It showed bad judgment and a lack of common sense.

The events that have taken place here were all avoidable. What that guard did to these people's daughter was grotesque and disquieting, he thought. It sent a chill up his spine to fathom such evil. Edward had gone and visited the girl. She was still unconscious at the time. He believed the young girl's suicide attempt to be an effort to escape a repeat attack. The information had been made known to him only early that morning. He was very thankful for the brave and conscientious inmate who came to him with the information and the letter. He contacted the authorities immediately. He would be meeting meet Officer Campbell after he finished with the Whites. The guard had already been arrested.

If it hadn't been for that letter... He brought his mind back from its tangent to the matter at hand.

Catherine's mind was stuck on the statement "suicide attempt" while Michael was remembering "early hours of the morning." Catherine reached for Michael's hand. Immediately she felt the tears, her eyes burned.

"Around three in the morning, I bet?" Michael ventured.

Catherine brought her hand up to grasp Michael's arm. She felt his goose bumps; they matched her own. They knew it had happened around three a.m. They were up then, praying. Now they knew why. Mr. Garret was puzzled. "How did you know the time?"

"We experienced something divine at exactly that time," Michael said.

"God is faithful, he protected our daughter," Catherine added.

Mr. Garret was relieved. It wouldn't be as weird as he thought to divulge the particulars of the event.

"Well, I guess this won't come as a shock to you then. I am choosing my words carefully, because what took place, as you may have guessed, was supernatural."

"We have a word for that," Michael offered. "It's called a miracle."

"Call it what you want, believe it, or don't believe it, but these are the facts as I know them to be." He pulled out a piece of white paper from his desktop and began to read. "Inmate 5777, Amber Aaron White, injected with a syringe a mixture of strychnine, used for pest control, mixed with morphine ..." He went through the details. "She regained consciousness on her own. She was immediately brought into the infirmary and checked over." He read off her stats and the other particulars of the medical report. "The blood tests revealed what she had put into her body and how much. We also have a formal confession regarding the attack on Amber that took place in the shower stall. There was a prison guard involved. He has been arrested. I am so sorry for the suffering you and your child must have endured due to the attack."

He went into detail regarding Amber's evaluation and what had happened with Kimberly, the psychologist. When finished, Mr. Garret apologized again for their suffering.

"Thank you."

"In regards to all these events, I have decided the best thing for your daughter is to have her moved to a new facility as soon as possible. It is a psychiatric hospital for offenders. The place is called Everbrook. It is an all-women's facility. Nothing is co-ed, guards included."

Edward Garret stared at the couple in front of him. He put his paper down and waited. Neither had a discernable expression. He was thankful for the lack of emotional display. It always made him uncomfortable when overemotional people carried on. He had read the file on Amber. A series of mishaps had led her to this place. Everbrook was a better route for her. He had a daughter himself; he was sure what had kept her out of trouble so far was luck, family outings to visit the downtown slums, and live encounters with drug addicts, prostitutes, and other barely existing forms of life. He was a firm believer in scaring kids straight. That was what he had attempted to do with Maya, his daughter.

Michael interrupted his private thoughts. "Is there anything else we need to know?"

"It really is a miracle."

Catherine wasn't quite satisfied. There was a question niggling her brain. "How do you know she did it? Maybe the same guard who attacked her did this to her."

Mr. Garret was silent for a moment and then perplexed. "You question the suicide, not the miracle?"

There was no surprise regarding the miracle, he could see that.

"Your daughter left a tell-all letter. Her roommate found it and turned it in. It was detailed. A lot of people are going to face criminal charges because of that letter."

Noting that the couple was satisfied with his explanation, Edward reached into a small box on the corner of his desk. He pulled a brochure out of the pile of papers. He offered it to Catherine and Michael. In bold letters across the top read Everbrook; there was a detailed map below.

"Read over the brochure. If you have any questions, please call."

Catherine and Michael browsed through the small pamphlet.

"If the man responsible for Amber's attack was already arrested," Michael asked, "why does she still need to be moved?"

"The psych analysis done by the psychiatrist conclusively found that your daughter is suffering from mental illness. She will go over her reports with you. Her phone number is attached to her requisition."

Amber would be escorted to her new residence that evening via police officer. Mr. Garret looked at his watch. He had to finish up, for his next meeting was very soon. He hurried the Whites to finish and directed them to the door.

Michael and Catherine left the building. The couple were nearly at their car when they noticed a young man approaching them. They recognized him as the man Amber had clung to inside the courtroom that day.

"Hi," he said.

They greeted him cordially.

"I just wanted to meet you. How is Amber?. I pray for her."

Catherine smiled up at him, tears glistening in her eyes. She was completely unashamed.

"Thank you."

Michael reached out his hand, and Jake gripped it firmly. "Yes, thank you," he reiterated his wife's gratitude.

"I have had a few occasions to get to know Amber." Jake looked at them both intently. "I am full of hope for her. God has something very special in mind for her. Especially after the other night." He caught himself before finishing. They might not know exactly what happened.

"What happened?"

Jake was exhilarated to share with the couple the miracle he had experienced through their daughter, confirming God's power, power that is governed by love. They listened as children at story time. It was easy to imagine the scene. Jake was so expressive; he left out no detail. It was nothing like the reading they had received from Edward. Jake had felt, witnessed, and experienced God's divinity. And he loved every moment.

They talked awhile longer, until Jake realized he was late. Mr. Garret was up there without him. He wanted to be with him when he got Amber. Jake explained that he was expected to meet his partner. He gave the couple his phone number. "If you ever want to go out for coffee or invite a bachelor over for dinner … " he said good-humoredly and then left.

Once inside the office building, Jake took the steps two at a time. Warden was always on the top floor. Matthew was just coming out.

"Sorry," he panted his apology. "I ran into her parents at the bottom of the stairs. I just had to say something."

"Not something stupid, I hope," Matthew teased. Jake smiled an uneasy smile. He didn't think so. He had been wrong before. He said nothing. Edward held a paper in his hands. It was small, unwrinkled, and written in pencil.

"It's addressed to you." Edward handed the letter over.
"What is it?"
"Check it out." He flipped Jake the letter. As he read the
letter, Jake's face went from anger to ashen to despair and ended
in tears. He got it. He finally got it. This was why he had never
been able to really break through. There had been too much. Her
life had started falling apart at sixteen and accelerated to almost
nothing by the mere age of what had recently become twenty.

Jake himself was twenty-four. He had been twenty when
he had gone through all the stuff with Sofia. He understood
how experiences could destroy you. One incident had stretched
out over a year, and he wondered at times if he would survive.
Amber's demise had stretched out over four years and was laced
with corruption and violation.

Those intended to help her had stolen from her—stolen her
soul, her youth, her value. His heart went out to her. His soul
struggled to comprehend. He wanted to beseech God. Why?
Why so much for one person. He turned his plea into a prayer.
*Why has she had to endure so much? And why alone? Let her feel
your presence, Lord. You do not let anyone suffer alone, just as you
promise. You will never leave nor forsake us.* He already knew the
answer. She hadn't been alone. Jesus was with her whether she
acknowledged it or not. He went through every pain, every
humiliation with her. He would carry its weight; all she had to
do was give it to him.

Jake drew in a deep breath. He wondered if Amber's parents
knew about the baby, that it was from her doctor. She had been
audacious enough to write in her letter that they hadn't believed
her about the doctor. He looked up at the warden. He could see
by the look on his face that reading that letter had caused him
a similar, though less-personal, reaction. Edward shocked Jake
further with his statement. "You realize that this was her suicide
letter, don't you? This was only meant to be found after she was
found."

Jake shut his eyes tightly. He recalled that every time he had tried to talk to her about those things, she had shut him down or lashed out. Of course she couldn't let him down; she would keep her end of the bargain. She had always fought so hard to maintain integrity. He recalled her last statement to him. *"You don't care what it costs me."* It suddenly all spoke so clearly. It was for him. This letter was for him. The confessions were for him. The secrecy was for him. She couldn't tell him earlier. She was weighted down with shame and the conviction of others' sins.

She had kissed him as an offering of herself to him. In her mind, he had rejected her. He had become everything to her. He had noticed the signs before. He recognized, but he hadn't fully seen. She had put him in the place where Christ was supposed to be. She had made him her savior. Jake felt the full weight of the pain. His chest was heavy, his soul reprieved. God had said, "Love her."

"You win." He clenched his jaw. He was angry at himself. He had been selfish. She had put him first. She had wanted to protect him. He had wanted to protect himself. Jake dug his hands into his scalp, squeezing, eyes clenched tight.

When he could trust himself to speak, he choked out, "Every name on this list. We nail … every name." He stated it so emphatically that Matthew felt it necessary to remind him, "The cops will handle it with me at the helm, okay. You can work with me all the way. Just don't do anything stupid."

Jake nodded, still looking like a deer in the headlights. He had so badly wanted this information from Amber. Now he had it, and he couldn't squelch the nausea it brought him. One element gave cause to hope. There would be retribution.

Amber sat down in the chair that was offered to her. Mr. Garret invited her into his office. She became suspicious and began looking around the room. She hoped to find an escape, a weapon. She didn't know what; she just knew she should have a plan.

Having read her letter, the warden was sensitive to her mind-set. He opened the door to the office and immediately sensed some relief in both her expression and her body language.

"How are you feeling?" he asked.

"Why are you asking?"

"I am wondering if you are up to discussing the analysis done by the psychiatrist."

Amber said nothing, waiting for Mr. Garret to continue. There was a long silence.

"So let's hear it," Amber finally said. She could see compassion on the warden's face. She didn't allow it to soften her. She knew it wasn't going to be good anyway. Still, sitting in silence, Amber grew impatient and tried to help the warden out.

"No matter what that letter says, my fate doesn't lie with you. I either do my time in prison or I do it in a nuthouse. So let's have it."

"I ... the prison, well, there are a network of people involved in these decisions. It is just that it falls in my lap to be the one to make you aware of them." He paused for a moment, uncertain of what to say. She looked expectantly, waiting for him to finish, so he tried. "You will be going to a place called Everbrook this evening. You can be properly treated there—"

"What exactly does 'treated properly' entail?" Her tone was harsh. The warden remained gentle as he tried to explain the details to Amber. She appeared apathetic, until he mentioned that Jake would accompany Matthew on the drive. They would arrive shortly after the dinner hour to take her to her new residence. She spoke quietly then, not in the harsh voice she had used only moments ago. "Has he seen the letter?" She looked at the paper in Mr. Garret's hand.

"Yes," he replied bleakly. Again, he noticed the change. She didn't wear the expression so much on her face as she exuded it from her soul. "He is certain of one thing. He will bring you justice."

I knew he would. He never lets me down. She knew she could count on him, and she found peace in that fact. However, she really had no desire to have to face him.

Mr. Garret continued. "It is four o'clock now. You will go back to your cell and pack anything that you own. Your personal belongings you came in with have already been packaged for you and are ready for pickup. Don't forget them on your way out." He stood up, signalling that they were done. Amber stood also. She reached out her hand to the warden. When he took it, she thanked him for being honest with her. He placed his hand on her shoulder and looked into her eyes. He didn't say a word. Amber felt it. He knew she didn't belong in prison. There was little comfort in that when the alternative was a nuthouse. To some that was better. Amber would soon find out.

Dinner in the mess hall was at five thirty. They were done by six precisely. The next dinner group would soon come in. When Amber got to her cell, Officer Johnson was already there, Jake in tow. Lauryn had been transferred to a different cellblock after finding and turning in Amber's letter to the warden. When Amber found out, she was selfishly terrified. What would she do without her cellmate? Never mind what would happen to her cellmate if inmates found out she had turned in the letter.

That question had been answered. She was going to be transferred to what would hopefully be a safe place. She was relieved for Lauryn that she would be safe also. For herself, she no longer had to wonder when or where her letter was going to turn up. It already had. She thought she was so clever. She hid it in a library book. While inmates may work in the prison library, they don't get to return books. They have to be checked in by a guard for small weapons or personal contacts, anything irregular. Lauryn had decided to read Amber's book. It must have taken so much courage for her.

Amber picked up her small box of stuff; she turned around to go. Jake took the small box, carrying it for her. They began the walk, leaving the prison behind forever.

As the three neared the cruiser, Charlie lagged behind. Jake paused in front of the cruiser door. Neither spoke. The silence was uncomfortable. Amber had felt so anxious about seeing him, especially after what had transpired after their last meeting. And now he was in possession of the letter. *He must feel as awkward as I do,* she thought.

"So I hear you received the letter I sent you?"

"Sent me?" He smiled. "It took some work to get a hold of this letter sent to me."

Amber smiled back. She was searching for signs that he felt differently about her. She was sure he must. He couldn't have read all those things and not be disgusted by her.

"I hope you understand. It was really hard for me ..." Jake wanted so badly to tell her that she didn't have to explain; he wanted to tell her it was going to be okay, that he was going to do something about every name on that list, but he couldn't. He knew it was his time to listen.

They got in the car and began driving. Amber regained her composure and continued. "You are the last person I wanted to know about that part of my life, and not for the reasons you might think." She spoke truthfully and unabashedly. "You were my lifeline. My last thread of hope. I couldn't bear it if you stopped looking at me the way you do. Like when I impress you with something that I have said that causes you to think a little deeper, or the way you look at me like I'm a person, and I don't disgust you. You look through the sin, through the ugliness, past all that you already know. When you look into my eyes, I know it is for my soul that you search."

Amber was glad Jake wasn't looking at her. She didn't want to feel that intense searching that he had in his deep eyes. She dared a glimpse at his face in the rear-view mirror. She was shocked at the way he allowed tears to flow freely down his face. He didn't fight them or hastily wipe them away. He allowed them to do their job: to cleanse, to alleviate. He still said nothing, so she continued.

"How much can I expect you to look past? How much can

I hope not to be judged for? It is too much. It's more than any man should be expected to cope with. I wanted to spare you that. I didn't want you to think all your effort on me had been futile, that you hadn't done any good. You need to know you kept me alive. Not just physically, but on the inside. I breathe for that next time I will see you, when you will make me feel like I used to. Free. Intelligent. Unashamed." She was going to that place again. Something she had said. She detected he was uncomfortable.

He wanted to interject. She was making him out to be her savior again. He had to say something. The timing wasn't right. He knew saying something now, when she had allowed herself to be vulnerable, could ruin all of this.

I have to trust my convictions, he convinced himself. *I have to have faith. Say something,* he commanded himself. *Lord, give me the words.* They were pulling into Everbrook, waiting for the gates to open. He turned around.

"I didn't save you, Amber." His voice was intense. "I have no power to do such a thing."

Charlie got out of the car quietly, giving the two of them privacy.

"If I could, I would have." Jake wanted to take hold of her and shake her. He got out of the cruiser and climbed in the seat next to her. He looked at her intently, beseeching her to acknowledge what she knew.

"There is only one power, the power of the cleansing blood of Jesus. When you look at me and you feel clean, you are feeling the forgiveness of Jesus. When you look into my eyes and see hope, you are seeing the mercy of your savior. When you're exhausted by this life and you feel like you don't want to go on, you think you search for me, but it is the reprieve and unconditional love of the sacrificial lamb that you seek."

The tears welled up in Amber's eyes. She wished she could let them spill down; she needed to feel the warmth on her cheeks, validating that she was alive inside, that not all she was had been slain. So she stared at him, jaw clenched, eyes wide, breathing short, panicked breaths. She wanted to believe, if only to make him happy. She was too far gone. God, if he was out there, had a lot to hold against her by now. If what Jake spoke of was real, God certainly wouldn't extend his grace to the likes of her. She hadn't earned it. She was certain God would have revoked any offer a long time ago.

Neither spoke. Jake led the way out of the cruiser. Amber looked at her surroundings, her eyes went wide, and then she lowered her head. Jake looked around. He wanted to see what she saw. He looked at the hospital-like building. Black iron bars were on every window and door. He knew that wasn't what had caused her to look away. Something in what he had said was the cause. What he really wanted to do was pull her into his arms and hold her. He wanted to reassure her, but he couldn't risk it. He refused to be responsible for leading her farther down the path of confusion. Jake began to lead the way up the small path, his heart breaking, his gut wrenching with every step. Why did it have to be so hard? He looked around. Aside from the iron bars and iron fence, Everbrook looked like a pretty nice place, he tried to convince himself. There was a flower garden along the path and little gardening areas all over. There were enormous trees, gorgeous willows, and colorful hydrangea bushes. It looked a lot less like a prison, yet it definitely bespoke hospital.

There were wheelchair ramps going up to the garden gazebo off in the near distance as well as up to the main entrance. Where there were stairs on the path, there was an alternate wheelchair-accessible route. There was the ambulance cross above the door, and there happened to be an ambulance parked in the emergency parking space.

Jake was nearly to the top of the four-step entrance. He felt Amber grab his arm. The look on her face gave way to all she was feeling. He went against his better judgment. He wrapped his arms around her and pulled her in. He held her tightly and allowed her to bury her face in his chest. He felt the heaving of her chest. Her breathing was slowing. She was able to relax there in the strength and comfort of this one man. He put one hand on the back of her head and coddled her there like a frightened child. He firmly placed a kiss on top of her golden hair. He drank in her scent, absorbing the moment. He didn't know how long it would be until he could hold her again. His heart felt near bursting as she wrapped her slender arms tightly around him.

She wanted to ask him if he would come visit her. She dared not hope. The moment was too precious to hurt with words. They heard Charlie approaching; he stepped in front of them, saying nothing. He knocked on the door. The door was unlocking, and they broke their embrace. Neither risked a glance at the other person. Once again, she would need to be strong. And once again, he couldn't help her. Charlie stared at the door. They awaited the face that would greet them on the other side.

New Places

"Remember this, whoever turns a sinner from the error of his way will save him from death, and cover over a multitude of sins."

James 5:20

Hannah opened the door and warmly greeted the police officer and the new patient. Hannah wore a typical nurse's uniform. She was a very pretty lady. She looked to be about twenty-four. Her hair was sunny blonde and pulled back in a smooth ponytail. Her eyes were round and expressive; her cheeks were rosy, accentuated by lightly tanned skin. She was a petite lady with a bright smile.

Hannah gestured to where Amber would go with Charlie to register. When that was completed, he turned to go. Amber glanced up at Jake. Before letting him go, she took his hand. Palm up, she kissed it and pressed it to her cheek. "Thank you," she said, quietly and sincerely. She walked away. She didn't look back. Her breath got caught up in her throat. She nearly choked when she heard the sound of the large door closing, followed by the clang and rattle of all the locks.

Jake barely made it out to the cruiser. He got in and sat down. Tears streamed down his face. They offered no solace. She had stirred something in him, yet a gentle voice strongly warned that he had to stay away for a time.

THIS ROAD I WALK

He had imagined coming to visit Amber here. He had to continue to instil hope in her. If he didn't, who would? The unmistakable message had come with the clatter of the locks after the door had closed.

"In my time." He would obey, hoping and praying that God would change his mind. "Love her."

"I don't know how."

"Through prayer and supplication."

"For how long?"

He didn't receive an answer.

"'My word that goes out from my mouth: It will not return to me empty. But will accomplish what I desire and achieve the purpose for which I have sent it,' Isaiah 55:11."

He would love her. He would wait as long as it took. Jake had already chosen obedience; now he had to rely on faith.

Charlie was driving. Jake was still deep in his personal reverie.

"Can you go to Thirty-second Avenue?"

Charlie nodded and followed the road to the requested destination.

"Hang a left here," Jake instructed. Charlie knew where they were headed.

"Why do you want to torture yourself?"

"I don't. I should have come down here a long time ago."

"Are you sure that's what is going on?"

Jake watched where they entered. It had been a while since he had come down this particular road. "That way," he said, pointing left.

Charlie turned and then parked the car. Jake got out. Charlie waited.

Jake walked. He counted two rows down. Then right. One, two, three, till he got to twelve. There it was. The place Sofia's body rested. There was no epitaph, just the year she was born and the year she died. He hadn't been back there since the day her body was lowered into the ground.

"Only a grieving man comes to visit the dead."

Jake was startled. He hadn't heard Charlie approach.

"I don't understand."

"In the infamous words of King Solomon, 'Some things are meaningless.'"

"Some things are painful."

"Lots of things are painful. A woman in the throws of labor, yet she brings forth a child. And when it is stillborn, it is meaningless. A loved one with a terrible disease. If the disease is overcome, he lives like he never lived before. If he loses the battle, nothing good comes from it. It is meaningless. But a man loving the woman God has chosen, though he may have to wait, it is not meaningless. 'There is a time for everything under heaven, a time to embrace, and a time to refrain. A time to tear and a time to mend. A time to be silent and a time to speak' (Ecclesiastes 3:1, 5, 7). After the mending, you will have great joy."

His friend spoke the truth. He had planted the seed. Someone else would water it. Then if the seed fell on a pliable heart, it would grow. He would wait and pray. Pray without ceasing.

Hannah showed Amber to her room and introduced her to her two roommates. Talia, a former meth user, was always twitching and wiggling. Too many "trips" landed her here. Her eyes were enormous, and she always looked terrified. She was chronically paranoid. She spoke in short, choppy sentences. "You hungry?" or, "You're new!" "Watch that one." She made Amber feel like she should constantly check over her shoulder.

Amber's other roommate was Fiona. She suffered from a major blow to the head. She stuttered a lot. One could scream from the frustration of waiting for her to spit out one sentence. Fiona was a redhead. Her hair was long and straight, but she usually wore it in a braid. She had brown eyes that were usually half closed. She was cute, and though having a conversation with her could be trying, in general she was sweet and likeable. This was Amber's new home.

Amber looked around her room. There were three single beds, hospital type. Drapes hung between each bed, providing mock privacy if one chose. There was a single toilet to share that had a shower in it. Amber noted the door, a welcomed privilege. There were metal lockers for clothes or anything personal.

Amber put her small box down on her bed and began unpacking her few personal belongings into her private locker. Hannah had left her with a key. Both Talia and Fiona tried telling Amber all she would need to know about the facility; which nurses were nice, which ones weren't, patients she should stay away from, ones who got in trouble a lot. Like an older lady named Kathy. She was near forty. She was always trying to climb the iron fences and escape. She would be taken down. Sometimes after an escape attempt she would be sent to "the room." They explained alternately to her how there were two rooms patients didn't want to get sent to.

The first one was all white. The lights were too bright. The walls were padded. Her voice, if she tried to yell, would bounce back at her off every wall, and she would know no one could hear her. But "they" were monitoring, watching.

The other room was for patients who cracked up, lost it big time. That was the worst room. The nurses would pump a patient full of drugs and then leave them strapped to a table until they calmed down and were no longer a threat to themselves or anyone else.

"The only thing you can move is your eyeballs," Talia said. Amber wondered if they might not be telling the truth. Maybe this was no better than prison. A nurse came by around nine. She informed Amber that she would have an appointment with a doctor in the morning. They would go over her specific care plan, what meds she would need, risk assessment, and whatever else would need tending to.

Nurse Michelle read some notes from her clipboard and said with a knowing smile, "It appears you have already met our psych doctor, Kimberly Alexander." She looked expectantly at Amber. She had to think for a moment before being clear on whom she was speaking of.

"That freaky lady is the regular doctor here?"

"She wrote a lot of nice things about you in her report," the nurse countered.

"I'm sure she did. That Kimberly chick is the reason I'm here," she stated harshly. She supposed she should be grateful. The nurse raised her brow, not wanting to get into a confrontation. She walked over to Fiona and Talia and gave them their meds. Both took them happily. Michelle checked under their tongues to make sure they had swallowed them. Then she was gone. On her way out, she said, "Lights out at ten o'clock."

"What's your problem?" Both girls were inquisitive. "How come you're here? You seem normal."

Amber had no desire to go into her personal life. At her silence they just talked more about themselves. Amber was once again confronted with how much home life had contributed to the demise of those youthful people.

Ten o'clock couldn't come soon enough; she was tired and hopeful for a peaceful night's sleep, something she hadn't had in a long, long time.

Ten may have been lights out, but Talia and Fiona continued to whisper and laugh for what seemed like forever. Once in while Amber would hear Talia get mad at Fiona and say, "Spit it out. You gotta stop stuttering."

"The d-d-d-octor says that if if if y-y-you make fun of me, it j-j-j-just makes it w-w-w-worse."

"It's in your head." Talia was certain. A nurse came in and announced that it was midnight. Anymore talking would result in a loss of privileges. Amber wanted to thank her but didn't want to make quick enemies with her roommates, so she bit her tongue.

Amber was pleased to discover that mornings at Everbrook didn't begin until seven thirty. Instead of a fire bell, it was a knock on the door that woke the girls up. Then a gentle-voiced nurse would come in, open the drapes, and make her med call.

"Come on, ladies, the time for beauty rest is over. Talia, I have your pills. Fiona, come on. Come get your pill. Amber, you will see Kimberly at nine thirty. That gives you half an hour for breakfast. Someone will come get you from the eating area and take you to her office. Girls, did you tell your new roommate what time she needs to arrive for breakfast."

"Nine o'clock," Talia spurted. Amber smiled and thanked her.

"Walk with us," Talia said. The nurse smiled her fake smile and continued down the hallway.

Amber went into the bathroom, delighted with the privilege of a shower, such a simple pleasure. Amber got out of the shower and realized that she had no towel. She hadn't grabbed one. She hadn't even looked for one, and there were none in the bathroom.

"Can one of you grab me a towel, please?" she yelled through the door. There was no reply. She was sopping wet. There wasn't even a towel on the floor. She stood behind the door and opened it a crack, trying to be modest and hide her naked self.

"Hey, can I please get a towel?" She looked at the faces in front of her and realized immediately she must have done something wrong. Both girls were staring at her. There were shocked expressions on their faces. Neither moved, and awkward silence filled the room.

Finally, Fiona ran out the door. As soon as she was gone, Talia said, "You're in trouble. Big trouble … No shower pass, no shower." She screwed up her face to let Amber know it was big trouble. Before Amber could defend herself, Fiona came into the room. She was carrying a towel for Amber. In tow was Nurse Hannah from the evening before.

"Has anyone told you about the rules here, Amber?"

"I have heard a few of them."

"I apologize. You should have received a booklet explaining our privileges and policies. I will get you one now. Someone can go over it with you, if you need. In the meantime, Fiona has a towel for you. You need to hurry now to make it down for breakfast." Hannah left. Fiona handed the towel to Amber.

"Thank you." She meant it.

Now that she had a towel, Amber realized a second problem. She only had the clothes she had worn yesterday, the same clothes she had been arrested in. She couldn't wear those clothes. Where was she supposed to get clothes? She looked at the dirty clothes on the bathroom floor.

The jeans were filthy, white crusted crystal meth stains still remained on the knees. The prison hadn't washed them before giving them to her to wear yesterday. It turned her stomach; she felt queasy. She steadied herself, gripping the towel bar.

"Get a grip," she scolded herself, picking up the jeans and using as little of her hand to touch them as possible. She dumped them into the shower and turned on the hot water. She would scald the pants clean. To her surprise, the water didn't get hot. She picked up the hoodie she had been wearing. It was still stained with vomit. She had thrown up outside the dingy apartment after she stuck Duncan with the needle.

She threw the hoodie on top of the pants. The room was steaming up. She knelt down on the floor. Looking at those clothes brought such truths to light. In a flash she saw her life, dirty and stained, like the clothes. That's how she must look to those on the outside, how she must appear to Jake. How was it that he still gave her so much value? He just gave.

Determined not to break down, she took the towel off her head and wrapped it around her body. It was an all-women's prison hospital, right? Just then she heard rushed footsteps coming into the room. There was a quick knock on the door, the jingling of the keys. Then the door flew open.

There stood Hannah. "What is going on?" As she asked the question, she took in the scene around her. The shower.

The dirty clothes from which, because of the steam, arose a repugnant odor. A look of understanding crossed Hannah's face as she noticed Amber's morose expression. She turned off the water. She would not scold or punish her this time. Instead, she led her down the hall into a huge linen room. There was an enormous trolley layered with different colored and sized uniforms. She grabbed one, looked at the size, and then tossed it to Amber.

"This should do. You are allowed to wear your own clothes as a privilege. In the case of disobedience, that privilege can be removed. Then you are back to our uniforms. There are strict guidelines regarding personal clothing. Your parents or an appointed guardian will receive a list. They can bring your clothes when they visit."

Amber, unsure of what to do and having had all her dignity stripped at Klahanee, dropped the towel and began to dress right there. Hannah averted her eyes. Once dressed, Hannah led Amber down to breakfast. She had ten minutes to eat before her meeting.

Unfortunately, breakfast was not held for latecomers at Everbrook, and there was nothing left for Amber. She was ready to make her way back to her room when a nurse spotted her. She began making her way to Amber.

"I will show you to Kimberly's office." Remembering who Kimberly Alexander was, her stomach knotted, and she felt a surge of anxiety.

They walked down a long corridor.

"If I scream from down here, can anyone hear?" Amber asked the question out loud but not to anyone.

"Your sessions are recorded and monitored," the nurse said flatly. Amber found little comfort in that.

The nurse guided Amber into a small room and she was gone. There were no windows; she began to feel panic claw at her stomach. Her head ached. She needed to sit down.

Amber stared wide-eyed at Kimberly as she entered the

room. Kimberly noticed and addressed the issue immediately. "We met briefly at Klahanee. You know it was my recommendation for you to be sent here. Amber, you are not prison material. I have seen your file. I have spoken with the arresting officers from the incident. I believe you acted in self-defense. I also think it is destroying you. I hope you desire to get well. You can achieve that here. You have hope for a normal life." Amber was listening intently, putting every effort into making it appear as though she wasn't. She looked around the room, staring at books in the huge bookshelf. She looked at the diplomas attached to the walls. Kimberly kept talking.

"Things will get better for you here. We'll meet once a week at first."

"Is that it?"

"I would like to record your account of that first time I interviewed you, if you can."

Amber couldn't decide how she felt about the meeting at all. She kept waiting for the rug to be pulled out from under her the way it had been last time.

The silence stretched until it became uncomfortable. Amber knew she was waiting for her to speak. She had nothing to say, not anything Kimberly would hope to hear.

"When am I allowed to have visitors?"

"That's not my decision, Amber. I only handle your psych file. You need to try talking to me. When you were at Klahanee, I know our meeting sent you reeling. It was something neither of us expected, I am sure. I want you to know I have no desire to use you sexually in order for you to receive something. The only way for you to succeed here is through hard work and devotion. I understand what you have been through. I hope you learn to trust me so I can help you."

Amber finally made eye contact with Kimberly. She was careful to hide anything she may have been feeling. "You don't look like you have that kind of time, Kimberly."

"Would it really be so hard for you to trust me?"

"Yes."

"Because I am a psychiatrist, or because of what happened at Klahanee?"

Amber continued to hold her gaze and, without batting an eye, retorted, "It's the hair!"

Her hair was funky, and she liked it that way.

"Style or color?" she asked, giving the question more genuineness than it evoked. Amber, impressed that she would continue the banter, answered seriously, "Preferably both, but I would settle for one or the other."

"Done," she replied. Amber hoped she wasn't making another promise she couldn't keep. The one she had made to Jake hadn't ended the way she intended. If this woman came back with a new hairdo, she would have to talk to her. Amber decided that if she was willing to change her hair, she could respect that, and she would talk to her. Kim handed Amber a piece of paper with her meeting time for early next week.

Amber had a hard time adjusting that first week, living with people who had no control over their lives and no desire to control their lives. The nurse said open up, and they opened up and in popped a pill. The nurse said lights out, and lights out it was. Everyone seemed like mindless drones to her. She wondered just how much medication the ladies in the facility received. She would not take any meds. She knew she had issues that needed to be worked on, but nothing in her life was messed up enough to warrant prescription medication.

Dr. Alexander prescribed meds for Amber, which she vehemently refused until she could speak with her. Kimberly came down to the floor right away to discuss the issue with Amber. The first thing Amber noticed was that Kimberly had already changed her hair. It looked nice. She wore a solid color, chestnut. It was cropped short and evened out. She had it gelled and styled.

Kimberly smiled at Amber. "Is this acceptable? 'Cause right now it would be useful if you chose to talk to me about what is going on here."

"A much-needed improvement, so here it is. This nurse is trying to cram pills down my throat. She won't tell me what they are or what they are for. She just keeps saying, 'This is what the doctor wants you to take.'" Amber made her voice high pitched and whiny, imitating the nurse. "Does she know I'm not retarded? I can make decisions by myself. I think, as a previous drug user, the last thing I need is another drug dependency for any reason."

"Good point. The pills that I prescribed for you are for your anxiety. You need to take them regularly for at least a week before they begin to work. Would you deny that you can be prone to anxiety attacks?"

"Is that what I keep having that make people think I'm insane?"

"I believe so. I will continue to analyze you."

Amber wasn't sure why that statement set her off. Maybe it was the way she referred to her as little more than a lab rat, but she blurted out harsh words without thinking.

"Analyze," she repeated the word, spitting it out like it was profane. "You can't analyze me like a rat and come up with a common denominator, then fix me and everyone who's like me with some group narcotic. You may not require anything from my body, but at least Gordon was educated."

She hoped the shock she felt at her own callous words wasn't revealed on her face. She had never, through any impassioned hatred of that man, spoken his name with such familiarity.

Kimberly looked at the nurse and ordered, "Until I have another session with Amber, she doesn't have to take those." Directing her attention back to Amber, she dictated, "We will have our appointment tomorrow." That was three days earlier than previously planned. Amber's heart began to race. Would she be sent to one of the "rooms" her roommates had warned her about? She wondered what Kimberly would do to her.

Amber bowed her head and went back to her room. Talia and Fiona were both there chatting. Amber's cantankerous mood made no allowances. She lashed out at her roommates, mimicking Fiona, "T-T-T-Talia, don't you g-g-g-et tired of l-l-listening to that?"

Talia looked horrified. She didn't speak. She just looked back at her friend and smiled. Fiona looked like it hadn't even fazed her.

"Oh, come on, I can't be the only person who notices the st-st-st-stuttering. I guess for a person who can't form a compound sentence, you are great company."

Of all the things Amber knew herself capable of, she had never been malicious. What had come over her? The nastiness continued as she hurled other insolent comments. Fiona began to cry. Talia wouldn't stand for any more. She pulled Amber's curtain closed.

Amber continued the verbal battery. "For Pete's sake, Fiona, don't be so sensitive. I can't be the only person to ever tease you. Toughen up. You two would never survive prison."

Talia noted her chance and took it. "Neither could you. That's why you're here. You went all nutso at the prison 'cause you couldn't handle it." She spoke more consecutive sentences than anyone had heard in at least two years, and the words struck their mark.

Amber whipped the curtain open. Seething with anger, she got on top of the girl who had only been protecting her friend and shook her shoulders with the strength that comes from pent-up rage. Talia's head shook and smacked again and again against the mattress, resounding dull thuds with every blow despite the softness of the landing. Amber's face contorted with fury. Fiona shrieked, a high-pitched, long scream easily heard by staff members.

A nurse came running in, followed by two other nurses. They grabbed Amber and pulled her off Talia, who continued to lay in shock. Fiona sobbed.

To Amber it was like watching something on television. She was just acting her part. Soon someone would yell, "Cut!" and then she would be herself again. She was brought to a pretentious reality by the sight of the large needle the nurse intended to inject into her flesh. She began thrashing and flailing. "You can't do this to me! Get off me! I didn't do anything! Please! Stop!" Her tangent was laced with expletives. No one was listening to her.

The needle went in. The nurse pushed the drug into her vein. It was effective immediately. Two of the nurses held Amber's limp body up while a third got a chair to put her in. They brought her to "the room," the one her roommates had warned her about. It was day seven at Everbrook.

Once again, Jake was accompanying Matthew on a ride-along. It was near the end of the shift. The two weeks since Jake had last seen Amber had gone by slowly. Their last conversation played over in his mind, and he wondered, *When? When will be the right time?*

He wanted to tell her the good news. Tyler Porter was charged, and so was Darryl Tate. Mostly because of the letter she had written. Her cellmate, Lauryn, had corroborated her stories; that helped. Jake hoped someone would pass the information on to her. She needed to know. He hoped that knowledge would grant her some peace.

One major name was left on that list: Gordon Forbes, and he was presently being investigated. It still made Jake sick to his stomach when he thought about it. At times he questioned God. He was angry; he would repent. He sought answers. None were good enough.

The most difficult information for him to cope with was the incident she described, where she "offered" herself to the repugnant doctor. It was condemning for her. Why would she include that? Did she hope that by making a complete confession, she would absolve herself of the guilt? Was she trying to offend him personally? Warning him of who she thought was her "true" self? Sorrowfully, that piece of the confession screamed of the unworthiness she felt for herself. It only saddened him further that she thought that was all she was worth.

He recently came across a passage in his devotions that renewed his hope. It was from Psalm 9:12 and 18. "He remembers who the evil doers are, he will not forget the cries of those who suffer, those who have trouble will not be forgotten, the hope of the poor will never die."

Matthew was talking, breaching his thoughts. "We need the full name of the girl Amber mentioned in her letter. Then we will try to find out if there are any more."

Breaking Ground

"Believe on the Lord Jesus Christ and you and all your house shall be saved."

Acts 16:32

Amber had already been at Everbrook for two weeks. Michael and Catherine were advised that there could be no visitors for the first three weeks. After that, as long as good character prevailed, they could come anytime between regular visiting hours.

Ruth and Linc were both excited to join Catherine and Michael on their first visit to see Amber.

"We all need to show our support for Amber," Ruth had stated.

Preparing for the visit, Catherine went into Amber's room to get some clothes. The nurse had explained to her about earning privileges. One of the privileges was wearing, within Everbrook's guidelines, her own clothing. She went through the drawers searching for anything appropriate. She pulled out a pair of jeans. They had been favorites not so long ago. She held them up. They would never fit. She must have lost near twenty pounds. They would have to stop at the mall and pick up some clothes on their way.

At the sight of her parents, the first words out of Amber's mouth were, "Get me out of this place!" followed by expletives. She had exploded before seeing her grandmother and her brother round the corner. She continued her tirade, leaving out the expletives. "Do you know what they do to you here? Do you know about 'the room'? I only got back from 'the room' yesterday. I was put on a table. My hands and my feet were buckled to the bed. At night a strap was placed around my head to keep my head from moving. This is not a place to be treated for insanity. This place will cause insanity."

Neither parent appeared sympathetic.

"You would rather be sent back to prison?" Catherine called her bluff.

Knowing she couldn't go back, Amber felt safe answering, "Yes!"

"We'll talk to someone before we leave," Michael reassured his daughter.

"Who? Who will you speak to? And what will you say? You can't help me here any more than you could help me at the prison." She looked away, demonstrating her disappointment in them.

"Amber, you will be here for a while. You need to figure out how to cope and get along with other people."

Her mother joined her father's rationale. "We looked into this place. It is really a great facility. You have to give it a chance. Aren't you worth more than what you have settled for? This is your second chance. *Make it work.*"

Amber's demeanor changed from belligerent to vanquished. Her parents were totally unsympathetic. Big surprise. Apparently guilt was short lived in her home. She wished it could be that easy for her.

Amber took the moment to acknowledge her grandmother. "Hi, Nan."

Lincoln looked up at her with huge, expectant eyes. It affected her, and her attitude quickly changed. "Linc!" She feigned enthusiasm. He looked up, delighted. His big sister wasn't mad at him for ratting her out. He had told about the phone call, the one about Amber wanting to kill someone. He wondered if that was the reason she got sent to this place that she hated.

Amber thrust out her arms. He responded immediately and bounced onto her lap, embracing her. She tousled his hair, hugging and kissing him. She told him how much he had grown, how handsome he was. She asked him about school and friends. He answered and asked questions of his own.

The adults made small talk. Nan came over to Amber and embraced her for a moment. Amber stiffened automatically. She ordered herself to relax and allow her grandmother to release her affection. Catherine handed Amber the bag of clothes. It was more than just clothes; they represented choice and that she had something of her own. One outfit was a velour sweatsuit in pale blue. There were a pair of loose-fitting capri pants and a matching T-shirt, some socks and underwear. What simple joy, having her own underwear. She wouldn't have to wear ones with the initials EPF, Everbrook Private Facility, in every pair. Michael and Catherine stood up to go. They were nearing the end of their visit.

Catherine hugged her daughter and placed a kiss on her cheek. "I will never stop loving you. I know you already know that, but I wanted you to hear it from me."

Amber thought about that. There had been times over the last years that she had given them reason to give up on her. Amber knew those words were sincere, coming from the deepest recesses of her heart. Where else could they come from after all she had put her mother through?

Michael handed Amber a beautiful handbound book. It had pressed flowers on papyrus paper in the front. It was full of blank pages. He and Nan had picked it out while Catherine and Linc had picked out the clothes. It came with a mini pen that slid perfectly between the seam.

"Thank you, Daddy. It's beautiful." She was sincere.

"You can write down all the things you've been afraid to feel. The words you record can be a source, an outlet for you. When you read back through what you have written and all the things you have endured and overcome, you will find encouragement."

Nan bent over and kissed Amber's cheek. "I love you, sweetie. Old Nan is praying for you. When this is all over, I know you will amaze us all, even yourself, with the person that emerges."

Amber had initiated the hug with her father; the book was so thoughtful. After everyone left, she thumbed through the pages. She noticed writing on some of the pages. She read one; it was a Bible verse, "If he stumbles he will not fall, because the Lord holds his hand" (Psalms 37:24).

A few pages over there were some words of inspiration. *I loved you from the moment I found out you were on the way. I loved feeling you kicking inside your mother's womb. I was thrilled by the miracle of your birth, what a joy to hear your first words, such pride in those first steps. My love for you continues to grow. You will always be my gift.*

In what appeared to be the exact middle of the book, he had written, "For the wages of sin is death, but the gift of God is eternal life in Christ Jesus our Lord" (Romans 6:23). She remembered back; she had tried to recall that verse once, but all she could remember was the death part. She realized now it would have been helpful to remember the rest of that verse.

There were more little inspirations jotted throughout the precious book. "I will put my laws on their minds, and write them on their heart. I will be their God, and they will be my people. For I will forgive their wickedness, and will remember their sins no more" (Hebrews 8:10, 12). Amber cherished the book.

Once back in her room, she tucked it under her pillow. Then she rested. She had lost her battle to stay off medication. She hadn't given in easily. In the end she hadn't really had a choice. The seventy-two hours she spent in "the room" had been one of a drug-induced haze. She now found that she wanted to take the Paxil. She was dependent on it.

As time went by, things began getting better. Amber did as her father had suggested. She wrote things down. When people made her mad. When she felt judged. When she had feelings of guilt. She wrote it all down. She was getting used to Everbrook. It was preferable over prison. Time seemed to be going by more quickly. There were routines and privileges at Everbrook. The thing she enjoyed most was outside. Amber hadn't realized how much she missed outside.

When asked to work in the yard one day, Amber remembered living at home, thinking yard work was a chore, but when Fiona had asked her to come out and help, she was excited. Fiona and Talia had quickly forgiven Amber for the incident that had sent her to "the room."

"A-a-a-Amber, d-d-d-o d-d-d-o you want to c-c-come to come out in in in the garden?" Fiona asked. Amber had happily gone. The job was tilling the soil, preparing it for planting. It was only April, but they would start planting in mid to late May depending on the weather. Fiona and Talia both described to Amber the lovely flowers that would grow in the summer. Fiona loved all the different floral smells, while Talia loved the radiant colors.

The large vegetable garden was around the side of the building on the east side, where the sun rose every morning. There were no trees on that side, so shade didn't come until evening, allowing an abundance of vegetables to grow. Amber was excited to watch the tiny plants as they would start, then struggle against the rampant growth of the weeds until someone came along to save them, plucking out the weeds by the root. They would be safe for a short time. Then new weeds would come. It was a bit of a metaphor for Amber's own life. In her mind the vegetables would win, she would make sure.

The girls worked, pushing, dragging, and pulling the tiller through the rough soil, using the shovel to mix in the big clumps of fertilizer. It was laborious, and it felt good to work up a sweat. Fiona had a large chunk of dirt stuck on her shovel. She lifted the shovel abruptly, hoping to bang it on the ground and knock the soil loose. The dirt did come loose. It flew right into Amber's face. For a moment Fiona looked terrified. Amber shrieked then giggled and lobbed a piece of dirt at Talia. The dirt-slinging match was on.

Before long, all three girls, and a few others who were also gardening, were covered head to toe in dirt. Hannah was on duty. She watched the fun, smiling to herself. The girls ran around, laughing, flinging dirt.

Amber flumped down on the ground. "I give up." She was still laughing. She hadn't felt so human since—her mind paused—she knew exactly when.

It was that night driving with Jake. Talking on the radio, she smiled at the memory. She wondered if she would ever see him again. A familiar pain tugged at her heart. He had saved her so many times. He was always there when she needed him. Her heart beat for him and, in her mind, because of him. It had been six months since she had seen him last, the night that he had dropped her off here. She closed her eyes, remembering how safe she felt with his strong arms around her. She wondered if he ever thought about her. She wondered what he was doing and if he had been true to his word about bringing her justice.

Michael and Catherine came regularly to see Amber. They had ever since she was taken there, so when she was told there was a visitor to see her, she assumed it was her parents. Visits with her parents were mostly enjoyable. They didn't preach at her like they used to, and they didn't make her feel guilty. She could visit with them without feeling like she had somehow ruined their lives or let them down. She no longer felt that she owed them an explanation for everything.

Amber walked down the corridor and reached the designated visiting room. The person waiting for her could not have been more of a surprise. Her eyes widened. She sucked up a breath and forgot to release it. It was a face from the past—one she hadn't been expecting. The smug expression on the other girl's face was exactly what Amber would have expected.

Amber recalled running into Kyle only weeks before her arrest for Duncan's murder. He told Amber about Wyatt being in jail. She was sure he had enjoyed telling her about Cody and his new sweetheart.

"You know her. Your friend, Jersey," he had eagerly pointed out. Of course she knew who she was. They had become good friends. Amber had been shocked but mostly heartbroken over the news.

She found herself face-to-face with Jersey. Amber sat across from her. No one spoke for a moment. The two girls held eye contact and waited for the other to speak. Finally, Amber broke the silence. "What?"

"I thought you would like to know something."

"Nope."

"Are you sure about that?"

Amber didn't answer. Jersey's expression made Amber feel less sure. Maybe she did have something good to tell her. She would wait her out, let her offer up the information. She could see she was dying to drop her secret. Jersey looked around and then spoke so quietly, Amber had to ask her to repeat herself.

"It's done!"

A shiver ran up Amber's spine. That moment she knew she didn't want to hear anymore; still, she had to ask. "What's 'done,' Jersey?"

Amber's stomach hit the floor. Cody had made her a promise, and he had used Jersey to fulfil it. She already knew the answer, and it made her sick.

"We got him, Amber. We did it for you. Cody did it for you."

"I didn't ask him to do anything for me, Jersey."

"But you'll be so glad when you hear."

"What did Cody do?"

"He got that doctor good. We got him for you, Amber."

Amber could feel her temperature rising. Her face flushed. *We*, she had said. How much did Cody tell Jersey?

"What did you do?" Amber was more insistent.

Jersey looked around again and then handed Amber a small newspaper clipping. The date on the top was only three days old. The writing appeared faded. The caption read *Doctor's Peril*, the Story Told of a Doctor, one who was presently under investigation for several counts of sexual misconduct. Amber read on. It appeared the doctor had committed suicide. Carbon monoxide poisoning was the vice. An autopsy would still be performed. Foul play was not anticipated.

"Know why there is no suicide note?" Jersey sounded evil. She loved this, and it wasn't even her life. She wasn't the one who had been humiliated. She hadn't gone through the torment. She wasn't the one he had raped. Her body hadn't carried his child. Her mind hadn't had to live through the repugnance of conceiving that child.

"He picked me up, thinking I was a hooker." Jersey didn't seem to notice the disapproval on Amber's face. "I got in the car with him. Cody told me to leave the window open, and while we were messing around, he put a tube from the exhaust into the window. Cody waited until we both passed out. Then he pulled me out of the car. Isn't Cody brilliant?" She was beaming.

Amber couldn't believe it. "Are you high?" she asked disgustedly.

Jersey giggled.

"Don't tell me this stuff, Jersey. I don't want to know. Whatever stupid thing you and Cody did I don't want to know about it."

Jersey's expression changed instantly, clouding over the exuberance. She seethed. "I risked my life for you. So did Cody. How can you be so ungrateful?"

Amber was dumbfounded. "I didn't ask anyone to do anything for me. This wasn't *your* problem. It wasn't even Cody's problem. There is an investigation, Jersey. I would have rather seen him rot in prison and be some guy's doll than slip comfortably into an eternal sleep. What justice is that? I won't get any vindication now. You can't prosecute the dead. You messed me up is what you did." Amber's voice had gradually reached a low growl. Careful to keep her voice down, she felt like grabbing Jersey by the throat and choking her. "Stupid bimbo," she hissed.

"I can't believe you, Amber," Jersey's annoyance with her only vexed Amber further. She came to a self-righteous realization: Jersey was just a victim of an excessive drug-induced stupor, so she explained carefully, as she would to an idiot.

"I would be grateful, really I would, but Jake was handling this. He would have nailed him. And a long, drawn-out punishment for what he did to *me* suits me a lot more than dying peacefully in his sleep. Get it?"

Then it all went bad. Jersey's eyes darkened and narrowed. "Who's Jake?"

Amber didn't catch the warning as she explained, "That aid guy who was always with Officer Campbell, whatever. Jake, black hair, brown eyes, nice bod. Young."

"That pig who arrested us when we were in the warehouse. He is doing this for you?"

"Not for me," Amber tried to explain. "It's his job."

"What's he get from you in return?" There was an accusation in that statement. Amber felt a sensation in her flesh. This was not right. "Amber, all you had to do was be thankful to me and Cody. We stuck our necks out for you."

"You moved in on my man the minute I was gone. I will be grateful to you for nothing." Even while she was saying it, she was aware that she had little feelings left for Cody. It was Jake's face that stayed vividly in her memory.

"You left him. But he still loved you. He took a huge risk. We both did. Do you know how bad this is gonna be?"

"I didn't ask either of you for this."

"What did you think would happen when you told Cody

about all those sick things that pig doctor did to you? He loved you. He told you he was going to do something"

"Jersey, we're done. You need to go."

"This is about to get really nasty. We aren't through yet." Jersey walked away. She headed straight for a nurse and spoke to her on her way out. Amber's blood went cold. She began rationalizing. "I'm locked up. They can't blame me for this." Her anxiety was peaking, ready to go. She walked back to her room as quickly as she could. She threw herself onto her bed, screaming into her pillow. She punched it. She had to make the hysteria go away. It was closing in around her, cutting off her air, squeezing her lungs, tightening around her throat. She gasped for air. She swung the pillow over her back and brought it down hard against the mattress. She swung at the fake brass headboard. It wasn't helping. She felt the guilt. She hadn't done anything. She hated him, but she didn't want him killed. She wanted him ruined. She wanted vindication. She wanted him to suffer like she had suffered. Now he had gotten off way too easy.

Then Jersey said they had done this *for* her. They had been bored and high and used her as an excuse to see what they could get away with. The rage continued to grow in Amber the more she recalled the conversation.

After the rage came bitterness. She had been ripped off. He would never suffer, and no one would ever know the truth. After the bitterness came fear. What if she got blamed? Especially after her accusations against him and the charges against her. It did make her look guilty. It ran through her head repeatedly. She flung the pillow across the room.

The rage grew stronger. She kicked the night stand beside her bed. The metal made a loud bang. She shoved the bed as far as she could across the room. The rage wouldn't stop. It picked up momentum. The more she fed it, the more it grew. She clenched her jaw and then punched the metal lockers. She picked up the book, the one from her daddy. She hurled it at the window. The Plexiglas window wouldn't break, but the loud bang brought the nurses running. There were four of them. They grabbed at Amber and tried to hold her. Her rage was powerful, and she fought them. The tirade had escalated into hysteria.

Eventually, a fifth person joined them, and they overpowered her. Exhausted and defeated, reacting to the recently injected medication, Amber went limp. For the second time since being at Everbrook, Amber was on a gurney being wheeled into a "special room." When she regained consciousness, she discovered she was in a white room. White lights, white walls, white floor, and a white ceiling. There was a small Plexiglas mirror. Unbeknownst to Amber, it was a two-way. She was being watched.

"You hear that a body was found on rounds last night?" Matthew cut into Jake's private thoughts.

"What's that?"

"Down the alley off McGillvery, they found Forbes' body in his car. Carbon monoxide poisoning. It's being called a suicide."

"Suicide? What a coward! This will destroy Amber and any other of his victims hoping for vindication. Did he leave a note? Or a confession?"

"He looks pretty guilty. The inquisition has just started, and he dies?"

"You're probably right, but what of his victims"

"They may be thankful for the trade-off."

Amber filled Jake's thoughts. She was counting on Forbes being proven guilty. She needed people to know she had told the truth. That wouldn't happen now. He hoped she would be okay when she found out. Her sanity had already been evanescent.

Evil, like darkness in every corner, had constantly lurked in Amber's life, always overshadowing the light. The confession she had written lit a fire in his soul. He read that letter daily; he would make good on his promise to her and pray continuously. At times all that enabled him to salvage sanity was faith in a just God and a promise of hell for those earning it.

Jake hoped Amber's parents would keep her aware of the arrests that had already been made, and now this. It struck him that people who seemed to have everything together, who seemed to do everything right, could end up with such a wild child. There were no certainties with children.

He got Charlie to drive him to Everbrook once. He remained in the car, looking out the window, unable to move. She had been right there, in the garden with some of the other girls. He watched her until Charlie drew in an exasperated breath, asking if his curiosity was replete? It was obvious the older man knew he had no intentions of approaching her. They drove off. That was the picture he carried with him. Her outside. Sun shining on golden curls. Genuine smile. If he had been closer, he may have heard her laugh. She had served almost half her sentence. She would turn twenty-one before being released.

Matt drove in silence, responding to the call they had received. Jake embraced the warmth of the sun. It tingled on his skin, like gentle hands caressing his face. The wind from the open window tousled his hair. It caused him to relax; he drank in the moment.

Amber wasn't sure if it was the white of everything that toyed with her sanity, or if it was her life and all the calamities in it. How long had she been in the rubber room, the second of the dreaded rooms at Everbrook? At first she just lay on the rubber floor, taking in all the white and the lights. The lights were so bright. She was groggy that first day. The next day she awoke a beast bent on rage and destruction. She flung herself into the walls, she spat, she screamed, she pounded her fists; all behaviors leading her further from the sanity she sought.

Weary and replete, she sat down on the floor. She was rest-less but had no energy left to fight. She was famished by the time food came. She ate it as though she had been starved for a week. She drank from the bowl and dug into the food with her hands. Food got into her hair, and by day four she began to smell. It was inhumane being left in there that long. She banged on the Plexiglas with whatever energy she had left. She screamed her accusations at whoever was watching. She cursed and pounded with her fists on every wall. She refused to be broken ... at first.

By day five with no contact from any other human, no toi-let, or bathing facilities, Amber was more insane than when she began. She did not want to be reduced to their mold, but she couldn't survive anymore. She curled into a ball, inside herself, where it was safe. Her mind sought comfort. Her body craved rest. Her soul yearned for solace. She stayed that way another day.

She awoke that sixth day with a spark of hope evoked through a dream, or perhaps it was a memory. Deep, dark eyes. Expression of love. Broad smile. A man. His hands extended toward heaven. He loved her. So he prayed for her.

She walked over to the windowed mirror and pushed her face up close enough to see a reflection. She began to speak to her reflection. There was no one else. "I never wanted this to be my life. I was full of life and hope once. This dead, empty life was not meant for me. You offer so much more. I need whatever you can spare me." Deep in her regret, sated by truth, she hadn't even realized she had prayed her first prayer in years. It came from within. Amber raised her hand and placed it on the two-way mirror, tracing her features with her fingertip. They didn't seem to resemble how she thought she looked.

She took a step back and gasped. Realization seeped in. She tried to cover the revelation with her hand. Too ashamed to be seen by the eyes of the One who knew. Eyes wide, yearning for acceptance, knowing she didn't deserve it. Her heart pounded at the realization.

She slumped. Sliding her body down the wall, her hand followed the conjectured profile of the One. The One who was still waiting for her. She curled up at the imagined semblance of his feet. She heard his voice; it whispered so kindly, full of the love and the hope she longed for. "I am waiting. I keep waiting." She knew. There was no mistaking Him. There is no mistaking Jesus.

An image of Jake freely, unashamedly allowing tears to fall flashed in her mind. Then curled at his feet the years of held-back tears pushed their way to the surface, a geyser of unreleased pain. Finally, Amber released hers. For so long she had used the scorching water of the shower to superficially cleanse all the filth away. She realized now that had provided her with a temporal bandage, not healing. The hot tears that flowed in a steady stream cleansed and purged. Her body racked with the sobs that should have been freed a long time ago.

"I am so sorry." She begged over and over. "Please, Jesus, forgive me. Forgive me. Make it go away. Make all the pain go away. I need you." The last revelation was the hardest. She needed. She needed Jesus. She felt it the moment it happened, the moment her prayer was answered. The weight lifted. She was finally free. Free of the pain. Free of the burdens. She raised her tear-streaked face to heaven. Still on her knees, arms outstretched, reaching back to the One who had been reaching for her. She rested her body against the white surface of the wall. She sobbed until her body was limp from exhaustion; she was replete.

Amber felt the change. It was palpable. She was clean. She was sinless before her God. She felt warmth in her soul. God's love shone on her like a ray of sunshine, simulating the new-found hope that burned in her heart. He had waited for her. He wanted her. Dirty, tainted, full of filth, guilty of a thousand sins, and he still chose her. Why had she clung so long to what burdened her? Why had she chosen bondage instead of freedom? It didn't matter. She was choosing now. She felt the sweet caress on her soul, like the morning after the rain. She felt the removal of her pain and her shame, the weight of guilt removed.

Amber felt something that she could only describe as weightlessness. She felt like she wanted to run, knowing she could run faster. She wanted to jump; she was sure she would jump higher. She would sing. She hadn't tried singing in a long time. Then there in the room of solitaire, she began to sing a song she remembered from her youth. "The flowers have the sunshine, and the earth has the rain, Lord, you know I love you without your spirit my life's so in vain. Melt me and mold me help me to be more like you. Make me an instrument of love brand new."

Amber felt so clean, she hoped the feeling would last forever. It must be like a newborn baby would feel. She knew her savior. She knew him by name, Jesus. She breathed the name again, "Jesus." Lying on the floor, she confessed every sin she could remember. "Take them away. And renew a right spirit in me. Don't just take them away, Lord; remove the memory and the feelings they bring with them. Whatever separates me from you."

She was still lying on the floor, arms outstretched, when the nurse came to let her out. It was as though Jesus himself had alerted her; the metamorphosis was complete. She was taken back to her room. Hannah was there. She noticed something as she looked into Amber's eyes. She couldn't explain what she saw, except to say, "She looked alive for the first time." That was exactly how she felt.

Renewal

"Therefore, if any man be in Christ he is a new creation, the old has gone the new has come. That God was reconciling the world to himself in Christ, not counting men's sins against them.

2 Corinthians 5:17, 19

Amber sat on her bed; she looked out the window. The serene blue sky was a metaphor for how she felt. Cloudless. She was embarking on a new journey. She was changed. That didn't mean she had to be perfect. It did mean she would put her hope and trust in God. She would have to be willing to let him make her into the person he had created her to be. God takes nothing by force. He gave free will, that his followers would come freely to him.

Amber asked Hannah if it were possible to get a Bible. The nurse got her one. Amber kept it under her pillow. She came across a verse that spoke directly to her: "But if a wicked man turns away from all the sins he has committed and keeps my decrees, he will surely live, none of the offences he has committed will be remembered against him" (Ezekiel 18:21–22). It didn't say there wouldn't be consequences, but her sins wouldn't count against her when she stood before God. It was so perfect. She felt the freedom in those words. She felt free. God's timing was perfect. The words from that verse strengthened and encouraged her; she was new … she felt it.

Talia and Fiona noticed the change in Amber. She was easier to live with; there was less walking on eggshells, unlike before, unsure of what could arouse an eruption. That had to be the most notable change. Instead of hitting adversity like the derailing of a locomotive, she walked away. The weight she had carried around her neck, like a noose ready to tighten and choke off the air at any second, was lifted.

She lived in bliss for three days, and her world was perfect. She was perfect. She saw herself as Christ *chose* to see her: created in the likeness of God. It enabled her to rise above conflict, to be more patient, to persevere. She wanted to always feel this way.

The afternoon of the third day came. Amber had maintained the steady, gradual improvements. She was reading her Bible daily, spending time talking with Jesus. She sought verses that would strengthen her.

Kimberly approached her at the lunch counter. She came under the guise of concern. Maybe it was genuine. Maybe she wanted the recognition for Amber's drastic change. And why shouldn't she? She was the one who had ordered her to 'the white room," the room where divine change took place. Leave anyone alone long enough, they will start talking to God. Why should this "God" get credit for her work?

"Has your medication been altered?"

"No, but I want to request my file be reviewed and my meds decreased."

"We have discussed this before, Amber. With your anxiety and violent history, you need medication." Her words brought up such fresh memories, things Amber wanted and needed to forget. A new weight was trying to take hold. It was guilt. She knew it was the devil's tool, and Kimberly was his vice, even if Kimberly didn't know it.

"I know. Hopefully we can discuss it at our next appointment anyway."

"Maybe."

Amber commanded herself to take deep breaths and repeated

in her head, *"Forgetting what is behind and straining toward what is ahead I press on toward the goal to win the prize for which God has called me heavenward"* (Philippians 3:13–14). She knew she had a lot to overcome, but she could do all things through Christ who strengthens (Philippians 4:13). She prayed silently, desperately. "Enable me, Lord. Don't let the guilt cause separation between us. Soften my heart to your will. Be gentle in your correction." God was gentle. He enabled Amber to deal with her past with patience. She knew God's promise to "remove her sins as far as the east is from the west" and "remember them no more." Laying her sins at the cross enabled *her* to "remember them no more" either.

Four weeks had gone by since Amber found salvation. She was sitting one evening watching television with the other residences. It was eight o'clock. Amber knew because everyone's favorite reality series, "Fear Factor," was starting. One of the nurses, Margaret, came up to Amber and whispered, "Someone is here to see you."

It was after visiting hours, and Amber's heart leapt. The only person she could imagine they would let in to see her after hours would be a professional of some sort. Her pulse raced. She had many times wished Jake would come see her. She wanted him to know that she had found Jesus. He would be so happy for her. He would only have to look at her, and he would know.

The thought of him and the probability of him waiting for her aroused new feelings. Not like before; she had misplaced her feelings for him. Now she would recognize him as what he was: a vision of Christ, an example of his pure love, and he was beautiful. He had done a lot to see her reach this point. He deserved to know his efforts had paid off.

Margaret led Amber to the waiting area. Catherine, Michael, Ruth, and Nina were all waiting expectantly; she knew something big was going on to bring in this particular group of people together at this hour. A moment passed in silence.

Finally, Amber spoke. "What are you all doing here?" Ruth walked up to her granddaughter. Their faces were only inches apart. She looked deep into Amber's eyes. Amber knew what she was searching for. She smiled lovingly at the amazing woman she was blessed enough to have as her grandmother. Ruth cupped Amber's face. "Precious gift," she whispered, then she drew her waiting granddaughter into her embrace. Ruth knew; there was no mistaking that clarity.

"Yes, Nan," Amber said softly. Both women allowed the tears of joy to validate the event. Ruth stepped back. It was then that Michael and Catherine could both see what all the emotion was for. They saw it too. It encouraged and strengthened Amber.

It validated faith for Michael and Catherine. They didn't ask questions. They knew their daughter well enough to know that she would volunteer any information she felt like parting with. They joined in and hugged Amber close.

"Glad to have you back," Michael said softly, his smile showing through his words. It was a sight to see, all four standing there, embracing each other. Tears flowed freely.

"Are we done with the drama?" Nina was still the same. She did notice that the family members appeared different somehow. Something unexplainable had taken place. Amber appeared softer somehow.

"We have come with some awesome news, so if you let me tell you what it is, hopefully you can all stop all this crying, and we can all be happy." Michael and Catherine smiled at Nina. Ruth just couldn't take her eyes off her granddaughter.

"Amber, Nina has some really great news." Her father sounded so happy.

"The girl whose name you supplied me with was willing to testify, and even though Forbes is dead, you knew that, right?" Nina kept talking, not even waiting for Amber's response.

"Candace had clothes shoved in her closet. One of her shirts contained semen. The DNA was a match to Forbes. You were right, she was only fourteen years old. So even if he is dead, he will be prosecuted. The good news is that you will get your exoneration. You will have the opportunity to have your story heard before a judge." Nina hesitated, then, looking at Amber, willing her to be agreeable, she continued. "The bad news is that you are going to have to testify in order to win. Court is in two weeks. If you agree to testify, it will be excruciating. The defense is going to bring up every sordid detail from your past. Defense will want to discredit you. You don't have much time to make a decision."

Amber thought. While she did, everyone remained silent. The expectancy stretched through the air like a tight rope. Amber knew she had to do it; she just hoped she was ready. She would have support. She had Jesus. He promised not to give more than she could handle. She would take him up on that promise. Amber, together with her savior, they could handle it.

"I can do it." She sounded certain.

"Great! I didn't expect such a quick answer. I hope it's one you can carry through." Nina paused, continuing cautiously. "It was only after she found out the doctor was dead that Candace agreed to testify." Nina questioned Amber seriously. "Do you know anything about his death?"

Amber's eyes shifted with nervousness. Was Nina accusing her? Amber was stuck; she didn't want to rat out Cody. She would have vengefully given up Jersey, but she was a different person now. She didn't know what was right. She conceded that the damage was already done; it probably didn't matter. She lied to herself further, recalling, *How many others did they save from suffering at those evil hands?*

Nina noted deep concentration in Amber's face. "Look, I am not accusing you. I just hope that if you have any information, you will share it."

Amber couldn't stop thinking about Candace. She was only

fourteen. She wondered how long it would take Candace to end up with an after-school habit. If she didn't already have one. Addiction would follow, leading to crime and self-loathing. Amber would think about that all through the night and into the next day. An idea was coming to light.

Court was in two weeks. Amber would meet a few times with Nina to go over her testimony. She was trying to prepare herself mentally but mostly emotionally for the trial. She wasn't ready to drudge out all the darkness in her life. Not yet. She hoped and prayed daily for the right words and for strength. Mostly, she prayed to overcome.

Amber had not spilled her guts to Nina about what she knew about Gordon Forbes' death. She made a conscientious decision. She would tell Jake Liddell if she ever got the chance to see him. She only had eight months left of her sentence; she would tell him then. *Unless,* she thought, *God could send him by sooner.* That way, if God wanted her to confess, she would know because he would come to her. She could confess and get to see Jake at the same time. She smiled to herself, knowing God didn't work that way. Still she enjoyed running the scenario through her mind.

Amber knew she had to tell Nina; certainly it would come up in court. She better deal with it and get it out in the open. Amber told Nina about the visit from Jersey and that Jersey had gloated to her about the death. Nina didn't look surprised. Amber figured she must have already known. Neither lady mentioned it again. Nina did tell Amber about the arrests. Tyler Porter, the case against him was so strong they hadn't needed Amber's testimony. Her mental state at the time of the trial would have done more harm than good. Jared had taken the stand; he was glad to be part of the team that put Tyler away for a long time. Darryl Tate was handed a suspended sentence for violating his position.

They went over all the questions she would most likely be asked by the defense. It was only the two of them, and Amber already felt the knot tighten in her stomach. She was going to throw up. It was too much. She was investing so much into forgetting.

The day of court finally arrived. Arrangements were made for Amber's pickup. A deep sorrow filled her as she remembered Charlie and Jake picking her up; it always lifted her spirits. Amber hoped that she would get to see Jake once they arrived at the courthouse. She thought about him for the entire drive. What she would say. What he might say. Would he notice the changes in her? She searched for him once she arrived. He was nowhere in sight. She should have spent the time praying.

The defense lawyer was a pit-bull named Lana Wilson. The toothpick of a woman stood around five foot nine. Her hair was short with frosted blonde spikes. Her eyes were a piercing blue, lined in thick black liner. She wore a deep crimson lipstick. She was nasty. Amber amazed herself at how calm she remained while on the stand. She remained poised through the questions and the accusations. Through all the probing and prodding, she was rational as Wilson tried to unnerve her.

Amber had not known until court that Dr. Forbes had two daughters. Both would take the stand: one for the defense, Claire, and one for the prosecution, Shelly. It was their courage as they took the stand that enabled Amber to remain undaunted by the lawyer tigress.

Claire claimed that her father had done those very things to her that he was being accused of by Amber, Candace, and a third victim, Dana, whom the cops had tracked down.

Claire talked about the rift in their family because of their father, how they always wanted to have friends over but were terrified that their father might do something to one of them.

Shelly was adamant that those things never happened, that her younger sister just needed attention. The rift in the family was because of her younger sister's accusations. Then family members were forced to choose sides.

Amber knew the truth; she recognized the deep lines in

their faces, scars only visible upon looking past the external, only evident to the eyes of one who has suffered. She felt more than she believed that both sisters had endured their father's abuse.

Nina was no lightweight as the prosecutor. She would not be outdone by the harshness of Wilson's attack. The hearings went on for two more days. According to Nina, they had been going on ten days before she had been called to take the stand.

After reliving every detail of the horrifying experience with the doctor and every other shameful thing from her past, Amber came down from the stand and walked up to Shelley. She looked into her eyes and gently said, "I know your pain." Tears welled up in Amber's eyes, but she wanted the young woman to know. "Maybe now just isn't your time to deal with it, and that's okay." She was genuine, gently placing her hand on top of Shelley's. Shelley didn't move it away; she looked at Amber. The room was silent. Amber felt Shelley's hazel eyes looking into her, through her. She was searching for unadulterated truth.

Four days had passed since the trial. Every time Amber thought about it, she prayed. She no longer felt the need for vindication. She prayed for Gordon Forbes' daughters, for Claire to stay strong and to find healing, for Shelley to find strength to deal with the pain. What would become of them after the trial?

Nina came by and informed Amber that, after she had spoken to Shelley, she refused to testify further. She retracted her statement and pled the Fifth Amendment. The implications of silence imprecated Gordon Forbes further. He was found guilty. Amber couldn't stop thinking about what that meant to his daughters. They had been so brave. She wondered if that truth, like her truths, had come with a price that was too high. Their father was dead. The epitaph proceeding him should read in the minds of many, "Child molester, incestuous, john. Heart of stone. Loved none, not even his own." She found no joy in a verdict that left two young women so empty.

Ten weeks had passed since Gordon's verdict had been handed down. Amber's experience with his daughters had validated what she already knew. God was directing her path. He had prepared her for something specific. She had been made wise through her experiences. She knew the look in Claire's eyes. The betrayal. The fear. She knew the look in Shelley's: *Please hear me. Listen to me.* They were all images she had once seen mirrored back at her. She was even more determined to begin courses and start training. She would be a counsellor, the profession of people she had once detested. She was meant for it.

Linc would be eight soon. At times it felt like he was going on thirteen. His questions about his sister required better answers than either Catherine or Michael were willing to supply. Catherine finally had the courage to bring it up with her daughter.

"Lincoln is still in the dark about a lot of the stuff that went on. We have kept our word and never told him much. He is less and less satisfied with our answers."

"Bring him in next time you come. You can find something to do for a couple hours, and I will spend some time alone with my brother." Amber was excited. Catherine was relieved. Next visit she would bring him in; that would be a week after Sunday.

Sunday came quickly. Linc had been excited all week about the promised visit to see his sister. He made mental notes to himself: *Don't ask too many questions. Don't stare,* and the hardest one, *Accept the answer you're given if you do ask a question.*

His big sister was thrilled to see him. She hugged him tightly and didn't want to let him go. "You are getting so big!"

"That's what Mom says."

"You look different too."

"Good." He smiled when his sister said that.

"How's school?"

"Good. I like P.E." Now his sister smiled and then she put her arm around him and got more serious.

"Linc, you know if you have any questions, about … about before, or about now, whatever."

"I know. I think you might like it better if I didn't though."

Amber was serious when she responded, "I would rather you knew an awful truth that would keep you from that path than not know and risk you repeating it."

All his preconceived ideas about how the day should go evaporated into a waterfall of questions overflowing into a sea of understanding as his sister revealed clandestine truths meant to deter him from a similar path. Having the question-and-answer period out of the way, they talked about much more pleasant things, like who was playing whom in hockey, what his favorite team was, and what he was learning in Sunday school. They would both eagerly await the next time they could have a day together.

Amber began work on her GED. She had seven and a half months left at Everbrook. She hoped to finish by the time of her release. When she told Kimberly of her plan to counsel young women who had survived sexual-related trauma, Amber got a surprise. Kimberly thought it was a great idea and even offered, "Why do you think I wanted to do this as a career choice? That's why it was so easy for me to believe you." Kimberly leaned back in her black leather chair, legs crossed. She was quiet a moment, transient. She finally spoke. "I had a similar experience, only it was from a coach on my basketball team. It happens, Amber. Young girls who have been through such ordeals need the chance to be heard and believed. Then they can start healing."

Amber left the office with renewed validation.

Upon finishing her GED, Catherine, Michael, Nan, and Linc came by with cake and a gift. Still Amber's thoughts fixated on Jake. *If only Jake were here to see this, he would be so proud.* Did he still think of her? Did he still pray for her?

"You look distracted." Nan noticed the look on Amber's face for the third time in the last hour. "Are you tired? We can go."

"I was just thinking. There's still so much to do."

"Yes! But your feet are pointing in the right direction, so every step takes you closer to the goal."

Amber looked on vacantly. Wisdom told Ruth not to pry, but she wondered what secondary thought was bothering her granddaughter.

Everyone was gone Amber fought the sleep that tried to overtake her. Closing her eyes, she began her prayer. *God, bring my family home safely. Continue changing me into the person you created me to be.* She paused. She knew what she wanted to say. God already knew. "He knows the desires of your heart. And when you pray, be thankful. As if your prayer has already been answered." She had read that in Matthew. It brought back past pain. Why was it so hard? Again she tried to convince herself. *God already knows, just ask.*

She knew what she lacked. *Humble yourself, then you can ask.* She took a deep breath. *God, you know, you know what my heart desires. If I can't have him, please take away this desire for him.*

TWYLA REMPEL-SADDUL

God expected more. She would have to be more specific. *Jake, God. Put Jake back in my life. Or remove this love for him. I am consumed with thoughts of him. Memories of him. You put this love in my heart. Don't let me hope if it is not in your plan. If it is in your plan, don't let me lose hope.*

Amber was nearing the end of her time at Everbrook. Fall would soon become winter, another birthday passed. She was now twenty-one, an adult. She maintained therapy with Kimberly, who informed her that it was a condition of her sentence that even once she was released, she would continue for a duration of two years. She hoped at that time to be receiving her diploma. Talia and Fiona teased that she should get an award for most improved roommate. The old Amber wouldn't have found that funny; now Amber herself laughed with the other women.

Amber still had the occasional bad day, but as time wore on they were fewer and further between. It also helped that she had goals, and she had a powerful way of dealing with her demons. They only had the power she gave them, and she was protected now. No way she was going down that road again. She was completely unaware of the foe that would soon beckon her.

It was a Saturday, middle of the afternoon. Amber was with Talia and Fiona outside. They were raking the very last of the autumn leaves and then running and jumping into the pile. They would rake them up again and the next person would get their turn.

Amber had noticed, even from a distance. Maybe it was the way Hannah walked as she crossed the leaf-strewn lawn. Her head lobbed to one side; she dragged her feet. Amber's entire body stiffened, anticipating the pain Hannah's message was sure to inflict.

Hannah stood silently in front of Amber, searching for

344

words. She had come to appreciate all the fire and passion in Amber. She had noticed the changes in her over the past while she was doing so well. Her faith really seemed to work for her, and at this moment she hoped it would be enough for her. She didn't want to be the one to drop the bombshell on Amber's seemingly wonderful new world. Hannah knew, from personal experience, what the young woman in a desperate situation was capable of. She chose her words carefully. "Amber, I need a moment with you privately." She looked at the two young ladies on the ground who seemed to be awaiting an explanation. "It is a private matter."

"What is it?" Amber already had a tone of concern in her voice.

"We should go somewhere else to talk about this. Please follow me." They walked around the building in complete silence, except for the crunching of autumn leaves underfoot, completely unaware of how they intruded on the purposeful silence.

Amber was anxious, wringing her hands as she walked. Finally, Hannah stopped walking and looked at her. She felt Amber's pain before the words were out of her mouth. Amber could see it in her expression.

"Your mother has just called ... "

Amber's heart was beating so hard, she could hear the pounding in her ears. She waited for Hannah to continue.

"Your grandmother passed away."

And Then

"Thy word is a lamp unto my feet and a light unto my path."
Psalms 119:105

Amber was in shock. She stared at the woman, jaw clenched, eyes narrowed. Hannah must be mistaken. Nan was such a strong woman. She was healthy. She loved Jesus. She couldn't be gone. Amber found her voice. "What happened?"

"Your mother said on the phone that this would be a shock. No one knew there was anything wrong. She had a blood clot, it burst. She died very suddenly. Amber, I am so sorry. You will be given a day pass to go to the funeral."

"Thank you," Amber whispered. It didn't make sense to Amber. A blood clot; one doesn't just not notice that. It would have been painful; there would have been such discomfort.

Hannah interrupted her private thoughts. "The funeral is Tuesday. Your mother was unable to come today."

Funeral. That word was so final. It left room for nothing. Amber closed her eyes; she pictured Nan, eyes shining, loving her. Amber would miss her dearly.

The rest of the weekend was a blur. Amber stayed in her room. She wrote stuff down in her special book. She slept a lot, having no energy, not even to eat. She just wanted to remember everything she could about Nan. Amber's sadness was compounded by the knowledge that she had missed out on the last five years of Nan's life, but Nan hadn't missed any of hers. She had stuck by through all of it. She had prayed for her; she had felt for her; she had hoped for her. She knew she had beseeched God on behalf of her. Now she was gone, and Amber would never be able to return any of her goodness.

"D-d-do you want t-t-to tell us about your g-g-grandma?"

"You can. I would like that. Would you?"

"Thank you. You guys are awesome roommates." She told Talia and Fiona a few stories, saying, "The thing I remember most, though, was her relationship with Jesus. They were best friends. Like the two of you. Nan was always praying and always hoping for someone, and often me."

Amber didn't think either girl understood what she was talking about. Nan could have made them understand. Doubt began to fill her heart, roiling into guilt. She knew somehow that Nan's death was her fault. Blood clots were probably stress related, and her dear Nan had loved her so much; she had done nothing but cause stress for five long years.

"You are unworthy," the voice whispered into the darkness. It came with a chilling breeze that pricked the hairs on the back of her neck. "You were unworthy before. How much less worthy are you now?" She curled into a ball on her bed and covered her ears with her hands. The voices, they were coming back; they had destroyed her before. She had to fight them this time; she had to win, so she prayed.

God, you have promised. You will provide my needs before I ask and will provide help while I am still asking, Isaiah 65:24. You promised, God. I am counting on your promise, it is all I have. Amber repeated the verse over and over. Eventually, the voices got quieter. Amber won this time.

Tuesday came fast. Amber felt exhausted. She jumped in the shower, feeling old habits clamoring for her heart as she turned the water up as hot as it would go. Her shower was quick. When she got out, she wiped the steam from the mirror and looked at her reflection. She pushed her face right up to the mirror, looking closely. Had the darkness won her soul while she slept?

"*I will never leave you nor forsake you*" (Matthew 1:5). The verse popped into her head; she had memorized it at camp one year. It comforted her while she felt so weak.

Catherine and Michael arrived early. Lincoln was with them. Amber could see in her mother's face that she had been crying. She probably hadn't stopped since the call. The guard that would be accompanying them arrived. They got into his SUV and headed for the church.

The church was full, and Amber knew so many of the people. She was encouraged by the many comments by those who sensed the change in her. Their prayers had paid off. It gave reason to smile on such a day of sorrow.

Mr. and Mrs. Farrell were there. It was good to talk with them. In this moment she was thankful she could talk with them face-to-face. They could look her in the eye, they could see, and they would know. Their son's death had been the pinnacle of her destruction. There was joy in the knowledge that she now belonged to Jesus.

The service was an accurate depiction of her grandmother. There was no need to embellish the life and the character of Nan. Following the service, the family made the twenty-minute drive to Orchard Flats, the burial site. The site was as lovely as the name implied.

Amber's guard was respectful, giving Amber space and time with her family. He was dressed for a funeral, not a prison or a hospital. Even now he hung back as everyone gathered to head back to the Whites', where hors d'oeuvres and beverages would be served. People milled around, talking about wonderful Nan.

As the crowd thinned and dispersed, Amber noticed the patrol car. It was pulled over. She wasn't close enough to see if anyone was inside. Her heart thumped with anticipation, her throat closed. She began looking at all the people, trying to find one, one in particular; she would know him immediately. She couldn't see him.

She recognized the calm, deep breathing that prickled the back of her neck. She turned around, and there right behind her, close enough to touch, was Jake Liddell. He stared at her. She didn't give him a chance to speak; she jumped into his arms, flung her arms around him, and breathed into his neck. "He found me, Jake. He found me!"

"I know, I know," he assured her. Holding on to her so tightly, it squeezed out what little air she had left in her lungs. Never before had she felt so right in front of this man. Never had she felt worthy of the look in his eyes; she did now. Amber lifted her head up off his broad shoulder. Her eyes shone; it wasn't just the tears; she shone with a purity, a newness, and he recognized it.

She was even more beautiful than he had remembered. Christopher, the guard, was approaching them. He was ushering her to keep up with her family. He placed his hand on her shoulder; that was it, that was all she got. Two minutes to catch up on two years. When would she see him again? They both remained in stunned silence.

"Wait, please wait." She was gentle in her tone. "Please." Christopher was uncertain, and in the moment's hesitation, her brother, who had headed back down the path, grabbed her hand and pulled her toward the SUV. She glanced over her shoulder. Jake stood motionless; he hadn't budged an inch in the moments since she had been herded away.

Christopher, upon being given directions by Michael, made his way to the Whites' home. Amber felt panicked; she was having to deal with so much all at once. There were so many painful memories she associated with the house, and it was her Nan's funeral. She was still reeling from her less-than-brief moment with Jake. It should have been enough that she got to tell him her news, their great news; he had been the light that led the way.

As the evening wore on, Amber found herself continuously looking out the bay window.

"Is there someone you expected to see?" Michael asked his daughter. When she looked at her father, he understood. "I noticed you and Jake."

Amber listened intently to the familiar way her father referred to Officer Liddell, as it should have been to him.

He observed her expression and offered explanation with a soft grin. "Your mother and I invited Jake over once for dinner, and we've gone for coffee a couple times. He is an impressive young man with a true heart for God. You don't find many men like him." He looked knowingly at his daughter; the young officer had been very forthcoming with his feelings for Amber.

"We invited him to come today, but he was on duty. That is why, I suppose, he stopped by at the burial site." Amber looked into her father's eyes; she knew he understood. She hugged her daddy; they stayed like that for an exaggerated moment. He gave her a squeeze, kissed her cheek, and then left her alone.

It was nearing eight o'clock. Christopher made his way over to her. "Time to say your good-byes, Amber. I have to have you back by eight thirty."

She kissed and hugged all her relatives; she held on to Linc so tightly that he finally had to squeak, "Amber, you're choking me,"

"Oh, I'm just going to miss you so much, little brother, but I'm home for good in eight weeks, so get ready," she said playfully.

"Your dad is going to go back to Everbrook with you and pick up our car." Her mother gave her a last kiss and hug, and they were out the door.

The drive to Everbrook was relatively quiet, and it seemed the drive went quickly. Amber was tired; she just wanted to go to bed and sleep for a week. She said goodnight to her father. Christopher left her outside the building while he walked Michael back through the iron gate to his car.

While the two men walked down the long drive, Amber looked after them. She heard unmistakable scuffing behind her.

Terrified that it might be vicious raccoons or a foul skunk, she whirled around. She gasped out loud, not even embarrassed by her show of emotion. Jake was three strides away. She made them quickly and was received passionately into his waiting arms. She burrowed herself there, deep in his warmth, encircling him with her slender arms. His arms felt so strong wrapped around her. When she backed up and looked into his eyes, searching for what he was feeling, she could see all the love he felt for her; it was their time.

He brought his mouth down on hers possessively; he had waited for the time to be right, and he had waited long. He kissed her with the passion that had waited two years to be released. She kissed him eagerly back. They held each other, enjoying the moment. They both gasped for air. Jake kissed her again. Having regained control, he kissed her gently this time, lovingly. They were still like that when Christopher returned to bring her back inside. They hadn't spoken a word to each other, and now she was going back inside. It didn't matter; she knew now how he felt about her; she knew God had put this man in her life for a purpose. He had prayed for her since she was sixteen. She was now a young woman. Everything was so right.

Amber entered her room, smiling. Talia and Fiona were both there waiting. Neither girl understood why she was smiling. Amber started her story from the beginning, how Jake had been the officer to bring her home one night. She talked and answered questions until she got to tonight.

"And then he kissed me."

Their eyes widened and their chins dropped. Amber smiled at them.

"I-i-if you are in l-l-love, why d-d-did he stay away so l-l-l-ong?"

"I made Jake into my savior, but he is just a man. The only name by which we are saved is Jesus. What I did was wrong. It would have been wrong for him to let me go on that way. I would have ended up very disappointed, because man will always fail; only Jesus doesn't. I had to find Jesus on my own and then I could be with my love."

Fiona, intrigued, said, "I-i-if J-J-J-Jesus made you b-b-better, could he, could he m-m-make me bet-bet-better?"

Amber's eyes went soft; her answer was full of love. "Absolutely." That didn't mean her stutter would go away or that the effects of the drugs she had used would be renewed; it meant just what she asked—he could make her better.

The last eight weeks at Everbrook had gone by slower than the twenty-two preceding months. It was February, and most of the snow was gone. The day finally arrived that Amber would be going home. She had prayed with Fiona and witnessed the change in her over the last eight weeks, the change that only comes from a relationship with Jesus. Talia had been curious; she had asked questions, but she had not made that commitment. Amber hugged them and said her good-byes; all three ladies had tears running down their faces as they embraced. Hannah surprised Amber, giving her a hug as well.

Michael showed up at eleven to pick up his daughter. It was the earliest he was allowed. He hugged her joyfully. Amber reassured Kimberly that she would be in for her appointments. The guard walked them to the huge iron gates, unlocked the large chain, and Amber walked out, finally free.

The realization hit her, and she began to sob. Michael put his arms around his daughter, comforting her, letting her weep in the safety of his embrace. She could finally be done with the past; she could leave it all behind. She had left it at the cross, but now she could walk away from it, no reminders.

"I'm okay now," she assured him.

Michael supported his daughter with his arms and led her to the car. He had already thought of the first thing he wanted to do to celebrate his daughter's freedom. He drove up to the

THIS ROAD I WALK

drive-thru window. "I'll take a combo number six, a number four no ketchup, and a number four with ketchup, and what would you like, Amber?" She was excited. She hadn't had fast food in literally years. She had always loved Wendy's.

"The biggest, juiciest burger you have, and Biggee size it," she said with a smile.

They got home and everyone dove into the bags, taking out their favorite orders.

"This one isn't mine. It has ketchup," Linc whined.

"Then I must have yours," Mom answered. They had their proper orders in front of them. Amber was ready to dig in; she had forgotten about grace. Her mouth was full. Everyone around the table was silent; they looked at her. Then they all began to laugh. Her mouth was so full she had to put her hand over it or lose her bite.

"I guess Amber volunteers to say grace," Linc was quick to point out, which she did after she swallowed her mouthful.

Amber wasted no time registering for courses and getting started on her educational goals. She enjoyed her first Sunday back at church. Being there made her think of Jake. She knew that somewhere in the city he was at a church as well.

That night he dropped by. The five of them sat around the table eating cake, sipping coffee. Linc had milk. After cake Amber and Jake took a walk. They walked and talked; they came to a small park and, after parking themselves on a bench, began to learn about each other.

Amber felt uncomfortable as Jake talked about Jersey.

"You remember Jersey?" he asked innocently. "She told the police that Kyle was your boyfriend and that he killed Forbes for you."

Amber had to be honest. "Cody, his twin, was my boyfriend, never Kyle."

Jake smiled. "So we put the right guy behind bars then. Cody is serving four years on a manslaughter charge."

Amber felt a pang of sadness.

Jake noted the expression. "With good behavior he could be out in two."

She smiled weakly.

Amber and Jake told each other of their passions and aspirations. They hoped to mesh them together. Jake already knew his intentions with Amber. He was planning a trip home in the summer; he hadn't seen his family in along time. He didn't say it that day, but he hoped Amber would make the trip with him … as his wife.

Epilogue

April second, Amber and Jake were married. The engagement was short, lest anyone stumble. Amber continued with her goal to become a counsellor. Two years into the marriage she became pregnant; she carried to second term and lost the baby. They were devastated. She suffered deep depression as she struggled with ideas of God punishing her for past sins. Jake supported his wife, encouraging her with the knowledge that God disciplines, he doesn't punish. He patiently explained that punishment is based on the past; discipline is to give you a better future.

When the time was right, Amber and Jake did have children, a girl to start with, and only seventeen months later, twin boys were born. Amber continued to counsel troubled young people. Jake continued as a police officer. They both experienced God's perfect love and tried to share that love with the many hurting people who need it.